THE FIRST HEROES

TOR BOOKS BY HARRY TURTLEDOVE

Into the Darkness

Darkness Descending

Through the Darkness

Rulers of the Darkness

Jaws of Darkness

Out of the Darkness

The Two Georges (with Richard Dreyfus)

Household Gods (with Judith Tarr)

Between the Rivers

(Writing as H. N. Turteltaub)

Justinian

Over the Wine-Dark Sea

The Gryphon's Skull

The Sacred Land

THE FIRST HEROES

EDITED BY

HARRY TURTLEDOVE

AND

NOREEN DOYLE

A Tom Doherty Associates Book
New York

This is a work of fiction. All the characters and events portrayed in these stories are either fictitious or are used fictitiously.

THE FIRST HEROES: NEW TALES OF THE BRONZE AGE

This book is printed on acid-free paper.

Edited by Patrick Nielsen Hayden

A Tor Book
Published by Tom Doherty Associates, LLC
175 Fifth Avenue
New York, NY 10010

www.tor.com

Tor® is a registered trademark of Tom Doherty Associates, LLC.

LIBRARY OF CONGRESS CATALOGING-IN-PUBLICATION DATA

The first heroes : new tales of the Bronze Age/[edited by] Harry Turtledove and Noreen Doyle. — 1st ed.
p. cm.
ISBN 0-765-30286-1
EAN 978-0765-30286-1
1. Fantasy fiction, American. 2. Prehistoric peoples—Fiction. 3. Historical fiction, American. 4. Bronze age—Fiction. 5. Heroes—Fiction. I. Doyle, Noreen Mary. II. Turtledove, Harry.

PS648.F3.F573 2004
813'.08766—dc22 2003071152

First Edition: May 2004

Printed in the United States of America

0 9 8 7 6 5 4 3 2 1

Copyright Acknowledgments

in memory of

POUL ANDERSON
1926–2001

Contents

BRONZE AGE:
(noun)

1) *archaeology/history*;
a period of cultural development
marked by the use of copper alloys,
such as bronze.

2) *Greek mythology*;
the era of the third race of humanity created by Zeus.
Their armor, their houses, and their tools were bronze,
for they had no iron.
Their strength was great, their arms unconquerable.
Terrible and strong,
they were followed by the nobler and more righteous
heroic race
that fought the Trojan War.

Introduction

Storytellers have been writing and rewriting the Bronze Age since the Bronze Age, and their enthusiasm shows no sign of waning.

Sometime before 1500 B.C. an Egyptian wrote down a series of stories about King Khufu, for whom the Great Pyramid had been built a thousand years before. In the seventh century B.C. Babylonian scribes incised onto eleven clay tablets their own adaptation of the much earlier Sumerian epic of Gilgamesh—and recorded a sequel on the twelfth. Homer's tales of the Trojans and Achaians inspired Mediaeval and Renaissance romances. All of this, and everything else you have ever read, is possible because literature itself was born during the Bronze Age. This singular invention, the written narrative, preserved for us the names and deeds and a little of the personalities of the first recorded individuals.

It was the beginning of history—literally, as archaeologists define the period before the development of writing as prehistory.

It was an age of new technology and experimentation (writing, metallurgy, the wheel) and evolving social forms (statehood, standing armies, the merchant class). It was an age of exploration, when Egyptian expeditions set sail for the incense terraces of Punt and Odysseus wandered his way home. And it was an age of magic: the gods so familiar to us, from Ishtar to Poseidon, attained recognizable name and form and power.

So we turn our eyes toward a past when kings were gods, voyagers were heroes, and tin was the key to cutting-edge technology. And as we look back—and forward and a little sideways—we see that Bronze Age figures, at once familiar and strange, remain around us everywhere.

THE FIRST HEROES

The past is a foreign country that cannot be visited but rather only glimpsed on the horizon. When we try for a closer view, through the spyglass of history or archaeology, our view is invariably distorted by distance, by our choice of focus, and by the curvature of our lens. If, however, we were to attempt landfall, could we navigate the currents of time to an intended moorage? And would we find a world any more familiar than might a sailor who, informed by rumor and legend and sightings through his telescope, has disembarked from his storm-swept ship onto an alien shore? Would the landscape around us remain distorted and strange to our expectations?

Renowned author Gene Wolfe takes us on such a voyage across the ancient Black Sea and the wider gulf of time itself. He shows us anew people, places, and events that, separated from us by more than three and a half millennia, authors and filmmakers have made unjustly familiar.

The Lost Pilgrim

Before leaving my own period, I resolved to keep a diary; and indeed I told several others I would, and promised to let them see it upon my return. Yesterday I arrived, captured no Pukz, and compiled no text. No more inauspicious beginning could be imagined.

I will not touch my emergency rations. I am hungry, and there is nothing to eat; but how absurd it would be to begin in such a fashion! No. Absolutely not. Let me finish this, and I will go off in search of breakfast.

To begin. I find myself upon a beach, very beautiful and very empty, but rather too hot and much too shadeless to be pleasant. "Very empty," I said, but how can I convey just how empty it really is? (Pukz 1–3)

As you see, there is sun and there is water, the former remarkably hot and bright, the latter remarkably blue and clean. There is no shade, and no one who—

A sail! Some kind of sailboat is headed straight for this beach. It seems too small, but this could be it. (Puk 4)

I cannot possibly describe everything that happened today. There was far, far too much. I can only give a rough outline. But first I should say that I am no longer sure why I am here, if I ever was. On the beach last night, just after I arrived, I felt no doubts. Either I knew why I had come, or I did not think about it. There was that time when they were going to send me out to join the whateveritwas expedition—the little man with the glasses. But I do not think this is that; this is something else.

Not the man getting nailed up, either.

It will come to me. I am sure it will. In such a process of regression there cannot help but be metal confusion. Do I mean metal? The women's armor was gold or brass. Something like that. They marched out onto the beach, a long line of them, all in the gold armor. I did not know they were women.

I hid behind rocks and took Pukz. (See Pukz 5–9) The reflected glare made it difficult, but I got some good shots just the same.

They banged their spears on their shields and made a terrible noise, but when the boat came close enough for us to see the men on it (Pukz 10 and 11) they marched back up onto the hill behind me and stood on the crest. It was then that I realized they were women; I made a search for "women in armor" and found more than a thousand references, but all those I examined were to Joan of Arc or similar figures. This was not one woman but several hundreds.

I do not believe there should be women in armor, anyway. Or men in armor, like those who got off the boat. Swords, perhaps. Swords might be all right. And the name of the boat should be two words, I think.

The men who got off this boat are young and tough-looking. There is a book of prayers in my pack, and I am quite certain it was to be a talisman. "O God, save me by thy name and defend my cause by thy might." But I cannot imagine these men being impressed by any prayers.

Some of these men were in armor and some were not. One who had no armor and no weapons left the rest and started up the slope. He has an intelligent face, and though his staff seemed sinister, I decided to risk everything. To tell the truth I thought he had seen me and was coming to ask what I wanted. I was wrong, but he would surely have seen me as soon as he took a few more steps. At any rate, I switched on my translator and stood up. He was surprised, I believe, at my black clothes and the buckles on my shoes; but he is a very smooth man, always exceedingly polite. His name is Ekkiawn. Or something like that. (Puk 12) Ekkiawn is as near as I can get to the pronunciation.

I asked where he and the others were going, and when he told me, suggested that I might go with them, mentioning that I could talk to the Native Americans. He said it was impossible, that they had sworn to accept no further volunteers, that he could speak the language of Kolkkis himself, and that the upper classes of Kolkkis all spoke English.

I, of course, then asked him to say something in English and switched off my translator. I could not understand a word of it.

At this point he began to walk again, marking each stride with his beautiful staff, a staff of polished hardwood on which a carved snake writhes. I followed him, switched my translator back on, and complimented him on his staff.

He smiled and stroked the snake. "My father permits me to use it," he said. "The serpent on his own is real, of course. Our tongues are like our emblems, I'm afraid. He can persuade anyone of anything. Compared to him, my own tongue is mere wood."

I said, "I assume you will seek to persuade those women that you come in peace. When you do, will they teach you to plant corn?"

He stopped and stared at me. "Are they women? Don't toy with me."

I said I had observed them closely, and I was quite sure they were.

"How interesting! Come with me."

As we approached the women, several of them began striking their shields with their spears, as before. (Puk 13) Ekkiawn raised his staff. "My dear young ladies, cease! Enchanting maidens, desist! You suppose us pirates. You could not be more mistaken. We are the aristocracy of the Minyans. Nowhere will you find young men so handsome, so muscular, so wealthy, so well bred, or so well connected. I myself am a son of Hodios. We sail upon a most holy errand, for we would return the sacred ramskin to Mount Laphystios."

The women had fallen silent, looking at one another and particularly at an unusually tall and comely woman who stood in the center of their line.

"Let there be peace between us," Ekkiawn continued. "We seek only fresh water and a few days' rest, for we have had hard rowing. We will pay for any supplies we receive from you, and generously. You will have no singing arrows nor blood-drinking spears from us. Do you fear sighs? Languishing looks? Gifts of flowers and jewelry? Say so if you do, and we will depart in peace."

A woman with gray hair straggling from under her helmet tugged at the sleeve of the tall woman. (Puk 14) Nodding, the tall woman stepped forward. "Stranger, I am Hupsipule, Queen of Lahmnos. If indeed you come in peace—"

"We do," Ekkiawn assured her.

"You will not object to my conferring with my advisors."

"Certainly not."

While the queen huddled with four other women, Ekkiawn whispered, "Go to the ship like a good fellow, and find Eeasawn, our captain. Tell him these are women and describe the queen. Name her."

Thinking that this might well be the boat I was supposed to board after all and that this offered as good a chance to ingratiate myself with its commander as I was ever likely to get, I hurried away. I found Eeasawn without much trouble, assured him that the armed figures on the hilltop were in fact women in armor ("both Ekkiawn and I saw that quite clearly") and told him that the tallest, good-looking, black-haired, and proud, was Queen Hupsipule.

He thanked me. "And you are . . .?"

"A humble pilgrim seeking the sacred ramskin, where I hope to lay my heartfelt praise at the feet of God."

"Well spoken, but I cannot let you sail with us, Pilgrim. This ship is already as full of men as an egg is of meat. But should—"

Several members of the crew were pointing and shouting. The women on the hilltop were removing their armor and so revealing their gender, most being dressed in simple frocks without sleeves, collars, or buttons. (Puk 15) There was a general rush from the ship.

Let me pause here to comment upon the men's clothing, of which there is remarkably little, many being completely naked. Some wear armor, a helmet and a breastplate, or a helmet alone. A few more wear loose short-sleeved shirts that cover them to mid-thigh. The most remarkable is certainly the captain, who goes naked except for a single sandal. (Pukz 16 and 17)

For a moment or two, I stood watching the men from the ship talking to the women. After conversations too brief to have consisted of much more than introductions, each man left with three or more women, though our captain departed with the queen alone (Puk 18), and Ekkiawn with five. I had started to turn away when the largest and strongest hand I have ever felt closed upon my shoulder.

"Look 'round here, Pilgrim. Do you really want to go to Kolkkis with us?"

The speaker was a man of immense size, bull-necked and pig-eyed (Puk 19); I felt certain that it would be dangerous to reply in the negative.

"Good! I promised to guard the ship, you see, the first time it needed guarding."

"I am not going to steal anything," I assured him.

"I didn't think so. But if you change your mind, I'm going to hunt you down and break your neck. Now, then, I heard you and Eeasawn. You watch for me, hear? While I go into whatever town those split-tailed soldiers came out of and get us some company. Two enough for you?"

Not knowing what else to do, I nodded.

"Me?" He shrugged shoulders that would have been more than

creditable on a bull gorilla. "I knocked up fifty girls in one night once. Not that I couldn't have done it just about any other night, too, only that was the only time I've had a crack at fifty. So a couple for you and as many as I can round up for me. And if your two have anything left when you're done up, send 'em over. Here." He handed me a spear. "You're our guard 'til I get back."

I am waiting his return; I have removed some clothing because of the heat and in the hope of ingratiating myself with any women who may return with him. Hahraklahs is his name.

Hours have passed since I recorded the account you just read. No one has come, neither to molest our boat nor for any other reason. I have been staring at the stars and examining my spear. It has a smooth hardwood shaft and a leaf-shaped blade of copper or brass. I would not have thought such a blade could be sharpened, but it is actually very sharp.

It is also wrong. I keep thinking of spears with flared mouths like trumpets. And yet I must admit that my spear is a sensible weapon, while the spears with trumpet mouths would be senseless as well as useless.

These are the most beautiful stars in the world. I am beginning to doubt that I have come at the right period, and to tell the truth I cannot remember what the right period was. It does not matter, since no one can possibly use the same system. But this period in which I find myself has the most beautiful stars, bar none. And the closest.

There are voices in the distance. I am prepared to fight, if I must.

We are at sea. I have been rowing; my hands are raw and blistered. We are too many to row all at once, so we take turns. Mine lasted most of the morning. I pray for a wind.

I should have brought prophylactics. It is possible I have contracted some disease, though I doubt it. The women (Apama and Klays, Pukz 20–25, infrared) were interesting, both very eager to believe that I was the son of some king or other and very determined to become pregnant. Apama has killed her husband for an insult, stabbing him in his sleep.

Long after we had finished and washed ourselves in this strange tideless sea, Hahraklahs was still engaged with his fifteen or twenty. (They came and went in a fashion that made it almost impossible to judge the exact number.) When the last had gone, we sat and talked.

He has had a hard life in many ways, for he is a sort of slave to one Eurustheus who refuses to speak to him or even look at him. He has been a stableman and so forth. He says he strangled the lion whose skin he wears, and he is certainly very strong. I can hardly lift his brass-bound club, which he flourishes like a stick.

If it were not for him, I would not be on this boat. He has taken a liking to me because I did not want to stay at Lahmnos. He had to kidnap about half the crew to get us out to sea again, and two could not be found. Kaeneus (Puk 26) says the crew wanted to depose Captain Eeasawn and make Hahraklahs captain, but he remained loyal to Eeasawn and would not agree. Kaeneus also confided that he himself underwent a sex-change operation some years ago. Ekkiawn warned me that Kaeneus is the most dangerous fighter on the boat; I suppose he was afraid I would ridicule him. He is a chief, Ekkiawn says, of the Lapiths; this seems to be a Native American tribe.

I am certainly on the wrong vessel. There are two points I am positive of. The first is the name of the captain. It was Jones. Captain Jones. This cannot be Eeasawn, whose name does not even begin with J. The second is that there was to be someone named Brewster on board, and that I was to help this Brewster (or perhaps Bradford) talk with the Lapiths. There is no one named Bradford among my present companions—I have introduced myself to all of them and learned their names. No Brewsters. Thus this boat cannot be the one I was to board.

On the positive side, I am on a friendly footing now with the Lapith chief. That seems sure to be of value when I find the correct ship and reach Atlantis.

I have discussed this with Argos. Argos (Puk 27) is the digitized personality of the boat. (I wonder if the women who lay with him realized that?) He points out—wisely, I would say—that the way to locate a vessel is to visit a variety of ports, making inquiries at each. In order to do that, one should be on another vessel, one making a long voyage with many ports of call. That is my situation, which might be far worse.

We have sighted two other boats, both smaller than our own.

Our helmsman, said to be an infallible weather prophet, has announced that we will have a stiff west wind by early afternoon. Our course is northeast for Samothrakah, which I take to be another island. We are forty-nine men and one woman.

She is Atalantah of Kaludon (Pukz 28–30), tall, slender, muscular, and quite beautiful. Ekkiawn introduced me to her, warning me that she would certainly kill me if I tried to force her. I assured her, and him, that I would never do such a thing. In all honesty I cannot say I have talked with her, but I listened to her for some while. Hunting is the only thing she cares about. She has hunted every large animal in her part of the world and joined Eeasawn's expedition in hope of hunting grups, a fierce bird never seen west of our destination. They can be baited to a blind to feed upon the bodies of horses or cattle, she says. From that I take them to be some type of vulture. Her knowledge of lions, stags, wild swine, and the dogs employed to hunt all three is simply immense.

At sea again, course southeast and the wind dead astern. Now that I have leisure to bring this account up to date, I sit looking out at the choppy waves pursuing us and wonder whether you will believe even a fraction of what I have to relate.

In Samothrakah we were to be initiated into the Cult of Persefonay, a powerful goddess. I joined in the preparations eagerly, not only because it would furnish insight into the religious beliefs of these amoral but very superstitious men, but also because I hoped—as I still do—that the favor of the goddess would bring me to the rock whose name I have forgotten, the rock that is my proper destination.

We fasted for three days, drinking water mixed with wine but eating no solid food. On the evening of the third day we stripped and daubed each other with a thin white mixture which I suspect was little more than chalk dispersed in water. That done, we shared a ritual supper of boiled beans and raw onions. (Pukz 31 and 32)

Our procession reached the cave of Persefassa, as she is also called, about midnight. We extinguished our torches in an underground pool and received new ones, smaller torches that burned with a clear, almost white flame and gave off a sweet scent. Singing, we marched another mile underground.

My companions appeared undaunted. I was frightened, and kept my teeth from chattering only by an effort of will. After a time I was able to exchange places with Erginos and so walk behind Hahraklahs, that tower of strength. If that stratagem had not succeeded, I think I might have turned and run.

The throne room of the goddess (Pukz 33–35) is a vast underground chamber of spectacular natural columns where icy water drips secretly and, as it were, stealthily. The effect is of gentle, unending rain, of mourning protracted until the sun burns out. The priestesses passed among us, telling each of us in turn, "All things fail. All decays, and passes away."

Ghosts filled the cavern. Our torches rendered them invisible, but I could see them in the darkest places, always at the edge of my field of vision. Their whispers were like a hundred winds in a forest, and whenever one came near me I felt a cold that struck to the bone.

Deep-voiced horns, melodious and tragic, announced the goddess. She was preceded by the Kabeiri, stately women and men somewhat taller than Hahraklahs who appeared to have no feet. Their forms were solid to the knees, where they became translucent and quickly faded to nothing. They made an aisle for Persefonay, a lovely young woman far taller than they.

She was robed in crimson, and black gems bound her fair hair. (Pukz 36 and 37) Her features are quite beautiful; her expression I can only call resigned. (She may revisit the upper world only as long as the pomegranate is in bloom—so we were taught during our fast. For the rest of the year she remains her husband's prisoner underground.) She took her seat upon a rock that accommodated itself to her as she sat, and indicated by a gesture that we were to approach her.

We did, and her Kabeiri closed about us as if we were children shepherded by older children, approaching a teacher. That and Puk 38 will give you the picture; but I was acutely conscious, as I think we all were, that she and her servants were beings of an order remote from biological evolution. You will be familiar with such beings in our own period, I feel sure. I do not recall them, true. I do recall that knowledge accumulates. The people of the period in which I find myself could not have sent someone, as I have been sent, to join in the famous voyage whose name I have forgotten.

Captain Eeasawn stepped forward to speak to Persefonay. (Pukz 39 and 40) He explained that we were bound for Aea, urged upon our mission by the Pythoness and accompanied by sons of Poseidon and other gods. Much of what he said contradicted what I had been told earlier, and there was much that I failed to understand.

When he had finished, Persefonay introduced the Kabeiri, the earliest gods of Samothrakah. One or more, she said, would accompany us on our voyage, would see that our boat was never wrecked, and would rescue us if it were. Eeasawn thanked her in an elaborate speech, and we bowed.

At once every torch burned out, leaving us in utter darkness. (Pukz 39a and 40a infrared) Instructed by the priestesses, we joined hands, I with Hahraklahs and Atalantah, and so were led out of the cave. There our old torches were restored to us and rekindled. (Puk 41) Carrying them and singing, we returned to our ship, serenaded by wolves.

We have passed Ilion! Everyone agrees that was the most dangerous part of our voyage. Its inhabitants control the strait and permit no ships other than their own to enter or leave. We remained well out of sight of the city until night.

Night came, and a west wind with it. We put up the mast and hoisted our sail, and Periklumenos dove from the prow and took the form of a dolphin (Puk 42 infrared) to guide us though the strait. As we drew near Ilion, we rowed, too, rowing for all we were worth for what seemed half the night. A patrol boat spotted us and moved to intercept us, but Phaleros shot its helmsman. It sheered off—and we passed! That shot was five hundred meters if it was one, and was made by a man standing unsupported on a bench aboard a heeling, pitching boat urged forward by a bellying sail and forty rowers pulling for all they were worth. The arrow's flight was as straight as any string. I could not see where the helmsman was hit, but Atalantah says the throat. Knowing that she prides herself on her shooting, I asked whether she could have made that shot. She shrugged and said, "Once, perhaps, with a quiver-full of arrows."

We are docked now at a place called Bear Island. We fear no bears here, nor much of anything else. The king is the son of an old friend of Hahraklahs's. He has invited us to his wedding, and all is wine and garlands, music, dancing, and gaiety. (Pukz 43–48) Eeasawn asked for volunteers to guard the boat. I volunteered, and Atalantah offered to stay with me. Everyone agreed that Eeasawn and Hahraklahs would have to be present the whole time, so they were excused; the rest drew lots to relieve us. Polydeukahs the Clone and Kaeneus lost and were then subjected to much good-natured raillery. They promise to relieve us as soon as the moon comes up.

Meanwhile I have been leaning on my spear and talking with Atalantah. Leaning on my spear, I said, but that was only at first. Some kind people came down from the town (Puk 49) to talk with us, and left us a skin of wine. After that we sat side by side on one of the benches and passed the tart wine back and forth. I do not think that I will ever taste dry red wine again without being reminded of this evening.

Atalantah has had a wretched life. One sees a tall, athletic, good-looking young woman. One is told that she is royal, the daughter of a king. One assumes quite naturally that hers has been a life of ease and privilege. It has been nothing of the sort. She was exposed as an infant—left in the forest to die. She was found by hunters, one of whom had a captive bear with a cub. He washed her in the bear's urine, after which the bear permitted her to nurse. No one can marry her who cannot best her in a foot-race, and no one can. As if that were not enough, she is compelled to kill the suitors she outruns. And she has, murdering half a dozen fine young men and mourning them afterward.

I tried to explain to her that she could still have male friends, men other than suitors who like her and enjoy her company. I pointed out that I could never make a suitable mate for a beautiful young woman of royal blood but that I would be proud to call myself her friend. I would make no demands, and assist her in any way I could. We kissed and became intimate.

Have I gone mad? Persefonay smiled at me as we left. I shall never forget that. I cannot. Now this!

No, I am not mad. I have been wracking my brain, sifting my memory for a future that does not yet exist. There is a double helix of gold. It gives us the power to make monsters, and if it exists in that age it must exist in this. Look! (Pukz 50–58) I have paced off their height, and find it to be four and a half meters or a little more.

Six arms! All of them have six arms. (Pukz 54–57 show this very clearly.) They came at us like great white spiders, then rose to throw stones, and would have brained us with their clubs.

God above have mercy on us! I have been reading my little book by firelight. It says that a wise warrior is mightier than a strong warrior. Doubtless that is true, but I know that I am neither. We killed three. I killed one myself. Good Heavens!

Let me go at this logically, although every power in this mad universe must know that I feel anything but logical.

I have reread what I recorded here before the giants came. The moon rose, and not long after—say, three quarters of an hour—our relief arrived. They were somewhat drunk, but so were we.

Kastawr came with his clone Polydeukahs, not wanting to enjoy himself without him. Kaeneus came as promised. Thus we had five fighters when the giants came down off the mountain. Atalantah's bow served us best, I think, but they rushed her. Kaeneus killed one as it ran. That was simply amazing. He crouched under his shield and sprang up as the giant dashed past, severing an artery in the giant's leg with his sword. The giant took a few more steps and fell. Polydeukahs and Kastawr attacked another as it grappled Atalantah. I actually heard a rib break under the blows of Polydeukahs's fists. They pounded the giant's side like hammers.

People who heard our war cries, the roars of the giants, and Atalantah's screams came pouring down from the town with torches, spears, and swords; but they were too late. We had killed four, and the rest were running from us. None of the townspeople I talked to had been aware of such creatures on their island. They regarded the bodies with superstitious awe. Furthermore, they now regard us with superstitious awe—our boat and our whole crew, and particularly Atalantah, Kastawr, Polydeukahs, Kaeneus, and me. (Puk 59)

About midnight Atalantah and I went up to the palace to see if there was any food left. As soon as we were alone, she embraced me. "Oh, Pilgrim! Can you . . . Could anyone ever love such a coward?"

"I don't ask for your love, Atalantah, only that you like me. I know very well that everyone on our boat is braver than I am, but—"

"Me! Me! You were—you were a wild bull. I was terrified. It was crushing me. I had dropped my bow, and I couldn't get to my knife. It was about to bite my head off, and you were coming! Augah! Oh, Pilgrim! I saw fear in the monster's eyes, before your spear! It was the finest thing that has ever happened to me, but when the giant dropped me I was trembling like a doe with an arrow in her heart."

I tried to explain that it had been nothing, that Kastawr and his clone had already engaged the giant, and that her own struggles were occupying its attention. I said, "I could never have done it if it hadn't had its hands full."

"It had its hands full?" She stared, and burst into laughter. In another minute I was laughing too, the two of us laughing so hard we had to hold onto each other. It was a wonderful moment, but her laughter soon turned to tears, and for the better part of an hour I had to comfort a sobbing girl, a princess small, lonely, and motherless, who stayed alive as best she could in a forest hut with three rough men.

Before I go on to speak of the extraordinary events at the palace, I must say one thing more. My companions shouted their war cries as they battled the giants; and I, when I rushed at the one who held Atalantah, yelled, "Mayflower! Mayflower!" I know that was not what I should have said. I know I should have said mayday, but I do not know what "mayday" means, or why I should have said it. I cannot offer even a hint as to why I found myself shouting mayflower instead. Yet I feel that the great question has been answered. It was what I am doing here. The answer, surely, is that I was sent in order that Atalantah might be spared.

The whole palace was in an uproar. (Pukz 60–62) On the day before his wedding festivities began, King Kuzikos had killed a huge lion on the slopes of Mount Dindumon. It had been skinned and its skin displayed on the stoa, no one in his country having seen one of such size before.

After Kaeneus, Polydeukahs, and Kastawr left the banquet, this lion (we were told) was restored to life, someone filling the empty skin with new lion, so to speak. (Clearly that is impossible; another lion, black-maned like the first and of similar size, was presumably substituted for the skin.) What mattered was that the new or restored lion was loose in the palace. It had killed two persons before we arrived and had mauled three others.

Amphiareaws was in a trance. King Kuzikos had freed his hounds, piebald dogs the size of Great Danes that were nearly as dangerous as any lion. (Pukz 63 and 64) Eeasawn and most of our crew were hunting the lion with the king. Hahraklahs had gone off alone in search of it but had left word with Ekkiawn that I was to join him. Atalantah and I hurried away, knowing no more than that he had intended to search the east wing of the palace and the gardens. We found a body, apparently that of some worthy of the town but had no way of knowing whether it was one of those whose deaths had already been reported or a fresh kill. It had been partly devoured, perhaps by the dogs.

We found Hahraklahs in the garden, looking very much like a lion on its hind legs himself with his lion skin and huge club. He greeted us cordially and seemed not at all sorry that Atalantah had come with me.

"Now let me tell you," he said, "the best way to kill a lion—the best way for me, anyhow. If I can get behind that lion and get my hands on its neck, we can go back to our wine. If I tried to club it, you see, it would hear the club coming down and jerk away. They've got sharp ears, and they're very fast. I'd still hit it—they're not as fast as all that—but not where I wanted, and as soon as I hit it, I'd have it in my lap. Let me get a grip on its neck, though, and we've won."

Atalantah said, "I agree. How can we help?"

"It will be simple, but it won't be easy. When we find it, I'll front it. I'm big enough and mean enough that it won't go straight for me. It'll try to scare me into running, or dodge around and look for an opening. What I need is for somebody to distract it, just for a wink. When I killed this one I'm wearing, Hylas did it for me, throwing stones. But he's not here."

I said I could do that if I could find the stones, and Atalantah remarked that an arrow or two would make any animal turn around to look. We had begun to tell Hahraklahs about the giants when Kalais swooped low and called, "It's coming! Path to your left! Quick!"

I turned my head in time to see its final bound, and it was like seeing a saddle horse clear a broad ditch. Three sparrows could not have scattered faster than we. The lion must have leaped again, coming down on Hahraklahs and knocking him flat. I turned just in time to see him throw it off. It spun through the air, landed on its feet, and charged him with a roar I will never forget.

I ran at it, I suppose with the thought of spearing it, if I had any plan at all. One of Atalantah's arrows whistled past and buried itself in the lion's mane. Hahraklahs was still down, and I tried to pull the lion off him. His club, breaking the lion's skull, sounded like a lab explosion.

And it was over. Blood ran from Hahraklahs's immense arms and trickled from his fingers, and more ran down his face and soaked his beard. The lion lay dead between us, bigger than any horse I have ever seen. Kalais landed on its side as he might have landed on a table, his great white wings fanning the hot night air.

Atalantah embraced me, and we kissed and kissed again. I think that we were both overjoyed that we were still alive. I know that I had already begun to shake. It had happened much too fast for me to be afraid while it was happening, but when it was over, I was terrified. My heart pounded and my knees shook. My mouth was dry. But oh how sweet it was to hold Atalantah and kiss her at that moment, and have her kiss me!

By the time we separated, Hahraklahs and Kalais were gone. I took a few Pukz of the dead lion. (Pukz 65–67) After that, we returned to the wedding banquet and found a lot of guests still there, with Eeasawn and most of our crew. As we came in, Hahraklahs called out, "Did you ever see a man that would take a lion by the tail? Here he is! Look at him!"

That was a moment!

We held a meeting today, just our crew. Eeasawn called it, of course. He talked briefly about Amphiareaws of Argolis, his high reputation as a seer, famous prophecies of his that had been fulfilled, and so on. I had already heard most of it from Kaeneus, and I believe most of our crew is thoroughly familiar with Amphiareaws's abilities.

Amphiareaws himself stepped forward. He is surprisingly young, and quite handsome, but I find it hard to meet his eyes; there is poetry in them, if you will, and sometimes there is madness. There may be something else as well, a quality rarer than either, to which I can put no name. I say there may be, although I cannot be sure.

He spoke very quietly. "We had portents last night. When we were told the lion had been resurrected, I tried to find out what god had done it, and why. At that time, I knew nothing about the six-armed giants. I'll come to them presently.

"Hrea is one of the oldest gods, and one of the most important. She's the mother of Father Zeus. She's also the daughter of Earth, something we forget when we shouldn't. Lions are her sacred animals. She doesn't like it when they are driven away. She likes it even less when they are killed. She's old, as I said, and has a great deal of patience, as old women generally do. Still, patience doesn't last forever. One of us killed one of her favorite lions some time ago."

Everyone looked at Hahraklahs when Amphiareaws said this; I confess I did as well.

"That lion was nursed by Hrea's daughter Hahra at her request, and it was set in the heavens by Hahra when it died—again at her mother's request. The man who killed it changed his name to 'Hahra's Glory' to avert her wrath, as most of us know. She spared him, and her mother Hrea let the matter go, at least for the present."

Amphiareaws fell silent, studying us. His eyes lingered on Hahraklahs, as was to be expected, but lingered on me even longer. (Puk 68) I am not ashamed to say they made me acutely uncomfortable.

"King Kuzikos offended Hrea anew, hunting down and killing another of her finest animals. We arrived, and she determined to avenge herself. She called upon the giants of Hopladamus, the ancient allies who had protected her and her children from her husband." By a gesture, Amphiareaws indicated the six-armed giants we had killed.

"Their plan was to destroy the *Argo,* and with most of us gone, they anticipated little difficulty. I have no wish to offend any of you. But had only Kaeneus and Polydeukahs been present, or only Atalantah and Pilgrim, I believe they would have succeeded without much difficulty. Other gods favored us, however. Polydeukahs and Kastawr are sons of Zeus. Kaeneus is of course favored by the Sea God, as are ships generally. Who can doubt that Augah favors Atalantah? Time is Pilgrim's foe—something I saw plainly as I began to speak. But if Time detests him, other gods, including Father Zeus, may well favor him.

"Whether that is so or otherwise, our vessel was saved by the skill in arms of those five, and by their courage, too. We must not think, however, that we have won. We must make what peace we can with Hrea, and so must King Kuzikos. If we fail, we must expect disaster after disaster. Persefonay favors our cause. This we know. Father Zeus favors it as well. But Persefonay could not oppose Hrea even if she dared, and though Father Zeus may oppose his mother in some things, there will surely be a limit to his friendship.

"Let us sacrifice and offer prayers and praise to Hrea. Let us urge the king to do likewise. If our sacrifices are fitting and our praise and prayers sincere, she may excuse our offenses."

We have sacrificed cattle and sheep in conjunction with the king. Pukz 69–74 show the entire ceremony.

I have been hoping to speak privately with Amphiareaws about Time's enmity. I know that I will not be born for many years. I know also that I have traveled the wrong way through those many years to join our crew. Was that in violation of Time's ordinances? If so, it would explain his displeasure; but if not, I must look elsewhere.

Is it lawful to forget? For I know that I have forgotten. My understanding of the matter is that knowledge carried from the future into the past is clearly out of place, and so exists only precariously and transitorily. (I cannot remember who taught me this.) My offense may lie in the things I remember, and not in the far greater number of things I have forgotten.

I remember that I was a student or a scholar.

I remember that I was to join the crew of a boat (was it this one?) upon a great voyage.

I remember that I was to talk with the Lapiths.

I remember that there is some device among my implants that takes Pukz, another implant that enables me to keep this record, and a third implant that will let me rush ahead to my own period once we have brought the ramskin back to Mount Laphysios.

Perhaps I should endeavor to forget those things. Perhaps Time would forgive me if I did.

I hope so.

We will put to sea again tomorrow morning. The past two days have been spent making ready. (Pukz 75–81) The voyage to Kolkkis should take a week or ten days. The capital, Aea, is some distance from the coast on a navigable river. Nauplios says the river will add another two days to our trip, and they will be days of hard rowing. We do not care. Call the whole time two weeks. Say we spend two more in Aea persuading the king to let us return the ramskin. The ghost of Phreexos is eager to be home, Amphiareaws says. It will board us freely. In a month we may be homeward bound, our mission a success. We are overjoyed, all of us.

Atalantah says she will ask the king's permission to hunt in his territory. If he grants it, she will go out at once. I have promised to help her.

This king is Aeeahtahs, a stern ruler and a great warrior in his youth. His queen is dead, but he has a daughter, the beautiful and learned Mahdaya. Atalantah and I agree that in a kingdom without queen or prince, this princess is certain to wield great influence, the more so in that she is reported to be a woman of ability. Atalantah will appeal to her. She will certainly be interested in the particulars of our voyage, as reported by the only woman on board. Atalantah will take every opportunity to point out that her hunt will bring credit to women everywhere, and particularly to the women of Kolkkis, of whom Mahdaya is the natural leader. Should her hunt fail, however, there will be little discredit if any—everyone acknowledges that the grups is a terribly difficult quarry. I will testify to Atalantah's prowess as a huntress. Hahraklahs offers his testimony as well; before our expedition set out they went boar hunting together.

We are loaded—heavily loaded, in fact—with food, water, and wine. It will be hard rowing, but no one is complaining so early, and we may hope for a wind once we clear the harbor. There is talk of a rowing contest between Eeasawn and Hahraklahs.

Is it possible to be too tired to sleep? I doubt it, but I cannot sleep yet. My hands burn like fire. I splashed a little wine on them when no one was looking. They could hurt no worse, and it may prevent infection. Every muscle in my body aches.

I am splashing wine in me, as well—wine mixed with water. Half and half, which is very strong.

If I had to move to write this, it would not be written.

We put out in fair weather, but the storm came very fast. We took down the sail and unshipped the mast. It was as dark as the inside of a tomb, and the boat rolled and shipped water, and rolled again. We rowed and we bailed. Hour after hour after hour. I bailed until someone grabbed my shoulder and sat me down on the rowing bench. It was so good to sit!

I never want to touch the loom of an oar again. Never!

More wine. If I drink it so fast, will I get sick? It might be a relief, but I could not stand, much less wade out to spew. More wine.

No one knows where we are. We were cast ashore by the storm. On sand, for which we thank every god on the mountain. If it had been rocks, we would have died. The storm howled like a wolf deprived of its prey as we hauled the boat higher up. Hahraklahs broke two ropes. I know that I, and a hundred more like me, could not have broken one. (Pukz 82 and 83, infrared) Men on either side of me—I do not know who. It does not matter. Nothing does. I have to sleep.

The battle is over. We were exhausted before they came, and we are exhausted now; but we were not exhausted when we fought. (Pukz 84, infrared, and 85–88) I should write here of how miraculously these heroes revived, but the fact is that I myself revived in just the same way. I was sound asleep and too fatigued to move when Lugkeos began shouting that we were being attacked. I sat up, blearily angry at being awakened and in the gray dawnlight saw the ragged line of men with spears and shields charging us from the hills above the beach.

All in an instant, I was wide awake and fighting mad. I had no armor, no shield, nothing but my spear, but early in the battle I stepped on somebody's sword. I have no idea how I knew what it was, but I did, and I snatched it up and fought with my spear in my right hand and the sword in my left. My technique, if I can be said to have had one, was to attack furiously anyone who was fighting Atalantah. It was easy since she frequently took on two or three at a time. During the fighting I was much too busy to think about it, but now I wonder what those men thought when they were confronted with a breastplate having actual breasts, and glimpsed the face of a beautiful woman under her helmet.

Most have not lived to tell anyone.

What else?

Well, Eeasawn and Askalafos son of Arahs were our leaders, and good ones, too, holding everybody together and going to help wherever the fighting was hottest. Which meant that I saw very little of them; Kaeneus fought on Atalantah's left, and his swordsmanship was simply amazing. Confronted by a man with armor and a shield, he would feint so quickly that the gesture could scarcely be seen. The shield would come down, perhaps only by five centimeters. Instantly Kaeneus's point would be in his opponent's throat, and the fight would be over. He was not so much fighting men as butchering them, one after another after another.

Hahraklahs fought on my right. Spears thrust at us were caught in his left hand and snapped like so many twigs. His club smashed every shield in reach, and broke the arm that held it. We four advanced, walking upon corpses.

Oh, Zeus! Father, how could you! I have been looking at my Pukz of the battle (84–88). King Kuzikos led our attackers. I recognized him at once, and he appears in 86 and 87. Why should he welcome us as friends, then attack us when we were returned to his kingdom by the storm? The world is mad!

I will not tell Eeasawn or Hahraklahs. We have agreed not to loot the bodies until the rain stops. If the king is among the dead, someone is sure to recognize him. If he is not, let us be on our way. A protracted quarrel with these people is the last thing we require.

I hope he is still alive. I hope that very much indeed.

The king's funeral games began today. Foot races, spear-throwing, all sorts of contests. I know I cannot win, but Atalantah says I must enter several to preserve my honor, so I have. Many will enter and all but one will lose, so losing will be no disgrace.

Eeasawn is buying a chariot and a team so that he can enter the chariot race. He will sacrifice both if he wins.

Hahraklahs will throw the stone. Atalantah has entered the foot races. She has had no chance to run for weeks, and worries over it. I tried to keep up with her, but it was hopeless. She runs like the wind. Today she ran in armor to build up her legs. (Puk 89)

Kastawr has acquired a fine black stallion. Its owner declared it could not be ridden by any man alive. Kastawr bet that he could ride it, laying his place on our boat against the horse. When its owner accepted the bet, Kastawr whistled, and the horse broke its tether to come to him. We were all amazed. He whispered in its ear, and it extended its forelegs so that he could mount more easily. He rode away bareback, jumped some walls, and rode back laughing. (Pukz 90–92)

"This horse was never wild," he told its previous owner. "You merely wanted to say that you nearly had a place on the *Argo*."

The owner shook his head. "I couldn't ride him, and neither could anyone else. You've won. I concede that. But can I try him just once more, now that you've ridden him?"

Polydeukahs got angry. "You'll gallop away, and my brother will never see you again. I won't permit it."

"Well, I will," Kastawr declared. "I trust him—and I think I know a way of fetching him back."

So the previous owner mounted; the black stallion threw him at once, breaking his neck. Kastawr will enter the stallion in the horse race. He is helping Eeasawn train his chariot horses as well.

The games began with choral singing. We entered as a group, our entire crew. I was our only tenor, but I did the best I could, and our director singled me out for special praise. Atalantah gave us a mezzo-soprano, and Hahraklahs supplied a thundering bass. The judges chose another group, but we were the popular favorites. These people realize, or at any rate most of them seem to, that it was King Kuzikos's error (he mistook us for pirates) that caused his death, a death we regret as much as they do.

As music opened the games today, so music will close them. Orfius of Thrakah, who directed our chorus, will play and sing for us. All of us believe he will win.

The one stade race was run today. Atalantah won, the only woman who dared run against men. She is celebrated everywhere. I finished last. But wait—

My performance was by no means contemptible. There were three who were no more than a step or two ahead of me. That is the first thing. I paced myself poorly, I know, running too fast at first and waiting until too late to put on a final burst of speed. The others made a final effort, too, and I had not counted on that. I will know better tomorrow.

Second, I had not known the customs of these people. One is that every contestant wins a prize of some kind—armor, clothing, jewelry, or whatever. The other is that the runner who comes in last gets the best prize, provided he accepts his defeat with good humor. I got a very fine dagger of the hard, yellowish metal all armor and weapons are made of here. There is a scabbard of the same metal, and both display extraordinary workmanship. (Pukz 93–95)

Would I rather have won? Certainly. But I got the best prize as well as the jokes, and I can honestly say that I did not mind the jokes. I laughed and made jokes of my own about myself. Some of them were pretty feeble, but everybody laughed with me.

I wanted another lesson from Kaeneus, and while searching for him I came upon Idmon, looking very despondent. He tells me that when the funeral games are over, a member of our crew will be chosen by lot to be interred with King Kuzikos. Idmon knows, he says, that the fatal lot will fall upon him. He is a son of Apollawn and because he is, a seer like Amphiareaws; long before our voyage began, he learned that he would go and that he would not return alive. (Apollawn is another of their gods.) I promised Idmon that if he was in fact buried alive I would do my utmost to rescue him. He thanked me but seemed as despondent as ever when I left him. (Puk 96)

The two-stade race was run this morning, and there was wrestling this afternoon. Both were enormously exciting. The spectators were beside themselves, and who can blame them?

In the two-stade race, Atalantah remained at the starting line until the rest of us had rounded the first turn. When she began to run, the rest of us might as well have been walking.

No, we were running. Our legs pumped, we gasped for breath, and we streamed with sweat. Atalantah was riding a turbocycle. She ran effortlessly, her legs and arms mere blurs of motion. She finished first and was already accepting her prize when the second-place finisher crossed the line.

Kastawr wrestled. Wrestlers cannot strike, kick, gouge or bite, but everything else seems to be permitted. To win, one must throw one's opponent to the ground while remaining on one's feet. When both fall together, as often happens, they separate, rise, and engage again. Kastawr threw each opponent he faced, never needing more than a minute or two. (Pukz 97–100) No one threw him, nor did he fall with his opponent in any match. He won, and won as easily, I thought, as Atalantah had won the two-stade race.

I asked Hahraklahs why he had not entered. He said he used to enter these things, but he generally killed or crippled someone. He told me how he had wrestled a giant who grew stronger each time he was thrown. Eventually Hahraklahs was forced to kill him, holding him over his head and strangling him. If I had not seen the six-armed giants here, I would not have believed the story, but why not? Giants clearly exist. I have seen and fought them myself. Why is there this wish to deny them? Idmon believes he will die, and that nothing can save him. I would deny giants, and the very gods, if I were not surrounded by so many of their sons.

Atalantah says she is of purely human descent. Why did her father order her exposed to die? Surely it must have been because he knew he was not her father save in name. I asked about Augah, to whom Atalantah is so often compared. Her father was Zeus, her mother a Teetan. May not Father Zeus (as he is rightly called) have fathered another, similar, daughter by a human being? A half sister?

When I congratulated Kastawr on his win, he challenged me to a friendly fencing match, saying he wanted to see how much swordcraft I had picked up from Kaeneus. I explained that Kaeneus and I have spent most of our time on the spear.

Kastawr and I fenced with sticks and pledged ourselves not to strike the face. He won, but praised my speed and resource. Afterward he gave me a lesson and taught me a new trick, though like Kaeneus he repeated again and again that tricks are of no value to a warrior who has not mastered his art, and of small value even to him.

He made me fence left-handed, urging that my right arm might someday be wounded and useless; it has given me an idea.

Stone-throwing this morning; we will have boxing this afternoon. The stadium is a hollow surrounded by hills, as my Pukz (101–103) show. There are rings of stone seats all around the oval track on which we raced, nine tiers of them in most places. Stone-throwing, boxing, and the like take place in the grassy area surrounded by the track.

Hahraklahs was the only member of our crew to enter the stone-throwing, and it is the only event he has entered. I thought that they would measure the throws, but they do not. Two throw together, and the one who makes the shorter throw is eliminated. When all the pairs have thrown, new pairs are chosen by lot, as before. As luck would have it, Hahraklahs was in the final pair of the first pairings. He went to the farther end of the stadium and warned the spectators that his stone might fall among them, urging them to leave a clear space for it. They would not take him seriously, so he picked up one of the stones and warned them again, tossing it into the air and catching it with one hand as he spoke. They cleared a space as he had asked, though I could tell that he thought it too small. (Puk 104)

He went back to the line at the other end of the field, picking up the second stone on his way. In his huge hands they seemed scarcely larger than cheeses. When he threw, his stone sailed high into the air and fell among the spectators like a thunderbolt, smashing two limestone slabs in the ninth row. It had landed in the cleared space, but several people were cut by flying shards even so.

After seeing the boxing, I wonder whether I should have entered the spear-dueling after all. The boxers' hands are bound with leather strips. They strike mostly at the face. A bout is decided when one contestant is knocked down; but I saw men fighting still when they were half blinded by their own blood. (Pukz 105–110) Polydeukahs won easily.

Since I am to take part in the spear-dueling, I had better describe the rules. I have not yet seen a contest, but Kaeneus has explained everything. A shield and a helmet are allowed, but no other armor. Neither the spears nor anything else (stones for example) may be thrown. First blood ends the contest, and in that way it is more humane than boxing. A contestant who kills his opponent is banished at once—he must leave the city, never to return. In general a contestant tries to fend off his opponent's spear with his shield, while trying to pink his opponent with his own spear. Wounds are almost always to the arms and legs, and are seldom deep or crippling. It is considered unsportsmanlike to strike at the feet, although it is not, strictly speaking, against the rules.

Reading over some of my earlier entries, I find I referred to a "turbocycle." Did I actually know what a turbocycle was when I wrote that? Whether I did or not, it is gone now. A cycle of turbulence? Kalais might ride turbulent winds, I suppose. No doubt he does. His father is the north wind. Or as I should say, his father is the god who governs it.

I am alone. Kleon was with me until a moment ago. He knelt before me and raised his head, and I cut his throat as he wished. He passed swiftly and with little pain. His spurting arteries drenched me in blood, but then I was already drenched with blood.

I cannot remember the name of the implant that will move me forward in time, but I hesitate to use it. (They are still shoveling dirt upon this tomb. The scrape of their shovels and the sounds of the dirt falling from them are faint, but I can hear them now that the others are dead.) Swiftly, then, before they finish and my rescuers arrive.

Eeasawn won the chariot race. (Pukz 111–114) I reached the semifinals in spear-dueling, fighting with the sword I picked up during the battle in my left hand. (Pukz 115–118)

Twice I severed a spear shaft, as Kastawr taught me. (Pukz 119 and 120) I was as surprised as my opponents. One must fight without effort, Kaeneus said, and Kaeneus was right. Forget the fear of death and the love of life. (I wish I could now.) Forget the desire to win and any hatred of the enemy. His eyes will tell you nothing if he has any skill at all. Watch his point, and not your own.

I was one of the final four contestants. (Pukz 121) Atalantah and I could not have been happier if I had won. (Pukz 122 and 123)

I have waited. I cannot say how long. Atalantah will surely come, I thought. Hahraklahs will surely come. I have eaten some of the funeral meats, and drunk some of the wine that was to cheer the king in Persefonay's shadowy realm. I hope he will forgive me.

We drew pebbles from a helmet. (Pukz 124 and 125) Mine was the black pebble (Pukz 126), the only one. No one would look at me after that.

The others (Pukz 127 and 128) were chosen by lot, too, I believe. From the king's family. From the queen's. From the city. From the palace servants. That was Kleon. He had been wine steward. Thank you, Kleon, for your good wine. They walled us in, alive.

"Hahraklahs will come for me," I told them. "Atalantah will come for me. If the tomb is guarded—"

They said it would be.

"It will not matter. They will come. Wait. You will see that I am right."

They would not wait. I had hidden the dagger I won and had brought it into the tomb with me. I showed it to them, and they asked me to kill them.

Which I did, in the end. I argued. I pleaded. But soon I consented, because they were going to take it from me. I cut their throats for them, one by one.

And now I have waited for Atalantah.

Now I have waited for Hahraklahs.

Neither has come. I slept, and sat brooding in the dark, slept, and sat brooding. And slept again, and sat brooding again. I have reread my diary, and reviewed my Pukz, seeing in some things that I had missed before. They have not come. I wonder if they tried?

How long? Is it possible to overshoot my own period? Surely not, since I could not go back to it. But I will be careful just the same. A hundred years—a mere century. Here I go!

Nothing. I have felt about for the bodies in the dark. They are bones and nothing more. The tomb remains sealed, so Atalantah never came. Nobody did. Five hundred years this time. Is that too daring? I am determined to try it.

Greece. Not that this place is called Greece, I do not think it is, but Eeasawn and the rest came from Greece. I know that. Even now the Greeks have laid siege to Ilion, the city we feared so much. Agamemnawn and Akkilleus are their leaders.

Rome rules the world, a rule of iron backed by weapons of iron. I wish I had some of their iron tools right now. The beehive of masonry that imprisons me must surely have decayed somewhat by this time, and I still have my emergency rations. I am going to try to pry loose some stones and dig my way out.

The *Mayflower* has set sail, but I am not aboard her. I was to make peace. I can remember it now—can remember it again. We imagined a cooperative society in which Englishmen and Indians might meet as friends, sharing knowledge and food. It will never happen now, unless they have sent someone else.

The tomb remains sealed. That is the chief thing and the terrible thing, for me. No antiquarian has unearthed it. King Kuzikos sleeps undisturbed. So does Kleon. Again . . .

This is the end. The Chronomiser has no more time to spend. This is my own period, and the tomb remains sealed; no archeologist has found it, no tomb robber. I cannot get out, and so must die. Someday someone will discover this. I hope they will be able to read it.

Good-bye. I wish that I had sailed with the Pilgrims and spoken with the Native Americans—the mission we planned for more than a year. Yet the end might have been much the same. Time is my enemy. Cronus. He would slay the gods if he could, they said, and in time he did.

Revere my bones. This hand clasped the hand of Hercules.

These bony lips kissed the daughter of a god. Do not pity me.

The bronze blade is still sharp. Still keen, after four thousand years. If I act quickly I can cut both my right wrist and my left. (Pukz 129 and 130, infrared)

The Zhou Dynasty of China came to an end during the Warring States Period (475–221 B.C.), when a number of vassals broke away from Zhou rule and fought vigorously among themselves. Amid this turmoil the arts thrived and the period came to be called "One Hundred Flowers Blooming." Brenda Clough, who has already brought elements of the Near Eastern Bronze Age into modern times in two recent novels, illuminates this contradiction, that art may indeed be born out of war, and serve it.

How the Bells Came from Yang to Hubei

BRENDA CLOUGH

I had never beheld such a miserable wretch. My master Chu gulped. The prisoner was bone-thin, the weeping sores easily visible through his rags. His dirty bare feet left red smears on the tile floor. "The carpet," old Lord Yang murmured, and servants carried the priceless textile aside. We ourselves had not dared to walk on it and had stepped around.

The soldier in charge jerked the rope attached to the unfortunate's leg shackle, and the prisoner fell flat on his face with no attempt to break the fall. I saw that his hands had been chopped off, the wrists ending in black cauterized stumps. How could one come to such a horrendous pass, the ultimate catastrophe for a handiworker? My own fingers twitched in sympathy. From my place just behind and to his left I saw Master Chu's cheek blanch. He is oversensitive, a true artist. Luckily he has me, young Li, for First Assistant. Discreetly I gripped him by the elbow to keep him upright. Lord Yang would not think a faint amusing.

"Tell your tale, worm," the soldier barked.

The prisoner's Chinese was accented but understandable: "The battle in Guangdong—we should have won. We were winning. Our arrows darkened the sky. We had a third again as many spears."

"And?" Lord Yang flicked a glance at my master. I squeezed his arm to make sure he was listening.

"The bells. They had sorcerers with bronze bells. Racks and racks of them, dangling like green skulls, carried into the field on wagons. And the sound . . ."

"Ah, the sound!" My master straightened. "Was the note high-pitched, or low?"

"Both. Neither. I cannot say. They beat the bells with mallets, and we fell down. Blood poured from our noses and assholes. Our guts twisted in our bellies . . ." The prisoner began to sob, muffling the noise in the crook of his elbow.

Lord Yang sighed. "This one's usefulness is at an end." The soldier hauled the prisoner roughly up, and the servants ushered them out. More servants crawled in their wake, silently mopping up the red stains with cloths. I tried not to look. "Now, Master Chu. You know of these bells that Lord Tso used to defeat Guangdong?"

"I can guess, my lord." My master would have scratched his head in his usual thoughtful gesture, but I twitched his arm down—you can't scratch in front of a warlord. "When I was First Assistant in his foundries, the Lord Tso was their most munificent patron."

"As I shall be yours." Lord Yang flicked a wrinkled finger. A servant came forward with two bulging leather bags. "Make me bells, Master Chu. Bells of war."

"My lord, the Lord Tso ordered a set of sixty bells."

"You shall make me eighty."

"Eighty!" My master drew in a deep joyful breath. "Such a commission—the foundry's resources will be yours alone, lord. And a huge ensemble like this—they must be *zhong* bells, of course, mounted upon racks for easy transport . . ."

It was just like Master Chu to immediately plunge into technical matters. He is like the phoenix, the bird that we inlay in gold upon the cylindrical sides of bells. The phoenix thinks only of its music, and flies higher and ever higher, singing. It doesn't worry about practicalities.

My thoughts ran otherwise. The Lord Tso was a warrior in his prime, reputed to be a tiger in both combat and peace. If he had devoured Guangdong, his power would be overweening. And we were going to fight him? "Then it is war, lord?" I burst out.

Lord Yang's lean mouth pursed in a smile. "High politics are for me to determine, apprentice. Do you stick to your master's craft, and I will hew to mine. You are but one tile in the mosaic, and who can say which tile is the most essential? Here is gold enough. And from my storehouses you may draw bronze and tin. In two years' time my armies shall march."

"Two years?" Master Chu nodded. "I must consult with your musicians . . ."

"My lord!" I licked my lips, which had gone unaccountably dry. "No one loves bronzework better than I. But—bells are only bells. They are only our plea to heaven, our voice to the gods. There is no power against mortals in them. The symptoms the prisoner described—could it be that his army merely had drunk bad water?"

When Lord Yang clapped his hands the sound was thin and dry as reed striking reed. "Let the prisoner be returned," he said. "You and your master shall question him closely. Wring from him all you can—indeed my spies brought him from Guangdong for this very purpose. Master Chu, you have my permission to have his captor exert whatever persuasion necessary."

The idea made me shudder, and my master stared. He is incapable of hurting a fly. But the servant returned and fell to his knees, crying, "My lord, you indicated the prisoner was no longer of use to yourself. He has already been executed. Perhaps your lordship would care to see the body?"

Lord Yang shook his head sadly. "Regrettable. No, have the useless carrion flung onto the midden. You must manage without, Master Chu. I look forward to seeing the bells. And—" He nodded at the servant. "You have served me long. Is it your wish to be executed for your incompetence, or to commit suicide?"

"I shall hang myself immediately, lord, thank you!" The servant kowtowed and scuttled away. We were dismissed with another gesture, and gratefully backed out of the room.

"Bells we can cast," I said, once we were safe in the forecourt. "Bells that will sing a true note clear as crystal, and not only a single note, but sometimes even two harmonious ones. But a bell that can kill? Master, are there secrets to the craft that you have not yet taught me?"

"Never, lad! I was First Assistant in Lord Tso's foundries, and I can attest that no magics were used in those bells. It's some fanciful story that our lord got into his head. He shouldn't have consulted that prisoner. Under threat of death a man will say any nonsense."

"But you didn't tell him that." I could not blame him. The fate of Lord Yang's servant did not encourage frankness.

"Bells are musical instruments, my boy. You could easier make a military weapon of needles and thread! I like your idea that the losing army had drunk bad water. And it could be that the music of Lord Tso's bells greatly enheartened the troops, urging them on to victory. If they believe it is magic, then it is so."

This was an encouraging line of reflection. "So perhaps our bells could be likewise," I said. "Like the jade button on the top of a mandarin's cap: not the cause of his greatness but an ornament upon it."

"Two years is a long time," my ever-hopeful master said. "Let us design and cast the bells, a fascinating project! And worry about slaying armies with them later—"

"Master?"

We both looked up from our talk. A maid beckoned from a circular archway in the wall. "Do I know you?" my master said uncertainly.

"Of course not. But surely you know of my mistress, Lady Yang. She summons you."

"I?" Bemused, my master followed her, and I fell in behind. Beyond the archway was a walled garden. A plum tree drooped over a carp pool bordered with elaborate stonework. Beside the tree sat a woman, almost lost in the amplitude of brocade sleeves and robe. The mere sight of the gold embroidery on her black satin slippers told us both that we should bow down to the pavement. "Great lady," my master murmured.

"Do it again, only this time don't let your butt stick up."

Astonished, I twisted around to stare up with one eye. The robe and cap and sash were huge, impossibly grand, but the little face beneath the cap was girlish, delicate and pale as plum blossom. "Go on," she commanded. "More elegantly this time."

The little foot in its satin slipper tapped impatiently. I hastened to set the example for my master, rising and then kowtowing again. Both of us tucked our sterns well under this time. I remembered now, how old Yang had lately married a new and exalted wife, a princess from Jiangsu. "Great lady, how may these humble ones serve you?"

"I wish to bear a son."

I could feel my stomach turning right over under my sash with a flop. Was she asking my master to father her child? Surely old Lord Yang could not be impotent—he was rich enough to buy aphrodisiacs by the cartload. And Master Chu has no interest in women, or in anything else for that matter. His love is given to his craft. It was his Assistant's job to take care of all the mundane details, which put me in the center of the target. Such things only happened in stories!

I said nothing and didn't look up, waiting for another clue. And thank the gods, here it was, the solid chink of gold on the pavement between us. I took a sideways peek: a gold bracelet, set with jade plaques.

"You will take this in payment, and you will engrave my wish upon the bell. Thus every time it is struck, my prayer will rise to Heaven."

I sagged so limply with relief that my bowed silhouette surely lost elegance. For once my master was the readier with words. "Willingly, great lady. Your august husband has commanded a set of eighty bells. Shall I have the prayer engraved inside each of them?"

"Oh, that would be very good! Nobody has ever had eighty sons before—I shall be the first!"

I risked looking at her again. This time I saw that her cheeks were round and babyish. Lady Yang must be scarcely twelve, too young to know what bearing ten children would be like, never mind eighty. On the other hand, she had the years before her to do it, if old Yang could keep his end up. For the first time my master's attitude of eternal hope seemed entirely sensible and wise. Not for us to argue childbearing with a princess and the wife of the warlord! "It shall be as you command, great lady," my master said. "Thank you." I hooked the bracelet with one sideswiping finger and tucked it into my sleeve as we rose and backed out.

Only when we were outside the gate did I say, "You realize we've just signed on to produce not one but two complete absurdities? To defeat armies with the sound of bells is impossible, as unachievable as using their music to make a bride pregnant. What are we going do?"

Thoughtfully scratching his head, my master hardly heard me. "This time I shall make all eighty of the bells two-toned. It will be a tremendous challenge! I can see in my mind's eye what the set should look like, cylindrical but slightly flattened. Inlaid gold phoenixes, the symbol of music, would be a proper decoration, sporting around the shoulders. My lady's prayer can be engraved on the inside of each bell, out of the way. The lower surface must be reserved for inscriptions of the *sui* and *gu* sites, so that the musicians may know where to strike for each note. Truly, this shall be magic."

"Just not the kind of magic they paid for!"

"You worry too much, Li," my master reasoned. "We have the job, and the money, and the materials. What more can we ask for? Let's just do our task. Lord Yang can deal with the wars, and his wife can worry about her babies. Do you think you can go to his storehouses and choose the best copper ingots today?"

Caring for nothing but its song, the phoenix soars higher and higher. Perhaps all would yet be well. Willing it to be so, I said, "Of course, master."

Safely secluded in our craft, Master Chu and I spent happy months compounding bronze alloys and casting test bells. The molten metal was poured into pottery molds so large they had to be made in sections, an exacting and difficult business. The largest bell would be chest-high. No one had ever attempted so large an instrument before. We practiced on the smaller ones, slowly perfecting the placement of the *mei,* the bronze bumps on the outside of the bell. Even such tiny details affected the tone.

The day we unmolded the first bell was like a birthday. Master Chu lowered the hot pottery mold into a sandbox and levered the halves apart with a stick. It was the tiniest bell, no larger than my hand, and the hot curve of metal rolled out of the dull mold glowing like a chestnut newly hulled. "Hot, hot!" my master exclaimed, patting it with his leather-gauntleted fingertips. He eased the tip of the stick into the *xuan,* the loop the bell would hang by. When he raised it from the surface of the sand the bell hung at a bit less than the ideal thirty-degree angle, counterbalanced by its heavy *yong.* "We can adjust that," he panted. "File the *yong* down a bit. Now, Li, strike!"

I had a tiny wooden mallet ready. The markings made the *sui* position perfectly easy to find on the flatter front surface of the curve. I have not the touch of a trained musician, but I knew how to tap the place. The sweet high note hung in the air and then faded. It's important that there be no prolonged echo that would interfere with the main melody. Then I struck the *gu* position. "Hah!"

"A perfect harmonic!" Master Chu grinned so widely the sweat dripped down into his open month.

The glorious pure sound made my vision blur, hope and joy bubbling up inside my chest. Perhaps the music of bells really did have some unknown power, unless it was only the heat radiating from the new metal to blame. I grinned too. "And it only took three months!"

"The next bells will be faster. Not easier, but faster. We can set the slaves to polishing this one and engraving Lady Yang's prayer inside."

There is no madness like love, and surely the love of one's craft is the maddest of them all. Master Chu would not have selected me as his Assistant if I did not also have something of the phoenix in me. Not a thought did I put into larger issues that year. To make the bells was enough; what others would do with them was unimportant.

Compounding this were the usual maddening delays and setbacks. The larger bells cracked or did not ring truly, and had to be cast and recast several times. Right up to the last moment we were adjusting tone by grinding metal from the insides. The Lord Yang had had three special wagons made with racks running down the middle, pegs for the different mallets, and space for the musicians to stand. When all the bells were hung in place and the wagons lined up, it looked very fine indeed.

The Director of the lord's orchestra came to the foundry to accept delivery. When I saw him in his full battle armor and helmet, it washed over me like cold water, what we had done. The phoenix fell to the ground with a thump. Impossible to tell myself that we were merely the ornamental button on Lord Yang's cap. My master was dashing from rack to rack, advising the players. So I was able to remark to the Director, "You are marching with the army, I see. Do you know, have these bells formed a vital part of our lord's battle tactics?"

"They are absolutely essential," the Director said cheerfully. "I've had the players perfecting their repertoire, practicing on clay dummy bells. On the way we shall do 'Carp and Bamboo' and 'Hands Like Lilies,' all the good old walking tunes. Then as they march to the actual battle we will play 'Spears of Gold' and my own special composition for the occasion, which our lord has graciously permitted me to title 'Thunder Dragon Yang' . . ."

More proof that love of one's work is madness! I could see that it would be the same whomever I queried. The generals would chatter of battle diagrams, the horsemen would drone on about saddlery, the sutlers would talk about supply trains until listeners wept with boredom. Every tile in the pattern believed passionately that it was paramount. There was no discreet way to find out whether our bells really were supposed to be magic. Suppose the Lord Yang truly was relying upon it? As well lean upon a sewing needle, as my master said. I could see it now, the crushing defeat, the carnage of the battlefield, Lord Tso marching upon our town, the sack and pillage. As his Assistant it would be my duty to defend Master Chu to the death. Perhaps we could escape before the victors put the city to the torch. Our tools could be loaded into a wagon . . .

It haunted me so much, I derived no pleasure from watching the army march away the next day. Everyone in town turned out to watch and cheer. Incense burners made the air blue with sweet smoke. Scarlet banners fluttered from spear points, and Lord Yang rode on a white stallion with slaves holding a green silk canopy over his head. "Magnificent!" my master yelled in my ear over the tumult. "Even that old warhorse 'Hands Like Lilies' sounds grand when played over a hundred and sixty tones."

"Will a hundred and sixty tones make Lord Tso's soldiers fall down and bleed?"

"There's always a sadness when a big project is finished," my master assured me. "Fear not—it passes off entirely when the next job turns up."

"My next job might be fleeing with you into the mountains. Could we perhaps buy a couple of mules, just in case?"

"Don't be silly, lad. Look, there's the palanquin with the Lady. Those gilded poles and rings must have cost a fortune."

"Is she pregnant?" I demanded gloomily. But with the flowing robes that princesses wore it was impossible to say.

With the passage of the ladies the most interesting part of the parade was over. "Look here, Li." My master patted me on the shoulder as we turned away. "You'll fret yourself into a fever. The odds are quite good. Either our lord wins the battle, or not. And either the babe will be a girl, or a boy. Fifty-fifty in both cases, and we can't affect the outcome either way."

"There's something wrong with your calculation," I grumbled, but couldn't put my finger on it.

As summer slid into autumn I became more and more uneasy. The war might be won or lost already, with no way to tell from this distance. The first word we got might be Lord Tso's regiments at the gate with fire and sword. I spent my own small savings on a good mule and its trappings, and packed food and clothing for us both, ready to be snatched up at a moment's notice. And I sorted all the tools in the forge into a pile to take, and those that could be left. "Perhaps you should marry," my master suggested mildly. "It's not healthy to bear the troubles of all the world on your back. A wife would help you sleep better."

"I don't want to sleep better. I want to keep an eye open for trouble."

"Always, you expect the worst!" Master Chu looked out over the silent workshop. "Another job, that's what we need. Perhaps you're right, and we should move on purely for professional reasons. Lord Yang probably has all the bells he will want for some time."

"Lord Yang has troubles enough on his hands—"

But he waved me to silence. "Listen. Do you hear?"

The sound suddenly resounded clearly in the empty room, the clamor of many voices and shouting. "News must have arrived! Quick, let's go to the marketplace and find out."

Forgetting the autumn chill we dashed bareheaded into the courtyard. But beyond the house gate horses milled, and armed men. Armored fists were raised to hammer for entry. "Oh gods, I knew it," I groaned. "All is lost. The town is being sacked. We're about to die. Run, master, run!"

"Wouldn't enemies loot the palace and the treasury first?" Master Chu raised his voice. "Sirs, who do you seek? This is the house of Chu the bronzeworker."

"Well met then, Master Chu. I bring you news from your Lord Yang."

"Me?" Trustfully my master unbarred the gate, while I peered out to see the soldiers' crests. These were not men of ours!

"Behold the orders of the victorious Lord Yang." The soldier swaggered in jingling and held out an enameled bamboo scroll-case. "He has lent you and your services to his triumphant ally, my lord the Marquis of Hubei. The fame of your war bells has inspired the Marquis with a profound desire for his own set."

"Gods!" My master goggled.

"Did you see them in battle?" I interjected. "Did the enemy fall down at the sound?"

At this the troops in the gateway yelled with laughter. "The enemy fell down all right, but it was at the sight of us!" "Oh, ho ho! We rattled our spears, and they wet their pants!"

For a moment I was speechless. Of course they would believe they were responsible. Everyone in the army probably did. Of all the tiles in the mosaic, which is the most essential? The only answer is all of them. "But then it was all by chance!" I cried. "We had nothing to do with the victory!"

"My Assistant is overwrought with relief," Master Chu said calmly. "Your news of victory relieves my mind tremendously, sirs."

The soldier chortled until his face was red. "My lord the Marquis is merely anxious to reproduce all the elements of this famous victory, when he marches against Zheng."

"Zheng!" I was aghast. Lord Zheng was the master military tactician of the western provinces, and we were going to fight him with bells? And there was another thing: "Does the lord Yang's wife enjoy good health, do you know?"

"She was delivered of a son last month." The soldier winked at me. "Word is you two had something to do with that, as well."

My master scratched his head thoughtfully. "I would be delighted to comply with the Marquis' behest. And by the greatest of good fortune my Assistant here has readied our tools and gear for travel."

"Good!" The soldier nodded to his men. "Fetch your baggage—we depart immediately!"

We hurried inside to gather up our bags. "The Marquis will not be satisfied to be outdone by Lord Yang," my master said happily. "We must make him a hundred bells, perhaps a hundred and twenty!"

"We don't know what we did or how we did it," I almost wailed. "But we're supposed to do it again, better?"

My master rolled the heavy leather forge aprons and gauntlets and crammed them into a sack. "What can we do, lad, but what we do best? The work is good, the bells as well made as can be. Mortals can ask for no more. When our best doesn't suffice, we shall die."

I sat down heavily on a box of metal scraps. The prisoner's fate could have been our own: brutal mutilation and slow death. Instead we had fame and possibly fortune. We had done nothing to either avert it or earn it. All our efforts were unavailing. "Is there anyone truly in control, then?"

"The gods, perhaps. No one less. Let it go, boy. The entire scroll of fate is too broad for our eyes. We view the world through a bamboo stem, a narrow circle of the picture, but it's all we can take in."

It came to me that the magic of the bells was not in the metal nor in their music nor in our crafting of them. The magic was in the hope they raised in the human heart. With it impossibilities became not certain but possible. My master's fathomless hope and ferocious concentration were the best wisdoms in this meaningless world. Wheat, he could bow to the wind; a phoenix, he could ride the storm. Five years I had been his Assistant, and I had not known that. "You are indeed my Master," I said humbly. "I have much to learn."

Master Chu smiled. "Now come, Li. Gather up those extra shovels. These soldiers can be useful—let us have them carry what we cannot. Surely the Marquis will build us a workshop!"

Chariotry became the hallmark of Bronze Age warfare, a status symbol from Egypt to northern Europe and far to the east. Some scholars argue that eventually new military tactics spelled the end not only of chariot-based warfare but of the Bronze Age itself. In the beginning, however, chariots promised protection from marauding tribes and commanded a great price. Judith Tarr demonstrates just how valuable by returning to the speculative Bronze Age of her Epona Sequence.

The God of Chariots

Enmerkar the king stood on the walls of Uruk. The hordes from the desert had withdrawn at last. In their wake they had left devastation: fields and orchards stripped of their harvest, villages burned, cattle slaughtered or stolen, and an echo of laughter as they marched away with their spoils.

He had hoped—gods, he had prayed—that if he raised the city's walls higher and doubled the guards on the fields, the Martu would give way. But they had only grown bolder, the more the city tried to resist them. Those who understood their language said that the raiders reckoned the city folk soft and their king a coward, too weak to put up a proper fight.

The men of Uruk were brave enough, but these savages were relentless. Their blades of flint and their spears of fire-hardened wood killed as thoroughly as the finest bronze. And there were so many of them. Uruk was a great city and powerful, but it could not send out the hordes of fighting men that these tribes bred like swarms of locusts.

Now they had gone away. A good half of the harvest was taken and much of the rest trampled and fouled. It was too much to hope that the Martu would not come back when the grain was tall again, as they had for year upon year, and each year in greater numbers and with stronger weapons and more outrageous contempt. The men of Uruk grew the grain; the men of the desert took it, as if the gods had given it to them as a gift.

Enmerkar stood under the open sky before the eyes of his people. He could not rend his beard in frustration, still less fling down his royal staff and trample it. He stiffened his back and squared his shoulders and made himself descend from the sight of a war that he could not, with all his wealth and power, hope to win.

"We need Aratta," the king's sister said.

She was Inanna, the living goddess, unlike Enmerkar, who was a mere king of men. In her divinity she could run far ahead of mortal understanding; she was not always patient, either. She glared at the blank faces of the king's council, a circle of round cheeks and round eyes, with no more wit in them than in a cairn of stones.

"Aratta," she said as if to children, "has wood. It has stone. It has metal. It has alliances with us from years before, oaths and promises of trade. Aratta will help us, if we offer a caravan of grain and the fruits of the south."

"A caravan?" said the king. "It will be a lean winter as it is. We can't spare even a tithe of the harvest—and Aratta will want more than that, if it knows how desperate we are."

"Then let us not be desperate," Inanna said sharply. "Let us be allies with trade to offer. Or are we truly defeated as the Martu declare? Are we their sheep, to be plucked of our fleece in season and led tamely to the slaughter?"

That made some of them bristle and others close their ears and minds against her. Lugalbanda, who had earned his place here by winning a battle or three but who was not the best or most eloquent of speakers, found himself unable to restrain his tongue. "I—I have heard," he said, battling the stammer that always beset him when he had to speak in front of people, "I have heard a story, a rumor really, but it has a ring of truth—that there is a new god in Aratta, a god of war."

"That's old news," said the councilor who had spoken first. "The god, if he is one at all, has been there for years."

"Indeed," said the king's sister. She turned her beautiful and terrible eyes on Lugalbanda. "Tell us what you have heard."

His knees were weak and his wits scattered, but those eyes compelled him. They drew words out of him, words that even made sense—and that was a miracle worthy of her divinity. "I—I have heard that the god came from the east, and he brought with him an art and a weapon. He forges bronze, they say, that is stronger and brighter and keener than any in the world. His swords are sharper, his spearheads more deadly. But even more than those, he has a craft, a thing of power and terror. It rolls like thunder over the earth. Great beasts draw it, swifter than the wind. Wherever it goes, armies fall like mown grain."

"Travelers' tales," said the king.

"Travelers who have been to Aratta," his sister said. "Is there more?"

Lugalbanda had an itch between his shoulderblades. It would have killed his dignity to scratch it, yet it was a miserable niggling thing.

It could not drive him any madder than the sight of her face. "There—there is a little, divine lady. They say the god rides in his great weapon, and rules it with the terror of his will. And—and they say that he is not alone. That he has made more of them, and taught the men of the city to master them, and they are unconquerable in battle."

"It is true," said the eldest of the council, who was deaf and nearly blind, but his wits were still as sharp as ever. "Even I hear a thing or two, and I have heard that no enemy has threatened Aratta since shortly after the god came to it. It's more than the terror of his presence; he has weapons that deter even the hordes of savages."

Enmerkar smote his thigh with his fist. "If Aratta has such weapons—if this is not dream and delusion—we need them. We need copper and stone, wood and bronze. We need strength to drive back the Martu and to keep them from coming back again and again."

Inanna clapped her hands together. "All hail to the king of Uruk! Yes, we need what Aratta has—and it would be best if our messenger went soon, before winter closes the mountain passes. As it is, he'll not come back until spring, but maybe he'll come to us with a hoard of god-forged weapons."

"And maybe he'll come back empty-handed, or never at all." But Enmerkar was less despondent than he had been in all this Martu-embattled year. "It's a risk I'm willing to take. But, lady, to send a caravan—"

"We can't send promises," she said. "We're too desperate. It must be sacks of wheat and barley, and jars of dates and baskets of apples and all the riches of the earth that we can possibly spare."

"And wine," the eldest councilor said. "Send the king a great gift of date wine, and see he drinks a good part of it while he haggles. That will bring him round if nothing else will."

He grinned a toothless grin. Some of them were outraged, but laughter ran round the rest of the circle, easing the mood remarkably. He had won them over more truly with laughter than she had with her fierce impatience.

She was in no way contrite, though she had the grace to acknowledge his wisdom. "We should leave as soon as may be," she said, "with as large a caravan as we can muster, under a strong guard. You"—she thrust her chin toward Lugalbanda—"will command the guard. See that you choose men brave enough, and hardy enough, for mountains."

Lugalbanda could find no words to say. He was the youngest and the least of this council. He was a fighting man, to be sure, and had led a company of stalwarts from the city with some credit and a number of victories the past few seasons. But to leave Uruk, to venture the mountains that walled the north of the world, to walk where all the gods were strange—

"I am not—" he began.

No one heeded him. The king had heard what Inanna had tried to hide behind the shield of Lugalbanda. "*You* are going? Lady, you cannot—"

"I am going," she said with divine certainty. "My temple will do well enough in my absence. The rest of the gods will look after the city. No one and nothing in Uruk will suffer because I have gone from it."

"No one but you," her brother said bluntly. "Lady, the journey is long and the road is hard. As great and powerful as you are, and as divinely blessed, still you walk in flesh, and flesh can be destroyed. We can't risk the loss of you."

"You can't risk a lesser messenger," she said. "You could send every wise man in this council, and that would be a noble embassy, but my heart declares that they would fail. I may not succeed, either, but the refusal may be less swift. Men will hesitate to refuse a goddess."

"I can't let you go," Enmerkar said.

She raised her chin. When she drew herself up, she was nearly as tall as the king. She met him eye to eye and will to will. "I am not yours to permit or deny," she said with dangerous softness. "I belong to Uruk, and Uruk has great need of me."

He was not struck dumb—far from it. But before he could burst out in speech, the eldest councilor said, "Certainly no man may oppose the will of a goddess. But, lady, Uruk will be a sad place without you."

"Uruk will be sadder when the Martu break down the gates," she said. "A god may address a god, even when kings are minded to be difficult. I will speak as an equal to the god in Aratta, and see what I may win for Uruk."

Even the king could hardly fail to see the sense in that. He scowled and snarled, but he no longer tried to forbid her. She rose from her chair of honor and shook out the flounces of her skirt. "We leave before the moon comes to the full," she said.

Whatever protest any of them might have uttered, she did not hear it. She had swept out, grand as a goddess could be, in every expectation that when she deigned to look again, all would be done exactly as she had ordered.

Mountains went up and up, but never quite touched the sky. Lugalbanda's men had known no height of land but what men made with their own hands: towers, and walls of cities. This lifting and tilting and tumbling of the earth robbed them of breath and sense, numbed them with cold and pelted them with stinging whiteness.

Snow, their mountain-born guides called that. They were casually contemptuous of the flatlanders, as they called the men of Uruk—but they were in awe of the goddess who traveled with them. Lugalbanda had deep doubts of their trustworthiness, but their fear of the goddess had proved thus far to be greater than either greed or malice.

He had been trudging upward since the world began, and wheezing for breath the more, the higher he went. Some of the men had had to turn back: they were dizzy, their heads were splitting, and when they tried to rise or walk they collapsed in a fit of vomiting. Lugalbanda was not much happier than they, but he had so little desire to eat that there was nothing to cast up.

There had been a raid or two, days ago; they had lost a pair of oxen and a drover. But since they had come to the top of the world, they were all alone but for the occasional eagle. Lugalbanda was sure by then that their journey would have no end, that they would climb forever and never find Aratta.

Inanna, being divine, knew no such doubts or weakness. She walked ahead of her people, beside or just behind the guides, wrapped in wool and felt and fleece, and nothing showing from the midst of it but her great dark eyes. She refused to ride on one of the oxen; she would not let one of the men carry her. Her legs were sturdy and her strides long; she breathed as easily on the summits as in the river valley in which she had been born.

Lugalbanda followed her blindly. The snow was so white, the light so piercing, that his eyes stabbed with pain. He wrapped them in folds of linen and followed the shadow of her, and knew little of where he went. He had no mind left; it was all burned out of him, there beneath the roof of heaven.

Even as dazed he was, he became aware, one bitterly bright day, that the ascent had stopped. They were going down, slowly sometimes, and at other times precipitously. Little by little the air warmed. The snow thinned. The sun's light lost its fierce edge. Lugalbanda's eyes could open again without pain, and his mind began to clear.

There came a morning when, having camped in a green and pleasant valley, they descended by a steep narrow track. It surmounted a ridge and, at midmorning, bent sharply round the knee of the mountain.

There before them was not yet another wilderness of peaks but a wide green country rolling toward a distant dazzle and shimmer.

"The sea," Inanna said. He had not heard or sensed her coming, but she was beside him. The mountainside dropped away almost beneath her feet, but she stood as calmly as if on level ground. "Look, do you see? There is Aratta."

He had seen it, but at that distance and out of the last of his mountain-born befuddlement he had taken it for an outcropping of rock. It was built on such, he saw as he peered under his hand, but its walls were deep and high, and within them he saw the rise of towers.

It was a greater city than he had expected. It was not as great or as noble as Uruk, but its splendors were manifold. Its walls were of stone, its gates of massive timbers bound with bronze. Its houses and palaces and the towers of its temples were built of wood and stone. The wealth of that, the extravagance, were unimaginable in a world of mud brick, but here they were commonplace.

They were three days on the road between the mountains and the city. Lugalbanda had sent men ahead, swift runners with strong voices, to proclaim the goddess's coming. They performed the task well: when the caravan came to Aratta, they found its walls hung with greenery and its processional way strewn with flowers.

Inanna allowed herself to be carried in like a sacred image, borne on the shoulders of the tallest and strongest of her guards. She had put on a gown of fine linen and ornaments of gold and lapis, and set a diadem of gold over her plaited hair, with golden ribbons streaming down her back and shoulders. She was as bright as a flame in the cool sunlight of this country, where everything was green, and the earth's bones were hidden beneath a mantle of grass and forest.

The king of Aratta received her at the door of his high stone house. He was a younger man than Lugalbanda had expected, tall and broad and strong, with the look of a fighting man and the scars to go with it. He watched Inanna's coming with an expression almost of shock, as if he had never seen a goddess before.

It was a remarkable expression, like none that Lugalbanda had seen before. After a while he set a name to it. It was hunger: not the hunger of the starving man who sees welcome sustenance, but of the rich man who thought that he had seized all the wealth that was to be had, but now he sees a treasure that is not his—and he must have it, whatever the cost.

As quickly as it had appeared, it receded into his eyes. He smiled the practiced smile of kings and greeted the goddess and her following in a fair rendering of the dialect of Uruk. She replied with dignity.

Lugalbanda did not listen to the words. He watched the faces. The god was not here: there was only one divinity in this place, and she had drawn every eye to her. No god would have borne such a distraction.

At length the king bowed and turned and led the goddess into his house. Lugalbanda followed at a wary distance. The caravan dissipated within the king's house; only Lugalbanda's own men followed the goddess to the depths of it, and there guarded her.

Embassies, even urgent ones, were leisurely proceedings. It would be days before anyone came to the point. Today they feasted and exchanged compliments. No word was spoken of the caravan of gifts and grain, or of the message that had come with it.

Nor did they speak of the god—not the king, and not the high ones seated near him, and certainly not Inanna. But in the farther reaches of the hall, among the young men, the talk was of little else. They were all wild to master the new weapon, which they called a chariot. "It is wonderful," they said. "Remarkable. Divine. To ride in it, it's like riding the wind."

"I should like to see this thing," Lugalbanda said. "Is it winged? Do the winds carry it?"

"Oh, no," they said. "You should see, yes. Come after all this feasting is over. We'll take you to see the chariots."

Lugalbanda made no secret of his pleasure in the invitation. They had no wariness in them, and no fear of betraying their city. They seemed as innocent as children. They were full of stories of the god: how he had come from a far country; how he had offended a goddess there and been broken for it, and still walked lame; how that curse had pursued him even to Aratta, and taken his consort and his daughter, and left him alone in a world of mortal strangers.

Lugalbanda must remember that these were strangers to him just as they were to the god, that even close allies could turn to enemies. Trust no one, the elders of Uruk's council had admonished him, and offer service to none but the goddess herself.

He was the elders' servant before all else. He exerted himself to be pleasant company and drank maybe a little more than was wise, but it was difficult to refuse his hosts' persuasion—and the beer was surprisingly good for an outland brew.

They were all much warmer than the sun warranted when the feast meandered to its end. Lugalbanda had a new band of dearest friends, each one dearer than the last, and all determined to show him their wonderful new god.

The god was in his temple, forging bronze. The roar of the forge and the ring of the hammer resounded in the courtyard, silencing even the most boisterous of the young men. Wide-eyed and mute with awe, they crept through the gate into the inner shrine.

In Uruk it would have been a place of beauty and mystery, glimmering with lapis and gold, and made holy with the image of the god. Here were walls of stone unadorned but for the tools of the smith's trade. The stone was dark with old smoke, but the tools were bright, with the look of frequent use. On the far wall, where would have hung a tapestry woven in honor of the god, was a wonder of work in gold and bronze and silver, brooches and ornaments and oddities that might be trappings for chariot teams.

Later Lugalbanda would marvel at the artistry of the work, but his eye was caught by the figure that bent over the forge. There were others in the hall, laboring as he labored, but they were mortal. This truly was a god.

He had come, they said, from the land of the sunrise. Its light was in him, shining out of him. His skin was the color of milk, his hair new copper shot with gold. His eyes when he lifted them were the color of reeds in the first light of morning, clear green shot through with shadow.

There was a great sadness in them, a darkness of grief, overlaid with pain. He lived, said that flat stare, because he had no choice. Life was a curse, and death was not granted him. The light was gone from the world.

"His consort," said one of Lugalbanda's new friends: "the greater gods took her to themselves—oh, a while ago."

"Five winters past," one of the others said. "A fever took her, and the daughter she had borne him. It was the fire of the gods, the priests said, taking back their own. There was nothing left of them but ash."

"They burned away to nothing?" Lugalbanda asked, barely above a whisper, although the others did not trouble to lower their voices.

"Not their bodies," his new friend said with a touch of impatience. "Their hearts and souls, their lives: all were gone in a day and a night. They were the breath of life to him, but they weren't permitted to linger here below. The gods wanted them back."

"But they didn't want him?" said Lugalbanda.

"My work is not done," the god said. His voice was soft and deep. He shaped the words strangely, but they were clear enough to understand.

Lugalbanda swallowed hard. He had thought, somehow, that the god was like his greater kin: oblivious to human nattering unless it was shaped in the form of prayer. But he wore flesh and walked visible in the world; of course he could hear what people said in his presence.

The god's expression was terrible in its mildness. "You would be from Uruk," he said. "Have you come to steal my chariots?"

Lugalbanda's shoulders hunched. But he had a little pride, and a little courage, too. "We are not thieves," he said. Then he added, for what little good it might do: "Great lord."

The green eyes flickered. Was that amusement? "You are whatever your city needs you to be," the god said.

"My city needs me to show you respect, great lord," Lugalbanda said.

The god shrugged. His interest had waned. He turned back to his forge.

He was making a sword, a long leaf-shape of bronze. Lugalbanda did not know what—whether god or ill spirit—made him say, "Don't temper it with your own heart's blood, great lord. That would cause grief to more cities than this one."

"I care nothing for yours," the god said. But he said no word of Aratta. Lugalbanda chose to find that encouraging.

Inanna's head had been aching since morning. It was worse now, between noon and sunset of this endless day. The sky beyond Aratta's walls was low, the air raw and cold. It would snow by evening, the elders had opined, somewhere amid their council.

She was wrapped in every felt and fleece she had, and seated in the place of honor beside the fire, but she did not think that she would ever be warm again. She clenched her teeth to keep them from chattering, though it only made her headache worse.

She had presented her embassy to the king and his council, offering her caravan of grain and wine and lesser treasures in return for wood and stone and bronze. The king's eyes had gleamed as her men laid gifts before him: fine weavings of wool and linen; ornaments of gold, copper, lapis, amber; a pair of young onagers, perfectly matched; and with them a pair of maidens from the south, so like to one another that only they themselves could tell for certain which was which.

The king was a man of strong appetites, as she had observed at the feast of welcome. He accepted the gifts with unconcealed pleasure, but when they were all given, he seemed faintly disappointed. That vague sourness persisted through the council. His elders haggled like women at market. They wanted as much as Uruk would give, in return for as little as they could manage. That was the way of commerce, even between kings.

She waited a considerable time before broaching the subject of chariots. Still, it seemed she had not waited long enough.

"No!" the king said firmly. Until then he had let his councilors speak for him, but in this he would speak for himself. "Those we do not sell or give away. The gods have given them to us, with one of their own to teach us their making."

"Indeed," Inanna said, "and the greater gods have let it be known to us that their gift resides in Aratta. Shall we not fill your granaries and adorn your women, and share this gift in return?"

Some of the council were wavering. One even said, "It will be a long winter. Our trade with the south was not as profitable as it might have been, nor are our storehouses as full as they should be. Surely—"

"We do not give our chariots away," the king said.

And that was all he would say, although the council stretched until evening. When it ended, he had not budged, and his elders had shifted equally immovably to his side.

Inanna was glad to leave the hall behind. She had thought only of food and a bed, but as she went to find both, she overheard two of the king's women whispering together in a corner. It seemed they had undertaken to console the god of chariots—a frequent venture, from the sound of it, but no more successful tonight than it had ever been.

"This time he was less angry," one of them said. "He's weakening, I can tell. One night he'll give way—and I'll be there."

"Not before me," her sister said.

They hissed a little as cats will, but amicably enough. They did not see Inanna's passing: she made sure that they were blind to her.

It was not difficult to find the god. Inanna had thought he might be still in his forge, where people said he always was, but he was in the priest's house behind it, attended by servants who were both loyal and discreet. But they could not stop a goddess.

When she came into the room in which he was sitting, he had been eating a little: there was cheese by him, and a loaf of bread, barely touched. He had an apple in his hand and was examining it, turning it with long clever fingers.

"One eats that," she said without thinking.

Lugalbanda had told her of those eyes, how they were as green as reeds by the river in summer. Even forewarned, she was astonished, taken aback by the light of them and by the grief that haunted them.

But she was a goddess, and his equal. She met him stare for stare. He blinked ever so slightly. She was careful not to let him see her smile.

"I will make an apple of gold," he said.

"Make it of bronze," she said, "and adorn a chariot with it."

"So you did come to steal my chariots." He did not sound dismayed by the prospect.

"I came to buy them," she said. "We're honorable merchants in our part of the world."

"Honor is a rare commodity," he said.

"Not in Uruk," said Inanna.

"Then yours must be a city of wonders," he said.

"We do think so," said Inanna.

He almost smiled—almost. She watched the wave of grief rise up and drown him, the memory so vivid and so bitter that it filled her own heart with sorrow. She could see the two who had died, how beautiful they had been, how deeply he had loved them—how grievous was their loss.

"Come with us to Uruk," she said. She had not plotted to say such a thing; the words escaped her of their own accord.

He did not laugh in her face. Neither did he reject her out of hand. He frowned, but not in refusal. "Are you so desperate for chariots?"

"We are desperate for something," she said. "A new weapon, new power to destroy our enemies. But I didn't ask for that. You would be welcome in Uruk for yourself, and not only for what you can give us."

"Why?"

This was a god of uncomfortable questions. She chose to answer honestly. "There are no memories in Uruk."

She had overstepped herself: his eyes hooded, and his face went cold. "The memories are within me," he said. "I thank you for your kindness."

It was a dismissal. She bridled a little, but she judged it wise to yield. She had much to think of, and little of that had to do with the need of Uruk or the greed of Aratta. She took with her a vision of eyes as green as reeds, and a long fair face, and sorrow that her heart yearned to console.

After the first storm of winter, the gods of heaven relented and brought back for a while the mellow gold of the season that, in this country, they called autumn. The king of Aratta seemed to soften with the sky. He accepted the riches of the caravan in return for an acceptable quantity of worked and unworked metal, quarried stone, and mountain gold. He would not sell his chariots or their maker, but he granted the king of Uruk a gift: a single chariot with its team and its charioteer.

Lugalbanda had grown uneasy as their stay in Aratta lengthened. There was nothing overt to object to; the people of the city were unfailingly courteous, and some of the young men had become quite friendly. But he was growing weary of the cold, the strangeness, even the way in which the trees closed out the sky. His new friends took him hunting in the forests, and taught him the ways of a country that he could never have imagined in his distant and treeless homeland.

He could have borne that, at least until spring, but he did not like the way the king watched Inanna. It never came to anything; it was only a constant, starveling stare. Yet it did not lessen at all as the days went on.

It was not Lugalbanda's place to bring it to her attention, but he suspected that there was no need. She had left most of the negotiations to the master of her caravan and withdrawn gradually from the daily councils. No one remarked on that. She was a goddess; she could set herself above mere human commerce.

It was assumed that she retreated to her rooms, which were warm, capacious, and adorned with every luxury. But Lugalbanda had discovered her secret: how she would put on a plain dark mantle like those worn by women here, and slip away. Sometimes she went into the city, but more often she sought the temple and the one who lived in it.

She would efface herself there, sit in a corner and watch the god and his servants at their work. The god did not appear to find her presence distracting. Often as time went on, she would linger after the day's labors were done and take bread with him, and then they would converse. It was easy conversation, as between friends, or between gods who understood one another. She did not press herself upon him as a woman might upon a man, nor did he seem to see her in that way.

And yet Lugalbanda, standing guard upon them—unmarked by the god and unforbidden by the goddess—saw too well how it was with her. She was a woman in love, hardly aware of it herself, but he knew the signs. He suffered them, too, with just as little hope of requital.

As the fine weather continued unabated, even the god tired of his temple and ventured out to the field on which the chosen of Aratta ran their chariots. His coming was a great occasion. He was brought there in a chair borne by strong young men, to find a chariot waiting, larger yet lighter and stronger than the others. The beasts harnessed to it were like onagers and yet unlike: horses, they were called, born beyond the eastern horizon.

When the god rose from the chair, he was very tall, taller than any man there, but he stooped somewhat as if in pain, and his steps were stiff and slow. He disdained the stick that someone offered, but accepted the shoulder of one of his young men, leaning lightly on it as he moved from the chair to the chariot.

However faltering his gait on the earth, when he had ascended into the chariot and taken the reins, his heart and body were whole again. His back straightened. His head came up. The darkness of grief faded from his eyes. His horses arched their proud necks and tossed their long, thick manes.

He did not let them run as they begged to do, not yet. Inanna had come, walking alone, dressed as simply as a woman of the city. Still there was no mistaking who she was, with the light in her eyes and the beauty of her face.

She spoke no word to the god and he none to her, but he held out his hand. She let him lift her into the chariot. There was space for two of them, if she stood close, within the circle of his arms. She, who was as tall as many men, was small beside him.

Then at last he gave the horses free rein. They leaped into flight, as swift as wind over the grass.

Lugalbanda's heart flew with them, but his eyes were not completely blind to what went on about him. They saw that another had come to see the god and the goddess together: the king of Aratta with his look of perpetual hunger. It was stronger than before, strong enough to fester.

The god and the goddess were far away, caught up in the glory of their speed. Lugalbanda, mere mortal that he was, was left to protect them as he could. It was little enough: a word to his men, a doubling of guards for when she should return, and a prayer to the greater gods for her safety and for that of the god of chariots.

When the god rode in his chariot, he was alive as he never was in his temple. Wind and sunlight lessened his sorrow. For once he saw Inanna, if not as a woman, then as an emissary from another, brighter world.

They rode far from Aratta, too swift even for men in chariots to follow. Inanna tasted the intoxication of speed and found it sweeter than wine.

He saw her delight and shared in it. His smile transformed him; his face that had been so grim and sad was suddenly far younger, and far more beautiful.

They slowed at last by the bank of a river, out of sight of the city. The river was narrow and swift and too deep to ford. The horses trotted beside it, tossing their heads and snorting, still as fresh as if they had just come from their stable.

"Come to Uruk with me," Inanna said with as little forethought as before. As soon as the words escaped, she regretted them, but there was no calling them back.

This time he heard her, and this time he answered. His smile did not die; the darkness did not come back to his face. He said, "Tell me—is it true? There are no trees there? No walls of mountains shutting out the sky?"

"No forests of trees," she said. "No mountains. Only long levels of land, green fields and thorny desert, and the many streams of our rivers, flowing into the sea."

"Only once have I seen the sea," he said. "My heart yearns for the open sky."

"That, we do have," she said a little wryly. "And heat, too, and flies, and mud or dust in season."

"Ah!" he said. "Are you trying to lure me there or repel me?"

"I'm telling you the truth of it," she said.

"An honest merchant," he said. He was chaffing her, but gently. He drew in a deep breath of the cold mountain air, and turned his face to the sun. "I will go to Uruk," he said. "I will make chariots for you."

"You will not."

The king's face was dark with rage; his eyes were glittering. But they were not resting on the god whom he had tracked to his temple to discover if the rumor was true: that Aratta was about to lose the blessing of his presence. They were fixed on Inanna.

"You will not take our god from us," he said.

"That is not for you to choose," said the god. "I have served you well, and given you great gifts. Now I am called elsewhere."

"You are seduced," the king said. "Your wits are clouded. Your place is here, where your destiny has brought you."

"You overstep your bounds," the god said very softly.

"You will not be taken from us," said the king.

He beckoned. His guards came, shaking with fear of the god, but their fear of the king was greater. They did not presume to lay hands on him, but they made it clear that if he did not let himself be led away, they would bind him like a common mortal.

No fire came down from heaven. No storm of wind swept them all away. The god went as he was compelled.

Inanna stood stiff in a temple now empty of its god, with her fists clenched at her sides and her face white and set. Her guards had closed in about her. The king's men surrounded them. None had yet drawn weapon, but hands had dropped to hilts.

A war was brewing, and she was in the heart of it. Her three dozen men stood against a hundred, and the whole city of Aratta behind them.

Long leagues lay between Aratta and Uruk, and seven mountains, each higher than the last.

Lugalbanda opened his mouth to speak. He did not know what he would say, but he could hope that the gods would grant him inspiration.

She spoke before any words could come to him. Her voice was clear and cold. "Lord king," she said. "I offer you a bargain."

The king's greed was stronger than his wrath. His eyes gleamed. "What can you offer, lady, that will buy a god?"

"Myself," she said. "A goddess for a god. Set him free; let him go to Uruk. In return I will stay, and serve you as best I may."

The king raked fingers through his heavy black beard. He was trembling; his breath came quick and shallow. "Indeed? You will do such a thing?"

She bent her head. "For Uruk I will do it."

"What? What will you do? How will you serve me?"

That was cruel. Inanna's back was rigid. "I give myself to you as your bride. I will be your queen, and the god of chariots will be free."

Lugalbanda cried out in protest, but no one heard him. He was nothing and no one in this battle of kings and gods.

The king could hardly contain himself. He must have prayed for this; his gods had given him all that he asked for. But the roots of his avarice were sunk deep. "Bring me a dowry," he said, "of the riches of Uruk. Every year a caravan of wheat and barley, with all the beasts that bear it, and a tribute of gold, and a mantle woven by the king's own women, a royal garment worked with images of the alliance between Aratta and Uruk."

Her lips were tight, her nostrils white, but she said steadily, "In return for the god of chariots, his art and craft, his chariot and his horses, and teams of onagers with their drivers and those who tend them, I will bring you such a dowry."

Lugalbanda watched the king reflect on the bargain, and ponder the riches that were laid in his hand—and what else might he win in this moment of her weakness?

He was a slave to his greed, but he was not a fool. He could see as well as any other man how far he had driven the goddess. He chose to desist while he held the advantage. "Done," he said, "and sworn before all who have witnessed it."

"Done and sworn," she said, still with that perfect, level calm.

"Lady," Lugalbanda pleaded. "Oh, lady. Nothing is worth such a sacrifice."

Inanna looked down at him where he knelt at her feet. She knew how he yearned after her; she would have had to be blind not to know it. But it was a clean yearning, the worship of a pure heart.

She raised him, though he resisted her, and laid her hands on his shoulders. "Uruk is worth any price."

"Uruk could find another way," he said. "You'll wither and die here, bound to that man."

"I hope I am stronger than that," she said.

She kept the quaver out of her voice, but he loved her well enough to see through her mask of courage. "Lady," he said, and he wept as he said it. "Lady, you don't have to do this."

"You know I do," she said. "Go now, prepare the caravan. The sooner you're out of this place with the god and his chariots, the better for us all."

But he was not her dog, to run tamely at her bidding. "I'm not going until the bargain is signed and sealed."

"If you wait," she said, "you may not be allowed to leave at all."

He did not like that, but he gave way to her wisdom. He must see what she saw: that the king of Aratta was not an honest merchant.

She prayed that it was not already too late. "Go," she said. "Be quick. Time is short."

He hated to leave her. She hated to see him go. But her choice was made, and his must not be made for him—to remain a prisoner in Aratta, with the god of chariots bound beside him.

The gates of Aratta were closed, and the guards were politely immovable. "After the wedding feast," they said, "you may go and welcome. The king requires the men of Uruk to witness the conclusion of the bargain, so that there may be no question in their city that it was truly fulfilled."

There was no arguing with that, or with arrows aimed at their throats and spears turned toward their hearts. The guards' courtesy was as honest as it could be, but so was their determination to carry out their king's orders.

"Do you solemnly swear," Lugalbanda asked their captain, "that when the wedding is over, when the price is fully paid, we will be allowed to go?"

"I do swear," the captain said.

Lugalbanda had to accept the oath. It was no more than his own heart had desired before the goddess commanded him otherwise.

The walls were closing in. This must be how it had been for the god of chariots, bound in forest and constrained by mountains. Had he felt the narrowness of Aratta's walls, and the will of its king crushing his own beneath it?

Inanna could not go to him to ask. She was shut within the women's house, surrounded by an army of servants. In a day and a night, in a fever of activity, they had made a royal wedding.

She had given herself up to them and let them make her beautiful, clothing her in the richest of the fabrics that had come from Uruk and adorning her with gems and gold. She fixed her mind on that and not on the man she had taken for Uruk's sake. She must not grieve; she must know no regret. This choice was made as it must be. She had been born into this world for such choices.

Even as strong as she endeavored to be, when the king's maids led her out to her wedding, it was all she could do to keep her head high and her shoulders straight. If she could have turned and run, she would have done it.

The king was waiting in his hall, naked but for the skin of a forest lion. She in linen and fine white wool, with her hair elaborately plaited and her face bravely painted, felt herself diminished by the raw power of this mortal beast.

She was a goddess, a daughter of heaven. She must not falter, even at the sight of Lugalbanda among the king's men with the rest of the guards from Uruk. She must not think of what it meant that Lugalbanda had disobeyed her command, or that the men about him had the look of men guarding a captive—or most disturbing of all, that the god of chariots was nowhere to be seen.

The chief of Aratta's priests set her hand in the king's and spoke the words that made her his wife. Her heart was small and cold and remote. She felt nothing, not even fear.

The king had joy enough for both of them. He took her as if she had been a great gift—and so she was, the greatest that had ever been given in this city. He neither noticed nor cared that she was silent. His delight was entirely his own.

The wedding feast was long and boisterous, but all too soon it ended. The women led Inanna away while the men were still carousing over date wine and barley beer. They had prepared the bridal chamber, hung it with fragrant boughs and adorned it with hangings of richly woven wool. The bed was heaped high with furs and soft coverlets, and scented with unguents from the south.

They took away her wedding garments but left the ornaments, and set her in the midst of the bed. They shook her hair out of all its plaits and combed the shining waves of it. Then they anointed her with sweet oils and bowed low before her and left her there, alone, to wait for the coming of the king.

She had hoped as a coward might, that he would lose himself in the pleasures of food and drink and lively company. But he had not forgotten why he celebrated the feast. He came as soon as he reasonably could. The sun had barely left the sky; it was still light beyond the walls. The king's men would carry on until dawn, but he had come to take what he had bargained for.

He was clean—that much she could grant him. He took no care for her pleasure, but neither did he cause her pain. He seemed not to notice that she lay still, unresponsive, while he kissed and fondled her. It was enough for him to possess her.

He was easily pleased. When he had had his fill of her, he dropped like a stone.

She eased herself away from his sleeping bulk. Her body was as cold as her heart. She wrapped it in one of the coverlets and crouched in the far corner of the bed, knees drawn up, and waited for the dawn.

With the coming of the day, Lugalbanda found the gates open and the way clear, as the captain of guards had promised. The caravan was drawn up, and his men were waiting. But the god of chariots was nowhere to be seen.

Lugalbanda was not in the least surprised. He called on the men he trusted most, who were his friends and kinsmen—five of them, armed with bronze. With them at his back, he went hunting the god.

The temple was empty, the forge untended. Its fires were cold. The god was gone. None of the king's servants would answer when Lugalbanda pressed them, and the king himself was indisposed. Still it was abundantly clear that the king of Aratta had not honored his bargain.

The god could have gone rather far, if he had been taken before the wedding feast. The gates were still open, the guards having had no orders to shut them. Lugalbanda stood torn. Go or stay? Take what he could and escape while he could, or defend the goddess against the man to whom she had bound herself?

He knew his duty, which was to Uruk. She was a goddess; he should trust her to look after herself. And yet it tore at his vitals to leave her alone in this city of strangers.

He did the best he could, which was to send the men he trusted most to stand guard over her door. They would take orders only from the goddess, and defend her with their lives if need be. "Let her know what the king has done," he said to them. "Do whatever she bids you—but if she tries to send you away, tell her that you are bound by a great oath to guard her person until she should be safe again in Uruk."

They bowed. They were hers as he was; they did not flinch from the charge he laid upon them.

He had done as much as he might in Aratta. He turned his back on it and faced the world in which, somewhere, the god of chariots might be found.

The king slept long past sunrise. Inanna, who had not slept at all, was up at first light. She called for a bath. When it came, she scrubbed herself until her skin was raw. The servants carefully said nothing.

When she was dressed, as one of the servants was plaiting her hair, a young woman slipped in among the rest and busied herself with some small and carefully unobtrusive thing. She had bold eyes and a forthright bearing, but she was somewhat pale. Her hands trembled as she arranged and rearranged the pots of paint and unguents.

Inanna stopped herself on the verge of calling the girl to her. If she had wanted to be singled out, she would have come in more openly.

It seemed a very long time before Inanna's hair was done. The servants lingered, offering this ornament or that, but in a fit of pique that was only partly feigned, she sent them all away.

The young woman hung back, but Inanna had no patience to spare for shyness—whatever its source. "Tell me," she said.

The girl's fingers knotted and unknotted. Just as Inanna contemplated slapping the words out of her, she said, "Lady, before I speak, promise me your protection."

"No one will touch you unless I will it," Inanna said. "What is your trouble? Is it one of my men? Did he get you with child?"

The girl glared before she remembered to lower her eyes and pretend to be humble. "With all due and proper respect, lady," she said, "if my trouble were as small as that, I would never be vexing you with it. Did you know that there are five men of Uruk outside your door, refusing to shift for any persuasion? Did you also know that the god of chariots has not been seen since before your wedding?"

Inanna had not known those things. The unease that had kept her awake had been formless; prescience had failed her. And yet, as the servant spoke, she knew a moment of something very like relief—as if a storm that had long been threatening had suddenly and mercifully broken. "Where have they taken him?" she asked.

"I don't know, lady," the servant said. "But I do know that most of your men went to find him. I also know—" She stopped to draw a breath. However bold she was, this frightened her. "I know that the king means no good to Uruk. He wants—needs—its wealth and its caravans of grain, but he would rather own it than buy it. Now that he has you, he'll seize the opportunity to make a state visit to your brother the king. If he happens to come attended by a sizable force, well then, isn't that an escort proper to a royal embassy? And if while he plays the guest in Uruk, your brother happens to meet an unfortunate accident . . ."

Inanna's hand lashed out and seized the girl by the throat. "Tell me why I should believe you. Tell me why I should not let my men have you, to do with as they will."

The girl was not the sort to be struck dumb by terror. Her eyes, lifting to meet Inanna's, held more respect than fear. "Because, lady, you know what a woman can hear if she sets herself to listen. The king never remembers that women have ears. I heard him boasting to one of his cousins. He swore by the gods of the heights that the god of chariots will never leave Aratta. But chariots will come to Uruk, armed for war."

However painful the truth might be, Inanna could not help but see it. The long levels of the river country were far better suited to the passage of swift battle-cars than these mountain valleys. They offered room for greater armies, faster charges, more devastating invasions. Aratta's king with his perpetual hunger would crave what he could gain with an army of chariots. And now he had free passage through the gates of Uruk by his marriage to its living goddess.

She did not berate herself for a fool. Her choice had been well enough taken. The king's might be less so.

"You have my protection," she said to the girl, "on one condition. Tell me the truth. Who are you and what is your grudge against the king?"

The girl flushed, then paled. Inanna thought she might bolt, but she lifted her chin instead and said, "My father was lord of a hill-fort that had been built above a mine of silver. The king sent envoys to him, who made bargains and failed to keep them. Now my father is dead and my brothers labor in the mines, and I was to be the king's concubine—except that you came, and he forgot that I existed."

There was truth in that, a passion that Inanna could not mistake. She laid her hand on the girl's bowed head. The girl flinched but held her ground. "You are mine," she said. "Your life and honor are in my keeping. Go now and be watchful. Bring me word of any new treachery."

Inanna's new servant bowed to the floor. In an instant she was up and gone, with a brightness in her like the flash of sun on a new-forged blade.

Inanna stood where the girl had left her. She knew what she must do. In her heart's wisdom she had already begun it, in making herself beautiful for the man who came shambling through the door, ruffled and stinking with sleep, wanting her again and with no vestige of ceremony. She suffered him as she had before, but more gladly now. Her purpose was clearer, her duty more immediate. In a little while, all bargains would be paid.

Lugalbanda found the god of chariots near a hill-fort a day's journey from Aratta. There was a mine below the fort, and a forge in it, to which the god was chained. His guards were strong, but Lugalbanda's were stronger—and they had unexpected aid: the slaves in the forge rose up and turned on their masters. The last of them died on Lugalbanda's spear, full at the feet of the god of chariots.

The god stood motionless in the midst of the carnage. He had an axe in his hand and a great bear of a man sprawled at his feet. The man's head had fallen some little distance from his body. Lugalbanda knew him even in livid death: he had been the captain of the king's guard.

The god's face was perfectly still. Only his eyes were alive. They burned with nothing resembling love for the men who had brought him to this captivity.

One of the freed slaves broke his chains with swift, sure blows. He walked out of them over the bodies of the slain, refusing any arm or shoulder that was offered. When he had passed through the gate into the open air, he let his head fall back for a moment and drank in the sunlight.

They had brought the god's horses, which some of Lugalbanda's men had reckoned madness, but Lugalbanda had trusted the urging of his heart. He had only and deeply regretted that they could not drag or carry a chariot up the mountain tracks. The god would have one with him, he had hoped, or would find the means to make one.

But the god needed no chariot. He took the rein of the nearer horse, caught a handful of mane, and pulled himself onto the broad dun back.

The horse tossed its head and danced. The men of Uruk stood gaping. The god swept them with his green glare. "Follow as close as you can," he said. With no more word than that, he wheeled the horse about and gave it its head.

The king was dizzied, dazzled, besotted. He lolled in the tumbled bed, reeking of wine and sweat and musk. Inanna rose above him. He leered at her, groping for her breasts.

She drove the keen bronze blade between his ribs, thrusting up beneath the breastbone, piercing the pulsing wall of the heart. It was a good blade. The god had made it, her servant said when she brought it, hidden in a bolt of linen from the caravan. It slipped through the flesh with deadly ease.

The king did not die prettily. Inanna had not wished him to. When his thrashing had stopped, when he had gaped and voided and died, she drew the blade from his heart and wiped it clean on the coverlets. Still naked, still stained with his blood, she walked out to face the people of Aratta.

The sun was setting in blood and the cold of night coming down, when the god rode through the gate of the city. His horse's thick coat was matted with sweat, but the beast was still fresh enough to dance and snort as it passed beneath the arch.

The god rode from the outer gate to the inner and into the citadel, and up to the hall. Inanna waited there, seated on the king's throne, with the bronze dagger on her knee, still stained with the king's blood. His body was her footstool.

She was wrapped in the lionskin that had been the king's great vaunt and the mark of his office. The king's body was wrapped in nothing at all. The five men of Uruk guarded them both, the living and the dead, but there was no defiance in Aratta, not before the wrath of a goddess.

She knew that she could expect treachery—she had braced for it, made such plans as she could against it. But the coming of the god of chariots had shocked them all into stillness.

His wrath was the mirror of her own. The marks on him told the cause of it. He had been taken and bound and forced to serve a mortal will. And she had robbed him of his revenge.

She offered him no apology. She had done what she must. He saw that: his eyes did not soften, but his head bent the merest fraction.

"The great gods bless your return," she said to him. "Have you seen my men? They were hunting you."

"They found me, lady," he said. "They set me free. I bade them follow as quickly as they could. They'll be here by morning."

"So they will," she said, "if Lugalbanda leads them." And tonight, she was careful not to say, she would have six men and a god to guard her, and a city that watched and waited for the first sign of weakness.

She would hold, because she must. The king's body at her feet, his unquiet spirit in the hall, were more protection than an army of living men.

She rose. She was interested to see how many of the king's court and council flinched, and how many watched her with keen speculation.

The god spoke before she could begin. His voice was soft, almost gentle. He was naming names. With each, the man who belonged to it came forward. They were young men, most of them; she remembered some of their faces from the field of chariots. These were his charioteers. There were a good half-hundred of them, many of whom advanced before he could speak their names, coming to stand beside her loyal few.

They were a fair army when they were all gathered, surrounding her in ranks as if they were ordered for a march, with the god on his horse in the midst of them. He smiled at her, a remarkably sweet smile, and said, "Hail the queen of Aratta."

"Hail," said the men whom he had summoned to her defense. "Hail the queen, lady and goddess, the glory of Aratta."

"A bargain is a bargain," Inanna said as they stood on the field of chariots, outside the walls of Aratta. A keen wind was blowing, with a memory of winter in it still, but spring softened it with the scent of flowers. "Uruk still needs Aratta—and I've made myself queen of it. Now my brother can trust that he will have the means to fight the Martu."

"But—" said Lugalbanda, knowing even as he said it that he could not win this battle.

"There are no buts," Inanna said. "I've won this city by marriage and by conquest. I dare not leave it to the next man who may be minded to seize it. It is mine—and its charioteers will serve me, because their god has bound them to it."

Lugalbanda let the rest of his protests sink into silence. She was not to be moved. She would stay and be queen, and teach these people to honor their bargains. The god would go, because he had promised.

"There will be a great emptiness in Uruk," said Lugalbanda, "now that you are gone from it."

"You've lost a goddess," she said, "but gained a god. It seems a fair exchange."

So it was, he supposed, if one regarded it with a cold eye. But his heart knew otherwise.

He bowed low before her, and kept the rest of his grief to himself. Winter was gone; the passes were open. He could bring the god of chariots over the mountains to Uruk. Then when the Martu came again, they would find a new weapon, and new strength among the soft folk of the city.

When he straightened, she had already forgotten him. Her eyes were on the god of chariots, and his on her, and such a light between them that Lugalbanda raised his hand to shield his face.

"I will be in Uruk," the god said, "for as long as I am needed. But when that need is past, look for me."

"You would come back?" she asked him. "You would suffer again the shadows of trees, and mountains that close in the sky?"

"Trees are not so ill," he said, "in the heat of summer, and mountains are the favored abode of gods."

"There are no mountains in Uruk," she said.

"Just so," said the god of chariots. He bowed before her as Lugalbanda had, but with markedly more grace. "Fare you well, my lady of the high places."

"And you, my lord," she said. "May the light of heaven shine upon your road."

He mounted his horse. The caravan was ranked and waiting, with a score of chariots before and behind. The new queen of Aratta was far more generous than the king had been: she was sending a rich gift to her brother, a strong force for the defense of Uruk.

She remained in the field, alone in the crowd of her servants, until the caravan was far away. Lugalbanda, walking last of all, looked back just before the road bent round a hill. She was still there, crowned with gold, bright as a flame amid the new green grass.

He took that memory away with him, held close in his heart. Long after he had left the city behind, as the mountains rose to meet the sky, he remembered her beauty and her bravery and her sacrifice. She would have her reward when the Martu were driven away: when the god of chariots came back to her. He would rule beside her in Aratta, and forge bronze for her, and defend her with chariots.

It was right and proper that it should be so. Even Lugalbanda, who loved her without hope of return, could admit it. A goddess should mate with a god. So the world was made. So it would always be.

Whether for tin or wine or gold or amber, commerce brought the Bronze Age cultures of northern and western Europe into contact with peoples of the south and east. With luxuries and staples, merchants wove vast webs of resources, creating an interdependence among powers great and small, far and near. How alien such travelers must have found the lands they visited and their inhabitants, and how strange these travelers and their goods must have seemed to their hosts. At such convergences foreign notions hybridized with one another and norms mutated as people were forced to adapt, embracing or rejecting influences far more profound than the material goods brought by merchant ship or caravan.

Harry Turtledove, master of the myriad its of history, explores how how much stranger still it might be if these Bronze Age peoples had not been—quite—human.

The Horse of Bronze

I knew, the last time we fought the sphinxes, this dearth of tin would trouble us. I knew, and I was right, and I had the privilege—if that is what you want to call it—of saying as much beforehand, so that a good many of the hes in the warband heard me being clever. And much grief and labor and danger and fear my cleverness won for me, too, though I could not know that ahead of time.

"Oh, copper will serve well enough," said Oreus, who is a he who needs no wine to run wild. He brandished an axe. It gleamed red as blood in the firelight of our encampment, for he had polished it with loving care.

"Too soft," Hylaeus said. He carried a fine old sword, leaf-shaped, as green with patina as growing wheat save for the cutting edge, which gleamed a little darker than Oreus's axe blade. "Bronze is better, and the sphinxes, gods curse them, are bound to have a great plenty of it."

Oreus brandished the axe once more. "Just have to hit harder, then," he said cheerfully. "Hit hard enough, and anything will fall over."

With a snort, Hylaeus turned to me. "Will you listen to him, Cheiron? Will you just listen? All balls and no sense."

If this does not describe half our folk—oh, far more than half, by the Cloud-Mother from whom we are sprung—then never have I heard a phrase that does. "Hylaeus is right," I told Oreus. "With tin to harden their weapons properly, the sphinxes will cause us more trouble than they usually do."

And Oreus turned his back on me and made as if to lash out with his hinder hooves. All balls and no brains, sure enough, as Hylaeus had said. I snatched up my own spear—a new one, worse luck, with a head of copper unalloyed—and would have skewered him as he deserved had he provoked me even a little more. He must have realized as much, for he flinched away and said, "We'll give the sphinxes some of *this,* too." Then he did kick, but not right in my direction.

In worried tones, Hylaeus said, "I wonder if what they say about the Tin Isle is true."

"Well, to the crows with me if I believe it's been overrun by monsters," I replied. "Some things are natural, and some just aren't. But *something's* gone wrong, or we wouldn't have had to do without tin shipments for so long."

Looking back on it, thinking about the Tin Isle while we were camped out not far from the sphinxes' stronghold, in the debatable land north and east of their river-valley homeland, seems strange. This is a country of broiling sun, and one that will never match or even approach the river valley in wealth, for it is as dry as baked straw. Only a few paltry folk dwell therein, and they pay tribute to the sphinxes who hold the land as a shield for their better country. Those folk would pay tribute to us, too, if only we could drive away the sphinxes.

They found us the next morning. Keeping our camp secret from them for as long as we had struck me as something of a miracle. With their eagle-feathered wings, they can soar high over a battlefield, looking for a fight. And so this one did. Hideous, screeching laughter came from it as it spied us. They have faces that put me in mind of our own shes, but lengthened and twisted into a foxlike muzzle, and full of hatred—to say nothing of fangs.

"Now we're for it," I said, watching the accursed thing wing off southward, listening to its wails fade in the distance. "They'll come by land and air, bedeviling us till we're like to go mad."

Nessus strung his great bow. When he thrummed the bowstring, he got a note like the ones a he draws from a harp with a sound box made from the shell of a tortoise. "Some of them will be sorry they tried," he said. Nessus can send an arrow farther than any male I know.

"Some of us will be sorry they tried, too," I answered. I had not liked this expedition from the beginning and never would have consented to it had I not hoped we might get on the scent of a new source of tin. That seemed more unlikely with each league farther south we traveled. Wherever the sphinxes got the metal to harden their bronze, it was not there.

But we were there, and we were about to pay the price for it. I had put out sentries, though our folk are far from fond of being so forethoughtful. One of them cried, "The sphinxes! The sphinxes come!"

We had enough time to snatch up our weapons and form the roughest sort of line before they swarmed upon us like so many lions. They are smaller and swifter than we. We are stronger. Who is fiercer . . . Well, that is why they have battles: to find out who is fiercer.

Sometimes the sphinxes will not close with us at all, but content themselves with shooting arrows and dropping stones and screeching curses from afar. That day, though, they proved eager enough to fight. Our warbands seldom penetrate so far into their land. I suppose they thought to punish us for our arrogance—as if they have none of their own.

The riddle of the sphinxes is why, with their wings and fangs and talons, they do not rule far more of the land around the Inner Sea than in fact they hold. The answer to the riddle is simplicity itself: they are sphinxes, and so savage and vile and hateful they can seldom decide what to do next or make any other folk obey them save through force and fear. On the one hand, they hold the richest river valley the gods ever made. On the other, they could be so much more than they are. As well they do not see it themselves, I suppose.

But whether they see it or not, they had enough and to spare that day to send us home with our plumed tails hanging down in dismay. Along with their ferocity and their wings, their bronze weapons won the fight for them. Oreus practiced his philosophy, if you care to dignify it with such a word, when he hit one of the sphinxes' shields as hard as he could with his copper headed axe. The metal that faced the shield was well laced with tin, and so much harder than the blade that smote it that the axe head bent to uselessness from the blow. Hit something hard enough and . . . This possibility had not entered into Oreus's calculations. Of course, Oreus is not one who can count above fourteen without polluting himself.

Which is not to say I was sorry he was part of our warband. On the contrary. The axe failing of the purpose for which it was intended, he hurled it in the startled sphinx's face. The sphinx yowled in pain and rage. Before it could do more than yowl, Oreus stood high on his hinder pair of legs and lashed out with his forehooves. Blood flew. The sphinx, screaming now rather than yammering, tried to take wing. He snatched it out of the air with his hands, threw it down, and trampled it in the dirt with all four feet.

"Who's next?" he cried, and none of the sphinxes had the nerve to challenge him.

Elsewhere in the field, though, we did not do so well. I would it were otherwise, but no. Before the day was even half done, we streamed north in full retreat, our hopes as dead as that lake of wildly salty water lying not far inland from where we were. The sphinxes pursued, jeering us on. I posted three hes beneath an overhanging rock, so they might not be easily seen from the air. They ambushed the sphinxes leading the chase as prettily as you might want. That, unfortunately, was a trick we could play only once, and one that salved the sore of our defeat without curing it.

When evening came, I took Oreus aside and said, "Now do you see why we need tin for our weapons?"

He nodded, his great chest heaving with the exertion of the fight and the long gallop afterward and the shame he knew that that gallop had been away from the foe. "Aye, by the gods who made us, I do," he replied. "It is because I am too strong for copper alone."

I laughed. Despite the sting of a battle lost, I could not help laughing. "So you are, my dear," I said. "And what do you propose to do about that?"

He frowned. Thought never came easy for him. At length, he said, "We need tin, Cheiron, as you say. If I'm going to smash the sphinxes, we need tin." His thought might not have come easy, but it came straight.

I nodded. "You're right. We do. And where do you propose to get it?"

Again, he had to think. Again, he made heavy going of it. Again, he managed. "Well, we will not get it from the sphinxes. That's all too plain. They've got their supply, whatever it is, and they aren't about to give it up. Only one other place I can think of that has it."

"The Tin Isle?" I said.

Now he nodded. "The Tin Isle. I wonder what's become of it. We paid the folk there a pretty price for their miserable metal. Why don't their traders come down to us any more?"

"I don't know the answer to that, either," I said. "If we go there—and if the gods are kind—we'll find out, and bring home word along with the tin."

Oreus frowned at that. "And if the gods are unkind?"

With a shrug, I answered, "If the gods are unkind, we won't come back ourselves. It's a long way to the Tin Isle, with many strange folk between hither and yon." That only made Oreus snort and throw up his tail like a banner. He has his faults, does Oreus, and no one knows them better than I—certainly not he, for lack of self-knowledge is conspicuous among them—but only a fool would call him craven. I went on, "And whatever has befallen the folk who grub the tin from the ground may meet us, too."

His hands folded into fists. He made as if to rear, to stamp something into submission with his forehooves. But there was nothing he could smite. He scowled. He wanted to smash frustration, as he wants to smash everything. Another fault, without a doubt, but a brave fault, let it be said. "Anything that tries to befall me will rue the day," he declared. Idiocy and arrogance, you are thinking. No doubt. Yet somehow idiocy and arrogance of a sort that cheered me.

And so we built a ship, something centaurs seldom undertake. The *Chalcippus*, we named her—the *Horse of Bronze*. She was a big, sturdy craft, for centaurs are a big, sturdy folk. We need more space to hold enough rowers to drive a ship at a respectable turn of speed. Sphinxes, now, can pack themselves more tightly than we would dream of doing.

But the valley in which the sphinxes dwell has no timber worth the name. They build their ships from bundled sheaves of papyrus plants. These strange vessels serve them well enough on their tame river, less so when they venture out onto the open waters of the Inner Sea.

We have fine timber in our country. The hills are green with pine and oak. We would have to cut and burn for years on end to despoil them of their trees. I do not like to think the dryads would ever thus be robbed of their homes. Not while the world remains as it is, I daresay, shall they be.

Once the wood was cut into boards and seasoned, we built the hull, joining planks edge to edge with mortise and tenon work and adding a skeleton of ribs at the end of the job for the sake of stiffening against the insults of wave and wind. We painted bright eyes, laughing eyes, at the bow that the ship might see her way through any danger, and the shes wove her a sail of linen they dyed a saffron the color of the sun.

Finding a crew was not the difficult matter I had feared it might be. Rather, my trouble was picking and choosing from among the swarm of hes who sought to sail in search of the Tin Isle. Had I not named Oreus among their number, I am sure he would have come after me with all the wild strength in him. Thus are feuds born. But choose him I did, and Hylaeus, and Nessus, and enough others to row the *Chalcippus* and to fight her: for I felt we would need to fight her before all was said and done.

Sail west to the mouth of the Inner Sea, then north along the coast of the strange lands fronting Ocean the Great—thus in reverse, it was said, the tin came down from the far northwest. What folk dwelt along much of the way, what dangers we would meet—well, why did we make the voyage, if not to learn such things?

Not long before we set out, Oreus sidled up to me. In a low voice, he said, "What do you think, Cheiron? On our travels, do you suppose we'll find—wine?" He whispered the last word.

Even if he had spoken more softly still, it would have been too loud. Wine is . . . Wine is the most wonderful poison in all the world, as any of us who have tasted it will attest. It is a madness, a fire, a delight beyond compare. I know nothing hes or shes would not do to possess it, and I know nothing they might not do after possessing it. As well we have never learned the secret of making the marvelous, deadly stuff for ourselves. Gods only know what might become of us if we could poison ourselves whenever and however we chose.

I said, "I know not. I do not want to find out. And I tell you this, Oreus: if you seek to sail on the *Horse of Bronze* for the sake of wine and not for the sake of tin, sail you shall not."

A flush climbed from where his torso rose above his forelegs all the way to the top of his head. "Not I, Cheiron. I swear it. Not I," he said. "But a he cannot keep from wondering . . ."

"Well, may we all keep wondering through the whole of the voyage," I said. "I have known the madness of wine, known it and wish I had not. What we do when we have tasted of it—some I do not remember, and some I wish I did not remember. Past that, I will say no more."

"Neither will I, then," Oreus promised. But he did not promise to forget. I wish I could have forced such a vow from him, but the only thing worse than a promise broken is a promise made or forced that is certain to be broken.

We set out on a fine spring day, the sun shining down brightly from the sky. A wind off the hills filled my nostrils with the spicy fragrance of pines. It also filled the saffron sail that pulled the *Horse of Bronze* across the wine-dark sea (an omen I should have taken, but I did not, I did not) fast enough to cut a creamy wake in the water.

The Inner Sea was calm. In spring and summer, the Inner Sea usually is. The *Chalcippus*'s motion was as smooth and gentle as an easy trot across a meadow. This notwithstanding, several strong hes leaned over the rail and puked up their guts all the way to the horse in them. Some simply cannot take the sea, do what they will.

I am not one who suffers so. I stood at the stern, one hand on each steering oar. Another he called the stroke. He set the speed at my direction, but I did not have to do it myself. I was captain aboard the *Chalcippus,* yes, but among us he who leads must have a light hand, or those he presumes to lead will follow no more. Not all hes see this clearly, which is one reason we have been known—oh, yes, we have been known—to fight among ourselves.

But all was well when we first set out. The wind blew strongly, and from a favorable direction. We did not have to row long or row hard. But I wanted the hes to get some notion of what they would need to do later, if the wind faltered or if we fell in with enemies. They still reckoned rowing a sport and not a drudgery, and so they worked with a will. I knew that was liable to change as readily as the wind, but I made the most of it while it lasted.

Some of the hes muttered when we passed out of sight of land. "Are you foals again?" I called to them. "Do you think you will fall off the edge of the earth here in the middle of the Inner Sea? Wait till we are come to Ocean the Great. Then you will find something worth worrying about."

They went on muttering, but now they muttered at me. That I did not mind. I feared no mutiny, not yet. When I set my will against theirs in any serious way, then I would see. A captain who does not know when to let the crew grumble deserves all the trouble he finds, and he will find plenty.

Oreus came up to me when new land heaved itself up over the western horizon. "Is it true what they say about the folk of these foreign parts?" he asked. He was young, as I have said; the failed attack against the sphinxes had been his first time away from the homeland.

"They say all manner of things about the folk of foreign parts," I answered. "Some of them are true, some nothing but lies. The same happens when other folk speak of us."

He gestured impatiently. "You know what I mean. Is it true the folk hereabouts"—he pointed to the land ahead—"are cripples? Missing half their hindquarters?"

"The fauns? Cripples?" I laughed. "By the gods who made them, no! They are as they are supposed to be, and they'll run the legs off you if you give them half a chance. They're made like satyrs. They're half brute, even more so than satyrs, but that's how they work: torso and thinking head above, horse below."

"But only the back part of a horse?" he persisted. When I nodded, he gave back a shudder. "That's disgusting. I can stand it on goaty satyrs, because they're sort of like us only not really. But these faun things—it's like whoever made them couldn't wait to finish the job properly."

"Fauns are not mockeries of us. They are themselves. If you expect them to behave the way we do, you'll get a nasty surprise. If you expect them to act the way they really do, everything will be fine—as long as you keep an eye on them."

He did not like that. I had not expected that he would. But then, after what passed for reflection with him, he brightened. "If they give me a hard time, I'll bash them."

"Good," I said. It might not be good at all—it probably would not be good at all, but telling Oreus not to hit something was like telling the sun not to cross the sky. You could do it, but would he heed you?

I did not want to come ashore among the fauns at all. But rowing is thirsty work, and our water jars were low. And so, warily, with archers and spearers posted at the bow, I brought the *Chalcippus* toward the mouth of a little stream that ran down into the sea.

As I say, fauns are brutes. They scarcely know how to grow crops or work copper, let alone bronze. But a stone arrowhead will let the life out of a he as well as any other. If they gave us trouble, I wanted to be ready to fight or to trade or to run, whichever seemed the best idea at the time.

It turned out to be trade. Half a dozen fauns came upon us as we were filling the water jars—and, being hes on a lark, splashing one another in the stream like a herd of foals. The natives carried spears and arrows, which, sure enough, were tipped with chipped stone. Two of them also carried, on poles slung over their shoulders, the gutted carcass of a boar.

"Bread?" I called to them, and their faces brightened. They are so miserable and poor, they sometimes grind a mess of acorns up into flour. Real wheaten bread is something they seldom see. For less than it was worth, I soon got that lovely carcass aboard the *Horse of Bronze*. My crew would eat well tonight. Before we sailed, before the fauns slipped back into the woods, I found another question to ask them: "Are the sirens any worse than usual?"

They could understand my language, it being not too far removed from their own barbarous jargon. Their chief—I think that is what he was, at any rate; he was certainly the biggest and strongest of them—shook his head. "No worser," he said. "No better, neither. Sirens is sirens."

"True," I said, and wished it were a lie.

An island lies west of the land west of ours. Monsters haunt the strait between mainland and island: one that grabs with tentacles for ships sailing past, another that sucks in water and spits it out to make whirlpools that can pull you down to the bottom of the sea.

We slipped past them and down the east coast of the island. The gods' forge smoked, somewhere deep below the crust of the world.

What a slag heap they have built up over the eons, too, so tall that snow still clings to it despite the smoke issuing from the vent.

The weather turned warm and then warmer and then hot. We stopped for water every day or two, and to hunt every now and again. There are fauns also on the island, which I had not known and would not have if we had not rushed by them while coursing after deer. Next to them, the fauns of the mainland are paragons of sophistication. I see no way to embarrass them more than to say that, yet they would not be embarrassed if they knew I said it. They would only take its truth for granted. They have not even the sophistication to regret that which is.

Maybe they were as they were because they knew no better. And maybe they were as they were because the sirens hunt them as we hunted that stag through the woods. We would not be as we are, either, not with sirens for near neighbors.

I wish we would have had nothing to do with them. What a he wishes and what the gods give him are all too often two different things. What the gods gave us was trouble. Hylaeus, Nessus, and I had just killed a deer and were butchering it when a siren came out of the woods and into the clearing where we worked. She stood there, watching us.

I have never seen a siren who was not a she. I have never heard of a siren who was a he. How there come to be more sirens is a mystery of the gods. The one we saw was quite enough.

In their features, sirens might be beautiful shes. Past that, though, there is nothing to them that would tempt the eye of even the most desperately urgent he. They are, not to put too fine a point on it, all over feathers, with arms that are half wings and with tail feathers in place of a proper horse's plume. Their legs are the scaly, skinny legs of a bird, with the grasping claws of a bird of prey.

But the eye is not the only gateway to the senses. The siren asked, "What are you doing here?" A simple question, and I had all I could do not to rear up on my hind legs and bellow out a challenge to the world.

Her voice was all honey and poppy juice, sweet and tempting at the same time. I looked at the other two hes. Hylaeus and Nessus were both staring back at me, as if certain I would try to cheat them out of what was rightfully theirs. They knew what they wanted, all right, and they did not care what they had to do to get it.

I glanced over at the siren. Her eyes had slit pupils, like a lion's. They got big and black as a lion's when it sights prey as she watched us. That put me on my guard, where maybe nothing else would have. "Careful, friends," I said. "She does not ask because she wishes us well." Roughly, I answered the siren: "Taking food for ourselves and our comrades."

By the way she eyed me, we had no need of food; we *were* food. She said, "But would you not rather share it with me instead?"

That voice! When she said something might be so, a he's first impulse was to do all he could to make it so. I had to work hard to ask the siren, "Why should we? What payment would you give us?"

I have lived a long time. One of the things this has let me do is make a great many mistakes. Try as I will, I have a hard time remembering a worse one. The siren smiled. She had a great many teeth. They all looked very long and very sharp. "What will I do?" she crooned. "Why, I will sing for you."

And she did. And why I am here to tell you how she sang . . . That is not so easy to explain. Some small beasts, you will know, lure their prey to them by seeming to be something the prey wants very much. There are spiders colored like flowers, but woe betide the bee or butterfly who takes one for a flower, for it will soon find itself seized and poisoned and devoured.

Thus it was with the siren's song. No she of the centaur folk could have sung so beautifully. I am convinced of it. A she of our own kind would have had many things on her mind as she sang: how much she cared about the hes who heard her, what she would do if she did lure one of them—perhaps one of them in particular—forward, and so on and so on.

The siren had no such . . . extraneous concerns. She wanted us for one thing and one thing only: flesh. And her song was designed on the pattern of a hunting snare, to bring food to her table. Any doubts, any second thoughts, that a she of our kind might have had were missing here. She drew us, and drew us, and drew us, and . . .

And, if one of us had been alone, she would have stocked centaur in her larder not long thereafter. But, in drawing Nessus and Hylaeus and me all with the same song, she spread her magic too thin to let it stick everywhere it needed to. Nessus it ensnared completely, Hylaeus perhaps a little less so, and me least of all. Why this should be, I cannot say with certainty. Perhaps it is simply because I have lived a very long time, and my blood does not burn so hotly as it did in years gone by.

Or perhaps it is that when Nessus made to strike at Hylaeus, reckoning him a rival for the charms of the sweetly singing feathered thing, the siren was for a moment distracted. And its distraction let me move further away from the snare it was setting. I came to myself, thinking, *Why do I so want to mate with a thing like this? I would crush it and split it asunder.*

That made me—or rather, let me—hear the siren's song with new ears, see the creature itself with new eyes. How eager it looked, how hungry! How those teeth glistened!

Before Nessus and Hylaeus could commence one of those fights that can leave a pair of hes both badly damaged, I kicked out at the siren. It was not my strongest blow. How could it be, when part of my blood still sang back to the creature? But it dislodged a few of those pearly feathers and brought the siren's song to a sudden, screeching stop.

Both my comrades jerked as if waking from a dream they did not wish to quit. They stared at the siren as if not believing their eyes. Perhaps, indeed, they did not believe their eyes, their ears having so befooled them. I kicked the siren again. This time, the blow landed more solidly. The siren's screech held more pain than startlement. More feathers flew.

Hylaeus and Nessus set on the siren then, too. They attacked with the fury of lovers betrayed. So, I daresay, they imagined themselves to be. The siren died shrieking under their hooves. Only feathers and blood seemed to be left when they were done. The thing was lighter and more delicately made than I would have thought; perhaps it truly was some sort of kin to the birds whose form and feathers it wore.

"Back to the ship, and quick!" I told the other two hes. "The whole island will be roused against us when they find out what happened here."

"What do you suppose it would have done if you hadn't given it a kick?" Hylaeus asked in an unwontedly small voice.

"Fed," I answered.

After that one-word reply, neither Hylaeus nor Nessus seemed much inclined to argue with me any more. They carried away the gutted stag at a thunderous gallop I had not thought they had in them. And they did not even ask me to help bear the carcass. As he ran, Nessus said, "What do we do if they start—singing at us again, Cheiron?"

"Only one thing I can think of," I told him.

We did that one thing, too: we took the *Horse of Bronze* well out to sea. Soon enough, the sirens gathered on the shore and began singing at us, began trying to lure us back to them so they could serve us as we had served one of them. And after they had served us thus, they would have served us on platters, if sirens are in the habit of using platters. On that last I know not, nor do I care whether I ever learn.

We could hear them, if only barely, so I ordered the hes to row us farther yet from the land. Some did not seem to want to obey. Most, though, would sooner listen to me than to those creatures. When we could hear nothing but the waves and the wind and our own panting, I had the whole crew in my hands once more.

But we had not altogether escaped our troubles. We could not leave the island behind without watering the ship once more. Doing it by day would have caused us more of the trouble we had escaped thus far by staying out of earshot of the sirens, for the creatures followed us along the coast. Had some foes come to our shores, slain one of our number, and then put to sea once more, I have no doubt we should have relentlessly hounded them. The sirens did the same for this fallen comrade of theirs. That she had tried to murder us mattered to them not at all. If they could avenge her, they would.

As the sun god drove his chariot into the sea ahead of us, I hoisted sail to make sure the sirens on the shore could see us. Then I swung the *Chalcippus'* bow away from the island and made as if to sail for the mainland lying southwest.

"You are mad," Oreus said. "We'll bake before we get there."

"I know that," I said, and held my course.

Oreus kept on complaining. Oreus always complains, especially when he cannot find something to trample, and not least because he never looks ahead. *It could be that he will learn one day,* I thought. *It could also be that he will never learn, in which case his days will be short*. To my sorrow, I have seen such things before, more often than I would wish.

A few of the other hes likewise grumbled. More, though, paid me no small compliment: they gave me credit for knowing what I was about. Now I had to prove I had earned their trust.

The sun set. Blue drowned pink and gold in the west. Black rose out of the east, drowning blue. Stars began to shine. There was no moon. Her boat would not sail across the sky until later. "Raise the sail to the yard, then lower the yard," I said, and pulled the steering oars so that the *Chalcippus* swung back to starboard.

"Very nice," said Nessus, who seemed to understand what I was doing.

"Is it? I wonder," I replied. "But we have need, and necessity is the master of us all." I raised my voice, but not too loud: "Feather your oars, you rowers. We want to go up to the shore as quietly as we can. Think of a wild cat in the forest stalking a squirrel."

At that, even Oreus understood my plan. He was loud in his praise of it. He was, as is his way, too cursed loud in his praise of it. Someone must have kicked him in the hock, for he fell silent very abruptly.

In the starlight, the sea was dark and glimmering. An owl hooted somewhere on the land ahead. I took the call as a good omen. Perhaps the sirens did as well, the owl being like them a feathered hunting creature. I have never understood omens, not in fullness. I wonder if ever I shall, or if that lies in the hands of the gods alone.

From the bow came a hiss: "Cheiron! Here's a stream running out into the sea. This is what you want, eh?"

"Yes," I said. "This is just what I want." Few folk are active by night. Fewer still are active both day and night. I hoped we could nip in, fill our empty jars, and escape the sirens without their ever realizing we were about.

What I hoped for and what I got were two different things. Such is the way of life for those who are not gods. I have said as much before, I believe. Repeating oneself is a thing that happens to those who have lived as long and have as seen as much as I have. And if you believe I have troubles in this regard, you should hear some of the gods I have known. Or, better, you should not. A god will tell the same story a hundred times, and who that is not a god will presume to let him know what a bore he is making of himself? Only one of great courage or one of even greater foolishness, for gods are also quick to anger. However boring they may be, they are also powerful. Power, after all, is what makes them gods.

My hes scrambled out of the *Horse of Bronze*. They set to work in as sprightly a way as any captain could have wanted. But they had not yet finished when another owl hooted. As I have remarked, owls crying in the night are said to be birds of good omen, but not this one, for his cries alerted the sirens. I *do* not understand omens. I have said that before, too, have I not?

The sirens rushed toward us, fluttering their winglike arms and then—far more dangerous—commencing to sing. For a bad moment, I thought they would instantly ensorcel all of us, dragging us down to doleful destruction. But then, as if a god—not, for once, a boring god—had whispered in my ear, I called out to my fellow hes: "Shout! Shout for your lives! If you hear yourselves, you will not hear the sirens! Shout! With all the strength that is in you, shout!"

And they did—only a few of them at first, but then more and more as their deep bellow drowned out the sirens' honeyed voices and released other hes from their enchantment. Shouting like mad things, we rushed at the sirens, and they broke and fled before us. Now they did not sing seductively, but squalled out their dismay. And well they might have, for we trod more than one under our hooves and suffered but a few bites and scratches in the unequal battle.

"Back to the ship," I said then. "We have done what we came to do, and more besides. The faster we get away now, the better."

Those sirens had nerve. They could not close with us, but they tried to sing us back to them as we rowed away. But we kept on shouting, and so their songs went for naught. We pulled out to sea, until we were far enough from land to hear them no more.

"That was neatly done, Cheiron," Oreus said, as if praise from him were what I most sought in life.

Well, this once maybe he was not so far wrong. "I thank you," I said, and let out the long, weary sigh I had held in for too long. "I wonder what other things we shall have to do neatly between here and the Tin Isle—and when we have got there, and on the way home."

We were not tested again until we left the Inner Sea and came out upon the heaving bosom of Ocean the Great. Heave that bosom did. Anyone who has sailed on the Inner Sea will have known storms. He will have known them, yes, but as interludes between longer stretches of calm weather and good sailing. On the Ocean, this business is reversed. Calms there are, but the waters more often toss and turn like a restless sleeper. Sail too close to land and you will be cast up onto it, as would never happen in the calmer seas our ships usually frequent.

The day after we began our sail upon Ocean the Great, we beached ourselves at sunset, as we almost always did at nightfall on the Inner Sea. When the sun god drove his chariot into the water, I wondered how he hoped to return come morning, for Ocean seemed to stretch on to westward forever, with no land to be seen out to the edge of the world. I hoped we would not sail out far enough to fall off that edge, which had to be there somewhere.

But for our sentries, we slept after supping, for the work had been hard—harder than usual, on those rough waters. And the sentries, of course, faced inland, guarding us against whatever strange folk dwelt in that unknown land. They did not think to look in the other direction, but when we awoke *someone had stolen the sea*.

I stared in consternation at the waters of Ocean the Great, which lay some cubits below the level at which we had beached the *Chalcippus*. I wondered if a mad god had tried to drink the seabed dry through a great rhyton and had come closer than he knew to success.

We tried pushing the ship back into the sea but to no avail: she was stuck fast. I stood there, wondering what to do. What *could* we do? Nothing. I knew it all too well.

As the sun rose higher in the east, though, the sea gradually returned, until we were able to float the *Horse of Bronze* and sail away as if nothing had happened. It seemed nothing had—except to my bowels, when I imagined us trapped forever on that unknown shore. Little by little, we learned Ocean the Great had a habit of advancing and withdrawing along the edge of the land, a habit the Inner Sea fortunately fails to share. Ocean is Ocean. He does as he pleases.

Here we did not go out of sight of land, not at all. Who could guess what might happen to us if we did? Better not to find out. We crawled along the coast, which ran, generally speaking, north and east. Were we the first centaurs to see those lands, to sail those waters? I cannot prove it, but I believe we were.

We did not see other ships. Even on the Inner Sea, ships are scarce. Here on the unstable waters of Ocean the Great, they are scarcer still. And Ocean's waters proved unstable in another way as well. The farther north we sailed, the cooler and grayer they grew—and also the wilder. Had we not built well, the *Horse of Bronze* would have broken her back, leaving us nothing but strange bones to be cast up on an alien shore. But the ship endured, and so did we.

We had thought to travel from island to island on our way to the Tin Isle. But islands proved few and far between on the Ocean. We did sail past one, not long before coming to the Tin Isle, from which small cattle whose roan coats were half hidden by strange tunics—I know no better word—stared out at us with large, brown, incurious eyes.

Some of the sailors, hungry for meat, wanted to put ashore there and slaughter them. I told them no. "We go on," I said. "They may be sacred to a god—those garments they wear argue for it. Remember the Cattle of the Sun? Look what disaster would befall anyone who dared raise a hand against them. And these may not be cattle at all; they may be folk in the shape of cattle. Who can say for certain, in these strange lands? But that is another reason they might be clothed. Better we leave them alone."

And so we sailed on, and entered the sleeve of water separating the Tin Isle from the mainland. That was the roughest travel we had had yet. More than a few of us clung to the rail, puking till we wished we were dead. Had the day not been bright and clear, showing us the shape of the Tin Isle blue in the distance, we might have had to turn back, despairing of making headway against such seas. But we persevered and eventually made landfall.

Oreus said, "Like as not, Ocean will steal the ship when our backs are turned. What would we do then, Cheiron?"

"Build another," I answered. "Or would you rather live in this godsforsaken place the rest of your days?"

Oreus shivered and shook his head. I did not know, not then, how close I came to being right.

Something was badly amiss on the Tin Isle. That I realized not long after we landed there and made our way inland. The Isle proved a bigger place than I had thought when setting out. Simply landing on the coast did not necessarily put us close to the mines from which the vital tin came.

The countryside was lovely, though very different from that around the Inner Sea. Even the sky was strange, ever full of fogs and mists and drizzles. When the sun did appear, it could not bring out more than a watery blue in the dome of heaven. The sun I am used to will strike a centaur dead if he stays out in it too long. It will burn his hide, or the parts of it that are not hairy. Not so on those distant shores. I do not know why the power of the sun god is so attenuated thereabouts, but I know that it is.

Because of the fogs and mists and the endless drizzle, the landscape seemed unnaturally—indeed, almost supernaturally—green. Grass and ferns and shrubs and trees grew in such profusion as I have never seen in all my days. Not even after the wettest winter will our homeland look so marvelously lush. High summer being so cool in those parts, however, I did wonder what winter might be like.

Hard winters or no, though, it was splendid country. A he could break the ground with his hoof and something would grow there. But no one and nothing appeared to have broken the ground any time lately. That was the puzzlement: the land might as well have been empty, and it should not have been.

I knew the names of the folk said to dwell in those parts: piskies and spriggans and especially nuggies, who were said to dig metal from the ground. Those names had come to the Inner Sea along with the hide-wrapped pigs of tin that gave this land its fame there. What manner of folk these might be, though, I could not have said—nor, I believe, could anyone from my part of the world. I had looked forward to finding out. That would have been a tale to tell for many long years to come.

It would have been—but the folk did not come forth. I began to wonder if they *could* come forth, or if some dreadful fate had overwhelmed them. But even if they had been conquered and destroyed, whatever folk had defeated them should have been in evidence. No one was.

"We should have brought shes with us and settled here," Nessus said one day. "We'd have the land to ourselves."

"Would we?" I looked about. "It does seem so, I grant you, but something tells me we would get little joy from it."

Oreus looked about, too, more in bewilderment than anything else. Then he said one of the few things I have ever heard him say with which I could not disagree, either then or later: "If the folk are gone out of the land, no wonder the tin's stopped coming down to the Inner Sea."

"No wonder at all," I said. "Now, though, we have another question." Confusion flowed across his face until I posed it: "*Why* have the folk gone from this land?"

"Sickness?" Nessus suggested. I let the word lie there, not caring to pick it up. It struck me as unlikely, in any case. Most folk are of sturdy constitution. We die, but we do not die easily. I had trouble imagining a sickness that could empty a whole countryside.

Then Oreus said his second sensible thing in a row. Truly this was a remarkable day. "Maybe," he said, "maybe their gods grew angry at them, or tired of them."

A cool breeze blew down from the north. I remember that very well. And I remember wondering whether it was but a breeze, or whether it was the breath of some god either angry or tired. "If that be so," I said, "if that be so, then we will not take tin back to the Inner Sea, and so I shall hope it is not so."

"What if it is?" Nessus asked nervously, and I realized I was not the only one wondering if I felt a god's breath.

I thought for a moment. With that breeze blowing, thought did not come easily, and the moment stretched longer than I wished it would have. At last, I said, "In that case, my friend, we will do well enough to go home ourselves, don't you think?"

"Do our gods see us when we are in this far country?" Oreus asked.

I did not know the answer to that, not with certainty. But I pointed up to the sun, which, fortunately, the clouds and mist did not altogether obscure at that moment. "He shines here, too," I replied. "Do you not think he will watch over us as he does there?"

That should have steadied him. But such was the empty silence of that countryside that he answered only, "I hope so," in tones suggesting that, while he might hope, he did not believe.

Two days—or rather, two nights—later, a nuggy came into our camp. I would not have known him from a piskie or a spriggan, but a nuggy he declared himself to be. I had sentries out around our fires, but he appeared in our midst without their being any the wiser. I believe he tunneled up from under the ground.

He looked like one who had seen much hardship in his time. I later learned from him that was the true aspect of nuggies, but he owned he had it more than most. He was ill-favored, a withered, dried-up creature with a face as hard and sharp as an outcropping of flint. In other circumstances, his tiny size might have made it hard for me to take him seriously; he was no larger in the head and torso than one of us would have been at two years, and had only little bandy legs below, though his arms were, in proportion to the rest of him, large and considerably muscled.

His name, he said, was Bucca. I understood him with difficulty. We did not speak the same language, he and I, but our two tongues held enough words in common to let us pass meaning back and forth. His rocky face worked with some mixture of strong emotion when he came before me. "Gods be praised!" he said, or something much like that. "Old Bucca's not left all alone in the dark!" And he began to weep, a terrible thing to see.

"Here, now. Here, now," I said. I gave him meat and bread. Had we had wine, I would have given him that as well. But for us to carry wine would have been like stags carrying fire with which to roast them once they were slain.

He ate greedily, and without much regard for manners. Though he was so small, he put away a startling amount. Grease shone on his thin lips and his chin when he tossed aside a last bone and said, "I hoped some folk would come when the tin stopped. I prayed some folk would come. But for long and long, no folk came. I drew near to losing hope." More tears slid down the cliffsides of his cheeks.

"Here now," I said again, wanting to embrace him yet fearing I would offend if I did. Only when he came over and clung to my foreleg did I take him up in my arms and hold his small chest against my broad one. He was warm and surprisingly hard; his arms, as they embraced me, held even more strength than I would have guessed. At last, when he seemed somewhat eased, I thought I could ask him, "Why did the tin stop?"

He stared at me, our two faces not far apart. Moonlight and astonishment filled his pale eyes. "You know not?" he whispered.

"That is the truth: I know not," I replied. "That is why I came so far, that is why we all came so far, in the *Horse of Bronze*—to learn why precious tin comes no more to the Inner Sea."

"Why?" Bucca said. "I will tell you why. Because most of us are dead, that is why. Because where *they* are, we cannot live."

I did not believe all Bucca told me. If I am to speak the whole truth here, I did not want to believe what the nuggy told me. And so, not believing, I told a party of hes to come with me so that we might see for ourselves what truth lay in his words—or rather, as I thought of it, so that we might see he was lying.

"You big things are bold and brave," Bucca said as we made ready to trot away. "You will have grief of it. I am no bolder or braver than I have to be, and already I have known griefs uncounted."

"I grieve for your grief," I told him. "I grieve for your grief, but I think things will go better for us."

"It could be," Bucca replied. "Yes, it could be. You big things still believe in yourselves, or so it seems. We nuggies did not, not after a while. And when we did not believe, and when *they* did not believe . . . we died."

"How is it that you are left alive, then?" I asked him. This question had burned in my mind since the night when he first appeared amongst us, though I had not had the heart to ask him then. Now, though, it seemed I might need the answer, if answer there was.

But Bucca only shrugged those surprisingly broad shoulders of his. "I think I am too stubborn to know I should be dead."

That, then, meant nothing to me. I have learned more since than I once knew, however. Even then, I wanted nothing more than to get away from the nuggy. And away we went, rambling east into one of the more glorious mornings the gods ever made.

It was cool. It was always cool on the Tin Isle, except when it was downright cold. A little mist clung to the hillsides. The sun had trouble burning it off. This too is a commonplace of that country. But oh! the greens in that northern clime! Yes, I say it again. Nothing round the Inner Sea can match them, especially not in summertime. And those hills were not stark and jagged, as are the hills we know, but smooth and round, some of them, as a she's breast. The plains are broad, and roll gently. Their soil puts to shame what goes by that name in our land. Yet it grew no wheat or barley, only grass. Indeed, this might have been a countryside forever without folk.

As we trotted east, we left the hills behind us. The plain stretched out ahead, far broader than any in our own homeland. But only a cold, lonely wind sighed across it. "Plague take me if I like this place," Oreus said.

"We need not like it," I answered. "We need but cross it."

Though I might say such things to Oreus, before long the stillness came to oppress me, too. I began to have the feeling about this plain that one might have about a centaurs' paddock where no one happens to be at a particular time: that the folk are but gone for a moment and will soon return. About the paddock, one having such a feeling is generally right. About this plain, I thought otherwise.

There I proved mistaken.

I found—the entire band of hes found—I was mistaken some little while before actually realizing as much. We hurried through the tall grass of the plain, making better time than we had before, and did not think to wonder why until Hylaeus looked down and exclaimed in sudden, foolish-sounding surprise: "We are following a trail."

All of us stopped then, staring in surprise at the ground under our hooves. Hylaeus was quite correct, even if we had not noticed up until that time. The earth was well trodden down, the grass quite sparse, especially compared to its rich lushness elsewhere.

Nessus asked the question uppermost in all our minds: "Who made it?"

What he meant was, had the trail survived from the days when folk filled this land—days Bucca recalled with fond nostalgia—or was it new, the product of whatever had driven the nuggies and so many other folk to ruin? One obvious way to find the answer crossed my mind. I asked, "How long has it been since any but ourselves walked this way?"

We studied the ground again. A trail, once formed, may last a very long time; the ground, pounded hard under feet or hooves, will keep that hardness year after year. Grass will not thrive there, not when it can find so many easier places close by to grow. And yet . . .

"I do not think this trail is ancient," Hylaeus said. "It shows too much wear to make that likely."

"So it also seems to me," I said, and waiting, hoping someone—anyone—would contradict me. No one did. I had to go on, then: "This means we may soon learn how much of the truth Bucca was telling."

"It means we had better watch out," Nessus said, and who could tell him he was wrong, either?

But for the trail, though, the land continued to seem empty of anything larger than jackdaws and rooks. It stretched on for what might have been forever, wide and green and rolling. Strange how the Tin Isle should show a broader horizon than my own home country, which, although part of the mainland, is much divided by bays and mountains and steep valleys.

There were valleys in this country, too, but they were not like the ones I knew at home, some of which are sharp enough at the bottom to cut yourself on if you are not careful. The valleys that shaped this plain were low and gently sloping. The rivers in them ran in the summertime, when many of the streams in my part of the world go dry.

And I will tell you something else, something even odder. While we were traveling across that plain, black clouds rolled across the sun. A cold wind from the north began to blow. Rain poured down from the sky, as if from a bucket. Yes, I tell you the truth, no matter how strange it might seem. I saw hard rain—not the drizzle and fogs we had known before—in summertime, when all around the Inner Sea a lizard will cook if it ventures out in the noonday sun. By the gods, it is so.

Truly I was a long way from home.

"Is it natural?" Hylaeus asked, rain dripping from his nose and the tip of his beard and the tip of his tail till he flicked it about, at which point raindrops flew from it in all directions. "Can such a thing be natural?"

"Never!" Oreus said. His tail did not flick. It lashed, back and forth, back and forth, as if it had a life of his own. "This surely must be some evil sorcery raised against us. Perhaps it is akin to whatever caused the nuggies to fail."

"I think you may be mistaken," I told him. He glared at me—until a raindrop hit him in the eye, at which point he blinked, tossed his head, and spluttered. I went on, "Look how green the land is all around us," emphasizing my words with a broad wave of my arm. "Could it be what it is unless rain came down now and again—or more than now and again—in the summertime to keep it so?"

Oreus only grunted. Nessus considered the greenery and said, "I think Cheiron may be right."

"Whether he is or not, we'll be squelching through mud if this goes on much longer." As if to prove Oreus's point, his hoof splashed in a puddle—a puddle that surely had not been there before the rain began.

The hard-packed trail helped more than somewhat, for it did not go to muck nearly so fast as the looser-soiled land to either side. We could go on, if not at our best clip, while the rain continued.

Little by little, the steady downpour eased off to scattered showers. The wind shifted from north to east and began to blow away some of the clouds. When we forded a stream, we paused to wash ourselves. I was by then muddy almost all the way up to my belly, and my comrades no cleaner. Washing, though, proved a business that tested my hardiness, for the stream, like every stream I encountered in the Tin Isle, ran bitterly cold.

In a halfhearted way, the sun tried to come out once more. I was glad of that. Standing under it, even if it seemed but a pale imitation of the blazing disk of light I had known around the Inner Sea, helped dry the water clinging to my coat of hair and also helped give me back at least a little warmth.

I was, then, reluctant to leave the valley in which that stream lay, and all the more so since it was rather deeper and steeper than most of the rest in the plain. "No help for it, Cheiron," said Hylaeus, who of the other hes had the most sympathy for my weariness.

"No, I suppose not," I said sadly, and set my old bones to moving once more. Some of the other centaurs went up the eastern slope of the valley at a pace no better than mine. Oreus, on the other hand, was filled with the fiery impetuosity of youth and climbed it at the next thing to a gallop. I expected him to charge across the flat land ahead and then come trotting back to mock the rest of us for a pack of lazy good-for-nothings.

I expected that, but I was wrong. Instead, he stopped in his tracks at the very lip of the valley, which stood somewhat higher than the western slope. He stopped, he began to rear in surprise or some other strong emotion, and then he stood stock-still, as if turned to stone by a Gorgon's appalling countenance, his right arm outstretched and pointing ahead.

"What is it?" I called grumpily. I had no great enthusiasm for rushing up there to gape at whatever had seized foolish Oreus's fancy.

But he did not answer me. He simply stood where he was and kept on pointing. I slogged up the slope, resolved to kick him in the rump for making such a nuisance of himself.

When at last I reached him, my resolve died. Before I could turn and lash out with my hind feet, my eyes followed his index finger. And then, like him, I could do nothing for long, long moments but stare and stare and stare.

How long I stood there, I am not prepared to say. As long as the wonder ahead deserved? I doubt it, else I might be standing there yet.

The great stone circle loomed up out of nothing, there on the windswept plain. Even in summertime, that wind was far from warm, but it was not the only thing that chilled me. I am not ashamed to say I was awed. I was, in fact, amazed, wondering how and why such a huge thing came to be, and what folk could have raised it.

The sphinxes brag of the monuments they have built, there beside their great river. I have never seen them, not with my own eyes. Centaurs who have visited their country say the image of one of their own kind and the enormous stone piles nearby are astonishing. But the sphinxes, as I have said, dwell in what must be the richest country any gods ever made. This . . . This stood in the middle of what I can best describe as nothing. And the sphinxes had the advantage of their river to haul stone from quarries to where they wanted it. No rivers suitable for the job here. And these blocks of stone, especially the largest in the center of the circle, the ones arranged in a pattern not much different from the outline of my hoof, were, I daresay, larger than any the sphinxes used.

Some of this—much of this, in fact—I learned later. For the time being, I was simply stunned. So were we all, as we came up the side of the valley one after another to stare at the amazing circle. We might have been under a spell, a spell that kept us from going on and bid fair to turn us to stone ourselves.

Brash Oreus, who had first seen the circle of standing stones, was also the one who broke that spell, if spell it was. Sounding at that moment not at all brash, he said, "I must see more." He cantered forward: an oddly stylized gait, and one that showed, I think, how truly impressed he was.

Seeing him move helped free me from the paralysis that had seized me. I too went toward the stone circle, though not at Oreus's ceremonial prance.

As I drew closer, the wind grew colder. Birds flew up from the circle, surprised and frightened that anyone should dare approach. *Chaka-chaka-chak!* they called, and by their cries I knew them for jackdaws.

I do not believe I have ever seen stonework so fresh before. The uprights and the stones that topped them might have been carved only moments before. No lichen clung to them, and I had seen it mottling boulders in the plain. Hylaeus noted the same thing at almost the same time. Pointing ahead as Oreus had done before, he said, "Those stones could have gone up yesterday."

"Yesterday," I agreed, "or surely within the past few years." And all at once, a chill colder even than the breeze pierced me to the root. That was the time in which the tin failed.

Again, Hylaeus was not far behind me. "This is a new thing," he said slowly. "The passing of the folk of the Tin Isle is a new thing, too."

Chaka-chaka-chak! the jackdaws screeched. Suddenly, they might have been to my mind carrion crows, of which I had also seen more than a few. And on what carrion had those crows, and the jackdaws, and the bare-faced rooks, and the ravens, on what carrion had they feasted? The wind seemed colder yet, wailing out of the north as if the ice our bones remembered lay just over the horizon. But the ice I felt came as much from within me as from without.

Oreus said, "Who made this circle, then, and why? Is it a place of magic?"

Nessus laughed at that, even if the wind blew his mirth away. "Could it be anything but a place of magic? Would any folk labor so long and so hard if they expected nothing in return?"

Not even quarrelsome Oreus could contest against such reasoning. I shivered yet again. Magic is a curious business. Some folk choose to believe they can compel their gods to do their bidding by one means or another rather than petition them in humble piety. What is stranger still is that some gods choose to believe they can be so compelled—at least for a while. Sometimes, later, they remember they are gods, and then no magic in the world can check them. Sometimes . . . but perhaps not always.

I looked at the stone circle again, this time through new eyes. Centaurs have little to do with magic, nor have we ever; it appears to be a thing contrary to our nature. But I believed Nessus had the right of it. Endless labor had gone into this thing. No one would be so daft as to expend such labor without the hope of some reward springing from it.

What sort of reward? Slowly, I said, "If the other folk of the Tin Isles fail, who will take the land? Who will take the mines?"

Once more, I eyed the stone circle, the uprights capped with a continuous ring of lintel stones, the five bigger trilithons set in the hoof-shaped pattern within. Of itself, my hand tightened on the copper-headed spear I bore. I thought I could see an answer to that. Had much power sprung from all this labor?

Chip, chip, chip. I turned at the sound of stone striking stone. Oreus had found a hard shard and was smacking away at one of the uprights. Before I could ask him what he was about, Nessus beat me to it.

"What am I doing? Showing we were here," Oreus answered, and went on chipping.

After watching him for a while, I saw the shape he was making, and I could not help but smile. He was pounding into that great standing stone the image of one of our daggers, broad at the base of the blade and with hardly any quillons at all. When he had finished that, he began another bit of carving beside it: an axe head.

"Not only have you shown we were here, but also for what reason we came to the Tin Isle," I said. Oreus nodded and continued with his work.

He had just finished when one of our hes let out a wordless cry of warning. The centaur pointed north, straight into the teeth of that wind. As I had with Oreus's before, I followed that outflung, pointing arm. There coming toward us were the ones who, surely, had shaped the circle of standing stones.

If dogs had gods, those they worshiped would wag their tails and bark. If sheep had gods, they would follow woolly deities who grazed. As the world is, almost all folk have many things in common, as if the gods who shaped them were using certain parts of a pattern over and over again.

Think on it. You will find it holds much truth. Centaurs and sirens and sphinxes and fauns and satyrs all have faces of an essential similarity. Nor were our features so much different from those of Bucca the nuggy on this distant shore. The differences, such as they are, are those of degree, not of kind.

Again, hands are much alike from one folk to another. How could it be otherwise, when we all must grasp tools and manipulate them? Arms are also broadly similar, one to another, save when a folk needs must use them for flying. Even torsos have broad likenesses amongst us, satyrs and fauns, nuggies, and, to a lesser extent, sirens as well.

The folk striding toward us through the green, green grass might have been the pattern itself, the pattern from whose rearranged pieces the rest of us had been clumsily reassembled. As bronze, which had brought us here, is an alloy of copper and tin, so I saw that sirens were an alloy of these folk and birds, sphinxes of them and birds and lions, satyrs of them and goats, fauns of them and horses. And I saw that we centaurs blended these folk and horses as well, though in different proportions, as one bronze will differ from another depending on how much is copper and how much tin.

Is it any wonder, then, that, on seeing this folk, I at once began to wonder if I had any true right to exist?

And I began to understand what Bucca meant. As a nuggy, he was no doubt perfectly respectable. Next to these new ones, he was a small, wrinkled, ugly *thing*. Any of us, comparing ourselves to them, would have felt the same. How could we help it? We were a mixture. They were the essence with which our other parts were mixed. They might have been so many gods approaching us.

Nessus shivered. It might have been that cutting wind. It might have been, but it was not. "When I look at them, I see my own end," he murmured.

Because I felt the same way, I also felt an obligation to deny it. "They are bound to be as surprised by us as we are by them," I said. "If we have never seen their kind, likewise they have never seen ours. So long as we keep up a bold front, they will know nothing of . . . whatever else we may feel."

"Well said, Cheiron," Hylaeus told me. Whether it would likewise be well done remained to be seen.

"I will go forward with two others, so they may see we come in peace," I said. "Who will come with me?" Hylaeus and Oreus both strode forward, and I was glad to have them (gladder, perhaps, of the one than the other). The reason I offered was plausible, but it was not the only one I had. If I went forward with only two bold companions, the new folk would have more trouble noticing how so many of my hes wavered at the mere sight of them.

We three slowly went out ahead of the rest of the band. When we did, the strangers stopped for a moment. Then they also sent three of their number forward. They walked so straight, so free, so erect. Their gait was so *natural*. It made that of fauns or satyrs seem but a clumsy makeshift.

Two of them carried spears, one a fine leaf-shaped sword of bronze. The one with the sword, the tallest of them, sheathed his weapon. The other two trailed their spears on the ground. They did not want a fight, not then. We also showed we were not there to offer battle.

"Can you understand me?" I called.

Their leader frowned. "Can you understand *me?*" he called back in a tongue not far removed from the one Bucca used. I could, though it was not easy. I gather my language was as strange in his ears.

"Who are you? What is your folk?" I asked him, and, pointing back toward the stone circle, "What is this place?"

"I am Geraint," he answered. "I am a man"—a word I had not heard before. He looked at my companions and me. "I will ask you the same questions, and where you are from, and why you have come here."

I told him who I was, and named my kind as well. He listened attentively, his eyes—eyes gray as the seas thereabouts—alert. And I told him of our desire for tin, and of how we had come from the lands around the Inner Sea to seek it.

He heard me out. He had a cold courtesy much in keeping with that windswept plain. When I had finished, he threw back his head and laughed.

If I needed it, I could have brought up my axe very quickly. "Do you think I jest?" I asked. "Or do you aim to insult me? If you want a quarrel, I am sure we can oblige you."

Geraint shook his head. "Neither, although we will give you all the fight you care for if that is what you want. No, I am laughing because it turns out those funny little digging things were right after all."

"You mean the nuggies?" I asked.

Now he nodded. "Yes, them," he said indifferently. "I thought they dug because they were things that had to dig. But there really is a market for tin in this far corner of the world that has none of its own?"

"There is," I said. "We have trade goods back at the *Horse of Bronze,* our ship. We will pay well."

"Will you?" He eyed me in a way I had never seen before: as if I had no right to exist, as if my standing there on four hooves speaking of trade were an affront of the deadliest sort. Worse was that, when

I looked into those oceanic eyes, I more than half believed it myself.

Oreus, always quick to catch a slight, saw this perhaps even before I did. "I wonder if this man-thing has any blood inside it, or only juice like a gourd," he said.

Geraint should not have been able to follow that. He should not have, but he did. His eyes widened, this time in genuine surprise. "You are stronger than the nuggies," he said. "Do any of them yet live?"

"Yes," I said, not mentioning that we had seen only Bucca. "Will you trade tin with us? If not, we will try to mine it ourselves." I did not look forward to that. We had not the skills, and the nuggies' shafts would not be easy for folk with our bulk to negotiate.

But Geraint said, "We will trade. What do you offer?"

"We will trade what we have always sent north in exchange for tin," I answered. "We will give you jewelry of gold and precious stones. We will give olive oil, which cannot be made here. We will give wheat flour, for fine white bread. Wheat gives far better bread than barley, but, like the olive, it does not thrive in this northern clime." I was sure the olive would not grow here. I was less sure about wheat, but Geraint did not need to know that.

"Have you wine?" Geraint asked. "If you have wine, you may be sure we will make a bargain. Truly wine is the blood of the gods." The mans with him nodded.

"We have no wine," I said. "We did not bring any, for it is not to the nuggies' taste." That was true, but it was far from the only reason we had no wine. I said not a word of any other reasons. If Geraint wanted to ferret out our weaknesses, he was welcome to do so on his own. I would not hand them to him on a platter.

I wondered what weaknesses the mans had. Seeing him there, straight and erect and godlike in his all-of-one-pieceness, I wondered if mans had any weaknesses. Surely they did. What those weaknesses might be, though, I had no idea. Even now, I am less certain of them than I wish I were.

I said, "You must leave off killing the nuggies who grub the tin from the ground. They have done you no harm. That will be part of the bargain."

One of the mans with Geraint did not understand that. He repeated it in their language, which I could follow only in part. I did not think he turned it into a joke or a bit of mockery, but the mans laughed and laughed as if it were the funniest thing in the world.

To me, he said, "You misunderstand. We did not kill the nuggies and the other folk hereabouts. They see us, and then they commonly die."

"Of what?" I asked.

He told me. I was not sure I followed him, and so I asked him to say it again. He did: "Of embarrassment."

I refused to show him how much that chilled me. These mans embarrassed me, too, merely by their existence. I thought of Bucca, who was somehow tougher than his fellows. I wondered who among us might have such toughness. I was not sorry these mans dwelt so far from our homeland.

Another question occurred to me: "Did you make this great stone circle?"

"We did," Geraint answered.

"Why?" I asked.

I thought he would speak to me of the gods these mans worshiped, and of how those gods had commanded his folk to make the circle for some purpose of their own. I would not have been surprised that he and the other mans had no idea what the purpose was. That is often the way of gods: to keep those who revere them guessing, that they themselves might seem the stronger. And I would not have been surprised to hear him say right out that the purpose of the circle was to bring a bane down upon the other folk dwelling in those parts.

But he answered in neither of those ways. And yet his words *did* surprise me, for he said, "We raised this circle to study the motions of the sun and moon and stars."

"To study their motions?" I frowned, wondering if I had heard rightly and if I had understood what I heard.

Geraint nodded. "That is what I said, yes."

I scratched my head. "But . . . why?" I asked. "Can you hope to change them?"

He laughed at that. "No, of course not. Their motions are as the gods made them."

"True," I said, relieved he saw that much. These mans were so strange, and so full of themselves, he might easily have believed otherwise. "This being so, then, what is the point of, ah, studying these motions?"

"To know them better," Geraint replied, as if talking to a fool or a foal.

For all his scorn, I remained bewildered. "But what good will knowing them better do you?" I asked.

"I cannot tell you. But knowledge is always worth the having." Geraint spoke with great conviction. I wondered why. No sooner had I wondered than he tried to explain, saying, "How do you know you need tin to help harden copper into bronze? There must have been a time when folk did not know it. Someone must have learned it and taught it to others. There must have been a time when folk did not know of wonderful wine, either, or of this fine wheat flour you brag you have brought to trade. Someone must have learned of them."

His words frightened me more even than his appearance. He carved a hole in the center of the world. Worse yet, he knew not what he did. I said, "Assuredly the gods taught us these things."

His laugh might have been the embodiment of the cold wind blowing across that cold plain. "No doubt the gods set the world in motion," he said, "but is it not for us to find out what rules they used when they did it?"

"Gods need no rules. That is why they are gods," I said.

"There are always rules." Geraint sounded as certain as I was. "At the winter solstice, the sun always rises in the same place." He pointed to show where. "At the summer solstice, in another place, once more the same from year to year." He pointed again. "The moon likewise has its laws, though they are subtler. Why, even eclipses have laws."

He was mad, of course, but he sounded very sure of himself. Everyone knows eclipses show the gods are angry with those whose lands they darken. What else could an eclipse be but the anger of the gods? Nothing, plainly. Quarreling with a lunatic is always a risky business, and all the more so in his own country. I did not try it. Instead, I answered, "Let it be as you say, friend. Will you come back to the *Horse of Bronze* and trade tin for our goods?"

"I will," he answered, and then smiled a very unpleasant smile. "We are many in this land—more all the time. You are few, and no more of your kind will come any time soon. Why should we not simply take what we want from you?"

"For one thing, we would fight you, and many of your hes would die," I said. "I do not deny you would win in the end, but it would cost you dear. And if you rob us and kill us, no more of our folk will come to this shore. You will have one triumph, not steady trade. Which do you want more?"

The man thought it over. By his expression, he had never before had to weigh such considerations. I wondered whether one orgy of slaughter *would* count for more with him than years of steady dealing. Some folk care nothing for the future. It might as well not be real to them. Were Geraint and his kind of that sort? If so, all we could do was sell ourselves as dear as possible.

In due course, he decided. "You have given me a thought of weight, Cheiron," he said. He pronounced my name oddly. No doubt his in my mouth was not fully to his liking, either. Our languages were close cousins, but not quite brothers. He went on, "Trade is better. Robbery is easier and more fun, but trade is better. Our grandsons and their grandsons can go on trading if we do well here."

"Just so," I said, pleased he could look past himself. Maybe all his talk of rules, rules even in the heavens, had something to do with it. "Aye, just so. Come back to the ship, then, and we shall see what sort of bargains we may shape."

We clasped hands, he and I. Though his body could not match mine for speed, his grip was strong. He and his followers turned and went off toward the rest of the mans, who were waiting for them. Oreus and Hylaeus and I trotted back to our fellow centaurs. "It is agreed," I called. "We will trade. All is well."

A jackdaw flew up from the stone circle. "Chaka-chaka-chak!" it cried. It seemed as if it was laughing at me. What a fool I was, to let a little gray-eyed bird prove wiser than I.

As I have said, we centaurs were quicker than mans. But Geraint's folk showed surprising endurance. We could do more in an hour. Over a day's journey, the difference between us was smaller, for the mans would go on where we had to pause and rest.

We did all we could to take their measure, watching how they hunted, how they used their bows and spears. They, no doubt, were doing the same with us. How folk hunt tells much about how they will behave in a fight. I learned nothing spectacular from the mans, save that they were nimbler than I would have guessed. With our four feet and larger weight, we cannot change directions so readily as they do. Past that, there was little to choose between them and us.

No, I take that back. There was one thing more. I had seen it even before I saw the mans themselves. The other folk of the Tin Isle could not abide their presence. I wondered if Bucca would call on us while we were in Geraint's company. He did not, which left me saddened but unsurprised. And of the other nuggies, or of the spriggans and piskies, we found not a trace.

Hylaeus noted the same thing. "Maybe the man spoke true when he said they died of embarrassment," he said worriedly. "Will the same begin to happen to us?"

"If it will, it has not yet," I answered. "We are stronger-willed than those other folk; no one would doubt that."

"True." But Hylaeus did not sound much relieved. "But I cannot help thinking they are all of what we are only in part. Does that not give them more of a certain kind of strength than we have?"

I wished that thought had not also occurred to me. Still, I answered,

"What difference does it make? What difference *can* it make? We will trade with them, we will load the *Chalcippus* with tin till she wallows like a pregnant sow, and then we will sail home. After that, how can the mans' strength matter?"

Now he did seem happier, saying, "True, Cheiron, and well thought out. The sooner we are away from the Tin Isle, the gladder I shall be."

"And I," I said. "Oh, yes. And I."

Geraint sent some of his mans off to gather the tin: whether to dig it from the ground themselves or to take it from stocks the nuggies had mined before failing, I could not have said. They brought the metal in the usual leather sacks, each man carrying one on his back. They had no shame in using themselves as beasts of burden. And the sacks of tin did not much slow them. They still kept up with us.

As with our home country, no part of the Tin Isle is very far from any other part. We soon returned to the *Horse of Bronze*. The hes we had left behind to guard the ship were overjoyed to see us and bemused to see the mans. Anyone of any folk seeing mans for the first time is bound to be bemused, I do believe.

The trading went well: better than I had expected, in fact. Geraint was clever, no doubt about that. But he had little practice at dickering. I gather, though I am not certain, that he was much more used to taking than to haggling. To him, the tin he gave us was almost an afterthought, nothing to worry about. He wanted what we had.

When the dealing was done, when we had loaded the sacks of tin aboard the *Chalcippus* and his mans had carried off the trade goods, he said, "Let us have a feast, to celebrate the hour of our meeting."

"You are kind and generous," I said, meaning it at least in part. The countryside belonged to the mans. If there was to be a feast, the burden of fixing it would fall on them. I did add, "But let it not be long delayed. The season advances. Ocean the Great was harsh enough on the northward voyage. I would not care to sail in a time when storms grow more likely."

"As you say, so shall it be," Geraint replied, and so, indeed, it was. Mans brought cows and sheep and pigs to the seashore for slaughtering as the sun went down. Others had slain deer and ducks and geese. Shes of the man kind—womans, Geraint called them—came to tend to the cooking. Many of them were as pleasing in face and upper body as any of the shes we had left behind so long ago. Below . . . Below is always a mystery. The mystery here was to discover whether one part would fit with another. Some of us, I am told, made the experiment, and found it not altogether unsatisfactory. I doubt we would have, were our own shes close by. But they were not, and so . . .

I do wonder if any issue resulted, and of what sort. But that is something I shall never know.

Along with roasting meat, the womans baked barley cakes and others from different grains they grow in that northern clime. Those were edible, but oats and rye are not foods on which I should care to have to depend. And the womans baked bread from the good wheat flour we had brought from our own home. The soft chewiness and fine flavor of the loaves occasioned much favorable comment from the mans.

In that part of the world, they use less pottery than we. Being rich in forests, they make wooden barrels in place of our amphorae. The mans brought several of them to the feast. I asked Geraint, "What do these hold?"

"Why, cerevisia, of course," he answered in surprise. "We brew it from barley. Do you not know it?"

"No, though we sometimes use barley-water as a medicine," I said.

He laughed. "Even as we do with cerevisia. Drink of it, then, and be . . . cured." He laughed again.

Some of the womans broached a barrel of cerevisia and used a wooden dipper to pour the stuff into mugs, most of them of wood; some of pottery; and a few, for the leaders, of gold. The stuff in the barrel was thin and yellow. It looked, to be honest, more like what we expend after drinking than anything we would have wanted to drink. But the mans showed no hesitation. In fact, they were eager. I also saw that the womans sneaked mugs of cerevisia for themselves when they thought no one was looking.

Geraint, then, had not brought this stuff forth with the intention of poisoning us. He could not possibly have given so many mans an antidote ahead of time, and he could not have known in advance which womans would drink and which would not. He had a mug of cerevisia himself, a golden mug. He lifted it to me in salute. "Your good health!" he said, and drank it down.

A woman brought me a mug of my own, a golden mug similar to Geraint's. Cerevisa sloshed in it. I sniffed the brew. We centaurs have keener noses than many other folk. It had a slightly sour, slightly bitter odor. I did not see how anyone could care to drink it for pleasure, but I did not see how it could hurt me, either.

As Geraint had done, I raised my mug. "And yours!" I said. I too drank down the cerevisia.

It was not quite so nasty as I had thought it would be from the smell, but it was definitely an acquired taste—and one I had not acquired. Still, for courtesy's sake I made shift to empty the mug. I even managed to smile at the woman who poured it full again. She was, I own, worth smiling at. I had made no surreptitious experiments with these womans. With this one . . . Well, I might even get used to the idea that she had no tail.

Looking around, I saw I was not the only centaur drinking cerevisia. Some of the hes who had sailed up to the Tin Isle took to it with more enthusiasm than I could muster myself.

A woman also refilled Geraint's mug. He drank deep once more. When he nodded to me, his face seemed redder than it had. "What do you think?" he asked.

"Of cerevisia?" I tried to be as polite as I could, for it was clear the mans were giving us the best they had. "It is not bad at all."

"Not bad at all?" As I might have known, that was not praise enough to suit him. "It is some of the finest brew we have ever made. I have drunk enough to know." But then he caught himself and began to laugh. "I forget. You who live by the Inner Sea are used to wine, and to those who have drunk only wine, cerevisia, even the finest, must seem nothing special."

I drained the golden mug once more. The cerevisia truly was not bad at all as the second serving slid down my throat. The woman smiled at me when she filled the mug again. My brain seemed to buzz. My whole body seemed to buzz, if the truth be known. I told myself it was the woman's smile that excited me so. On the Tin Isle, I told myself any number of things that were not true.

One of the centaurs let out a great, wild whoop. Another he howled out a similar cry a moment later. The buzzing that coursed through me grew stronger. I tossed back the mug of cerevisia. No, it was not bad. In fact, it was quite good. Without my asking, the woman gave me more. And the more I drank, the better it seemed.

Geraint had said something. I needed to remember what it was. It had mattered, or so I thought. But thought was . . . not so much difficult, I would say, as unimportant. I managed, however, and laughed in triumph. "Cerevisia and wine!" I said, though my tongue seemed hardly my own or under my will. "Why do you speak of cerevisia and wine together?"

I was not the only one who laughed. Geraint all but whinnied, he found that so funny. "You should know," he told me when he could speak again.

"What mean you?" I was having trouble speaking, or at least speaking clearly, myself. Drinking cerevisia was easier and more enjoyable. Yet another mug's worth glided down my gullet.

Geraint laughed once more. "Why, they are the only brews I know that will make a man drunk," he replied. "And I see they will make your folk drunk as well. In truth, they must mount straight to your head, for the cerevisia makes you drunk far faster than it does with us."

"Cerevisia . . . makes for drunkenness?" I spoke with a certain helpless horror. I knew then what was toward, and knew myself powerless to stop it.

"Why, of course." Geraint seemed tempted to laugh yet again, this time at my foolishness. And I had been a fool, all right. The man asked, "Did you not know this?"

Sick with dread, I shook my head. The buzzing in my veins grew ever higher, ever shriller. Many folk around the Inner Sea make wine, drink wine, enjoy wine. We centaurs fight shy of it. We have good reason, too. Wine does not make us drunk, or not as it makes them drunk. Wine makes us mad. And cerevisia seemed all too likely to do the same.

I tried to say as much, but now my tongue and lips would not obey the orders I gave them. Not far away, a woman squealed. Oreus—I might have known it would be Oreus—had slung her over his shoulder and was galloping off into the darkness with her.

"What is he doing?" Geraint exclaimed. I knew perfectly well what he was doing (as did Geraint, no doubt), but I could not have told him. The man drew his sword, as if to stop Oreus, even though Oreus was now gone. I could not speak, but my hands and hooves still obeyed my will. I dealt Geraint a buffet that stretched him on the ground. When he started to get to his feet, I trampled him. He did not rise after that. No one, not from any folk, could have after that.

The woman who had served me screamed. I trotted toward her. Would I have served her as Oreus was surely serving the other woman? I suppose I would have, but I found myself distracted. There stood the barrel of cerevisia, with the dipper waiting for my hand. I drank and drank. The woman could wait. By the time I thought of her again, she had—quite sensibly—fled.

All over the feasting ground, madness reigned. Centaurs fought mans. Centaurs fought other centaurs. I do not know if mans fought other mans, but I would not be surprised.

A man speared a centaur in the barrel. The centaur, roaring, lifted the man and flung him into a pit of coals where a pig was cooking. The savor of roasting meat got stronger, but did not change its essential nature. Man's flesh on the fire smells much like pork.

Some centaurs did not bother taking womans into the darkness before taking them. The mans attacked these very fiercely. With madness coursing through them, the centaurs fought back with an animal ferocity I had rarely known in us before.

Shrieks and screams and howls of rage from both sides profaned the pleasant seaside feasting ground. There were more mans than centaurs, but the centaurs were bigger and stronger—and, as I say, madder. We cared nothing for wounds, so long as we could wound the enemy in return. We drove the mans wailing into the night, the few we did not slay.

Then we were alone on the beach, along with those wonderful barrels of cerevisia. To the victors, the spoils of battle. For us, these were enough, and more than enough.

I came back to myself thinking I had died—and that the gods of the afterlife were crueler than I had imagined. The pale sun of the Tin Isle beat down as if on the valley of the sphinxes. By the way my head pounded, some demented smith was beating a hammerhead into shape just above my eyes. The taste in my mouth I will not dignify with a name. Like as not, it has none.

The sun was just rising. It showed me that not all the horror, not all the nightmare, dwelt within me. Mans and womans and centaurs lay sprawled and twisted in death. The blood that had poured from them was already turning black. Flies buzzed about the bodies. Rooks and carrion crows and ravens hopped here and there, pecking at eyes and tongues and other exposed dainties.

Not many centaurs had died. This, I think, was not only on account of our advantage in size but also because we had been full of the strength and vitality of madness. Looking around, I saw ovens overturned, barrels smashed, and much other destruction for the sake of destruction. This is not our usual way. It is not the usual way of any decent folk. But when the madness of wine—and, evidently, also the madness of cerevisia—struck us, what was usual was forgotten.

Other centaurs were stirring, rousing, from what had passed the night before, even as was I. By their groans, by the anguish in their voices and on their faces, they knew the same pain I did. Awakening from madness can never be easy, or sweet. You always know what you are and, worse, what you were.

My fellows gazed on the devastation all around as if they could not believe their eyes. Well, how could I blame them, when I had as much trouble believing as the rest of them? Nessus said, "Surely we did no such thing. Surely." His voice was as hoarse a croak as any that might burst from a raven's throat. Its very timbre gave his hopeful words the lie.

"Surely we did not," I said, "except that we did." I wish I could claim I sounded better than Nessus. In fact, I can. But claiming a thing does not make it true. How I wish it did!

He turned his tail on the chaos, the carnage, the carrion. It was as if he could not bear to see himself mistaken. Again, blaming him is not easy. Who would wish to be reminded of . . . that?

"Did we slay all the mans?" Hylaeus asked.

"I think not." I shook my head, which sent fresh pangs shooting through it. "No, I know not. Some of them fled off into the night."

"That is not good," Nessus said. "They will bring more of their kind here. They will seek vengeance."

There, he was bound to be right. And the mans would have good reason to hunger for revenge. Not only had we slain their warriors, we had also outraged and slain their shes. Had some other folk assailed us so, we too would have been wild to avenge.

I looked inland. I saw nothing there, but I knew the mans did not yet thickly settle this part of the Tin Isle, the other folk who had lived hereabouts having only recently died out. I also knew this did not mean vengeance would not fall upon us, only that it might be somewhat delayed.

"We would do well not to be here when more mans come," I said. "We would do well to be on our way back toward the Inner Sea."

"There is a coward's counsel!" Oreus exclaimed. "Better we should fight these miserable mans than run from them."

"Can you fight five mans by yourself? Can you fight twenty mans by yourself?" I asked him, trying to plumb the depths of his stupidity.

It ran deeper than I had dreamt, for he said, "We would not be alone. The other folk of this land would fight with us, would fight for us."

"What other folk?" I inquired of him. "When the other folk of this land meet mans, they perish." Perhaps the madness of the cerevisia had not worked altogether for ill for us. Mad with drink, we had not fretted over our place in the scheme of things and that of the strange folk who sought to find rules (rules!—it chills me yet) in the gods' heavens.

Oreus would have argued further, but Nessus kicked him, not too hard, in the flank. "Cheiron is right," he said. "Maybe one day we can sail back here in greater numbers and try conclusions with these mans. For now, though, we would be better gone."

The thought that we might return one day mollified the young, fiery he. Nessus knew better than I how to salve Oreus's pride. "Very well, let us go, then," Oreus said. "The mans will not soon forget us."

Nor we them, I thought. But I did not say that aloud. Instead, I helped the rest of us push the *Horse of Bronze* into the sea, which luckily lay almost under her keel. With all those sacks of tin in her, the work still was not easy, but we managed it. The gods sent us a fair wind out of the east. I ordered the yard raised on the mast and the sail lowered from it. We left the Tin Isle behind.

Our homeward journey was neither easy nor swift. If I speak of it less than I did of the voyage outward, it is because so many of the hazards were the same. For the first two days after we left the Tin Isle, I do admit to anxiously looking back over my tail every now and again. I did not know for a fact whether the mans had mastered the art of shipbuilding. If they had, they might have pursued. But evidently not. We remained alone on the bosom of Ocean the Great, as far as my eyes could tell.

Sailing proved no worse—and possibly better—than it had on our northward leg. We stayed in sight of land when we could, but did not stay so close that we risked being forced onto a lee shore by wind and wave rolling out of the west. And *rolling* is truly the word, for we saw waves on Ocean the Great that no one who has sailed only the Inner Sea can imagine.

With the *Chalcippus* more heavily laden than she had been while we were outward bound, I did not like to bring her up on the beach every night. I had learned to respect and to fear the rise and fall of the waters against the land, which seems to happen twice a day in the regions washed by the Ocean. If the waters withdrew too far, we might not be able to get the galley back into the sea. To hold that worry at arm's length, we dropped anchor offshore most nights.

That too, of course, came with a price. Because we could not let the ship's timbers dry out at night, they grew heavy and waterlogged, making the *Horse of Bronze* a slower and less responsive steed than she would otherwise have been. Had a bad storm blown up, that might have cost us dear. As things were, the gods smiled, or at least did not frown with all the grimness they might have shown, and we came safe to the Inner Sea once more.

As we sailed east past the pillars said to hold up the heavens, I wondered once more about the mans, and how *they* escaped the gods' wrath. Most folk—no, all folk I had known up until then—are content to live in the world the gods made and to thank them for their generous bounty. What the gods will, lesser folk accept, as they must—for, as I have remarked, the essence of godhood is power. Were I as powerful as a god, what would I be? A god myself, nothing else. But I am not so powerful and so am no god.

Nor are these mans gods. That was plain. In our cerevisia-spawned madness, we slew them easily enough. Yet they have the arrogance, the presumption, to seek out the gods' secrets. And they have the further arrogance and presumption to believe that, if they find them, they can use them.

Can a folk not given godlike powers arrogate those powers to itself? The mans seem to think so. How would the gods view such an opinion? If they did take it amiss, as I judged likely, how long would they wait to punish it?

Confident in their own strength, might they wait too long? If a folk did somehow steal godlike power, what need would it have of veritable gods? Such gloomy reflections filled my mind as we made our way across the Inner Sea. I confess to avoiding the sirens' island on the homeward journey. Their temper was unpleasant, their memories doubtless long. We sailed south of them instead, skirting the coast where the lotus-eaters dwell. I remember little of that part of the voyage; the lotus-eaters, I daresay, remember less.

I do remember the long sail we had up from the land of the lotus-eaters to that of the fauns. The sail seemed the longer because, as I say, we had to keep clear of the island of the sirens. We filled all the water jars as full as we could. This let us anchor well off the coast of their island as we traveled north. We also had the good fortune of a strong southerly breeze. We lowered the sail from the yard, then, and ran before the wind. Our hes were able to rest at the oars, which meant they did not grow thirsty as fast as they would have otherwise. We came to the land of the fauns with water still in the jars—not much, but enough.

That breeze had held for us all the way from the land of the lotus-eaters to that which the fauns call home. From this, I believe—and I certainly hope—the gods favored our cause and not the sirens'. This I believe and hope, yes. But I have not the gall to claim it *proves* the gods favored us, or to use it to predict that the gods would favor us again in the same way. I am not a man. I do not make stone circles. I do not believe a stone circle can measure the deeds and will of the gods.

By what has befallen the other folk on the Tin Isle besides the mans, I may be mistaken.

From the easternmost spit of the fauns' homeland to ours is but a short sail. Yet the *Horse of Bronze* came closer to foundering there than anywhere on turbulent Ocean the Great. A storm blew up from nowhere, as it were. The *Chalcippus* pitched and rolled and yawed. A wave crashed over the bow and threatened to swamp us. We all bailed for our lives, but another wave or two would have stolen them from us.

And then, as abruptly as it had sprung to life, the storm died. What conclusion was I to draw from this? That the gods were trying to frighten me to death but would spare me if they failed? That drawing conclusions about what the gods intend was a risky business, a fool's game? I had already known as much. I was not a man, to require lessons on the subject.

We came home not only to rejoicing but to astonishment. Most of the hes we left behind on setting sail in the *Chalcippus* had expected to see us no more. Many of the shes we left behind also expected to see us no more. That led to several surprises and considerable unpleasantness, none of which deserves recounting here.

It often seemed as if the tin we brought home was more welcome than we were. Few cared to listen to our tales of the great stone circle or of the strange mans who had built it. The fauns, the sirens, the lotus-eaters we centaurs already knew. The stay-at-homes were glad enough to hear stories about them.

Certainly the smiths welcomed the tin with glad cries and with caracoles of delight. They fell to work as if made of bronze themselves. We have a sufficiency of copper—more than a sufficiency—for we trade it with folk whose land gives them none. But tin is far less common and far more dear; were it otherwise, we would not have needed to fare so far to lay hold of it.

Spearheads and shields and swords and helms began to pile up, ready for use against the sphinxes or whoever else should presume to trouble us. Now we could match bronze against bronze, rather than being compelled to use the softer copper unalloyed. Some of the younger hes quite looked forward to combat. That far I would not go. I have seen enough to know that combat too often comes whether we look for it or not; what point, then, in seeking it?

The smiths also made no small stock of less warlike gear. I speak of that less not because I esteem it less, but only because, when bronze is not measured against bronze, its hardness as compared to copper's is of less moment.

Not too long after our return, I learned that we in the *Chalcippus* were not the only band of centaurs to have set out in search of tin. A he named Pholus had led a band north by land. There are mountains in those parts that yield gold and silver, and Pholus hoped he might happen upon tin as well.

Although those mountains are not far as the raven flies, our folk seldom go there. The folk who live in those parts are strange, and strangely fierce and formidable. They come out only at night, and are often in the habit of drinking the blood of those they kill. And they are persistent of life, though sunlight, curiously enough, is alleged to slay them.

This Pholus affirmed for me, saying, "After we caught a couple of them and staked them out for the sunrise, the others proved less eager to see if they could sneak up and murder us by the light of the moon."

"Yes, I can see how that might be so," I told him. "Good for you. But I gather you found no tin?"

"I fear me we did not," he agreed. "It is a rich country. Were it not for these night skulkers, we could do a great deal of trade with it. They care nothing for bargaining, though. All they want is the taste of blood in their mouths." His own mouth twisted in disgust.

"Many good-byes to them, then," I said. "Maybe we ought to send a host up that way, to see how many we could drag out for the sun to destroy."

"Maybe." But Pholus did not sound as if he thought that a good idea. "If we did not get rid of them all, they would make us pay. And besides—" He did not go on.

"Besides, what?" I asked when I saw he would not continue on his own.

He did not answer for a long time. I wondered if he would. At long last, he said, "I swore my hes to secrecy, Cheiron. I did not take the oath myself, for I thought there was no need. I knew I could keep a secret. Perhaps the gods foresaw that I would need to speak one day, and did not want me forsworn. I know you can also hold a secret close at need. The need, I think, is here. I have heard somewhat of your voyage, and of the peculiar folk you met on the Tin Isle."

"The mans?" I said, and he nodded. "Well, what of them?"

"That is the secret we are keeping," Pholus replied. "Up in the mountains, we met some of what I think must be the same folk ourselves. They were coming down from the north, as much strangers in those parts as we were. They did not call themselves mans, though; they had another name."

"Why did you keep them a secret?" I asked.

He shivered. Pholus is bold and swift and strong. I had never thought to see him afraid, and needed a moment to realize that I had. "Because they are . . . what we ought to be," he answered after another long hesitation. "What we and the satyrs and the sphinxes and those troublesome blood-drinkers ought to be. They are . . . all of a kind, with more of the stuff of the gods and less of the beast in them than we hold."

I knew what he meant. I knew so well, I had to pretend I knew not. "More of the gall of the gods, if they truly are like the mans I met," I said.

"And that," he agreed. The hard, bright look of fear still made his eyes opaque. "But if they are coming down from the north—everywhere from the north—how shall any of the folk around the Inner Sea withstand them?"

I had wondered that about the mans, even on the distant Tin Isle. If they had also reached the mountains north of our own land, though, there were more of them than I had dreamt, and the danger to us all was worse. I tried to make light of it, saying, "Well, the blood-drinkers may bar the way."

Pholus nodded, but dubiously. "That is the other reason I would not go after the blood-drinkers: because they might shield us. But I do not think they will, or not for long. The new folk have met them, and have plans of their own for revenge. Do you think the night-skulking blood-drinkers can oppose them?"

"Not if they are mans of the same sort I knew," I said. "Are you sure they are the same? What *did* they call themselves?"

"Lapiths," he answered. The name meant nothing to me then. But these days the echoes of the battle of Lapiths and centaurs resound round the Inner Sea. We are scattered to the winds, those few left to us, and the Lapiths dwell in the land ours since the gods made it. And Pholus knew whereof he spoke. The Lapiths *are* mans. They remain sure to this day that they won simply because they had the right to win, with no other reason needed.

They would.

The Indo-European-speaking ancestors of the Hittites probably brought their culture into Anatolia during the late third millenium B.C. *After several hundred years, their descendants established an empire that rivaled and sometimes destroyed other, older Near Eastern kingdoms until they themselves fell to foreign enemies at the end of the Bronze Age. Despite their ancient (and modern) reputation as warriors, their culture was first and foremost agricultural. They were also literate, and among the Hittite texts is the story of one Hupasiya summoned to aid the gods. The original text is, like so many others from antiquity, broken, and the ending is lost, but Josepha Sherman, with her expertise in folklore and the ancient world, here attends to that.*

A Hero for the Gods

Hupasiya stepped out of his farmhouse, then stopped dead, grabbing for his old woolen mantle and hastily wrapping it around himself. Gods, it was cold out here!

He still looked very much like the true Hittite warrior he'd been just a few short years ago: burly and muscular, black of curly hair and beard, with a narrow scar like a white blaze of lightning seaming his face. His bronze sword hung on a wall inside, and he still kept it polished and oiled as befitted a good blade. But the battles he fought these days were only with the fields and the harvests, and no regrets about it.

Almost no regrets, he corrected wryly. Springtime—ha. Not a touch of softness to the biting air, not a hint of greenery poking up out of the frozen fields. And the snow on the towering mountains of Anatolia all about him hadn't even begun its retreat up to merely cap them, but still gleamed blazing white halfway down the slopes.

"Husband?"

Hupasiya turned at the sudden voice. Even now, as always, he felt a smile curve his lips at the sight of Zaliya. Still lovely, so lovely, even after having borne them a daughter and a son. Lovely even with her hair in a simple braid and dressed in a simple gown of undyed wool. Once she'd worn more elegant clothes, and gleamed with gold as befitted an officer's wife . . .

Then Hupasiya saw the worry in her dark eyes, and the smile faded. "Nothing," he told her reluctantly. "Just like the day before, and the day before that. Nothing but this dry, endless cold."

Zaliya shivered. Hupasiya held open a fold of his mantle, and she gladly huddled against him, letting him wrap the wool about them both. "It's never stayed so chilly this late in the spring," she murmured. "If the crops don't sprout soon . . ."

He shrugged helplessly.

"Hupasiya . . . you don't suppose . . ."

"What?"

"The gods—"

"Are angry with us?" Hupasiya snorted. "Then they are angry with all who live near or in Ziggaratta. We all suffer the same weather." He looked sideways at her, suddenly anxious. "Zaliya . . . are you regretting this?" His sweep of an arm took in their farm. "I mean, you had a fine life as an officer's wife—"

"I had a terrible life!"

"What—"

"You'd go off to war against the Akkadians or the Egyptians or the gods only know who else, and me, I'd be left back in Ziggaratta with the other wives, wondering if a living husband would return to me, a husband with arms and legs and—"

"And all the necessary parts. Hey!"

Zaliya had pulled a hand free to smack him on the arm. "You do not show the proper respect." But she was smiling.

"Papa?" a sleepy voice asked from within the sturdy farmhouse. A second voice added quaveringly, "Mamma?"

"Hush, loves," Zaliya called back. "Nothing's wrong. Papa and I are just talking."

"That's why I left," Hupasiya murmured, gesturing with his head back into the house. "Not just for us. So that they could have a normal, happy life." *And if it demeans me to be a farmer instead of a warrior, so be it.*

But Zaliya's eyes were still worried. "And what's to happen to them if the crop fails? We don't have enough from last year's harvest to tide us over."

Yes, his mind chided, *and at least in the army you drew steady wages. And a pension for your wife were you slain.*

Oh, and there was cold comfort for Zaliya and the children.

I am a husband and father, not some fool of a hero with his gleaming bronze sword—

"It's too early to worry," Hupasiya said.

I will protect them. Even if I must sell what may be left of honor. I will protect them.

The mountaintop was slick with ice and chill with bitter wind, and not quite in the mortal world. She who paced angrily back and forth, never slipping on the icy footing, never risking a fall, was Inaras, daughter of the Storm-God and Goddess of the Wild Beasts. Beautiful as a wild thing in her long-fringed robes, she was all sleekness and peril, with dark hair glinting with hints of light and eyes the ever-changing colors of her father's stormy skies. "We cannot let this be!"

The other gods would not meet her angry glare.

"Hebat, wife of my father! You know we cannot suffer this! My father cannot be defeated yet again!"

The Storm-God's wife, all matronly curves and fullness, suddenly became very busy combing knots out of the mane of the sacred lion that lolled at her feet.

Inaras let out her breath in an angry sigh, and turned sharply to another deity. "You, Telepinus, you know what happens when the proper order is overturned!"

Green-robed and handsome, he was Lord of Agriculture, and Inaras's brother. And yes, Inaras thought, he certainly did know. Once, when he was angry, he had hidden from the world. The crops had suffered, and the human people with them, until Telepinus had guiltily returned.

"What is there to be done?" he muttered. "The Dragon has already defeated our father once."

And that is why Father does not even dare to show his face at his meeting! Inaras thought. "That is because we thought to fight Illuyankas as though he were one of us. He is not!"

Kamrusepas frowned. "What are you proposing?" Goddess of Healing though she was, there was a hint of warrior anger in her voice. "There are none of us who are not divine."

Inaras turned sharply to her. "And that was where we made our first mistake. This time the Dragon will be slain—because this time I will bring us the aid of a mortal. Yes, yes, I know, it has never been done. Mortals are fallible, mortals are unpredictable—that uncertainty is exactly what will make this man so valuable!"

Kamrusepas raised one elegantly curved eyebrow. "What's this? Have you already chosen your hero?"

Hebat made a soft, disapproving *tsk*. "This does not surprise me. When has Inaras *not* chosen herself a mortal man?"

"A hero!" Inaras corrected angrily. "I chose only heroes!"

"If that's what you wish to call them."

"Listen to me, all of you! Do you not see what has happened to the mortal world since the Dragon came to power? There is no spring, no ripening crops, nothing for the beasts of earth to eat! Telepinus—"

"You are right," he agreed reluctantly. "I say yes, let it be done. Bring us your mortal hero and see what he can do for us."

Hupasiya bent over the frozen furrow, trying to see if maybe, *maybe*, that tiny speck of green was actually something he'd planted starting to grow. He straightened with a grunt, working a knot out of his back with one hand, and—

Found himself without warning facing a woman who had appeared without a sound. She was tall and eerily beautiful, high and wide of cheekbone, full and lush of figure, the woman of whom any man might dream. No . . . a chill ran up his spine as he realized that this was never a woman. Never a human one, Hupasiya corrected uneasily.

She was simply too *alive* for any mere mortality, fairly radiating a force that was sheer Life. It crackled in the ringlets of her long, blue-black hair and in her gleaming dark eyes. The curves of her body, clearly outlined under the folds of her lightweight robes, were all that was woman yet more perfect than any human woman could ever boast. In that moment of awareness, in that sudden state of nearly helpless awe and lust, Hupasiya threw up his hands in a ritual gesture of respect. It seemed the safest thing to do.

"Hail, Divine One!" he gasped, since not trying for a name that might be wrong seemed safest, too.

"Yes, indeed, I am divine," she said impatiently, as though the fact of his worship and blazing desire were hardly important. "I am Inaras, you are my hero, and let us be away from here."

She gestured, and the world dazed him with a sudden flare of light. Hupasiya blinked—

—blinked again.

And let out his breath in a slow gasp of wonder, all lust dashed from him by the suddenness of change. A moment ago, he had been standing amid his fields, yet now he was . . . wherever this was. A mountain peak . . . yes, with sharp rocks and ice all around him, and gusts of wind sending snow whirling up in little spirals, but he wasn't cold, only . . .

Only scared out of my senses. Scared as I never was in the heart of battle. This is a god, a goddess, the Goddess Inaras—what does she—

"What do you want of me?" he burst out before he could control himself. And then, heart pounding, waited to be destroyed for his impertinence.

But Inaras said only, "Illuyankas threatens."

"Your pardon, but I don't—"

"Have you mortals no wisdom at all? Learn!"

She seized him in her arms. Her lips met his in a savage, sensual, demanding kiss, and in that instant Hupasiya saw, knew—

It was Illuyankas the Dragon. Mighty being, terrible being, all strength, all hunger for power mortal and divine. Illuyankas, who had defeated the Storm-God himself, and with that defeat of the normal order of Nature had caused both the immense insult to the gods and the unnaturally long chill of winter.

Inaras released him, and Hupasiya fell helplessly to his knees, gasping for breath. That kiss had nearly been strong enough to force the life from him. And yet, and yet, he was a man, a mortal man, and there was a thought deep in his mind that would not be denied: What would it be like to know that kiss again, what would it be like to feel those limbs about a man, to know the passion of a goddess . . .

"I've been recruited." Those were the only reasonably sane words he could find that would come forth. "Your pardon for any rudeness, great one, but—you want me to conquer *that*?" How could a mortal ever possibly succeed when the gods themselves could not?

To Hupasiya's immense relief, the goddess didn't blast him where he stood. "It is precisely because you are mortal that you shall succeed."

And are you also so sure that the mortal will survive? But sarcasm almost certainly *would* get him turned to ash. At least Inaras didn't seem able, or at least willing, to read the thoughts in his mind.

"I know how mortals think," she said, and disdain was in the words. "Name a reward."

What reward is worth my life? Hupasiya wanted to say something about his wife and children, anything to ensure their safety, but confronted by all that too-living, too-perfect female splendor, he could not focus his mind on them, or on his love for them. Instead, he heard himself say, "You, gracious lady. The price I name for my aid is a night with you."

He waited, heart pounding with renewed force. Oh, fool, fool! Surely she, goddess that she was, would refuse him, and he could only pray that she would not strike him down for his impertinence, and not take vengeance on his family, either.

But to Hupasiya's astonishment, after the briefest of silences, Inaras merely said, as though it meant nothing to her, "Done."

So fierce and hot a stare did she give him in the next instant that lust beyond all controlling blazed up in Hupasiya. His last clear thought as the goddess opened her arms to him was, *And here I worried about a Dragon?* This *will probably kill me!*

At least he would die happy.

But . . . he hadn't died. He was himself, waking and standing without any memory of awakening and getting to his feet, yes, and with only the dimmest, most unsure memories of . . . of . . . a wife . . .? Children . . .? He couldn't even be sure about what had just happened. And he—

He was standing among others—

The gods! He was surrounded by gods! These so very fierce with Life folk were never, never human men and women! That tall, handsome young deity in the fringed robes of a hundred different shades of green could only be Telepinus, he who oversaw all that grew. For a mindless instant Hupasiya wanted to ask, "What happened to this year's harvest?" But he already knew the answer to that question: Illuyankas.

Besides, Hupasiya really didn't think this was the time to ask any deity anything, not after . . . well, the details still weren't at all clear in his mind, but whatever had happened . . . had happened.

Hot breath on the back of his neck made Hupasiya whirl, going almost instinctively into a warrior's crouch. He nearly let out a shout to find himself nose to nose with a lion, and sprang back a step, just barely keeping from landing on his rump. The lion gave a rumbling purr, almost as though laughing at him.

"And *this* is your hero," a woman murmured from behind the beast.

That was Hebat, surely, since who else but she would keep a lion as a pet? Who else but Hebat could look so motherly and dangerous at the same time, she who was the Storm-God's wife. And, for that matter, she who was Inaras's mother—gods, had she, did she—did she know what her daughter and he had—

What nonsense! These *were* the gods, and they would hardly be interested in anything so petty as human morality.

"Glorious Lady," he said, making a raised-hands gesture of reverence, "I make no claims of being a hero, nor do I make any claim to understand the ways and wishes of the divine. But surely we do share this one thing: We both wish an end to the Dragon to avenge a wrong and return the rightful order to the world."

"And how, little mortal," Telepinus asked, "is that to be accomplished?"

You didn't snap back at someone who could easily destroy you. But something in Telepinus's jeering tone struck an odd chord of memory in Hupasiya's mind. He'd heard the same sort of so-superior backtalk from superior officers in the Hittite army. Then, too, he'd been unable to say what he was thinking. But he'd handled the situation then, and by the—by the gods, he'd handle it now.

Crouching down, he cleared a patch of ground with a stick, then used the same stick to cut symbols in the earth. As he did, Hupasiya spoke in his most no-nonsense military voice, "To destroy a foe, we must first know his strengths and weaknesses."

When the gods were silent, Hupasiya prodded them, "I am, as you remind me, a mortal. What may seem quite ordinary to you will be new and unknown to me."

"Shall we then waste our time educating you?" Telepinus asked.

Calmness. Can't strike back at a superior officer. "It may seem a waste, Divine One, but the smallest of details so familiar it has been overlooked may provide us with a clue—and a weapon."

"The mortal shows a good line of reasoning," Hebat murmured. "Let us agree with him and begin listing what we may know of the Dragon."

The gods listed feature after feature: Illuyankas's strength; Illuyankas's fury; Illuyankas's envy of the gods. Obvious features, useless features. Hupasiya kept silent all the while, forcing himself to keep his uneasiness and growing despair from showing. Nothing here, nothing at all. But if he didn't find some weapon against the Dragon, they were going to throw *him* against the Dragon, and there was a knife's edge difference between being slain by Illuyankas or by angry gods.

Eh, wait—Hupasiya held up a hand, not caring in that moment of sudden hope that he was interrupting Inaras. "What was that? What did you just say?"

She stared at him, clearly too startled to be angry. "Why, that Illuyankas is large in all his appetites."

"Ah, yes, there it is! O Divine One, you have just given us the weapon we need!"

As the gods listened, frowning slightly, Hupasiya told them his newly born plan.

"That's impossible!"

"It can never work!"

"There is no honor in this!"

"I am but human," Hupasiya reminded them all. "It is my honor, not yours, Divine Ones, that is at stake. And I dare risk it." He could feel the gods uncertainty as a chilly wind prickling his skin, so Hupasiya added, "What harm to this? If my plan fails, why, you are no worse off then you were before my arrival. But if it succeeds, then you are avenged."

"Interesting," a stern voice said.

The newcomer was a tall, powerfully built god, the dark masses of his hair like gathering storm clouds, his eyes flashing with the blue-white fire of the lightning. Even as Hupasiya bowed low before the Storm-God, he thought, at the point of terror when one is utterly calm, *I was wondering when he would appear.*

"Let it be done," the Storm-God said.

I hoped that the invitation would be made, Hupasiya thought. *I knew that the invitation had to be delivered. I just never thought that* I *would be the one to deliver it.*

It was hardly work for a warrior. And yet it made sense, in a purely unemotional way. Illuyankas would never believe any offering made directly from the gods.

And of course if something happens to the messenger, why, that is merely the inconvenient loss of a human.

He hadn't expected Illuyankas to live in a palace. And sure enough, this was a cave. A cavern, rather, he realized, once he had gotten through the narrow entrance. Excellent defense to keep enemies from following the Dragon into his home. His dark, chilly home.

Illuyankas suddenly loomed up before him, a great mass of darker shadow against the darkness. Other shadows moved behind him.

Wonderful. The Dragon has a family.

Hupasiya promptly abandoned all thoughts of being a dragonslayer. One did not go up against an army with only one sword. Either deliver his message or die.

"O great Illuyankas, the Storm-God sends you humble greetings."

That eerie repetitive snarl could almost have been a laugh. "Indeed . . ." It was the softest, coldest whisper of sound.

"And to show you his sincerity," Hupasiya continued, keeping his voice steady, "he has invited you to a great feast in your honor, out on the mountaintop where you two once fought. Will you not join him, O mighty Illuyankas?"

He heard that eerie snarl-laugh echo in the darkness. "Warn the god of faintest breezes that I am coming."

Not only Illuyankas but his whole family followed Hupasiya out into the light. Nightmares, he thought, living nightmares, sleek and sinuous, scaled and furred, and impossible to see as any one kind of being. Hupasiya knew for the first time why even a god had been overcome.

Something so fully a thing of old Chaos has no right still existing in the world of gods and mortals.

Now, if only the gods have kept up their side of this trap . . .

And if only their judgment of his character is correct . . .

It was, it was! The Dragon and his children were not wasting time on gloating or threatening. They threw themselves on the food like so many starving creatures, gorging themselves on the meal.

Gorging themselves as well on the drugs within the food. One by one, they staggered from the feast and fell. One by one, Hupasiya bound them with rope. Only Illuyankas did not fall. The Dragon stumbled and staggered toward his lair. But he was too bloated from his meal to slip through the cave's narrow entrance. As the other gods slew the Dragon's brood, the Storm-God fell upon Illuyankas like a thunderbolt, and slew him.

Only Hupasiya did nothing. It was not a warrior's way to slay a bound captive.

I . . . am something other than a warrior . . . am I not? I cannot remember.

"Come," Inaras told him with a purr in her voice. "I have a reward for you, my hero, a fine house here in the mountains, on a cliff overlooking all the world, balanced on the four directions, with windows facing all of the four. You shall live here and want for nothing. And perhaps, perhaps, my hero, I shall visit you. I ask only this one thing of you, a little, little thing. Do not look out of the western window. That is the window of death."

Hupasiya felt nothing. He had done the gods' bidding, he had been rewarded, and yet . . . nothing.

"I will not look out of the western window," he agreed, since that, too, meant nothing.

It was a fine house, indeed, with servants to pamper him and fill his every wish. But he had no wishes. Inaras did visit him when the whim struck her. Each time she would warn him not to gaze out of the western window. But when she left, he once again would feel nothing.

"I will not look out of the western window," Hupasiya murmured.

Why should he not? What else was there for him to do?

He threw aside the curtain covering the western window and looked out and down to the foot of the mountains. A small farm nestled down there among the fuzz of new green growth, and if he stared, he could almost see a woman . . . two children . . .

"Zaliya . . .?"

As he said her name, memory returned with a rush. His wife, his family. "Inaras!" he shouted, brushing aside the servants who tried to silence him. "Inaras!"

She was before him in a rush of air. "My hero, what is wrong?"

"Let me go. I beg you, let me go!"

Inaras straightened, looming over him. "You have disobeyed me."

"Yes, I admit it. I have seen my wife and family—Inaras, Lady, Divine One, I love them! Let me go."

Her hair swirling about her, her eyes blazing with blue-white fire, Inaras shouted, "I treat you as I treat no mortal man! I give you the love of my body. And you—is this treason my repayment?"

"I am mortal, yes. I cannot live as a god. Inaras, please, you do not need me and my family does."

"They shall want for nothing ever again!"

It took him only a moment to realize the possible threat latent in that statement. The dead want for nothing. "No!" And was that why he felt . . . nothing? Was he already dead? "It doesn't matter if I am one among the dead if my family is safe. Take my life if you must—but let them live!"

It took greater courage than ever it had to face down the enemy, but Hupasiya dropped to his knees, head bent, waiting for the blow that was sure to come.

There was utter silence for an agonizingly long time. "You are dead to me," Inaras said at last. "This shall not have happened."

Hupasiya stepped out of his farmhouse, then stopped dead, breathing deeply. He still looked very much like the true Hittite warrior he'd been just a few short years ago: burly and muscular, with a narrow scar like a white blaze of lightning seaming his face, although his hair had turned in one short night from black to white.

"Husband?"

He turned to face Zaliya with a smile. "Smell the air, love. The springtime has come at last."

In the opening volume of S. M. Stirling's Nantucket series, the Information Age found itself confronting—and entirely surrounded by—the Late Bronze Age of the thirteenth-century B.C. *Even as guns, germs, and steel (not to mention three-masted barques, radio, and a money economy) bring about a completely different kind of Iron Age in the course of the novels, no one, not even the Nantucketers, must ever underestimate the timeless power of cunning.*

Blood Wolf

His name was *Kreuha Wolkwos*—Blood Wolf, in the tongue of the Keruthini folk—and he was the greatest of all the warriors of his people, although still unwedded and barely old enough to raise a thick yellow down on his cheeks. Even before that fuzz sprouted he had been called a man in the *korios,* the war-band of the youths who spent the summer living like a wolf pack in the woods off what they could hunt and steal. Now even householders and the clan chiefs called him a man, for six heads of his taking—the oldest weathered down to a skull, the newest still ripe—were spiked to the lintel above his father's house-door. This year he had come to his full height, a finger's-span below six feet, rangy and long-limbed; agile enough to run out on the yoke-pole of a chariot while the team galloped, fast enough on his own feet to chase down deer and cut their throats with his knife. At a full run he could throw his narrow-bladed javelins through a rolling hoop of rawhide half a hundred paces distant, and in a wrestling bout few men could keep their shoulders off the ground once Blood Wolf's hands closed on them. At the Sun Festival he had thrown the sacrificial bull by its horns and then danced the night through by the side of the Spring Queen.

Two horses and eight cattle were his by *soru-rechtos,* booty-right, taken in lawful raids, besides sheep, bronze, cloth, and a girl who would be valuable if she lived to womanhood. Many men hated him for his toploftiness, but none had dared face him for some time. Two of those heads on his father's lintel were fellow-tribesmen, slain within the sacred wands after due challenge. His name was often spoken around the hearthfires, and all knew that—if he lived to be a householder—the ruler of the tribe, the High *Reghix,* would make him successor to the broad lands of his father. Then he would surely become a great chief whose name lived forever.

Right now that pride was lost in a dull misery as he scrambled to the lee side of the boat and puked helplessly, bringing up only a spatter of thin, bitter bile into an ocean that heaved gray and white with foam beneath a cold October sky of racing gray cloud.

His stomach had been empty since the first few minutes of the day-long voyage from the mainland to Alba, the White Isle. One of the boatmen pushed him aside as he adjusted a rope, and he was too weak to return a blow for the insult. Only when the fifty-foot length ceased moving beneath him did he raise his head.

"Get your arse out of our boat, wild-man," the crewman said.

His accent was strange to the young man's ears, and the order and sometimes the endings of the words he used, but comprehensible—many tribes distantly related to the Keruthinii folk had settled across the salt water in Alba, the White Isle. That didn't mean they were his friends; the opposite, if anything.

The seaman also scooped up the horsehide bundle that held Blood Wolf's goods and threw it on the planks of the dock. Two more grabbed the youth by the belt of his wolfskin kilt and half-carried, half-threw him out on worn oak-wood. That done, the crew ignored him as he crawled up the splintery surface toward his goods. Gradually the shaming weakness left him, and he could sit, then stand, spit some of the vile taste out of his mouth, begin to feel like a man once more. He had crossed the Channel to Alba; beyond Alba lay the Summer Isle, and beyond that the River Ocean, and the Island of Wizards, Nantucket.

First he looked to his weapons: round shield, spear, a light bronze-headed axe, and his precious steel knife, bought from Alban traders. Then he swung his pack onto his back and walked landward as he gazed around, trying hard not to gape at the magical city of Southaven. The shore tended north and south here, but little of it could be seen; great piers of timber framework filled with rock stretched out into the water. Beside them lay ships, more than he could count on fingers and toes both, many times more, their bowsprits looming over the broad cobbled harborside street thronged with folk and beasts and wagons. There were more folk here than in his whole tribe—six or seven tens of hundreds.

The ships' masts were taller than trees, their rigging and yards a spiky leafless forest, but that was nothing beside the ones out on the water with chimneys of *iron* sticking up from their middles and belching black smoke, and great wheels on either side churning up foam.

"True wizardry," he murmured to himself, grinning.

And in the tales, didn't the great warrior always come off well from his meeting with wizards? Either gaining their friendship and battle-luck, or overcoming and plundering them. He snuffed deeply—silt, fish, salt water, horse-manure, odd sulfur-tinged smoke, but less sweat and ordure stink than you'd expect—and looked along the street. At the thronging folk dressed more richly than great chiefs or tribal kings and more strangely than his eyes could take in; everything from home-like kilts and shifts to shameless string skirts on bare-breasted cloaked women, long embroidered robes, with the odd-looking trousers and jackets and boots that the majority favored, making a dun-colored mass. And at the nets of cargo swinging ashore, laden with sacks and bales and kegs of the Gods alone knew what unguessable wealth; at buildings of baked brick, some five times a man's height, with great clear windows of glass—and remembered the price the Keruthinii chieftains paid for a single tumbler or goblet of it . . .

His belly rumbled. It had been more than a day since he'd eaten, and that had gone to the Channel fish. It was a cool brisk day with a strong wind under scudding cloud, enough to awaken any man's appetite.

"*Stop, thief! Stop him!*"

Kreuha's head whipped around. The cry had been in En-gil-its, the tongue of wizards and wizard traders; he'd learned a little of it. And the call was repeated in half a dozen other languages, two of them close to his own:

"*Kreuk! Kreuk!*" That was the ancient call to raise the hue-and-cry after one who stole by stealth.

A man came pushing through the crowd, vaulted a pile of barrels, leapt and scrambled over a four-wheeled wagon piled with bales of some dirty-white fibre; that gave him space to pick up speed, heading for the frayed edge of town south of the small-boat docks. He was holding a sword in his hand; Kreuha's eyes narrowed at the sight. The blade was like none he'd seen, slightly curved and as long as a man's leg, with a round gold-chased guard and a hilt made for two hands. Sunlight glittered on the bright metal, picking out a waving line in the steel a little back from the cutting edge.

Kreuha laid his pack and spears down and ran three bouncing strides to put himself in the man's way. The thief stopped, sweating and snarling; he was a few years older than the newcomer, shorter but broader, with a shock of dark-brown hair and beard. The arms below his sleeveless singlet were thick with muscle and lavishly tattooed. But there was something about the way he stood, the sweat and desperation that made him blink—

"Give me the sword," Kreuha said, crouching slightly and spreading his hands so the man couldn't dodge past him. "And I will return it to the owner."

And be richly rewarded, he thought. He'd heard of such weapons. The lords among the wizard-folk wore them. *This one is no warrior, only a thief.*

"If you try to strike me, I will kill you and take it," the Keruthinii tribesman continued calmly.

The man hesitated for an instant and then cut desperately, a sweeping two-handed roundhouse blow at waist level. It was clumsy, and Kreuha could see the prelude coming a full three heartbeats before the steel began to move, but it was hard enough to slice him to the spine if it landed—the more so as the blade looked knife-sharp. Kreuha leapt straight up as the sword moved, and it hissed like a serpent as it passed beneath the calloused soles of his feet. One long leg smashed out, and his heel slammed into the thief's breastbone with a sound like a maul hitting a baulk of seasoned oak and a crackling noise beneath that. The man was shocked to a halt, staggered backward with his face turning dark purple, coughed out a spray of bright arterial blood, and fell bonelessly limp.

Kreuha landed on his feet and one hand, then bounced erect. The sword spun away, landing on the cobbles and sparking as steel struck flint-rich stone. The tribesman winced at the slight to a fine weapon and bent to retrieve it, marveling at the living feel it had in his hands. He was considering whether he could take the head when a party of strangers came up, breathing hard from their run.

"Oh, hell," Lucy Alston-Kurlelo said, looking down at the body of the dead thief. He was extremely dead, and stank. "I *knew* I shouldn't have hired him."

She turned to glare at the Southaven policeman. He spread his hands, including the one holding a revolver: "I offered you hands from the lockup willing to sign up rather than work off their sentences here. Ardaursson was a brawler and a drunk and a thief, and this looks like a clear case of self-defense. I didn't say anyone you bought out of lockup would be any good."

Lucy shrugged. That was true enough; there simply weren't enough deckhands to go around, with demand so high; more so as the *Pride* was going far foreign, a long high-risk voyage, not schlepping back and forth across the Pond between Alba and Nantucket. The thief had been a fisherman by trade, worth any dozen farmers or dockside sweepings . . . if he'd been honest.

"No charges?" she said.

"No charges. Plain enough case of taken-in-the-act; I'll file the report."

And you did *supply this piece of garbage yourself,* she thought to herself. Instead of arguing with the peace officer—officials in Southaven had gotten very assertive since the local Town Meeting was admitted to the Republic two years ago, and though young, the policeman came of a prominent local family—she looked at the kilted youngster who'd kicked in the luckless thief's chest.

Pretty, she thought. In a chisel-faced blond athletic way. And he was obviously fresh off the boat from the European mainland. No east-Alban tribesman would still be carrying bronze-headed spears, even in the backwoods of the north; hell, most of them were in trousers these days, some building themselves brick houses and sending their children to missionary schools.

Not from anywhere near the trade-outposts at the mouth of the Loire and Seine and Rhine, either, she thought.

At a guess—

"*Khwid teuatha tuh'on?*" she said: What tribe is yours? Of what people do you come? "*Bawatavii?*" she went on: "*Jowatani?*"

Those were the nearest coastal groups over the water, but he looked a little too raw for that. He'd been staring at her in wonder from the moment she showed up. Lucy was used to that; black people weren't common in Nantucket and extremely rare elsewhere. Her own birth-mother had been Alban, her father an American—a Coast Guardsman who later turned renegade and eventually ended up as a king on the upper Nile. One of her two adoptive mothers had been true coal-black, as opposed to Lucy's own light milk-chocolate, and there were still people in Alba who thought Marian Alston was some sort of spirit or demigoddess . . . though her deeds had more to do with that than her appearance.

"*Keruthinii teuatha eghom h'esmi,*" he said, shaking his head and visibly gathering himself. "I am of the Keruthini folk." He drew himself up proudly: "Those who drove the Iraiina to Alba in my grandfather's time."

She grinned; that had happened just before the Event landed the late-twentieth-century island of Nantucket in 1250 B.C.E. It'd been a typical tribal scuffle between two small bands of scruffy bandits.

Evidently it was a legendary battle-of-the-heroes thing with this boy's people, now that the tribal bards had had a generation to work it over.

Then his jaw dropped a trifle more as he noticed she was a woman; he might not have at all, save that her jacket was open on a well-filled sweater.

Still, he recovered fairly well. "This is yours?" he said, turning the *katana* and offering it hilt-first—and surprised her by saying it in gutturally accented but fairly good English. "You are from the Island of Wizards?"

Well, not just pretty, but fairly smart, she decided, carefully examining the edge—this was a pre-Event heirloom, carried back in time with the island of Nantucket to the Late Bronze Age—and then wiping it clean with a cloth before slipping it into the sheath whose lip rode over her left shoulder.

Not *just* an heirloom, though. The layer-forged metal had minute etchings along three-quarters of its length, where the salt and acids of blood had cut into the softer layers between the glass-hard edge steel. Only some of them were from her mother's time.

"It is and I am," she said. "Lucy Alston-Kurlelo, captain of the merchantman *Grey Lady's Pride* . . ." She saw his eyes open slightly at the family name; curse of having two famous mothers. "And I'm shipping out soon. Interested in a berth?"

For a moment the man's face—he looked to be in his late teens, considerably younger than she—grew keen. Then he looked wary.

"On . . . ship? Ocean?" He pointed out toward the salt water. At her nod he raised his hands in a warding gesture and swallowed.

Lucy laughed and flipped him a gold ten-dollar piece. He caught the small bright coin and nodded with regal politeness. She sighed as she turned and led her people back toward the ship.

"Well, let's go see what other gutter-scrapings, shepherdesses, and plowboys we can rustle up," she said to her companions—first mate and bosun and two senior deckhands; her younger brother Tim was supercargo and in charge back at the dock.

They nodded in unison. The Coast Guard kept the North Atlantic fairly free of pirates, and Tartessos did the same for the waters south of Capricorn and the western Mediterranean. You could take a chance and sail shorthanded on the crowded runs between here and home, and you needed to squeeze every cent until it shrieked to meet your costs even so.

Where the *Pride* was going, Islander craft were all too likely to meet locals who'd acquired steel and even gunpowder without developing any particular constraints on taking whatever they wanted whenever they could. You needed a crew big enough to work the guns and repel boarders; the extra risk and expense was what kept competition down and profits high on the Sumatra run and points east. It was also one reason she and her sister-cum-business-partner Heather never shipped together on these long voyages.

No sense in making *two* sets of children orphans with the same shower of poisoned blowgun darts.

The strangers departed while Kreuha was marveling over the gold-piece; he had seen copper and silver coins from Alba and the Isle of Wizards, Nantucket, but this was the first one of gold he'd ever held. He held it up to the fading light of afternoon; there was an eagle clutching a bundle of arrows and a peace-wreath on one side, and strange letters and numbers on the other.

One of the strangers had remained, a young brown-haired man in blue tunic and trousers, with a wooden club and one of the fearsome-wonderful fire-weapons at his belt—the awesome type called *revolver,* which let the bearer hold the deaths of six men in his hand. He pulled a metal whistle free and blew three sharp blasts on it.

"*Ual kelb soma krweps,*" he said, to Kreuha in something close to the warrior's own language: "To summon help with the body."

Blood Wolf nodded, although he didn't offer to help himself—dead bodies were unclean, and he didn't know how he'd get a purification ceremony done so far from home. The man went on:

"I am . . . you would say, a retainer of my chief. A warrior charged with keeping order and guarding against ill-doers among the people. In English, a *policeman.*"

Kreuha's brows rose. *That* was a duty he didn't envy; you'd be the target of endless ill-will if you had to offend people as part of your duty. He'd never walked away from a fight, but now that he'd come to man's estate he didn't go looking for them, not *all* the time. His lips moved, as he repeated the word softly several times, to add to his store of En-gil-its terms.

"It's also my duty to advise strangers," the armsman went on. "No slight to your honor, stranger, but it's forbidden here to fight unless you are attacked." He looked at Kreuha's spears. "How were you planning on finding your bread in this land?"

Kreuha drew himself up. "I am Kreuha Wolkwos, the Blood Wolf," he said. "Son of Echwo-Pothis, Horse Master; son of a chief who was son of a chief, and I am foremost among the men of war of my people.

I come to find some great lord of the wizard-folk who needs my arm and faith, so that I may win fortune and everlasting fame."

The armsman—*policeman*—made a wordless sound and covered his brow and eyes with a hand for a moment. Then he sighed. "You think that, do you?"

"How not?" Kreuha said, puzzled. "Already a lord . . . well, lady, mistress . . . from Nantucket itself wished me to follow in their fighting-tail. Surely I would quickly rise in any such band."

"Oh, Captain Lucy," the policeman said, nodding. "Well, you *were* lucky to get that offer, and you'd probably see some fighting on the *Pride*. Hard work too, but she's run on shares." At Kreuha's look, he went on: "You get a share of the gain at the end of the voyage."

Kreuha nodded—a lord always shared booty with his sworn men. But then he remembered the *voyage* here to Alba, and gulped again. "I cannot . . . not on the sea. A lord by land, yes."

It was more than the memory of his misery; it was the *helplessness*. How could the Blood Wolf be mighty if his belly made him weaker than a girl?

The policeman grinned, the more so at Kreuha's black look. "Nobody ever dies of seasickness," he said. "They just wish they would—until it passes, which may take a day or two."

He pointed out a building with a tall tower attached to it, a street or two back from the dockside. "That's the Town Meetinghouse. It's a hiring hall, too. If you can't find work, go there and mention my name: I'm Eric Iraiinisson. They can always find something for a strong back, enough for stew and a doss, at least." Sternly: "Remember also that here robbers are flogged and sent to the mines for many years, and robbers who slay or wound are hung up and their bodies left for the crows."

Kreuha nodded with stiff dignity; just then two more men and a woman dressed alike in the blue clothes came up. They had a horse with them, and tossed the corpse onto its back with brisk efficiency.

"I have gold," he pointed out. "Cannot gold be bartered here?"

Eric Iraiinisson nodded. "While it lasts," he said.

Kreuha saw eyes upon him. This *tavern* was full of men who looked a little less alien than the smooth folk of the upper town; there he'd noticed stares and smiles at his dress and manner. Here there was a dense fug of sweat and woodsmoke from the hearth, and plain rushes on packed dirt below, and plain stools and benches. He had feasted well on beef roasted with some spice that bit the tongue, and beer that was good though strange. Now a man had offered to pay for his drink; he knew of coined money, but such was rare and precious in his tribe still, not something to be casually thrown about on an evening's bowsing. Still, the amber drink was *whiskey,* something that only the High Reghix had tasted at home . . .

"I will drink, if you will drink with me again afterward," he said. "Drink from my bounty. I have gold!"

Remember that whiskey *is more potent than beer,* he reminded himself. Still, it couldn't be *much* stronger than ice-mead, and his belly was full of bread and meat to sop it up.

"Arktorax thanks you," the man said, then grinned at him and tossed off the small shot-glass, breathed out satisfaction, then followed it with a long swallow of beer. Kreuha imitated the stylish snap of the wrist, throwing the amber liquid at the back of his throat.

"*Ai!*" he wheezed a moment later, when he'd stopped coughing. "What do you make this out of, dragon's blood?"

"Barley," Arktorax laughed; he fit his name of Lord Bear, being bear-tall and thick. "It's made from barley. But if it's too strong for you—"

Kreuha's fist thumped the table. "By He of the Long Spear, nothing's too strong for a Keruthinii of the Wolf clan! I've drunk the vats dry and danced all night, at our festivals."

He soothed his throat with a long draught of the beer. It made a pleasant coolness after the fire of the whiskey, but the flame had turned to a comfortable warmth by now.

"That's the problem with being a Keruthinii," he went on, signaling to the wench who served the tables. "You're so tough and hardy you can't get drunk."

His new friend laughed long and loud. "Are you boasting, or complaining?" he said, and tossed off his glass in turn.

Kreuha missed the considering look in his eye, and the glance he exchanged with the impassive figure behind the plank bar. Instead he laughed himself, until the tears ran from his eyes. The next whiskey went down far more smoothly than the first, and tasted good: there was a peaty, sweetish flavor to it he hadn't noticed the first time. That called for another beer, and when it came he stood, swaying a little.

"Drinks for all!" he said. A roar of approval went up, bringing a flush of happiness to his cheeks. Everlasting fame was the warrior's reward. "Let no man say Blood Wolf son of Horse Master son of Stone Fist is a niggard with sword-won gold!"

"Sword-won?" Arktorax said.

"Aye!" Kreuha shouted. "Gold won by winning a sword!" He was also accounted something of a poet, at home. "Listen and I will tell you of how I won it, bare-handed against a wizard blade—"

He was half-chanting it by the time he was finished, and men crowded around to slap him on the back and shout their admiration. *A fine lot, a fine lot,* he thought a trifle blurrily. His boon companion looked a little wary when he mentioned the black warrior-woman, but not everyone could be as stout in the face of the unknown as Blood Wolf. "—and so I came here, that men might know of my deeds," he said.

"So you're the one who killed Frank Athadaursson with one blow of his foot!" a woman said admiringly. "You must be a *real* man, beard or no . . ."

Hours later he lay with his head on his hands in the quiet of the near-deserted tavern, giggling occasionally. His stomach threatened to rebel, but even that thought was funny. . . . His eyes crossed as he watched his own reflection in the glass before him. It was that that saved him, an image of an arm raised behind him.

Reflex pushed him to one side, falling to the rushes of the floor as the small leather sack of lead shot cracked down on the beer-stained wood of the table rather than the back of his head. He lay gaping as the barkeeper turned and raised the cosh again, then lashed out with one foot. By purest luck that plowed into the fat man's groin, and he doubled over in uncontrollable response. Kreuha scrabbled away on his backside, as the woman and his friend Arktorax—the man he'd thought was his friend—came at him with ropes and a canvas hood.

His back hit the rough brickwork of the wall, and he scrabbled upright, lashing out left and right with his fists. Another man's fist thudded into the tough muscle of his belly, and he felt the night's drinking and the long-ago meal leave in a rush of sour bile. That saved him; Arktorax stepped back with an exclamation of disgust, and Kreuha turned and turned again along the wall, as if he were rolling down a slope. His hand found the latch and he fell forward with a splash into a muddy street under a thin cold rain that shook him back to the edge of consciousness. He rose, plastered with a thin layer of earth and horsedung churned to gray slime, and turned to meet the rush from the tavern, trying to scream out the war-howl of his clan.

Where is my axe? he thought. *Where—*

Shadowy figures rushed at him. He lashed out with a fist, head-butted an opponent who tried to grapple with him, then screamed with shocked pain at what that did to his drink-fuddled head. Blows landed on him in turn, many, more than he could begin to count and from all directions. He went down again, and feet slammed into body and head—feet encased in hard leather boots. Instinctively he curled himself into a ball and covered his head with his arms.

Blackness, shot through with the sound of a whistle.

Kreutha came back to consciousness slowly. He recognized the symptoms—splitting headache, nausea, blurred vision—of a bad hangover combined with being thumped on the head. The place where he woke was utterly unfamiliar; there were strange shouts, metallic clangs, stenches. And bright light, light that hurt like spears in his eyes. Despite that he opened them—and saw a cage of iron bars not far away, with men inside gripping the metal with their hands. He bolted straight upright, letting the blanket fall away—

"Easy friend, easy!" said a voice in his own language.

Blood Wolf looked around, blinking and squinting and holding up a hand against the light of the bright mirror-backed coal-oil lamps. The voice came from Eric Iraiinisson, still dressed all in blue, jacket and trousers. A hand rested on his revolver, and Kreutha forced himself to wariness. Then he noticed that he was *outside* the cage, unbound, and that a corridor led to a door that swung open and closed as folk passed by. A woman dressed in blue like the man sat behind a table, writing on many papers before her; even then Kreutha shuddered a little at the casual display of magic. The Alban traders he'd met had carried revolvers, some of them . . . but the knowledge of writing on paper had proved to be a weapon nearly as strong and far harder to understand. He'd heard that the priests of the wizard-folk would teach it to those who took the water-oath to their God. It might almost be worth it.

"You're safe here," the man in blue said. In English, he continued: "I'm chief policeman of the dockside station . . . in your language . . . hard to say. I guard the peace in this area. I found you in the street."

I am *safe,* Blood Wolf thought; and with that the nausea came back, redoubled. It showed on his face.

"The bucket, use the bucket!"

It was a big wooden one, but already half full; he knelt in misery and then staggered erect when the last cupful of sour stomach-acid had come up; he was spending far too much time these days puking. That thought made him smile a little, a very little, as the policeman guided him back to the bench and handed him a blanket; Kreuha clutched it around his shoulders, and took the cup of hot steaming . . . something-or-other that he was handed. Sipping cautiously, he found it unlike any of the herbal teas wisewomen had given him for childhood complaints.

It had cream in it, and a delicious sweetness without the musky flavor of honey, and under that a bitterness. Still, it warmed him and diminished the pain in his head and brought something like real wakefulness. The two tablets he swallowed with it seemed to help as well, for all that they were tiny, white, and tasteless; the effect was like willowbark tea, but stronger and quicker.

When he had climbed far enough out of wretchedness to talk, he looked up to find the man-at-arms also dealing with papers. Occasionally other armed men—and a few armed women—would come in, sometimes leading prisoners in the manacles known as *handcuffs;* many of the captives were drunk as well.

"Is it the custom here to make men drink and then fall upon them?" he asked the . . . *policeman, that is the word.*

Eric Iraiinison laughed. "No, it's the custom to arrest men who break the town's peace," he said. "This is a seaport, and a fast-growing one, with many folk who are strangers to each other and many rootless young men. When ships come in and crews are paid off, we get a lot of traffic here."

"I broke no peace!" Kreuha snapped. "I was set upon dishonorably, by stealth!"

Eric nodded. "And so you're not under arrest. The three assaulting you would be, if I could find them—and evidence against them."

"Ai!" Kreuha's head came up; he was owed vengeance for this indignity. "I can give you faces, and names. Arktorax son of—"

He told all he knew, then scowled as Eric shook his head.

"I know those three," the policeman said. "They're *criminals—*" he dropped the English word into the conversation, then paused to search for an equivalent "—evil-doers, breakers of taboo and custom. If you were to take them to court, they'd lie truth out of Creation. They're crimps, among other things. If you'd fallen asleep, you'd have woken up in the foc'sle of a sealer or a guano-boat, with a thumbprint on a contract and no way back until you'd worked a year for a pittance and daily swill."

Fury flushed more of the pain out of Kreuha's system. "They sought to make a slave of me?" he cried, springing erect, his hand reaching for a missing axe. "I will take their heads! I will feed their living hearts to the Crow Goddess! I will kill, kill—"

Eric's hand went to his revolver; Kreuha considered that, and the blood-debt he owed the man, and sank back.

"Not quite a slave," the policeman said. "If I could get them on *that,* I'd be a happy man; the penalty's death. Or if I could prove crimping charges, that would be nearly as good—ten years' hard labor. But they're careful, the swine; they never pick on citizens and never do anything before witnesses. We don't keep track of every stranger who wanders in here—we can't."

"Is no man here *man* enough to take vengeance on them?" Kreuha said indignantly. "Or to call them doers-of-naught before the folk? I will challenge them to fight me between the wands—the men, of course, not the woman."

The policeman chuckled. "You remind me of my grandfather," he said. "Or me as I might have been, if Nantucket hadn't come out of time. . . . Fighting to the death is against our law here. It's treated like murder, killing-by-stealth. You could invite them to meet you outside our Township boundary." He pointed northward. "The Zarthani still allow death-duels. Arktorax and his friends won't do it, of course. They'll laugh at you, no more, and so would most other people."

Kreuha stared in horror. "Did the wizard-folk take all honor from you Iraiina when they overcame you and ground you beneath their heel, then? You were warriors in our grandsires' time, even if we prevailed in the end."

To his surprise, the policeman's chuckle turned into a full-throated laugh. "You *do* remind me of my grandfather's grumbles," he said, then held up a hand. "No offense. No, we fled here after you put defeat upon us, took in the Nantucketer renegade Walker, and he led us to war and yet more defeat, and then the Nantucketers did something far more . . . *drastic*"—that was in English—"more *powerful*, you might say, than grinding us down."

Kreuha shivered, imagining the vengeance of wizards. "What?"

"They lifted us up again, helped, taught us their faith and all their secret arts." He pulled a silver chain around his neck, showing a crucifix. "My father they took to Nantucket—he was young, our chief's nephew and heir—and the sons and daughters of many powerful men—and sent them to their . . . *schools*, places of learning. My father lived for years in the house of the Republic's chief like one of his own sons. When he saw all that they had, how could he be content to sit in a mud-floored barn and think himself grand because it was the biggest barn? And so he sent for teachers and missionaries, and . . . well. *My* sons could be Chief Executive Officers of the Republic, if they desire to go into politics."

The conversation had mostly been in something close to Kreuha's tongue, which Eric spoke easily enough. The young warrior noted that when the policeman spoke to his own subordinates—who must be his own tribesfolk, or mostly—he used English.

He shivered slightly, he who had never known fear before a mortal foe. *Mighty wizardy indeed, to make a whole tribe vanish as if it had never been*. Then he shook his head. That was an Iraiina problem, not his. Or perhaps not a problem for them either.

"I thank you for your courtesy to a stranger," he said formally and began to rise.

Eric reached over and pushed him firmly down again with a hand on one blanketed shoulder. "It's a cold wet night to go out with nothing but a kilt—and if you are truly grateful, you could help me deal with that God-damned crimp and his gang."

Kreuha's eyes went wide. "I thought you said—"

"I said you couldn't chop them up with a war-axe in fair fight," the other man replied. "But we in the Republic have a saying that there is more than one way to skin a cat."

Slowly, as Eric outlined his idea, Kreuha's smile matched that of the man across from him. If the wizards of Nantucket had taught the Iraiina all their arts, then they must be a crafty, cunning, forethoughtful crew.

I like it, he thought. Aloud: "Tell me more."

"Arktorax!" Kreuha called jovially.

The little tavern was half empty on this afternoon; with the tide beginning to make in a few hours, crews would be back on their ships and fishing boats, and most ashore were at work. The big hearth on the inner wall had a low coal fire burning, and two big pots of stew simmering on iron hooks that swung out from the chimney wall. The tables were littered but mostly vacant, their few occupants looking to be oldsters or idlers, and a harlot or two.

Arktorax was sitting with a cluster about him, throwing dice from a leather cup; he rose, his expression a little wary, one eye puffed up and discolored. Long greasy blond hair swirled about his face as he turned to face Kreuha, carefully putting his back to the wall without seeming to hurry about it.

"Ah, I see you took some blows also," Kreuha said. "Shame and eternal shame to me that I was too drunk to ward you—or myself. Between the whiskey and the crack on my head, I don't even know how badly I did! But I did remember I left my gear with your friends here."

He seated himself, and Arktorax took the bench across the table, waving a hand. A wench—it was probably the same one who'd helped to befool him last night—brought a plate with a loaf of bread and lump of cheese, and two thick glass steins of foaming beer. The barkeeper called her over, and after a moment she returned with his spear, axe, dagger and bundle of goods. They might be wealth in the Keruthinii lands, but here they were only a pittance of scrap metal.

Kreuha made himself smile as he lifted the stein. In daylight, he could see what a shabby den this was—his mother would never have allowed rushes this fusty or garbage-strewn—but the crofters and gangrels here drank from glass mugs! And the beer was better than any his father brewed, as well. For a moment he saw himself as this Arktorax did, as a woods-running savage to be plucked and sold.

No, he thought. *Lord Bear here thinks he has fallen on a sheep in a pen. He will find it's a wolf—a Blood Wolf.*

"The police took you off," Arktorax said, relaxing a little and cutting a slab of the bread and cheese. "Officer Iraiinisson, that would be."

"Yes," Kreuha said, and scowled with rage. It was a genuine enough expression; the other man didn't need to know it was directed at *him*. He went on, his voice rough:

"And threw me in a cage full of vermin, and barked questions at me as if I were some thrall to be thrashed for not shoveling out the byre! By He of the Long Spear, by the Crow Goddess, I swear I will have my vengeance for last night's work!"

Arktorax nodded. "He's given to questions, is our officer Iraiinisson, and no mistake," he said genially. "You told him all, I suppose."

Kreuha grimaced. "I did not, not even what little I knew. I am not a spear-captive, to be kicked and cuffed. And he said he would not let me leave this place, so long as I did not tell him what he would know!"

"There've been complaints about him in the Town Meeting more than once. I complained, the last time he ran me in on suspicion—and had to let me go," Arktorax said. "He's had a feud with me for years, the son of a pig, but he and his kin have too many votes behind them."

"Why don't you kill him, if he's defamed your honor before the folkmoot?" Kreuha said. "I would give much to see his blood."

The big burly man looked at him blankly for a moment; they were speaking the same language, more or less, but it was as if Arktorax had just heard words without meaning to him. He smiled, shrugged, and switched to English:

"Was your mother a whore by choice, or did her father sell her?"

"I'm sorry," Kreuha said, with an effort at self-control greater than he'd needed to remain motionless on night ambushes. Eric had warned him they'd probably test him so. "I speak none of the wizard tongue."

Arktorax chuckled. "I asked if you would like me to assist in your vengeance," he said smoothly, with a genial grin.

"I would like that very much," Kreuha said. "Very much indeed."

The planning went swiftly. This time Kreuha turned down whiskey;

that would not arouse suspicion, not after last night. He did grumble a little, as the urchin Arktorax hired sped off toward the police station and they left the tavern, the barkeeper and the woman in tow.

"Can you shield me from the blades of his kin?" he asked. It wasn't a question he would have made, or at least put that way, on his own.

"Just this way—" Arktorax said.

The building they entered was large and dim; empty as well, up to the high beams that held the ceiling. Mysterious piles of boxes and barrels hid much of the floor, stretching off into dimness.

"Yes, of course, my friend," he went on, clapping Kreuha on the shoulder. "You will vanish from this place as if you had never been."

The fat man chuckled, and spoke in English: "Just as we planned; Captain Tarketerol will be most grateful."

Kreuha smiled and nodded, the skin crawling between his shoulders. That was a Tartessian name; the wizard-folk of Nantucket kept no thralls, but the men of the far southern kingdom most assuredly *did*. Perhaps the villainy of these three was worse than Eric had thought . . . which was very good.

"And Officer Iraiinisson will be dead," Arktorax said. "We three can swear you were with us—and that's the truth, isn't it?"

He laughed, and then there was a long while of tense waiting, until a knock came at the door. The woman swarmed up a ladder to peer down at the doorway, and then turned to give a signal: the policeman was alone. That had been likely anyway, since there were only a score of the blue-clad armsmen in Southaven.

"Kreuha Wolkwos?" Eric Iraiinisson's sharp voice came through the boards.

"I am here," Kreuha said, taking stance in an open space not far from the portal.

The light was dim and gray, through small windows high up around the roof, but there was enough for someone who'd hunted deer and men by moonlight.

"And the Blood Wolf is ready to speak as you wished," Kreuha went on.

The door opened, letting in a spray of light along with a mist of fine rain. Kreuha poised with his spear, and the policeman staggered back—

"Kill!" Arktorax shouted, pushing him with a heavy hand between the shoulders. "What are you waiting for?"

Kreuha dove forward, rolling around the spearshaft and flicking himself back erect, facing the man who'd pretended friendship. The

Keruthinii grinned like his name-beast and bayed laughter that might have come from his clan totem indeed.

"I am waiting for you to put your head in the rope," he said—in English, thickly accented but fluent enough. "Arktomertos," he added, in a savage play on the man's name: *Dead* Bear.

The crimp roared anger, turned, snatched up a barrel and threw it. That took strength; it was heavy, and the policeman dodged, falling backward into the street. When the wood staves struck the thick timber uprights of the door they cracked open, and fine-ground flour exploded in all directions. The fat man who'd been Arktorax's henchman turned to flee; Kreuha's arm cocked back as he squinted through the dust, then punched forward with smooth, swift grace. The flame-shaped bronze head took the barkeeper between the shoulders and he fell forward with the spearshaft standing up like the mast of a ship sailing to the ice-realms where the spirits of oathbreakers dwelt.

That left Arktorax. The big man drew a broad-bladed steel knife from beneath the tail of his coat and lunged, holding it underarm and stabbing upward in a stroke that would have opened the younger man like a fish filleted for the grill. Kreuha bounded back with panther ease beyond the reach of the blow, his hand unslinging the bronze-headed axe slung over his back as, for the first time since he'd set foot on the boat that brought him to Alba, he felt at ease: here was something he understood.

Arktorax wailed as he stumbled forward, drawn by the impetus of the failed stroke. The keen edge of the bronze skittered off his knife and gashed his forearm. He dropped the knife and tried to catch it with his left hand; Kreuha struck backhanded, then again, and again, smiling.

He was holding up the head when Eric Iraiinisson came through the door—this time with his revolver drawn. He swore in English, then by the hooves of the Horse Goddess.

"I didn't mean you to kill them!" he said at last. "We were to capture them for trial—"

"You didn't mean to kill them," Kreuha grinned. "I did, Eric son of the Iraiina—and ask your grandfather why, some day."

The policeman shook his head. "This means trouble."

"Didn't you say your law allowed a man to fight in self-defense?" Kreuha said. *No. I can't keep the head,* he decided regretfully; he did spit in the staring eyes before tossing it aside, and appropriating the dead man's knife and the contents of his pockets.

"Yes . . . but there's only one witness, and I'm known to have accused him before," Eric said. "It could be trouble for me as well as you—he does have kin, and friends of a sort here."

Kreuha grinned. "Then let me not be here," he said. "I've been thinking of what you said earlier."

Eric looked at him, brows raising. "Now that's forethoughtful," he said. "Maybe you'll go far, young warrior. If you live."

"All *right,*" Timothy Alston-Kurlelo said.

Lucy and her younger brother both stood in the forward hold, watching a cargo-net sway down. It dangled from a dockside crane, which made the rate of descent something she needed to keep an eye on—if they'd been using one of the *Pride*'s spars as a derrick, she'd have trusted her deck-crew.

Two sailors had ropes on the net and were guiding it to the clear space at her feet; orderly stacks of other goods rose fore and aft, covered in tarpaulins and tightly lashed down. The early morning air was cold; the first week in November was usually chilly and raw here in southern Alba, and she could scent the faint mealy smell of snow.

"I'll be glad to get out of the harbor," she said, mentally running over the list herself.

Simple goods for the raw-native trade: spearheads and axe-blades, saws and hammers, kegs of nails, chisels, drills, printed cotton cloth, glassware and ornaments, cheap potato vodka. Wind-pumps and ore-breakers and stationary steam engines for the mining dredges Ellis & Stover had set up out east these last five years; treadle sewing machines and corn-shellers and cotton-gins, threshing engines and sugarcane crushers for the Islander settlements in the Indian Ocean. . . . She took a deep satisfied sniff of the smells, metal and oil and the pinewood of boxes and barrels. Even the bilges were not too bad; the *Pride* had been hauled out for complete refitting in the Fogarty's Cove shipyards on Long Island not four months ago.

"Won't we all," her brother said; he was a slim dark young man in his teens, chin blue-black with stubble despite his youth, holding his clipboard with a seriousness that made her smile.

"This is the last of the chocolate," Tim said as the net creaked to the decking.

Longshoremen sprang to unhitch it and begin stacking the cargo under the direction of the bosun and his mates; they knew the captain's fanatical insistence on neatness and having everything precisely in place. She grinned inwardly; that was another reason she and Heather didn't ship together if they could avoid it. She drove Heather crazy by being finicky, and Heather's blithe confidence that everything would come right in the end with a lick and a promise infuriated *her,* the more so since it seemed to work about as well as her methods instead of resulting in the immediate ruin it should. They'd been raised like twins—they were the same age almost to the day, as close as they could figure it—and loved each other dearly, as long as they didn't have to watch each other work too closely.

It's a very good thing Alston-Kurlelo Shipping and Trading has three merchantmen and a headquarters to run, now, she thought.

Lucy nodded to Tim, then sprang and planted a foot on the hook of the line that had held the cargo net and a hand on the cable. A man on deck whistled and waved, and the line jerked upward. She judged her distance easily as her head came above the hatch coaming, then jumped down to the deck, her mind on her return cargo. Tin, of course—alluvial tin washed from the streams was cheap enough to compete with the hard-rock mines here in Alba, with their high fixed costs. The West Alba Mining and Smelting Corporation had annoyed everyone during the long years it had a virtual monopoly.

Hmm. Can't expect more than a few hundred tons ready for loading. What else? There was always market for teak, but it was bulky in relation to its value. Would it be worth another thousand miles of easting to top up with cinnamon and cloves in the Celebes, then return via the Horn? If she did that, she could make a brief stopover on the coast of Peru; the locals there had silver in the ingot, and cocoa, and some excellent handicrafts. . . . *Best keep a careful eye on prices via radio.* That helped only so much, though. You still had to take months covering distance.

The deck was busy too, with sailors making all secure for their departure on the evening tide. The mates and the senior hands were busy as well, showing newcomers how to coil a line, or shoving them into position to clap onto a rope and haul. There was an occasional foot to a backside as well; she frowned, but there wasn't much alternative until the raw hands learned enough to be useful. Until then everyone was doing their own work and half the trainees' as well, and there weren't as many even for simple pull-on-this as she'd have liked. Another group were being shown down the line of guns bowsed up against the bulwarks, sleek blue-black soda-bottle shapes, thirty-two-pounders bought surplus from the Coast Guard a year ago. She suppressed a wish for a Gatling; that would eat half the voyage's profits, and she had over a hundred employees, two children, and four nieces and nephews to support.

"All's well, Mr. Hands?" she called to the master-gunner.

He turned and touched a knuckle to his forehead. "As well as can be expected, ma'am. Arms drill as soon as we make open water? These handless cows—"

"A week or two after," she replied. "When they can be trusted to go aloft and reef."

She was *very* unlikely to meet a pirate before then, but sailing into a bad blow was entirely possible. And when she'd reached the Roaring Forties and started to run her easting down before the endless storms . . . then she wanted every jack and jill able to hand, reef, and steer.

"In the meantime, signal the tug we're ready," she said, as the crew began to batten down the hatchway. "Prepare to cast off!"

A noise on the docks drew her head up. A man was running down the quay, dodging carts and goods and passersby; a young man, with long fair hair and a mainlander's leather kilt. Her eyes widened slightly. *That's the woodsrunner, the Keruthinii,* she thought. And despite the recent rain, looking rather ghastly with flour-paste; doubtless there was a story behind that. He dashed for the gangway where crewmen were unfastening the lashings.

"Belay that!" she called, as they snatched up cargo-hooks or put their hands on their belt-knives. "Let him on board!"

She went over to meet him; her first mate fell in behind her, and a pair of the older hands with belaying pins from the rack around the mainmast, held casually but ready. He bounded up the plank with a stride that made him look as if his legs were rubber springs, then halted and cried her hail.

"What are you doing on my ship?" she asked quietly.

The young man—*Blood Wolf,* she dredged out of her mind; typical melodramatic charioteer-tribe name—was breathing deeply but easily, and he grinned with a cocky self-confidence.

"I came to see if you still wish my allegiance, chieftainness," he said. "For I wish to leave this *dunthaurikaz,* and see far lands."

Lucy snorted, hooking her hands in the brass-studded belt she wore over her long sea-sweater. "I'm not taking you on board if you've broken Southaven law," she said.

He offered her a piece of paper. She snorted again; it had the municipal stamp, and the Republic's eagle; she recognized Eric Iraiinisson's handwriting and signature, as well. Apparently the youngster wasn't wanted . . . exactly.

And I could *use another hand. This one looks to be quick-thinking as well as strong.*

"It's fifty cents a day and your keep," she said, and looked him over.

"Eight months to a year round-trip and a share of the take to depend on how you're rated when we make the chops of Nantucket Channel and pay off. And you do what you're told when you're told, or it's the rope's end or the brig. Understood?"

He grinned again. "Command and I obey," he said with a grandiloquent gesture, then went down on one knee and placed his hands between hers.

She knew the ceremony; this wasn't the first time she'd gone through it, either.

"Mr. Mate!" she called.

"Ma'am?"

"Sign this man on; rate him ordinary and see he's issued slops and a duffel." Louder: "Prepare to cast off!"

The crew bustled about; Lucy went up the treads to the quarterdeck, taking her place beside the wheel, with the helmsman and pilot. She looked southward, to where the gray water of Southaven Water waited, and the world beyond. Down on the deck, Blood Wolf was looking in the same direction, and she could hear his clear, delighted laughter.

After the Old Kingdom, when the world entered a period of climate change that some researchers speculate was precipitated by the near passage of comet Hale-Bopp, Egypt slipped into a century and a half of political chaos (c. 2190–2040 B.C.). Local lords fought for and against a quick succession of kings who claimed to rule Upper and Lower Egypt. Noreen Doyle introduces us to one of these lords loyal to the king: Ankhtifi, who, in his tomb at modern-day Mo'alla, was the first Egyptian to take the epithet translated as "the Hero" or "the Brave."

Ankhtifi the Brave is dying.

Yet he is not an old man. He can hold his back straight. He does not lean so very much upon his long staff. The two loaves of *khenmet*-bread and the foreleg of a calf he carries in a finely woven basket do not cramp his arms. It is, he supposes, the wounds of campaigns festering invisibly beneath his skin. They have violated his body, pierced his shadow, created windows through which his *ba*-soul would fly, as he has defended his King. Or perhaps it is the scarcity of bread, the thinness of cattle and fowl, the filth in the water. In time, he allows his fluttering *ba*, in time. Not yet. It is dawn, not dusk.

The sun mounts the eastern horizon, over the steep cliffs toward which he walks on a path carefully beaten down and clean, on which oxen will someday drag a sledge and his coffin from the town of Hefat. Unlike other lords in other districts, he keeps no sunshade-bearer to follow him: now that man sits at the door of Idy's house, giving out grain to the needy, of which there are so many in these days. Ankhtifi himself shades Hefat. Does the mountain that shades the city need a fan of ostrich feathers held over its peak?

Only falcon wings shade his head, great ones, perfumed.

Soon they will fly away, Ankhtifi thinks as the scent of incense fills his nose, warmed by the morning sun. They will fly away to the far-off Residence until sleep and desire draw them back again to these two *khenmet*-loaves and the foreleg of a calf.

Spearmen walk behind him, one on the right, one on the left. It is a small display of the force he can muster at an instant. Everyone loves

Ankhtifi here in Hefat and in the Districts of Nekhen and Edfu, but men from other districts and other cities sail upstream and moor here, from Thebes and from Koptos, and those men must not forget.

Oh for the days when one cast arrows and spears at one's foe and received them in return, rather than bags of barley and chickling peas. Oh for the days when all the falcons in the sky were little ones, whose shadows frightened only geese, although Ankhtifi is not afraid, not so very much.

The track takes him from brown fields that crack like bread left too long in the oven to the desert, where life has forever been even sparser. A pyramid of a mountain rises before him, quite apart from the enormous cliffs to the east: a pyramid built by the gods, Ankhtifi's way to heaven when his body is interred here and his *ba* at last flies away from this droughtened earth to the Field of Offerings, eternally moist, forever green.

Every season the Red Land creeps a little nearer to the river. The withered roots of lentils and lettuce and weeds cannot hold it back. Only the river, rising from its bed like an army, can do so, and so within his tomb there is a prayer invoking the name of the King: *May Horus grant that the river will flood for his son Neferkare*. It has not done so very well, not for a very long time.

Ankhtifi enters his little valley-temple, where someday priests will present offerings, but today it is unfinished and empty: the priests are not yet appointed, and the workmen labor elsewhere in the tomb. From this chapel a paved causeway leads partway up the steep mountainside. Ankhtifi walks this way, knowing someday he will be carried, and arrives in the forecourt, where, at his signal, the spearmen pound their piebald shields with the butts of their weapons. With his staff Ankhtifi traces out the threshold of Elephantine granite at the entrance of his tomb, mindful of the royal uraei raising their hooded necks on the architrave above his head.

"Great Overlord!" comes a cry from deeper shadows. Voices echo from within the tomb.

A man emerges with a broom in his hand and bows low before Ankhtifi. He is thin.

"You may speak," says the Royal Seal-bearer, Lector-priest, General, Chief of Scouts, Chief of Foreign Regions, the Great Overlord of Edfu and Nekhen, Ankhtifi.

"My lord," says the man, Sasobek, showing dusty tongue and teeth, "you are welcome in your house of eternity. We did not expect you so early in the day, or else we would have brought a leg of beef and beer sweetened with date juice."

More intention than promise fills Sasobek's words; there is little beer and less beef in Hefat or elsewhere in the districts, and the dates have not ripened well. Sasobek would offer them if he could.

The antechamber spreads wide before them, aglow in a patchwork of lamplight: thirty columns hewn from living rock hold aloft its ceiling; its floor is swept clean of any trace of dirt.

"My name is here, coupled with your dearest desire," says the falcon that has shaded him, now settling into a particular darkness. No one else hears this voice or sees the bright eye and the brighter eye staring at the two loaves and the leg Ankhtifi has set down at his own feet. "Take care."

"In your name, my lord, I have always taken care," Ankhtifi whispers. The workmen hear but say nothing because he is their overlord and a lector-priest, and they know that he speaks to the god.

In pools of light stand and crouch men, all thinner than they once were, scraping out their lives in the drought and the famine that has worn them down as if they were chisels and brushes. They bow before him, careful amid their bowls of paint. Ankhtifi takes stock of them not as though they were tools but as though they were his sons. He knows them, every one, and their wives and sisters and aged parents, their sons and daughters, their cattle and their fields, their skills and their follies.

He is surprised to find the son-of-his-body Idy here among the outline-draftsmen and painters.

Brightly colored scenes surround them, painted on plaster, newly finished, their figures bold and vigorous. The festival of the falcon-god Hemen of Hefat is celebrated in paddled boats. Fatted cattle are herded and butchered, fish harpooned and netted in abundance. Porters bring bag after bag after bag of emmer on their shoulders to be emptied into the granaries. Once it was so. Idy and his three brothers accompany Ankhtifi. Once that, too, was so.

What, Ankhtifi wonders, is his last surviving son doing here? Why is Idy not at home before the door from which barley is handed, or inspecting the granaries, or overseeing the riverbank? He taps his staff upon the immaculate floor of his tomb.

"My son, my heir."

"My lord, my father."

"Tell me your business. I would know what occurs in my domains and what you have seen, for soon you will stand in my place and see what I see. I would see by your eyes while I'm still among the living."

Idy's gaze drifts, for a moment into light, for a moment into shadows. Does he see the god? His lips part, so that Ankhtifi sees Idy's tongue before he speaks.

"I came to account for the workmen's rations."

Good, then, good, Ankhtifi thinks. There is enough in Hefat that none go entirely without, but only because for enough the hungry do not mistake excess nor do the treasurers mistake too little. And Idy does not see the god, not yet.

Idy goes on: "What work these artists do at your word! O you will dwell contentedly in the Field of Offerings, my lord, my father, and none shall ever dishonor your name, nor pollute your house of eternity." He turns away from Ankhtifi to gesture at the painted plaster on the western wall. "You are forever young, and your beloved wife stands here, and your beloved daughters, and your beloved sons, my brothers, here and here and here—and I! Since the days of our forefather Sobekhotep, no one here has ever seen the like of this tomb or its owner."

"Since?" Ankhtifi rasps. Is this doubt in his son's voice? Could it be? Ankhtifi's next breath catches in his throat.

But Idy says, "Not even then—not ever, before or after! Did Sobekhotep call himself Great Overlord? Did the god Horus plan out his tomb? Did the god Hemen dictate a spell to guard it? Did any god ever proclaim anyone other than Ankhtifi to be peerless, whose like has never before been seen nor ever will be seen? Who else has ever called himself the hero, the brave?"

With his staff Ankhtifi strikes a pillar with such force that a little yellow paint scrapes away. It does not matter. The relief carved upon its face will endure for a million years.

There are murmurs in the dark. Sasobek comes forward with his broom and sweeps the imperceptible flecks from the floor. Sand has come along on Ankhtifi's sandals, and Sasobek discreetly attends to that, too.

The falcon stirs in the shadows, rasping claws along the standard upon which he perches when at rest. None sees him, none hears him, but Ankhtifi, and none but he and the falcon is party to the agreement between them.

Ankhtifi walks to the edge of the burial shaft cut into the center of the floor, like a black pool that gives no reflection, that refuses the light. His staff prods its darkness. "Do you remember Khuu, the wretch of Edfu?"

"Yes!" the workmen cry, and Idy says, "I do."

"Men killed their neighbors, the fields of Edfu were left untended like marshland. This is the state of affairs that those in Thebes would wish upon the entire countryside. They deny our rightful King Neferkare, a child of the House of Khety, and would place their own line of wretches upon the Horus-throne. Horus himself summoned me, Ankhtifi, to sail upstream and free knives from men's palms and make men embrace those who had slain their brothers."

"We remember that day," says Idy. The others echo him. "You spoke when all of us were silent, when the other lords had lost their speech and could not raise their arms."

"I led you to the river," Ankhtifi says. "It was a little higher in those days." A little, he thinks, just a little. "Do you remember?"

"We remember!" the men cry, and, as the falcon—it is full daylight; why is he still here? will the King in his Residence sleep the day through?—makes a noise like the bending of a copper saw, Ankhtifi remembers.

People were less hungry in those days. Boats were sailed upstream and rowed downstream, rudders set at sterns or quarters with less concern for sandbars and stones. There had been even better years with abundant harvests and fatted cattle and nets burdened with fish of all kinds, but those were all lost to living memory and known only through tales of the days of kings named Khufu and Unas and Pepy, when men were called northward to labor on great pyramids.

One day—*that* day—a boat came downstream. Its spars were laid across its beams, but there was no sail or rigging. Eight men manned its oars, a ninth kept his hand at the tiller, and women and many children huddled in its wet bottom, for most of the deck planking had been taken up.

"Where is the Great Overlord? We have sworn not to take our hands from looms and tiller until we have come to the city where the Great Overlord lives! Our hands bleed! We have passed by Nekhen because he was not there! Is he here in Hefat?" cried the helmsman as the rowers pulled in their oars. Two of them leapt into the river and drove the boat ashore as the children dumped themselves overboard and splashed in the water until their mothers joined them and herded them to land. They crouched in a place of a little shade of a tree, where they looked like twigs broken from its branches. The helmsman said, "Where is the Great Overlord of this district?"

"The Great Overlord is where he should be, attending to trouble when it comes to his shore," said Ankhtifi. These were not fit men: like the women and children, their limbs were thin, their stomachs distended, and they wore cloaks of bruises and welts. "Where are you from? Are you people of mine?"

"Would that we were," said the helmsman, "or else we would not have trouble to bring to your shore, my lord. We come from Edfu in this old boat that we took from a boatwright before he could break it up for timber."

"If the boatwright should come in search of his craft, you might be punished. I may punish you for theft anyway."

"He won't come after it, my lord. He's dead, but not by our hands. His brother killed him, because he would not pledge his heart to Khuu's new lord."

"New lord!" Ankhtifi exclaimed. "Our lord, Neferkare, still wears the crowns in the Residence at Neni-Nesut, so the administrator of Edfu has no new lord. I, the King's Seal-bearer, would have been informed if he had flown to heaven."

"Neferkare is king in Neni-Nesut and Lower Egypt, and here in the District of Nekhen if you say so, but he is not the king of Edfu any longer," said the helmsman. "Khuu has declared it."

"What manner of abomination is this? Has some vile Lower Nubian sorcerer laid a spell on Khuu's heart?"

The helmsman did not know; he had spoken all that he could of the matters of big men, and he, a little man, was tired and hungry and his wife and children were crying on the shore. Ankhtifi learned the helmsman was in fact a potter and, although Hefat had potters already, Ankhtifi appointed him a place where he might build a little house and workshop beside the rest.

That evening Ankhtifi laid a banquet for these people on the riverbank and another in his pillared hall, where he summoned his sons and his council. They ate choice cuts of beef, drank good beer, ate white bread, and spoke of what the potter had told them.

The Overseer of Troops of Hefat, Minnefer, said, "The District of Edfu lies at the southern border of our district, and we are very near the northern. It is a long way."

"Khuu is like a wound in the foot of the King," Ankhtifi said. "We are the hands of the King."

"And where is the King's heart but in the Residence at Neni-Nesut," murmured Minnefer, "far to the north at the entrance of the Faiyum. He might as well dwell in Syria."

"He is near the gods and honors them, to ensure that the river floods in its season. That inundation must pass Edfu before it reaches us. Would you have a rebel between us and the first floodwaters?"

"The vile Lower Nubians lie between us and the first floodwaters, and what ill is that? Unless they're drinking up the water of the river, to make it rise so poorly as it does nowadays." Everyone laughed, even Ankhtifi.

"If Edfu falls," Ankhtifi said, as his smile withered word by word and the laughter drained out of his voice, "what of Elephantine, to the south? Will it fall to Khuu? Will Khuu then join with the Nubians upstream? Will they together push north with the current and attempt to crush us?"

"Ha," said Minnefer, slouching on his stool, "for once in your life you're too ready for a fight, Ankhtifi! Usually you're all speech and council. Life is good in Hefat. I am old enough to know. Don't go looking for death in Edfu. Death is bad anywhere, but worst away from home. A rebel against our King would have to arise in Elephantine for there to be any real trouble. It will not happen."

"And did you think a rebel would arise in Edfu?"

"Oh, no, but you did, Ankhtifi the Brave!" the workmen say, and for a moment Ankhtifi does not know where he is: why is his hall so dark, why has the smell of the roast evaporated, replaced by the taste of dust in his mouth, and why are workmen here in the place of his councilors? Why are these men so thin? Where are his other three sons?

"Khuu was ever a wretch and a rebel," Idy says. "You could not fail against him."

Could he? No, he could not, because the god said so. And suddenly it is as if he stands not on the perfectly clean floor of a nearly finished tomb but on the dusty pyramid mountain that workmen's picks and chisels have not yet carved out. It is as if the title Great Overlord of Edfu is not yet his, and as if the falcon does not yet follow him in shadows.

The falcon came to him *that* night for the first time, when the councilors had returned to their homes and his wife, Nebi, had gone to bed, as had his sons and his daughters. Ankhtifi went out to the hills to watch over this place where life was good. The lay of the land was perfect here, farmland and hill-country each in good measure, shady stands of trees fringing the riverbank. Minnefer had argued the truth: it was good, very much so.

And as Ankhtifi was thinking these things, a bird descended from the sky. For a moment he thought it was a bat, or a swallow that had lost the way to its nest in the riverbank, but it was too large, and the markings on its face were those of the most perfect falcon Ankhtifi had ever seen. What could it be but a god? Horus or Hemen? One and the same? And if it were not, if it were merely some exceptional bird with most perfect markings on its face—who would know if the Great Overlord Ankhtifi went to both knees and pressed his face to the ground before it? No one, unless the bird might tell its master, in which case Ankhtifi would still be justified indeed.

So he did, then brought his hands up before his face in a gesture of praise. There was a scent about the falcon, a remarkable odor of sadness and age, as if it had flown over all the incense-terraces of the God's-Land.

Ankhtifi bowed again. Even as a lector-priest, he did not know what to say before a god.

"So," said the falcon, "here are my hands!"

Into the aromatic lull that followed, Ankhtifi offered these words: "The King willing, here is my lord!"

"Are you so certain?"

"You are god, or you are as god. Such would be my lord, if it is the King's will."

"My hands, with such wisdom you would do well as my heart! I am your King. Behold me, *Ankhtifi*, He-Who-Shall-Live."

Ankhtifi, who was accustomed to receiving no direct command, did as commanded. Ankhtifi, who feared none, worried that his gaze might be too direct or too deferent. But he looked upon this god and saw that it had perched upon a standard. Indeed, Ankhtifi noticed as he drew his eyes away from the ground and up its length, that this standard was set upon nothing, being merely balanced above the rocky ground, as if the weight of the bird upon it were so perfect that the world would forbid it to fall, and if by some device of the god it did fall, the world itself would move aside, lest the standard come to harm.

And he saw, too, that every feather was as white as alabaster or blue like lapis lazuli, that its feet and beak shone like the green gold of Amau, that its talons were silver, that its right eye was bright as the noon sun, its left eye as bright as the full moon.

"Well, what is the matter, Seal-bearer of mine? Answer."

"I had thought that my lord, my King, was the son of Re but born of a woman's womb. No queen could have brought you into the world, my lord. You are a god, fashioned in the time of creation."

"I emerged from the womb of Iput and six years later began the first of my ninety-four years upon the throne. No king does that without learning a trick or two. When I was a boy, my Seal-bearer Harkhuf—Warden of Nekhen, Lector-priest, not so unlike you—went down to Nubia to fetch me a pygmy from beyond the land of Yam. I worried mightily for this divine dancer from the Horizon-Dwellers. 'Don't let him drown!' I begged Harkhuf, 'Keep a guard with him night and day.'"

Until this moment Ankhtifi had thought nothing could amaze him more than what had already happened, but the falcon, god or King or both, outdid himself. Ankhtifi had heard of this Harkhuf, and of the pygmy of the Horizon-Dwellers, and of the King, all generations past. But he knew nothing more of the story, so bit his tongue.

"That pygmy was a marvel, worth more than every resin-tear from every incense-terrace, more than every green nugget from every gold mine in Amau, more than every black log from every forest of ebony. I was so very young, still suckled at my mother's breast, and even then I recognized his preciousness. What dances he danced! He pleased the gods mightily, my hands. Perhaps that is why they allowed him to work the magic that he knew, the magic of the Horizon-Dwellers that is not known in the land of Egypt or indeed anywhere else in the world. In secrecy he taught me how to live in three years as other men live in one, and thus I sat upon the Horus-throne for four years and *ninety*. Not until then did I fly to the West."

Well, then, that was it, Ankhtifi thought, strangely mollified that this was not *his* King, Neferkare of the House of Khety, but rather Neferkare Son-of-Re Pepy, the old king of many years ago when kings were still building pyramids of size. This must be his *ba*, wandering about the world. In any case, Ankhtifi had done very well to bow and would continue to treat the falcon thus.

"My lord, if my King should permit, I will be your hands, even as I am the hands of the successor of your successors."

"Successors!" The falcon laughed, a sound like the bending of a copper saw. "I have no successors; those who have upon occasion occupied the throne in my stead have been little men and one little woman."

"Is my King Neferkare so weak that you, his forefather, do not acknowledge him? Should I disavow my allegiance to him? I would not do so with a willing heart, for he is indeed my King."

The falcon's copper laughter turned to a proper hawkish shriek.

"I am your King Neferkare."

"That pygmy knew death nearly as well as he knew life. Not once but ten times have I sat upon the Horus-throne! I have been one more than the Ennead!" And the falcon proceeded to name his old name and recount those of the Great Nine Gods, interspersed with the names of kings, some of which were known to Ankhtifi, others not: "Neferkare Pepy—Atum! Neferka-the-child—Shu! Neferkare—Tefnut! Neferkare Neby—Geb! Neferkare Khenedy—Nut! Neferkare Terer—Osiris! Neferkare Pepysonby—Set! Neferkaure—Isis! Neferirkare—Nephthys! Neferkare—wait, there is no more. One more than the Ennead."

Then his timbre changed, becoming darker or tired. "It is enough now. The tenth time shall be the last time, the perfected time, and for ten times four-and-ninety years I now will reign. Those Amenemhats and Senwosrets and Amenhoteps and Thutmoses and *all* those Rameseses! They think they will succeed me. Let them pass their lives away as fishermen, as arrow makers, as boys of the horse-stables."

Ankhtifi did not think he knew any of these men, and he did not know what a horse was, but he let the falcon speak; what else could he do?

"But you, Ankhtifi, you are my loyal hands, ready to bind up the wound in the sole of my foot."

"I am ready to do anything that pleases you, my lord, my King."

"Of course you are; you've proven yourself no fool. How much like Harkhuf you are! Go to Edfu with your troops. Tell your councilors and your soldiers that Horus himself dispatches you there. Defeat Khuu, who is a rebel and a wretch and who has stolen much of what belongs to the shrine of Horus-Behdeti, the god of that place. And every third night, from next one forth, bring to me two *khenmet*-loaves from the altar of Re and an offering of flesh. Do this, and my hands shall be rewarded."

"It will be done," Ankhtifi pledged, bowing to the ground again, and when he raised himself once more, the standard was gone and the falcon was gone, and just the slightest essence of the incense-terraces hung heavy in the still night air.

He was eager for morning and, having returned home to his bed, tried not to sleep, but sleep he did, and when he awoke he was not entirely sure if it had all been a dream. It did not matter, dream or otherwise, and Ankhtifi thought otherwise. Horus—the King!—had ordered him to Edfu.

When his council heard this, they did not know properly what to say. Even as Ankhtifi had never before spoken to a god, awake or dreaming, nor had any of these men spoken to someone who had spoken to a god, not on such intimate terms. So, although they still believed that Ankhtifi was for once in his life too ready to fight, they declared that they would make themselves ready, too.

Ankhtifi and his sons and all the troops mustered their boats and their spears and their bows and their shields. They stepped their masts and raised their sails, but the wind died.

"This is," said Minnefer, looking northward, "an evil sign."

"The wind always dies when you most want it," Ankhtifi said, looking southward. "Take out the lines and we'll track."

So some of the men took out the ropes and pulled the boats from shore, hour by hour, up the river. Each of Ankhtifi's four sons, all strong young men, took their turn at the lead of the trackers. Ankhtifi prayed to Horus, Hemen, Neferkare, whatever he should call the falcon, to restore the wind, that they might all the sooner be upon the border of the district of Edfu. Shadows and clouds passed along the sky, as if the god Set were up to a storm. A great flock of geese flew up the river. In their wake the wind rose—from the west and dusty, useless and dangerous like Libyan tribes. The geese followed them in the days that they tracked, and even at night as they camped, Ankhtifi could hear their cackle, *negeg-negeg-negeg*.

Then, at last, as one evening they tracked past the city of Nekhen, the flock scattered. Ankhtifi sighted a falcon, the north wind returned. The square sails grew rounded and the trackers joyfully leapt aboard. Ankhtifi drew a deep breath, filling his nose with the fragrance of the God's-Land.

"Sail," he said, "even into the night." The sailors did as he ordered, without argument that there might be shallows the pilots could not see, obstacles the helmsmen could not avoid. He longed to ask them if they disregarded their sailor's instincts because their noses were filled with incense from the wind—or perhaps it was now upon his own breath and they obeyed him on that account. But he did not ask, for by the time he thought to, they were on the borders of Khuu's district and one word might give them away to the rebels. Under the cover of night and silence they passed by crumbling villages and wastelands; dark, stinking things floating in the river; piles of grain rotting on the shore; until they came to the fields and the city of Edfu.

The sky was yet dark to the west; the east was just giving birth to the sun, which had yet to warm the moist morning air. Baboons, stirred into worship of the sun as shadows crept away from the hills, barked across the river.

Ankhtifi broke his men into four ranks and placed himself before the first. He led the first up the riverbank through the fields that were green with bindweed and cornflower, clover and vetch. His eldest son, Sobekhotep-the-younger, led the next line, Hotep-the-younger the next, Sanebi the last, and Idy held the rest of the troops back along the river, guarding the boats.

They came upon bodies along the way: a man and young girl, left there to rot, fly-blown father and sister to the stinking, swollen forms that had floated by on the river.

Smoke rose from beyond the wall of Edfu. A dog yapped, a bitch answered. The high voices of children carried in the still morning air. Such ordinariness in a day when the dead lay unburied troubled Ankhtifi deeply.

Where were the men to tend the fields? Callous and lazy, too, the grip of the rebel had made them. Truth had been overthrown and abandoned like the corpses. Evil spread like a weed in the fields.

"Khuu!" Ankhtifi called. "Where is Khuu?"

For an hour, like an eternity, Ankhtifi and his troops stood there before the wall. Living in the shadow of a rebel had made even the soldiers slothful. They would rather drink beer and chew melon seeds.

"Ankhtifi of Hefat has come to Khuu! In the name of the King!"

Now Khuu's men took notice. They whooped and ran to the walls, pouring through the gate while others crouched atop the walls.

"Halt, you of Khuu!" cried Ankhtifi, raising his battle-ax. "In the name of the King of Upper and Lower Egypt, Neferkare, put down your spears, lay aside your bows, and drop your slings!"

The men of Khuu did halt, and although they did not put down their spears, nor lay aside their bows, nor even drop their slings, they did not immediately press their attack. Instead, they laughed.

"Neferkare is not king here," cried an archer from the wall. Others took up the reply like a chorus, weaving into it insults: "Neferkare-who-has-lost-his-testicles is not King here, Neferkare-who-drinks-urine is not King here, Neferkare-who-eats-filth is not King here."

"Then," Ankhtifi replied, "there can be none here who can stand against me, because the only one who can best me is a man worthy of Neferkare, King of Upper and Lower Egypt. Lay aside your weapons and take up Truth once again."

The troops of Edfu who were assembled before the gate made way for a man. This man wore a starched-white kilt, heavy rings and armlets of Nubian gold and precious stones, and carried a fine battle-ax of bronze. Ankhtifi thought he saw red hairs among the black of his head.

"Khuu, I have come to weed your fields," Ankhtifi said.

Khuu laughed. "I would not trust a man of Neferkare with a sack of barley on his back."

"Why have you made a wasteland of your district?"

"There will be a harvest of grain after the next inundation. This year it has been necessary to winnow the chaff that covers my district. No doubt you have seen stray bits lying about. Like the wind I will take you out, too, Ankhtifi of Hefat, unless you prove yourself to be other than straw. There is a new lord in Egypt, and he performs in Truth before the gods. Let him lay mud upon your fields, Ankhtifi, let him bless the District of Nekhen."

"The District of Nekhen is already blessed, by Hemen, by Horus, by

Neferkare. We are civil in Nekhen and do not leave our dead for the carrion-birds and the flies, nor let the fish nibble upon their backs. This is not Truth. This is chaos. The stench of it fills my nostrils, Khuu. You and your name and your district, they reek."

Khuu raised his ax, and as he did so, slings and arrows and spears came up in the arms of his men.

"Beware, Khuu, for Horus himself—your own god!—brings me to Edfu. I am the hands of the King."

"Then I will deprive this so-called king of his hands and of that shriveled sack of skin that hangs empty between his legs."

Khuu overtook the distance that had separated them, and Ankhtifi took up his shield. With a yell from Khuu, arrows rained from the walls and slingstones came like bees to chicory. Ankhtifi's men stood still until, in the moment after, Ankhtifi gave the order to defend, and they raised their shields.

Khuu pressed his shield against Ankhtifi's, trying to bring him to ground. "You're a fool," he said between his teeth as Ankhtifi resisted. "Beside Montu of Thebes, god of war, another god stands behind the new lord, a Great Cackler, one self-created, the Hidden."

"Have you seen this god?"

"No one has. No one can see this Amun."

"I have seen Horus, spoken to Hemen, and he stands behind no one but Neferkare! But—" Ankhtifi pressed harder now "—but—" to give room to his ax "—but this god flies above me!"

His ax hit hard into the stiff cowhide of Khuu's shield, which was torn away by this blow. At that strike, and one word from Ankhtifi, the troops of Nekhen broke from their defense and returned the assault.

In the end, Khuu and thirty of his troops lay dead. Khuu's sons were slain, and all of his brothers. And so were Ankhtifi's sons, all but Idy, who had remained behind to guard the boats.

Ankhtifi, wounded but standing like many of his own troops, summoned together the men of Edfu. His heart ached to strike blows at these men who had killed his sons, but he had to do otherwise, in the name of his King, lest civil strife burn forever across the District of Edfu. He would take his sons home and give them good burials and mourn them and miss them and rule justly over their slayers.

"Now embrace your neighbors. You will bury all of your dead," Ankhtifi said, wiping the blood from his ax but ignoring that which spilled down his thigh. "There will be no more filth upon the land. Cleanse the District of Edfu."

The men of Edfu complained bitterly. "He killed my brother," said each man, pointing to another.

"And you," replied Ankhtifi, pointing at them with his clean ax and they shied away, "have killed my sons. I will deal with you, the slayers of my sons, as you deal with the slayers of your brothers."

Leaving Minnefer behind to implement his orders, Ankhtifi went home to Hefat.

"And so you won Edfu," Idy says. "Great Overlord of the Districts of Edfu and Nekhen." He pronounces this dual title as if he can taste it in his own mouth at once with his own name.

Ankhtifi's mouth is too dry to taste anything. Sasobek is sweeping again, and it is as if he has brushed away all the moisture from Ankhtifi's tongue. His thigh aches.

Ankhtifi says, "Edfu was given to me. By Horus, by Hemen."

Why? He would ask the King but the falcon is gone now. In the Residence far downstream the King has awoken.

"Because," says Idy, as if Ankhtifi spoke his question aloud, "you are the hero without equal!" And he goes about pointing to where the texts say this very thing, here and here and here.

Ankhtifi-*nakht*. The Brave. Ankhtifi-*nakht*. The Hero. *Ankhtifi*. He-Who-Shall-Live.

The fields grew a little better in those days than now, but only a little. The days when the floodwaters reached all of the good fields and blessed them with new black mud were generations past, the memories of forefathers long ago laid into the tomb. Ankhtifi dispatched scribes to account for the grain in the granaries, not only in the District of Edfu but likewise in the District of Nekhen, so that he knew his resources to the smallest detail. He ascertained what was in Khuu's treasury, and made note of mines and the places of good clay and the herds of cattle in Edfu. He became aware of the smiths and the potters, of the fishermen and the hunters, of the scribes and the priests. And he noted what goods came down from Elephantine and Nubia beyond it, and what goods came up through the Districts of Thebes and of Koptos and from the Faiyum far beyond them. He noted what came from the Sand-farers of the Eastern Desert and what came from the Libyans of the Western Desert.

He appointed treasurers to oversee the granaries, ordering them to take a fair measure of each harvest and set it aside. No one questioned his demands because Ankhtifi ever took but a fair measure.

Ankhtifi marveled that his power stretched so far from the District of Nekhen, and that he was well-loved, even by those whom he had made to bury the murderers of their brothers. As Ankhtifi gave an order, so it was carried out by those far distant from him, his judges and his treasurers and his troops. And it was always well done, because he was well-loved.

Every third night, even as a few hungry men watched after him, he went out to the pyramid of a mountain, where he set out two *khenmet*-loaves and the foreleg of a calf for the falcon. And every third morning, unlike any other offering Ankhtifi had ever set out for any other god, these were gone, vanished from the earth, devoured in their entirety, the basket clean and undisturbed.

"This is the secret to power," said the falcon one evening when Ankhtifi again met him on the pyramid-mountain with these offerings, "its judicious giving-away. I was profligate in my youth, before I flew to the sky, and I gave too much to too many. The kingship suffered and so Egypt is now in such a state that rebels defy Truth. I diluted rather than tempered. This is not a mistake I will make again. You are well-chosen, Ankhtifi."

"I am touched by the trust you have put in me, my King."

"As I give to you, Ankhtifi, so you give to me. That is the agreement between us. I give you authority, for I am the arms at the end of which are you, my hands. And in turn you give me effectiveness, for you are the hands upon my arms." He blinked his eyes, the bright and the brighter, toward the offerings in the basket.

"There has never been another man like you, Ankhtifi. Not even Harkhuf, who so dutifully brought me my pygmy from beyond Yam. You have no peer. You are to be my sole receptacle, you, and yours ever after, in ways that not even my favorite general from the days of my first youth could ever be. In the earth beneath my perch, within this pyramid-mountain, build yourself a tomb, which I will guard with spells taught to me by the pygmy of the Horizon-Dwellers. He knew these spells as well as he knew life.

"No, he knew them better than life," the falcon said, thinking perhaps of the eight short reigns that had been his after the first lengthy one. "This is my boon to you. By the hand of men your house of eternity will be hewn, by the spells of gods it will endure and protect you and yours. Even as you and yours will protect me."

And the falcon described the tomb as it was to be, hewn from the earth itself, columns growing thick like reeds in the swamp on the day of creation, a roof of stone, a great copper door, a burial shaft sunk into its floor. The threshold must be of stone brought from Elephantine, the architrave carved with uraei, like the cobra that guards the

King's brow. Ankhtifi took due note of everything and planned for how to acquire it.

"Everything must be honestly gotten, in accordance with Truth, and maintained in Truth and purity," said the falcon. "That is why I have chosen you, Ankhtifi, for you are not only brave but trustworthy. You are unique and have no peer."

Ankhtifi bowed before his lord, his god, his King.

Subsequently he took a fair measure of the fair measure of the harvest for himself, and he did the same with every trade-good that came into his districts and the livestock and the catch of the hunters and fishermen, the products of the mines. Carefully he apportioned the labor of stonecutters and masons, and when they might be spared from erecting defensive walls, he set them to hewing his tomb exactly as the falcon had dictated. They did precisely what they were told, for to do otherwise would be disobedience, and they loved Ankhtifi too much for that.

Traders did not complain of what they had to give to Ankhtifi, but they voiced bitter opinion of what they had to give to others, even when it was less. Ankhtifi listened carefully to what they had to say, to learn what was happening in Elephantine and Nubia, in Thebes and Koptos.

"The Great Overlord of Thebes," travelers said, "he claims control of the ways of the Eastern Desert. The King may not pass to the God's-Land."

At this Ankhtifi might have laughed, for every third night the falcon came to him perfumed with incense of the God's-Land, but matters were too serious for that. He spoke of this to the King.

"With Thebes and Koptos together, Antef grows," the falcon replied. "He threatens to fill up the land with his vile seed. The House of Khety is not big enough to contain him."

"Khuu called him lord and spoke of a Great Cackler, a Hidden god."

"Khuu is a wretch and dead, deader than you will ever know, boiled in the lake of fire, which was all too good for him. His name, *Khuu*, means *baseness* and *wrongdoing*. You do not remember, but that was not always his name. You will never remember that name given him by his mother." And indeed, such was the strength of the King's words that Ankhtifi could never remember any name but *Khuu*.

"Be judicious, my hands, my precious hands. Make peace with them to the south, make war with them to the north, and make your tomb here exactly as I told you. Now I will tell you what must be written within it. This is Truth, all shall believe, there will be no doubt:

"You are the beginning of men and the end of men. Such a man as you has never before been born and will never after be born. You will have no peer in the course of this million of years. You, Ankhtifi, are the hero without equal."

The falcon flew into the air, circling Ankhtifi's head, filling his nose with perfume.

"And as for any overlord who shall be overlord in Hefat and who commits a bad deed—"

Ankhtifi breathed in the perfume, memorizing and wondering at the terribleness in the falcon's next words and not for a moment doubting the truth of them.

In the following days Ankhtifi gathered his scribes and his overseers about him at the necropolis. The mountain where he had first met the falcon swarmed with men, smelling sharply of salt and urine, a stink that obliterated the lingering trace of the incense-terraces. But these were the strong arms of the Districts of Nekhen and Edfu. *That smell should be as a perfume to me,* Ankhtifi thought.

And he told his scribes everything the falcon had ordered inscribed within the tomb. They agreed with every word, peerless, beginning and end, the hero.

Three times they had him repeat the last of the falcon's words: "As for any overlord who shall be overlord in Hefat and who commits a bad deed or an evil act against this tomb—" and then the butchery that would be performed upon him in the netherworld, an arm struck away for each offense. "Hemen will refuse his offerings on his festival-day, Hemen will not accept any of his offerings, and his heir will not inherit from him."

The scribes took note, collating their copies in order that the text might be perfect, murmuring approval of its thoroughness and efficacy.

When the scribes had gone off to their work, Minnefer came to Ankhtifi. "Your troops are eager to go north, my lord. Every sailor who comes from the north with tales of Thebes and Koptos only blows his breath across the fire in their hearts. They would fight and defeat Antef for you and the King."

Ankhtifi told Minnefer what the falcon had said, that together these two districts made Antef too great to fight at this moment. "And to think that once you said that I was too eager to fight, Minnefer!"

Minnefer made no jest in return, as once he might have. He only smiled and obeyed.

As Ankhtifi bided time, earth came away from the tomb like the swollen river receding from the fields, and the smells of labor became Ankhtifi's perfume.

It did not go as well with the river, which he watched with hope. It had not risen well, and this was the second month of Inundation. With offerings farmers tried to coax the waters to rise a little higher, to stand a little deeper, on the fields to lay down more precious, fertile mud. One might as well have tried to coax a flood down from the sky. Ankhtifi even dared to hope that while digging the burial shaft in the floor of his tomb-chapel the workmen would strike water and so make a well. But they did not. Peerless that he might be—peerless that he was, the falcon had so said—such things were not within the purview of Ankhtifi's authority.

Boats yet came and went with little trouble along the river, and one windless morning a boat tracked from the north by six men put to shore at Hefat. There was nothing special with regard to this: boats tracked by six men or four came and went by Hefat every day that the wind did not blow exactly right. This boat had a round-topped cabin woven of reeds, with shields of cattle-hide covering its windows. From this cabin emerged a man with a quiver of arrows and a good bow. Sailors of other boats who were at the riverbank called for Ankhtifi, for they recognized this man as the Overseer of the Troops of Armant. Armant was a town of the District of Thebes, its Overseer a follower of Antef.

"Come!" the Overseer called, waving his arms.

Ankhtifi watched from the apex of his pyramid-mountain. The Overseer's voice was small to him.

"Come!" the Overseer called again.

Because he did not nock an arrow or leave his boat, Ankhtifi did not come. He went about his business at the tomb and then, after a time when the Overseer had finished shouting and sat down at the bow, Ankhtifi made his way to the river. When he came to the shore, the Overseer leapt up.

"Come, you hero!" he said, swinging his bow like a sickle. "I have come to bid you north to our camp."

"Have you come or have you been sent?"

"*You* are bade to Armant," the Overseer replied evenly. "My lord Antef would speak with you."

"This Antef may speak with me here, at Hefat. His district is not so very far. Even your sailors have scarcely beaded their brows with sweat."

The Overseer dropped his voice, but not so much that Ankhtifi could not hear him clearly. "Thebes and Koptos have parted ways. Antef dares not come farther south than the Mount of Semekhsen, does not dare pass the boundaries of his district, for fear that Koptos will attack while he's away. Come, in my boat or your own. Armant is not so very far."

Ankhtifi demanded of the sailors of other boats who had lately come from the north what they knew of this, but none could say. The lords of those districts were like lions, they said, and when lions gorged on a single kill, who was to tell at what moment they might argue over the choicest bits and part company?

"I will not come," said Ankhtifi.

He sent the Overseer of the Troops of Armant back the way he had come; he knew that by nightfall the man would be back in the District of Thebes. It was not so very far indeed.

Idy and Minnefer and his councilors came to him and, having learned the Overseer's news, offered to ready the boats so that, if it was true, Ankhtifi might take advantage, in the name of the King.

Ankhtifi shook his head. "I will not come," he said, "but in my own time, I will go."

He offered loaves and a foreleg to the falcon that night. "It is your time," he said to Ankhtifi, his eyes shining more brightly. "This is a boon I grant you: your opponents will always fall to you in battle. You have no equal."

And he went the next day, before dawn, with two boats and twenty men. They rowed with stealth, the spoon blades of their oars kissing the water and speeding the craft along faster than the flooding current. Here the river branched, and Ankhtifi's boats slipped into the little channel that flowed nearest the Mount of Semekhsen.

There were men at the hill, many men and a half-built fortified camp, with the standards of Thebes and of Koptos.

"He lied!" Idy said, as if such a thing had never before occurred to him.

"He lies, like a hippopotamus in the mud," Ankhtifi said. He hefted his spear, the shadow of which grew longer in the morning light. "And like a hippopotamus in the mud, he dies."

They disembarked, having staked their boats out of sight. A shadow fell over them, winged, perfumed, like a moment of night that was not yet scattered by dawn. His troops did not question Ankhtifi, although he was leading them, a trustworthy band of twenty, against five, six, seven times as many, or more, as they counted by the growing light.

They came to the boundary of the camp, which had stirred and began to break fast. Men scratched themselves and shoved bread into their mouths. The Overseer of the Troops of Armant walked among his soldiers, shoulder to shoulder with other overseers of troops from other towns. These men were the nose, the breath, of this army. The soldiers among whom they walked were the tusks and the flesh, lolling in the mud. Yet there was no sign of the heart, no sign of Antef of Thebes.

"Stand beside me, my strong arms, my harpoons," Ankhtifi said, "and I will pierce the nose."

Ankhtifi stood tall, like the sun suddenly birthed from the horizon, and the scented shadow fell away: the King, far away in the Residence, awoke and rose from his bed.

Cries of terror rose from the troops of Armant and their allies. These quickly turned to whoops and they grabbed their weapons.

"You! You there!" Ankhtifi called, giving them neither name nor title nor sobriquet. "I am Ankhtifi, Seal-bearer of the King of Upper and Lower Egypt, Lector-priest, Great Overlord of the Districts of Edfu and Nekhen. I have prevailed in the south over Khuu the wretch of Edfu. I am the hero without peer. By Horus and by Hemen I am here to fight you, all of you, and I will smite you, all of you, and I will carry north through your own districts your herds and your fleets and present them before King Neferkare in the Residence at Neni-Nesut! I will fight all of you. Who among you will fight me?"

The Overseer of the Troops of Armant came forward and quieted his men. If he gave his name, now or ever, Ankhtifi has long ago forgotten it, perhaps at the falcon's word. "Neferkare, so far as we are concerned, is as dead."

Ankhtifi laughed now, and laughed and laughed, for the Overseer spoke more truth than he could ever know.

"Antef is our lord," the Overseer went on, sounding something less than certain in the face of Ankhtifi's laughter. "You would be wise to make him your own. Join Thebes and Koptos, Ankhtifi. Would you rather that Antef overrun Nekhen and Edfu and leave you and your heirs with nothing at all?"

"Will you fight me?"

The Overseer perhaps thought of Khuu, or perhaps he thought of the victorious troops of the Districts of Nekhen and Edfu. Or perhaps he thought of the god that had brought Ankhtifi unseen to the boundary of his camp. Whatever he thought of, at the end of it he said: "I will fight you. My troops will fight you."

And they did.

At Ankhtifi's signal the trustworthy troops of Nekhen and Edfu stormed the encampment, piercing it like harpoons. They brought down their axes upon the shields and the arms and the heads of Armant and Thebes and Koptos. Their slingstones smashed in eyes and tore off ears, their arrows pierced limbs and chests and skewered the very hearts of men, and their spears transfixed whatever they touched.

What the spears did not transfix, and what could move eyeless or earless or with arrows feathering their arms, and what had lost merely hands and not limbs to axes, these fled north, like a single wounded beast. Ankhtifi pursued their leaders, the overseers of troops, and fixed *them* with his spear. He laid waste to their camp, destroying it utterly, carrying away whatever of value could be carried away, burning whatever would burn.

Then Ankhtifi's men went home, injured but valiant. They went against the current, and this time no wind filled their sails, but they did not care. Home was near, and all the way the trackers hauled while bleeding and singing, "Ankhtifi the Brave, the hero who has no peer."

"Seven, perhaps eight, perhaps nine, against one," Idy says, marveling at the memory to which he himself was witness, of which he himself bears old scars. Ankhtifi is startled: has he been speaking? He thought the dryness in his throat was from crying battle-orders to his men. "You have no equal, my lord, my father."

Ankhtifi looks at his son, who stares at him wide-eyed, adoring, no different from the workmen. It is so now. But someday men will not question *Idy,* when *he* is overlord and the authority of Neferkare, of Horus, of Hemen, fills *him.*

Ankhtifi steps away from the burial shaft in the spotless floor of his tomb.

For some time no one came south from Koptos or Thebes. No one traveled south at all, unless they began in the District of Nekhen or Edfu and went upstream to Elephantine. Scouts dispatched by Ankhtifi through the desert to look upon the District of Thebes reported that Antef strangled the ways of the desert, that King Neferkare had but hard access to the mines and quarries in the east. When boats came again, their crews and passengers said the same.

The falcon did not speak of these things. Ankhtifi wondered if they felt it showed some weakness the King did not wish to admit, or if he did not so keenly feel this loss, or if there were simply more pressing matters always at hand. And there were. The river was sluggish. Each year it rose as high as it had the year before, but it never seemed quite so high as the year before that. Ankhtifi ordered his treasurers to appropriate a little more than a fair share, and farmers complained to the treasurers. Ankhtifi sent men among them to tell them that this share was going into the granary like the rest, as proof against the fickleness of the river, and the farmers gave even more than they were asked.

Ankhtifi marveled at this with the falcon as he laid before him offerings.

The falcon said, "A king's strong arm is his tongue."

"And the strength of the land is the river," Ankhtifi replied. "It is low, even at its height."

"Horus grants the flood."

"You are Horus. You are Hemen. Grant us the power of the river. Give it away, make us, make yourself, thereby all the stronger."

The falcon blinked his bright eye, then his brighter one. "Put my name into your tomb, just once, asking Horus to grant in my name what you most desire. There is power in that."

"Once only?"

"It will be for your son to multiply my name, and for his son, and his son, they who will be overlords after you. Fear will be in them, and love and respect. Your tomb will be unpolluted until the end of time, because none will ever question your authority. Even as I have assured their inheritance, so they will assure mine. The Thebans would take this from me. They would take this from us both."

It startled Ankhtifi to hear the falcon speak of this now. It had been such a long time since the falcon had spoken of Thebes.

"I have thought to go north," said Ankhtifi. "My troops, I can call them from their fields for a little while. The time to plant comes earlier and earlier each year, yet the growing season is shorter and shorter. The river is quick to retreat from the land, and the drought of summer is quicker to descend upon it."

"Go north, then, hero," the falcon said. "Go north and lay my hands about the throat of my enemy."

Before going north, Ankhtifi went to his scribes and told them what to write upon one wall of his tomb: "May Horus grant that the river will flood for his son Neferkare."

Then, over the course of ten days, he summoned his trustworthy troops from their fields and their barracks and from their labors. They rowed past the Mount of Semekhsen, where it seemed that the smell of burning staves and a whiff of incense lingered still. They slipped past the town of Armant on the great channel of the river. Those who were along the riverbank in the dark hours gasped in fear. They sent runners northward.

Then Ankhtifi's best archers made ready to shoot them. They were sure of their mark even in moonlight because confidence in their overlord filled them, but Ankhtifi stopped them.

"Someone must tell Antef that I have come to challenge him. Let them go. Their fear will inform him well."

They rowed until at dawn they came to Tjemy's fine estate on the west bank, whose fields were not so deeply flooded as once they might have been, whose quay was no longer so convenient as once it might have been. Soldiers stood along its walls.

The fleet moored at the riverbank, and out poured the valiant troops of Edfu and Nekhen. Ankhtifi at their lead, they marched to the walls.

"Come out, you! Come out! Who will fight Ankhtifi the Brave, the Great Overlord of Edfu and Nekhen? Tjemy! You, there! Who?"

Ankhtifi raised his ax.

None replied. Even a volley of arrows, aimed at the walls, did not stir the soldiers from their places. Shadows grew short and then long again, now stretching back toward the river. The runners from Armant at last came by and Ankhtifi let them pass.

"Let them tell Antef of Thebes," he said. "Let them proclaim in Thebes that cowardice perches like sparrows on the walls of Tjemy." Then he turned to the walls again:

"I thought Montu was the god of Armant and the god of Thebes! Have you abandoned the god of war for a cackling goose? This Hidden god of Thebes has hidden your courage!"

When none replied he divided his troops. Southward again he sent them, with Idy and Minnefer. By foot and by boat they went, seeking villages and farms, estates and camps. For two days they scoured the western shore of the river, north and south, the muddy fields and the sandy hills. None came out to fight them.

So they crossed the river and went to the north, to that place where one Imby had built his tomb. A camp had been made there not long ago. Warm ash from campfires still lay in little pits, and the tracks of men and donkeys were still fresh. The camp-men had come from the north, but they were gone now, headed south, and, on the river, Ankhtifi's fleet followed while scouts marked the trail of footprints and hoof prints.

They led to the plain of Sega.

Here stood a small fort the height of four men, its merlons biting the sky like teeth. The bricks were new, forming plumb-straight faces violated only on the northern side, by a single doorway. Acaciawood planks, hewn smooth and joined tight, fit between thick jambs no battering ram had ever rattled. With a noise like thunder, that door was now barred shut from within.

Ankhtifi stared at the wood and the brick. Not so much as a hair of a soldier, not the tip of an arrow, peered down over the walls at them.

"I am Ankhtifi the Brave! Who among you will challenge me?"

No one answered.

"Who will come out to fight me and my trustworthy troops?"

No one answered.

Ankhtifi brought forward those who had axes and they beat at the door, but it was so well-barred that they could not break it.

No one answered.

So began the siege.

Ankhtifi's troops camped outside the walls, beyond bow-shot, beyond the range of a slingstone. Evening came and their campfires burned, and they could smell the fire and see the smoke rise from behind the walls of Sega.

As he stood on a rise and surveyed the little plain and the fortress he thought he saw the falcon. Perfume carried on the night air and there was something in the dark.

"My lord?"

A great cackle, an enormous flap of wings—

"My lord?"

A goose flew up from the river, near enough that its wing brushed the top of Ankhtifi's head as he threw himself to the ground.

He whispered, "My lord?"

No one answered.

He went back to his campfire and lay on his side, even as he imagined the King, lying on a golden bed in the Residence, sleepless through the night.

For ten days they camped at Sega, and for ten days they heard men behind the walls, smelled bread at the cook-fires, saw the smoke rise after dark, and heard the cackle of a goose. On third evenings Ankhtifi left *khenmet*-loaves and a foreleg, the latter wrapped in linen against the flies. Although the falcon never spoke to Ankhtifi at Sega, each of those mornings these were gone, only stained linen wrappings strewn about the ground.

Each morning the men of Edfu, and each afternoon the men of Nekhen, scaled the walls, one atop another's back because they had no ladder, and each time they were repelled by Antef's men, though none ever could claim to have seen their weapons or their faces.

Idy said, "So much do they fear you that they dare not show even their noses!"

Three times Ankhtifi walked around the walls, seeing only his own shadow cast upon the bricks. West, south, east, north, there upon each face stood Ankhtifi's shadow.

His shadow was so strong that it cast itself upon all of Sega! Did those within the wall not realize this? Or perhaps they did, and were seized with the terror of it.

"Bring out your goose and wring its neck before me!" Ankhtifi cried before the door of Sega, raising his ax as his shadow did likewise. "Do honor to Horus and to your King! Come out! Wring its neck! Roast it! We will feast together and then decide who will fight Ankhtifi the Brave!"

A goose cackled. Like laughter. Noise from the throat that would not be strangled. *Negeg-negeg-negeg*.

The troops of Nekhen and Edfu began to array themselves around the fort of Sega, drawn closer by Ankhtifi's agitation. He directed them to bring the boats spars and rigging, which they fashioned into ladders that could be quickly climbed by two men abreast. Ahead of his troops, Ankhtifi would ascend one and, at his signal, the soldiers would scale the rest. They would clear the wall, they would defeat Antef's men, and Ankhtifi himself would strangle the goose and offer it to the falcon with two *khenmet*-loaves.

Idy climbed the rungs beside his father but Ankhtifi proceeded to the top alone. "They fear you," Idy cried from below, echoed by the troops waiting at their ladders. They will drop dead the moment your face appears at the height of their wall!"

Ankhtifi looked over the wall of Sega.

And he slid down again, throwing his troops into confusion and chaos.

"Go!" he yelled to his men. "To the east and to the west, apart from Sega, find those who will fight you! Find them, find them and know that if they do not come out, if they will not fight you, it is through fear. It is not because they are obeying their hidden god! They cannot hide our victory.

His trustworthy troops did as he commanded. Like flies they swarmed the district, challenging at every village, at every estate, at every fortification, but no one answered.

And when they gathered again at Sega, before they went home Ankhtifi reaffirmed that it was fear that kept the Thebans behind their walls, because Ankhtifi was a man whose like had never been known before and would never be known again, not for this million of years.

"You have never said, my lord, my father," says Idy, "what you saw beyond the walls of Sega."

No, he never has. Ankhtifi does not deny it. He wonders if, like the name of Khuu, like the name of the Overseer of Armant, it is something he cannot remember but in this peculiar way because the falcon has made it so. He replies, "I saw the birthplace of languish, the cause of lack, the wellspring of privation."

Hiddenness, like a god who cannot be seen, unrevealable but for the goose that Ankhtifi saw and wished to strangle, laughing from a green field of barley and lentils and lettuce, *negeg-negeg-negeg*.

When the falcon was not speaking of Antef of Thebes, and he often was not, or of the wonders of the God's-Land, or of how he wished that all his court was as efficient and insightful and brave and trustworthy as Ankhtifi, he spoke of his pygmy from the Horizon-Dwellers. The gods delighted in his dance above all else, the falcon said. Nothing on the earth pleased them nearly so much, and indeed, the falcon himself had loved nothing better. "Not Ipuit, Wedjebten, not even Neith, favorite of my wives. Not even my dear mother or my brother.

"My fiftieth year of kingship came, and I was as an old man, but not as a man who had sat upon the throne for so long. Feebleness was itself weak in my limbs. The pygmy from beyond Yam had taught me what to eat and how to pray and how to sleep and what spells to recite in what hours of the day on what days of the year. *I might live forever,* I thought. One day the pygmy came to me and asked if he might return home to the Horizon-Dwellers. 'Soon,' I promised, for he had served me well, though thought of his departure filled me with unutterable sadness, such was the depth of my love. Then the royal barber found a white hair growing among the black that he so carefully shaved from my head. I had him let it grow and then pluck it when it was the length of one finger. I showed this white hair to my pygmy. 'No man may live forever,' he said, 'not even the King. From clay our bodies are fashioned, to clay they all decay.' When he saw that this did not please me, he said, 'But because I love you, and because you love me, I will teach you how to live again on the earth, after your *ba* has flown from your body.' Over the next ten years he taught me these spells, and I learned them.

"When I had proven to him and to myself that I had learned them beyond forgetfulness, he came to me and again begged to return home to the Horizon-Dwellers. I was loathe to let him go. He had for so long been my friend and my confidant and my teacher! I wished to share eternity with him. His wisdom was boundless; I wished to know all he could teach me. His dances pleased the gods, they pleased me, and I wished that they would do so forever. He told me, wagging one finger, 'I am going to call upon a god. The god will teach you a lesson, a lesson that I myself cannot teach you. Which lesson the god teaches will depend entirely upon which lesson you learn.'

"One night of my eighty-seventh year of kingship, he took me into the desert. He pointed to the sky, and I saw this god of his, a pale streak in the sky. I had seen such things before and shrugged. The pygmy said, 'That is my god. Will you let me return home to the Horizon-Dwellers?' My heart could not bear to let him go. For eighty-five of my years he had been beside me. He was like my shadow; what would I do without him?

"The month and the days passed, and the pale streak remained in the sky, growing brighter, until one night it was enormous, brighter than the moon, and then the pygmy said to me, 'My god has arrived! Now I will go home.'

"And he jumped. The pygmy from beyond Yam jumped out of his skin. I saw his *ba,* or something very like his *ba,* fly so very, very high! For two days I stood there watching him, neither sitting nor eating. He landed upon the great, bright streak with such force that some of it broke away and fell beyond the western horizon. He rode it like a boat, this god of his, back to the Horizon-Dwellers.

"The earth tossed dust upon its head in bereavement. To this day, to this very day, the gods and the earth mourn the loss of my pygmy. And so do I. In the fullness of my power I learned the lesson that the god taught.

"Power is sacrifice. To gain power one must give it away in due proportion. To gain the utmost power one must be denied that most desired thing. I loved the pygmy more than I loved my own everlastingness. And in my longing for him, from the heat of the unquenchable fire within my heart, my power will last forever. And in your longing, Ankhtifi, so will yours."

And since those days the river has lain quietly in its bed, listless and bereaved. Sandbars do not submerge, but loll like hippopotami in the water. Soon one will be able to walk from east to west and back again with a dry kilt, and after that, with dry sandals. Boats sail carefully, with a pilot ever at the bow taking soundings with his pole. Ankhtifi has been a pilot for Hefat. He once thought he had found the deepest channel. Today, dying of wounds from old campaigns and of privation, he doubts.

"Ankhtifi the Brave, the hero without peer," Idy says when Ankhtifi's story has come to the deep droughts and the years of failing crops and starvation, when it is with barley in their arms and not bows that the troops of Nekhen and Edfu meet the troops of Koptos and Thebes. Inglorious, ignominious years. Suffering years. Years of languish and lack.

Through this Idy has remained as certain as ever. And so have the men, everyone of the Districts of Edfu and Nekhen, even as their children grow sickly and their pregnant wives die and their arms grow weak.

How certain are they of Ankhtifi's authority? Could there not be some doubt?

He points to written words and reads them aloud: "As for any overlord who shall be overlord in Hefat and who commits a bad deed or an evil act against this, my tomb, Hemen will refuse his sacrifices on his festival-day, Hemen will not accept any of his offerings, and his heir will not inherit from him."

He turns this finger upon the workmen, upon his son. "Do you doubt this?"

The men are dumbstruck. It is their own handiwork the god has so guarded, and if they have not thought of this before they think of this now, and tremble.

"Would any of you do such a thing ever, in a span of a million of years?"

Idy blinks. He steps away and stands apart from the others. Will he speak? Ankhtifi wonders. Idy will, he must speak out while the people are silent, on the day of fear. He must not be afraid. He must doubt. He will be the next to see the falcon and receive the King's boon. He must see what Ankhtifi has come to see, to know what Ankhtifi has come to know.

Idy replies.

"No, my lord, my father. For you are the hero who has no equal. No one like you has existed before nor will he exist ever after. You have accomplished more than your forefathers, and coming generations will never be able to equal you, not for a million years."

Ankhtifi leans on his staff, bowing his head to the truth of it. By covenant it has been so written, upon the walls and upon the columns of this tomb, and thus it is so in the world. The men whisper that he is listening to the god; Ankhtifi the Brave would never otherwise bow his head.

But, now gesturing toward the doorway with his staff, he says, "Look, the sun has set while we have stood here talking. The light dims over the hills in the west, and it is time to eat, soon time to sleep. Go home. I would be alone in my house of eternity."

They leave, without question, even the spearmen who would sooner see their sons die and lie unburied than allow any harm to Ankhtifi. Idy looks back before he has passed over the threshold, which Sasobek sweeps clean of wind-borne dust, but he does not linger. They know that Ankhtifi speaks with the god. They love Ankhtifi. They fear him. Neither they nor their children, born and to be born, will ever do anything against him, disobey, violate.

Ankhtifi the Brave is alone. The falcon has not yet returned this evening for the two *khenmet*-loaves and the foreleg. The King, still wakeful, paces the Residence, perhaps, or receives tribute from men of far-off lands. He yet counts the oil jars in the great storehouses of Neni-Nesut, makes love to a queen he does not love so much as his pygmy.

Whatsoever else he does, the King does not raise the river, and never will.

Ankhtifi raises his hands toward the ceiling, as if he might reach out through its stones to heaven. He raps the ceiling with his staff. "All I asked from you was this one thing, O King! O lord! O god! Do not deny me what I most desire." His staff clatters to the floor. He clutches at his own image on the pillar and presses his cheek upon it. "I do not want your authority. What has it given me? Might my own tears raise the river? Must I myself lay new mud upon the fields?"

Ankhtifi's fingers trace the hieroglyphic script upon the pillar. He is He-Who-Shall-Live, the brave, the hero, whose equal cannot exist. These are the King's own words, uttered with the King's own authority. These are the god's own boon.

Into the shadows he whispers, "What you have given to me, O lord, I now give to you in kind."

He turns from the pillar. It is cool, and he presses the carved signs into his back. They scratch his skin as he squats.

His bowels move. He is an old man. He is dying.

It is dark and soft like Nile mud. It reeks.

And, leaning heavily on his staff, his back bent, with the two *khenmet*-loaves and the foreleg of a calf burdening his arms, Ankhtifi walks toward the west, home to share one last meal with Idy.

The emergence of a writing system dramatically alters the record of human activity. Not only does it preserve more detail, such as names and activities that might otherwise leave no trace in the archaeological record, but those details are skewed to the interests of those for whom the accounts are kept. This has meant that, unlike the prehistoric period when men and women equally laid their traces (although archaeologists have not always paid them equal attention), historical records are overwhelmingly biased toward the activities of men. Literary glimpses of Bronze-Age women are usually veiled by the male point of view, whether of their contemporaries or of much later authors. One such author was the Roman poet Vergil, whose epic Aeneid *(composed for none other than Augustus Caesar) follows the Trojan hero Aeneas to the shores of Italy. There he wins the daughter of the Latian king and ultimately founds the Roman people. Katharine Kerr and Debra Doyle lift the veil to take another look at the story of fair Lawinia, daughter of Latinus, heir to Latium.*

The God Voice

On her hands and knees the old woman scrubs the wood floor of the shrine. She dips her wad of linen rags into the leather bucket of water, then scours each plank in turn. Her back aches, her calloused knees burn with pain, but if she omitted this daily ritual, her dreams would torment her with work left undone. Sunlight streams in through the western window and falls across her back, the touch of the god Dian, easing her pain.

"I'm gray and wrinkled and twisted in the bone," Watis says aloud, "but you love me still."

In this warmth she can finish her task. Getting to her feet presents a challenge, but by clinging to the windowsill she manages to haul herself up. She sets the bucket and the rags outside for her slave—a woman nearly as old and bent as she is—to take away, then pauses to look over her work. In the sunset light the oak planks, polished daily for over forty years, gleam like the pure yellow sun-gold of Witelli. On her bare feet the wood feels smooth and cool, scoured down to a surface as sleek as metal. She turns in a way that mimics Dian's path across the sky, first east, then south, then west, and back, finally, to the north.

Across the little shrine stands a block of gray stone, and behind it on wooden shelves sit the offerings that suppliants have given the god: a beaten silver bowl, a bronze dagger with a blade shaped like a bay leaf, a tripod of bronze and a bronze cauldron to go with it, and a bulbous ingot of pure tin, brought all the way from the edge of the world by a dark-haired trader from the land of Hatti.

The strangest gift of all hangs nailed to a side wall. Sea-bird feathers, stuck with wax, cover leather straps and thin strips of wood to form two huge wings, big enough to support a man in the air—or so they seemed to have done. She did see a man glide from the sky and stagger, dragging his wings, down the hillside one bright morning, a half-crazed fellow whose outpouring of speech she found incomprehensible. He wept and moaned, then with a stick drew pictures in the dirt; a huge bull, a man with a bull's head, a boy falling from the sky as his wax wings shed feathers like tears. At last she decided that he had given either the bull or the boy or both to Dian as a sacrifice. In return she fed him and blessed him when he left, still babbling in his strange tongue.

Other suppliants have brought other gifts, but those she bartered to build this shrine, to get a slave, to feed them both in the lean winters. The god never begrudged her the use of his gifts. If he had, Dian Farseer would have slain her and the slave both with his black arrows; Watis is sure of that. But just as Dian pours his golden light freely upon the earth, to her, his priestess and his voice, he has given gold and amber to trade as she needed, and his sister Diana has never begrudged her silver as well. The sun and the moon, the holy twins, their wishes and their supplicants—these have been her entire life. Once she had another name, but the years have scoured it away. As she stands in the doorway to the shrine, the only name she knows is Watis, the seer, the god voice.

When she turns to leave the shrine, the pain in her back stabs her and steals her breath. For a moment she clings to the rough wood of the doorway and gasps. It's time for me to die. That thought has become familiar over the past few months. Whenever her back twists and sags, whenever she cannot breathe from the pain of a back breaking under its own frail weight, the thought comes to her, and she longs for death, for rest deep in the earth. Yet she cannot die and will not die until she has found another woman capable of taking up the god's work.

"It will be soon." The words pour from her own mouth, but they are in the god's voice, deep and hollow. Her body trembles, and she feels sweat trickle down her back and between her breasts. "She will come soon. Her feet are upon my road."

When the god leaves her, Watis staggers outside, calling for the slave. The shrine perches on a ledge halfway up a mountain, overlooking the sea. Above it, steps cut in rock lead to the mouth of a cave. From the ledge she can see down to a village, thatched houses the size of fists from her distance. Two fishing boats, draped in drying nets, stand on the narrow pale beach. The old slave is climbing the twisted path; she puffs and gasps, but she carries only a basket, balanced on one hip. Over the years, she too has lost her name and become merely the slave woman.

"Fish," Serwa gasps. "For dinner."

"Good. They'll make a nice change from barley porridge."

Serwa nods and smiles. Together they turn away from the sea and follow the narrow path that leads past the shrine and down. Already evening's shadows have filled the grassy valley where they have a little square house, shaded by olive trees. Past their cottage lie the fields, all green with tall wheat and barley, that belong to the farmers in the village beyond. Fishers and farmers make up the twin villages of Cumae.

"The god spoke to me today," Watis says. "He's promised me a successor. When she comes, you'll be free."

"And where will I go?" Serwa turns to her, and her voice rises in panic. "They took me so long ago, the raiders! Do you think anyone on the island will remember me, even if I could get back there?"

"No, they probably won't. Stay here, then. I'll tell the new priestess to find a young slave to wait on both of you."

As she speaks, Watis feels a comfortable warmth like remembered sunlight. Soon the new voice will come. She's sure of it. The god, after all, told her so.

Whether or not Dian has sent her, a young woman does appear some days later. The god hangs low in the sunset sky when Watis leaves the house to climb to the shrine to scrub the floor. Leaning on a stout stick, she clambers up the path; every now and then she stops to rest. Just as she reaches the ledge where the shrine perches, she realizes that someone sits sprawled all in a heap by its door—a woman, her long brown hair a tousled mess, her tunic filthy and torn, her face streaked with dirt and old tears. At the sight of Watis hobbling toward her, the woman hauls herself up to a kneel. She looks familiar, Watis realizes, though she cannot find her name in her memory.

"Sanctuary," the woman gasps. "I beg you, please, please help me." Her voice too strikes a familiar note.

"What's so wrong, child?"

"They say I murdered my husband, but I never did. They won't listen. They're right behind me on the road. The gods—our gods, the true gods—hid and helped me, Grandfather Faunus the most, but Dian and Diana came to my aid as well. The men rode right past me. I stood at the forest edge and watched them clatter by without a glance in my direction. Dian must have blinded them with his light. How else could such a thing happen?"

"Slowly, slowly, hush! Who are 'they'? When did—"

"You don't remember me." The young woman's eyes fill with tears. "You don't remember."

"I'm very old, child. I forget everything but those things I need to serve the god." Yet a memory is stirring in her mind, like the flicker of sunlight on a stream. "Wait. You were brought to me as a child for the omens."

"Yes, by my father, Latinus."

"Lawinia! Forgive me, child. So many people have come here since."

"Of course. I should have thought of that. I'm sorry."

"Now, what's this about your husband? I've had news of the wars, and I know that the men from Wilion conquered Latium. Aeneas himself came here, you see, before he reached you. The god told me that he was fated to take your lands."

"And so he did, and me with them." Lawinia sits back on her heels. "My mother hanged herself. The war drove her to it. Did you know—"

"That I'd not heard, no. What a sad, sad thing!"

Lawinia nods, staring down at the rocky ledge in front of her. "It's all been horrible," she whispers. "I never wanted to marry Turnus, but I didn't want to see him dead. I never wanted Aeneas, either, but I didn't murder him, I swear it!"

"Who thinks you did?"

"His son, of course. Askanios."

"He was always devoted to his father, and his father to him."

"Oh, I'm sure of that! You won't let them take me, will you?" Lawinia's upturned face runs with tears. "Please, please, don't let them take me."

"That's not my decision, child. It's up to the god."

"But—"

"Don't argue! If the god decides you're a murderer, and I lied to save you, then he'd leave me and never speak through me again. I absolutely must tell the truth. Do you understand?"

Lawinia's words dissolve into one long sob. She tips her head back further and stares up at the gleaming dome of the sky. "Yes, of course," she says at last. "I'll accept whatever the god decides."

"Good. Now get up. I hear horses coming."

They walk to the head of the seaward path. Far below, horsemen are heading their way on the hard damp sand at the edge of the foaming water. Two young men ride in front, their purple boots dangling under their horses' sleek bellies. Directly after comes a man driving a two-horse chariot, a young man with slicked-back dark hair. Over a fine white tunic he wears a purple cloak carelessly slung from one shoulder. Four more horsemen, one leading a laden pack horse, ride after him. All of them carry long swords in sheaths slung from baldrics across their chests. The charioteer has a pair of spears as well, standing upright next to him in the vehicle. The bronze buckles and chapes, the bronze spear points, all glitter in the sunlight. Lawinia sobs once.

"There they are, then," Watis says.

Lawinia nods, staring down at the beach. The horsemen are coming to a stop and dismounting. The man with the purple cloak steps out of the chariot and tosses the reins to one of his men. He lays a hand on the hilt of his sword and looks up the path toward the two women.

"We'll receive them in the shrine," Watis says. "Come along."

When they go inside they leave the door open. Watis stands in front of the altar. Lawinia sits at her feet. Together they listen to the sound of footsteps trudging up the hill.

"Holy one! Servant of Dian!" The man's voice bristles with anger. "Are you in there?"

"Come in and see," Watis calls back. "But watch your words in the god's house."

Flipping back his purple cloak, the young man strides in, and two of his men follow. Askanios. She remembers him as a child on the edge of manhood. Now stubble darkens his chin, and he stands tall.

"Give me that woman," Askanios says. "She's a murderess."

"Oh?" Watis crosses her arms over her chest. "She says otherwise."

Askanios lays a hand on his sword hilt and takes one step forward, but at that moment the sunlight reaches the west-facing window. Like a spear a long gleam falls across his eyes and blinds him. Blinking he turns sharply away. One of his men, a solid-looking fellow with gray in his hair, catches his arm and whispers urgently in their peculiar language.

"My apologies, Holy One," Askanios says. "I forgot myself."

"I'm glad you remember yourself now. Now. You say this woman murdered your father. She denies it. She tells me that she'll abide by the god's decision in the matter. Will you?"

"Yes, I will. If the god tells us that she killed my father, will you give her to me?"

Lawinia sobs once.

"Yes," Watis says. "If the god tells me. Not if you tell me, mind. Come with me into the cave. We'll see if Great Dian will speak to us."

The mouth of the cave is a narrow opening in the mountain above the shrine. "Go up," Watis says to Lawinia. "The rest of us will follow." Then, to Askanios, "The caves are dark. If you want light, you must bring it with you."

If Askanios takes any deeper meaning from the words, he gives no sign. "Light a torch," he says to one of his men, and it is done. The flame is pale against the daylight, but when the little procession—Lawinia, Watis, Askanios and his torchbearer, and a straggling tail of armed men—passes into the depths beyond the mouth of the cave, the smoky orange glow pushes back the darkness ahead of them.

The cramped entryway widens out into a large open area—the god's grotto, where his voice speaks truth through his servant to those who come willing to hear. The air is cool, freshened day and night by the breezes that issue, like the breath from a hundred mouths, out of the cracks and channels and narrow passageways that lead from the grotto to the world outside.

Watis seats herself on the tall chair where she will wait for the coming of the god. "Speak," she says to Askanios. "The god will listen."

"I always knew that the woman Lawinia held some grievance against my father," Askanios says. He speaks formally and in measured words, as men will speak before their gods. "I saw it in her face and heard it in her voice, though she never spoke it. What grudge she could possibly hold against the husband who had saved her from marriage to Turnus—a man whose very allies thought him a brute and a danger!—and made her part of his own high destiny, I cannot say, but a grudge there was, and it broke forth at last in anger. I was not there to hear it, but the women of the household say that she and my father quarreled over the morning meal, and that my stepmother ran from the house alone. My father went after her; and I, a newcomer to their troubles, followed too late and too far behind.

"I saw her standing on the high cliff above the sandy beach, with her hands upraised and her hair unbound, and I heard her voice rise and fall as she called out to the wind. My father was on the narrow path below, toiling upward to reach her—and when my stepmother's chant ended he fell as if struck by a javelin, toppling down from the path to his death below. He was a good man, faithful to his gods and to his duty, and this woman has worked his ending by witchcraft."

Watis does not like Askanios—he is arrogant, and he lacks the respect that should be paid to one through whom the god speaks—but she hears the faint hoarseness in his voice that tells of grief, and the god whispers to her that he has told his part of the story honestly.

"Well," she says to Lawinia, who is pale and set-faced now, and no longer crying at all. "You've heard what the son of Aeneas has to say. Now let the god hear your side of it."

Lawinia faces Askanios to look him over with narrow eyes. Askanios looks back at her with lips shut hard, and his hand never leaves the hilt of his sword.

"My life has been nothing but a length of thread spun by the Fates to hold omens like beads," Lawinia begins. "My husband complained constantly of the Fates. They had driven him over the seas, he told me, and goaded him with plague and shipwreck. They had stripped him of everything he had ever loved, all for some destiny that he would not live to see. Never once did he think that I too might have a destiny, because he saw me only as the gods' assurance that he had finally accomplished his own. I knew better."

Askanios steps forward, his lips parted, but Watis raises a hand. "Be silent and listen to her," she says. "The god will decide when he's heard enough."

"Very well." Askanios steps back with a bob of his head. "Never would I cross the god's wishes."

Watis turns to the girl. "No one will interrupt you again."

And so Lawinia speaks:

I will tell you how I first heard the Fates speak to me. They came not in a dream or vision. They spoke in a borrowed voice, but I heard the message between and behind the words, even though the speaker was full of malice.

I was still a child. We lived then in the compound of the Woodpecker clan, which stood on a low hill, a mere swelling in the earth like a breast, not far from the banks of Father Tiber. Our house sprawled at the crest of the hill, because my father, Latinus, was clan chief. On a hot summer's day my mother, Amata, and her two slave women had taken their spinning out to the courtyard. In the shade of an olive tree they perched on high stools, their laps full of carded wool which they fed to the drop spindles a bit at a time. Our house bounded the court on three sides, but the fourth lay open; I was sitting on the ground nearby and playing with my wooden doll when I heard horses coming.

I looked up to see a man and a boy, or so I thought them, leading their mounts into the court. Another look, and I saw that the boy was no boy at all, but a girl, wearing a short tunic and high-laced leather sandals. Her short black hair clustered in loose curls like a cap of hyacinth blossoms, and her skin was sun-brown as new-baked bread. This was Camilla as I first saw her, her own childhood not far behind her and her name not yet known outside the circle of her kin.

"Now what's this?" Mother said. With a flip of her wrist she brought the spindle back to her lap and laid it on the mat of wool. "Metabus?"

The man frowned. I could tell he didn't like it that my mother was the first to speak. "Where is your husband? I need to talk with him."

"Very well." Mother glanced at Favva.

The slave woman stood down from her stool and laid the wool and spindle upon it, then hurried into the house. My mother and Metabus waited, saying nothing, she with her hands folded and Metabus scowling and pacing. Camilla looked bored, and I saw that she had moved closer to where I sat.

I stole another look at her short tunic. "Why are you dressed like that?"

Mother started to hush me, but Camilla only smiled. "I'm dressed like this because I belong to the goddess Diana. She hunts in the forest, and so do I."

I had never heard of anyone belonging to a god before, and it fascinated me. "You belong to her? Like a slave?"

"Yes. My father gave me to her." The thought didn't seem to bother Camilla very much. "But because I'm her slave, I'm really free. I never have to get married and worry about babies and things like that."

"That's splendid!" I said. But I was still curious. "Were you in the marketplace? Did she barter for you?"

Metabus had kept an ear open despite his scowling, and my question made him laugh, showing strong teeth like an animal's in the black of his beard. "The gods don't stoop to haggling over eggs and lettuces, girl. I was pursued by enemies, and my infant Camilla with me—she could have fit into a market basket, that much is true enough—when we came hard up against a river too fast and deep for a man to wade across. There was nothing left to do but ask the gods for help, and since we were in Diana's forest, it was she I asked, saying that if she would only keep us both safe she could have my daughter for a servant ever after."

Camilla took up the tale; her eyes were dancing, and I could tell that she'd heard the story many times before. "He unbelted his tunic," she said, "and used the belt to tie me to his spear, and threw the spear across the river. That was no easy cast, with the spear so weighted and out of balance, but the goddess guided and strengthened his arm. The spearhead lodged in the dirt of the riverbank and I hung there, howling, until he swam across to take me down. Since then I honor his promise, and serve Diana out of gratitude."

Nothing that exciting had ever happened in the compound of the Woodpecker clan. I thought for a moment and asked, "When I get big can I worship Diana?"

Metabus was laughing again, even though my mother's face had knotted in disapproval. I think it amused him that his daughter's story had put Amata out of pleasure with me. "Maybe you can," he said to me. "I wouldn't know. Or maybe you'll serve some other god, her twin brother, maybe."

My mother had heard enough. She slid down from her stool and grabbed my arm so tightly that it hurt and gave me a shake. "Winni, go into the house! Tell Favva to bring some cups and a pitcher of water to offer our guests."

I trotted off, rubbing my arm, but at the doorway I looked back. My mother was shaking her finger in Metabus's face and talking fast and angrily. Metabus, however, was still laughing. That he would dare laugh at the wife of a headman just as if she were a foolish child stunned me—but Camilla's little smile as she watched them shocked me even more. When I saw it, I truly understood that yes, as she'd told me, she was free.

I want to be free, too. The thought came to me like a traitor's whisper, and I ran into the house.

I don't remember what Metabus came to ask my father about that day, except that it had to do with one of the feuds in which Metabus, with his violent nature, often found himself embroiled. What I do remember clearly, even across the gap of years, is how beautiful and strong all of my family looked when they stood together in the sunlight by the olive tree. My father had already gone heavily gray—my mother, much his junior, was his second wife—but still he stood tall and straight, and to me he was the handsomest man in Latium. Even my brothers, young and vigorous as they were, yielded pride of place to him in my mind. As for my mother, I had always thought that she was the most beautiful woman in the world, young and slender, always laughing, her pale brown hair pulled back carelessly with a pair of bone combs. My father's thinning hair was the color of silver, and his face was marked by thoughtful lines, but I remember him as happy then, when my brothers were still alive.

Yet before three winters had come and gone, everything changed. My younger brother caught a fever and died. My elder brother, my father's heir, drowned as he swam in the river. Although my father prayed, and my mother worked charms, and both made sacrifice after sacrifice to the gods, she never conceived again. I felt each winter passing without a new heir as a chain, binding me around. I was afraid that I'd never be allowed to serve a god or goddess if I were the only living child of Latinus.

The second of the omens that were to rule my life came here, in Cumae cave. I was on the threshold between child and woman when my father and mother came to ask the god voice what should be done if my mother could not conceive another heir. Almost, they left me behind—but my father said, "She is Latium, if there is no one else," and so I traveled with them.

I remember the heat of the summer day and the flat pale blue of the sky. The sweat ran down the back of my neck and in between my breasts, and the bright sun blinded me and made my head ache. The cool air inside the cave felt pleasant against my skin and the darkness soothed my burning eyes, and I thought how kind it was of the god to shelter his voice from the full strength of his power in the heat of the day.

We waited together in a circle of torchlight, my mother and father, the god's voice, and I, and Latinus spoke. "Great Dian," he said, "no man lives forever, and I grow old. Once I had two sons, either one well-suited to take my place as chief of the Woodpecker clan, but the Fates saw fit to take them before me, and only a daughter remains. I ask now for some omen or word of guidance. Show me, great Dian, what I should do—for the sake of my family, and for the people of Latium who look to us for help and safety."

My father finished speaking, and there was silence. Even the air inside the cave, which had flowed about us like the cool breath of the mountain, drying my sweat and making the flame of the torch bend and waver, ceased moving and grew still. The pause lengthened and tightened like wool turning into thread on a spindle, and still nobody moved or spoke, only waited on the coming of the god.

He came in a great outrushing of air from all the hundred mouths of the grotto, a roaring blast that whipped my hair loose from its bindings and extinguished the torch altogether. For an instant we stood in total darkness. Then the fire came, and I was enveloped in blue-white flames that licked and played around my body but did not burn. I held up my arms, and the blue fire ran down them like water, and Latinus and Amata gazed at me wide-eyed in its light.

It seemed forever that I stood there wrapped in the god's fire, but it can only have been for the space of a few heartbeats. Darkness came again, and the wind stopped, and I fell half-fainting to the cavern floor.

"The god has spoken," the seer told my father. "You have your answer."

It settled nothing, of course. The gods give us omens, but men—and women—interpret them. My mother and father argued with each other all the rest of that summer and into the winter of the year about what the god had intended. On one thing only were they agreed: when I dared to voice my own belief, or perhaps hope, that Dian Farseer had marked me for his servant, my words found no hearing with either Latinus or Amata.

"You are all that is left of the family in your generation," my father said. "For the sake of the whole clan, you must marry, and to the right husband."

"To a strong husband," my mother said, and they began the argument anew as though I had never spoken. I gave up my thoughts of entering the god's service and resigned myself to marriage. I could only pray that I would find the man pleasing—or at least, pleasing enough.

I had no lack of suitors. More than one man found the thought of ruling Latium through me desirable. But my father cared for none of them, dismissing one man as too weak and another as too prone, like Metabus, to feuds and quarrels, and yet a third as unkind to his horse, until I began to think that no one could please him. My mother, on the other hand, cared for only one of my prospective husbands; from the beginning, with her, it was Turnus.

I never completely understood why she was so intent on the marriage—they were distant kin and much of an age, but the same could have been said of half my suitors. She told me that they had played together as toddlers, and perhaps that had some influence. When I once said, in a fit of impatience, that if she loved Turnus so much she could marry him herself, she grew red and slapped me in the face.

Still my father fretted and delayed, while I grew older and left childhood behind completely. "She's ripe for marriage," Turnus said to my mother one day. "Latinus will have to see it now."

"I'll speak to him again," Amata said. "He's put off making a decision for long enough."

She never had the chance. The third of my life's omens came that night, when Latinus had a dream. He told us all about it in the morning—Grandfather Faunus had spoken to him, he said, and had advised him that I should not marry Turnus or any other man from Latium, but should take a foreigner for a husband.

Turnus left our house in anger, and my mother sulked for a week. For my part, I was grateful to Grandfather Faunus. Foreigners were rare, and it stood to reason that foreigners in search of wives must be rarer still.

Then Aeneas came, and the men from Wilion with him.

Not for a long time did I understand why Grandfather Faunus spoke to my father as he did. The men from Wilion had a destiny, they said, a command from their gods to make a new homeland in this place where our people were already living, and they were men hardened by long years of wandering. If we could not drive them away by force, perhaps it was better to draw them in. Aeneas would rule Latium through me, and through me the line of Latinus would continue.

Such, at least, my father must have hoped. My mother saw things otherwise, and who can say, now, that she was not right all along? Because it came in the end to war despite his efforts, and the destruction of the world of my childhood—even Camilla, whose service to Diana should have kept her away from such things, died on a battlefield before it was done. But you know all this, and what matters is that the men from Wilion prevailed. Aeneas killed Turnus, and my mother hanged herself in rage and shame, and I was dragged forth from hiding to marry the foreign invader, whether I wanted him or not.

I had not wanted Aeneas, any more than I had wanted Turnus or any of the other, lesser men whom my father had sent away, but I found marriage to him less of a burden than I had feared. He was kind, and he saw to it that the men from Wilion treated me with respect and honor, as the one through whom the rule of Latium had come into his hands. His son Askanios did not like me—Aeneas's first wife had died when Wilion fell, and, since Askanios could not truly remember her, he had made her perfect in his mind, and a stepmother could never equal perfection—but the young man's love for his father was strong enough that he was respectful to me for Aeneas's sake.

At first, when my husband did not come to me in the marriage-bed, I thought it was yet another of his acts of kindness—for he could be kind, when thoughts of the Fates and his destiny were not oppressing him. The brutal war, and the sudden unexpected horror of my mother's death, had left me easily frightened and prone to nightmares. For a long time, I do not think I could have made myself lie quiet and accepting underneath any man, let alone the killer of Turnus—whom my mother had, perhaps, loved as more than just an old playmate and distant kin. It was good of my husband, or so I thought, to give me the time I needed in which to heal.

The healing came slowly, but it came. I do not think I would ever have come to enjoy lying with a man, but with Aeneas, who was always gentle to me, I could have learned to tolerate it, and perhaps to give him pleasure even if I found none. And in time there would have been children, which I had begun to want a great deal. Children of Aeneas, out of my body, would carry out my father's old hopes for Latium, and at the same time would bring my own life full circle, creating anew the family grouping of my early childhood.

The Fates who had so beset Aeneas must have found me amusing as well: now that I was, finally, ready for my husband, it seemed that my husband was not ready for me. I waited patiently, supposing that his difficult life had left him with ghosts and nightmares of his own, but the months went past and still he did not approach me. I decided at last that patient waiting had failed, and that—since I lacked the talent and the knowledge for seduction—nothing was left but to ask outright.

I waited until a morning when Askanios was away, and Aeneas and I, except for the servants, were alone. We had taken our morning meal in the courtyard, in the shade of the olive tree, and had talked of everyday matters, the summer weather and the health of the crops and whether the household would need to trade for anything before winter came. When he finished the last of the bread and rose to go, I stopped him.

"Husband," I said. "There is another thing."

His brows drew together in a worried frown. "Is there trouble again with the clans?" He had come to rely on me, since we were married, to keep him informed about their shifting feuds and alliances. No man not born to Latium could keep them unentangled in his mind.

"No," I said. "This concerns the two of us alone." I took a deep breath, and knotted my hands together in my lap. "Aeneas, when will you give me a child?"

He became very still, as a man does who spies an adder coiled beneath his descending foot. "Lawinia," he said. "I thought that you understood."

The day was hot and bright, but I felt suddenly cold. "What was it that I was supposed to understand?"

"This marriage," he said. "How it would have to be."

"No. I don't understand." I began to feel a new emotion stirring in me, one that I was unaccustomed to feeling—the deep, bitter anger that comes from loving and from being betrayed. "Explain it to me."

Say whatever else you want about Aeneas the son of Anchises, but he was a man honest enough to speak the full truth when it was demanded of him, even though he knew the telling would destroy whatever harmony had grown up between us.

"Everything I have done," he said, "from the burning of Wilion until this moment, I have done because the gods desired it and commanded me. They intended this homeland in Latium to be for Askanios and his progeny; I will not go against their will by giving him younger brothers whose claim through you is greater than his own."

That was the start of our quarrel, and the sum of it, though it lasted longer and grew worse. In the end I left him, running from the house in the wildness of my anger, not caring who if anyone might follow. I took the winding path to the cliff above the ocean. There, in the solitude of the high place, I unbound my hair and lifted up my hands to pray to the god who had marked me once in the cave at Cumae.

"Great Dian," I said, "if it is your will that I am to be neither your priestess nor any man's true wife, then help me at least to bear the pain. Love for Aeneas sits in my heart like a stone, and does me no good; end it, Great Dian, I beg of you, take it away from me so that at least I will not care."

Thus I prayed, even while Aeneas was climbing up the path from the beach below—whether he intended to comfort me or to chastize me, or whether he feared that, like my mother, I might do myself an injury out of despair, I cannot say—and as I prayed, Great Dian reached out with dazzling light and blinded him for an instant so that he slipped and fell.

That is what Askanios, following after, saw. Not witchcraft, but the hand of the god, struck down Aeneas and sent him to his death.

She finishes speaking and lifts her head to stare at Watis. Torchlight gilds her face. The young chief and his retinue are watching the elderly seer, but none of them speak, not even Askanios.

"Do I lie?" Lawinia said. "I submit myself to the judgment of the god."

And the god comes to judge her. Watis feels the icy touch of his hands along her face and neck. She begins to tremble; she tosses her head back and pants for breath as the power takes her. Her head snaps forward, but its seems that she is seeing them all from a great height. The girl crouches at her feet, the men step back, jostling each other in fear. Her mouth opens at another's will, and another's voice speaks.

"She is mine. Will any mortal man harm her? She will serve me. Will any mortal man prevent her? She will speak for me. Will any mortal man silence her?"

Watis gasps for breath. The power slides from her like a wet dress, leaving her shivering. Her hands clasp each other like claws, then release. She is seeing them all from the height of her chair and nothing more. The girl sighs once in sharp relief. The blood has drained from Askanios's face. He crosses his arms over his chest and tucks his trembling hands into his armpits, perhaps to hide their involuntary motion from his men.

"Well, Teukrianos?" Watis says. "Man from Wilion, far sailing, Aeneas-son, will you challenge the god for this girl?"

"Never!" He gulps for breath. "May she serve him well." He turns to his men. "We'll camp down on the sea coast. Let's go. We've troubled the holy one too much as it is."

To save their dignity they leave slowly, filing out of the cave with their heads held high. Watis waits until their footsteps die away, then stands and hobbles to the mouth of the cave. Lawinia follows. The men are striding down the path, heading for their horses tethered on the beach below.

"They're gone," Watis says. "Tell me the truth. The god never did say whether you lied or not."

"My story's true." Lawinia pauses, staring down at the floor. "All except the very end. In my anger, I wished Aeneas dead. That's what I prayed for. And the god gave it to me."

"I thought so. Very well."

"You won't—"

"Won't what? Berate you? Condemn you?"

"Just that."

For an answer Watis says merely, "The cave gets cold and damp once the sun sets. I need to show you your first task."

"Will the god come to me?" Lawinia looks up, her eyes wide.

"No." Watis pauses for a smile. "First you need to learn how to scrub the shrine's floor."

In the western hemisphere, the Bronze Age was confined to the Andes, including the Inka people and their neighbors. Spanish chronicles preserve the complexity of their oral history, including the troubled succession of Pachakuteq (who reigned c.A.D. 1438–1471). *The colonial writers also described the quirks of their subjects' personal lives in devastating detail. Although considered one of the greatest indigenous rulers of the Americas, Pachakuteq and his family did not escape their scrutiny, nor that of Karen Jordan Allen.*

Orqo Afloat on the Willkamayu

The icy waters of the Willkamayu closed over Orqo as he fell. He still gagged from the blow to his throat, and when the freezing current flooded his mouth and nostrils, he thought himself dead. Then rage filled him, pouring a last, desperate strength into his arms and legs. He clutched his heavy mace and lunged for the surface. Damn you, Kusi, he thought. You haven't won. Not yet.

He reached the air, coughing desperately and shuddering as the frigid water chafed his skin. Then he heard a splash beside him, and a *thunk* behind. Stones dropped into the river all around him. He gulped as much air as he could and dove under the surface. A rock glanced off his back. He kicked and kicked until his lungs were ready to burst, then lifted his face just out of the water. He looked quickly over his shoulder, searching the high riverbank for the man who so enraged him, the half-brother who stood with his army between Orqo and the *maskapaycha,* the insignia of the Inka, Qosqo's rightful ruler.

He could see figures on the bank high above, silhouetted against the stone-gray sky, but he could not say which might be Kusi. Only one was unmistakable, the tall form of Roqa, their older brother. He had slung the stone that caught Orqo in the throat. Orqo raised and shook his mace. Let Roqa see that. Let him tell Kusi, Orqo is not defeated.

A handful of stones pelted the water between him and the watchers. He turned and kicked, swimming hard, for his defiance would come to nothing if he lingered, or let the river swallow him, or went ashore too soon.

For a time his anger powered his body, and he swam as if he raced the fish. This is not right, he complained to himself as he churned through the water. *I* am the chosen heir. My father, the eighth Inka, Wiraqocha, named *me* to follow him. Why do the gods scorn the Inka's will and side with Kusi?

He paused once more to look back; he could no longer see the riverbank at Yukay, where he had fallen, nor was anyone in sight. For the moment, he could breathe. But how long would it take Kusi to follow and find him? He gazed up at the green, implacable mountains, the rocks that tumbled down their sides and spilled into the river. The gods knew every crevice and current. Was any place safe?

Orqo's feet hit rock. He put out a hand and caught himself on the suddenly shallow bottom, then stood. He cupped one shaking hand around his mouth, and with the other held his mace aloft. Its star-shaped bronze head glistened. "Speak to me!" he screamed to the mountains. "Tell me! What must I do?"

And he waited, breathless, in case the gods finally broke their silence. But the stillness swelled and grew until he felt himself sinking in a bottomless river of it.

Orqo's shoulders sagged. He pulled off his heavy, sodden tunic, which made it hard to swim, then threw himself back into the freezing water wearing only his loincloth.

So. He fought alone, or nearly so. Kusi had most of Qosqo on his side, the generals, the *pururawka-kuna*—the warrior stones—and the gods. He, Orqo, had only himself, his mother, and an aged father whose grasp on power was slipping, and whose judgment had already proved disastrous.

Father, Father, we should have stayed in Qosqo and fought the Chankas, Orqo thought. We should have defended the city with Kusi. No matter how fierce the enemy. Did you think the people would love us better for deserting them to save ourselves? Did you truly believe they would accept your peace treaty at the cost of their freedom?

No, Orqo mused bitterly, we should have fought. And if Kusi had died—heroically in battle, of course—then there would have been no question about who would succeed Inka Wiraqocha as ruler of Qosqo.

Damn you, Kusi! Orqo thought again. And then, Damn you, too, Father. Damn you, damn you.

The news from Qosqo had reached the fortress of Hakihawana in the morning, suddenly.

"Kusi is coming! With his army!" The messenger skidded into the Inka Wiraqocha's private courtyard, pulled off his sandals, and bowed hastily.

Orqo dropped his half-eaten maize cake and looked sharply at the intruder. His mother, Qori Chullpa, who leaned against her son's back as she ate, stiffened but said nothing. Orqo glanced from the panting messenger to his father, and finally to Waman Waraka, the Chanka envoy who shared their morning meal. The envoy slowly set his plate on the blanket that was spread over the ground. The evening before, he and Wiraqocha had concluded a peace treaty between the Inka people and the Chankas, providing, of course, for a great deal of tribute to go to the Chankas. But, Orqo thought, if Kusi had accomplished the unthinkable, and successfully driven the Chankas from Qosqo—

A contingent of guards dashed in, grabbed for the messenger, and shrugged in apology, but Wiraqocha stilled them with a gesture. The man bowed again, but his eyes were still wide with the enormity of his news. "The Chankas are defeated," he gasped. "A great victory. Qosqo is saved. Even the stones—"

He stopped and looked at Waman Waraka. The Chanka man's face had paled, but he stood up quietly. "I think this message is not for my ears. I will return to my apartments." His mantle flapped as he left the courtyard.

Orqo unfolded his legs and rose slowly. "The stones *what?* Go on."

Wiraqocha touched Orqo's foot and whispered to him to sit down, but Orqo straightened and folded his arms. The messenger threw himself to the ground. "The stones themselves. The *pururawka-kuna*. Kusi commanded them. They became warriors, fierce warriors, men and women, and they fell upon the Chankas like wild animals. I saw them, lords."

A dusty silence settled. Orqo felt the guards staring at him. He leveled his gaze at the nearest one until the man looked away.

"So Kusi marches from Qosqo?" Wiraqocha's voice was quiet, dangerously quiet.

"Yes, my lord."

"How far is he from here?"

"Half a day's march from Hakihawana, lord."

"Then we must prepare for his arrival." Wiraqocha held out a hand to Qori Chullpa, who helped him to his feet. He moved stiffly, but his back remained straight and proud, Orqo noted. When Kusi arrived, Wiraqocha would remind him who was Inka, still. And who was to become Inka.

"How fares Mama Runtu?" Qori Chullpa asked. "I know she stayed in Qosqo, at her son's side." Orqo looked at her. Why would she ask about Wiraqocha's official wife?

"The Qoya is well, and still at her home in Qosqo."

"Well, it is good news, is it not? Qosqo remains in our hands, and the Qoya is unharmed." Qori Chullpa's smile rebuked Wiraqocha and Orqo for not pretending, at least, to be glad for the victory. Orqo flushed. His mother poured a cup of *aqha* and handed it to the messenger, who gulped the fermented maize drink greedily. Then she gathered up the breakfast things. "I will see to the preparations for the feast," she said, and she disappeared into the shadows.

Orqo waited for his father to say something, but Wiraqocha just stared into the sky over the fortress walls. The guards shifted nervously. Finally the Inka gave them his attention. "You may go," he said. "Find this man a room where he may rest, and give him food. Then bring him to me again. I wish to question him further."

"Yes, lord."

"And send fresh messengers to watch Kusi's approach. They must watch secretly. I want to know everything."

"Yes, lord."

Wiraqocha dismissed them with a nod, and the guards and messenger departed. For the first time since the news had arrived, Wiraqocha looked at Orqo. His eyes were opaque, his expression betrayed nothing. Orqo clenched his fists. *This is not what you promised!* he wanted to shout to his father. *The Chankas are fierce, you said. Let Kusi stay and fight them if he insists, you said—the Chankas will kill him for us. We will treat for peace. Then when our neighbors have their fill of Chanka cruelty, they will come to us for aid, and you, Orqo, you will lead them to victory.*

Then, Orqo remembered, his mother—listening, as always—had whispered, *This is a dangerous plan, lord. I fostered Kusi and taught him. I know him better than any woman, better even than his own mother. He is—different.*

But Wiraqocha had remained stubborn, and the three of them had fled Qosqo for Hakihawana, where they could treat for peace in safety. Yes, safety, thought Orqo, but at the cost of what later danger?

Orqo could no longer swallow his bitterness. "We should have listened to my mother," he said. "We should have stayed."

Wiraqocha shook his head. "The Chankas threatened to destroy Qosqo. You know their numbers, and their skill in fighting—to challenge them without allies would have been foolishness for an experienced general, let alone a boy." He crossed his arms. "I will believe this victory when I see the Chankas dead at my feet, and touch the mummy of Osqo Willka with my own hand."

Orqo wished his father to be right. But he remembered the messenger's urgent haste, and he was afraid. "If Kusi has won, Father," he said slowly, "the people of Qosqo will never accept me as Inka after you, no matter what you say. Many of them already prefer Kusi."

"*If* Kusi has won," Wiraqocha said, "we will find other ways to deal with him."

Yes, thought Orqo, swimming slowly now. Other ways to deal with Kusi! Which did his father mean? The botched ambush? The hasty and disorganized campaign that had led Orqo to defeat above the river at Yukay?

A cold ripple slopped over his face. Ambush, he thought. Again he scanned the rocky riverbanks, and the steep slopes beyond. Still he saw no one. His mind raced ahead, trying to follow the sacred river, to remember anything about its course or the terrain along its banks—rapids, bridges, fords, shrines. But he had not explored it, not as Kusi had. Their father had let Kusi come and go as he pleased, but kept him, Orqo, the future Inka, all but tethered, training him in arms but refusing to let him go to war, teaching him geography but trapping him at home, schooling him in languages but sending other envoys to their allies for fear of ambush or treason.

I will not lose you as Inka Yawar Wakaq lost his sons, Wiraqocha would say when Orqo protested. *Six young men, murdered or killed in battle. Any one of them*—

Would have made a fine Inka, Orqo would finish. *But had they lived,* he would add, *the council of chiefs would not have elected you Inka, Father, and I would not be dying of boredom!* The first time he said that, his father had struck him. The second time, Wiraqocha only said mildly, *When you are Inka, you will understand.*

But it was Wiraqocha who had not understood, Orqo thought. He had not seen how Orqo's confinement isolated him from the people he was to rule and made them distrust him. Or how Kusi, happy little Kusi, used his freedom to run about the city befriending every artisan and merchant, warrior and beggar, farmer and priest, winning the hearts of all, high and low.

Again Orqo's feet scraped against rocks, but this time he kicked himself toward a deeper channel. The current dragged his mace toward the bottom, and he held its shaft tightly.

No, Wiraqocha hadn't understood. He had only said, *Be kind to your brother; befriend him now and you may not have to kill him later.* So Orqo had allowed Kusi to follow him like a skinny little dog, devoted and cheerful. Annoyingly cheerful.

And then one day they had argued about their mothers.

That was where the trouble between them had begun. With their mothers—

Qori Chullpa stepped into the courtyard where Orqo and Kusi crouched on the dirt rolling dice. A gameboard dotted with colored beans sat between the two boys.

"Come in soon, Orqo," she called. "Your father wishes to see you before the evening meal." Her shiny black hair spilled over her *lliklla,* which was fastened in front with a long golden pin. Both her outer mantle and the dress under it hung in soft, finely decorated folds. Qori Chullpa had woven them herself; Orqo had watched her. He felt a surge of pride. Her cloth was worthy of the gods.

"Yes, Mother," he said.

"One more game, please?" Kusi pleaded.

Orqo opened his mouth to refuse, but Qori Chullpa silenced him with a brilliant smile. "Of course, Kusi, he has time for one more game."

Kusi's face lit up. "I've already won four!"

Orqo rolled his eyes and pretended he didn't care.

"Your brother has taught you well, then," she said, and she winked at Orqo. He studied the dirt. "Don't forget, Orqo. Your father." And she stepped back into the palace.

Orqo gathered the beans into two piles and handed Kusi the dice. Kusi beat him quickly, ending the game with a delighted laugh. Orqo tried not to look angry. It was getting harder and harder to beat Kusi. Orqo was glad to be entering the Yachay Wasi soon, to earn the golden earplugs of a noble Inka warrior. Kusi could not follow him to school, not until he, too, came of age.

But Kusi seemed to read his thoughts. "Will you come play with me even when you study to be a warrior?"

Orqo stood up, and stamped his feet to shake off the dust. "No, Kusi, the *amauta-kuna* will keep me very busy." Truthfully, he was not eager to come under the tutelage of the Yachay Wasi's famously zealous teachers, but if they would keep Kusi from him, perhaps school would be worth the trouble.

"Don't go, Orqo. Let's spin our tops again."

Kusi looked at him with big, eager-puppy eyes. Suddenly Orqo could bear him no longer, his victories, his unrelenting cheerfulness, his constant presence.

"No, Kusi. My father is waiting."

"*Our* father." For the first time that day, Kusi sounded annoyed.

Orqo tried not to smile. "All right. *Our* father. But he's waiting with *my* mother."

"Yes. So?"

"She's very beautiful, isn't she?" Orqo allowed himself to gloat a little.

"So?" Kusi said again, sounding even more irritated.

Orqo pressed his advantage. "I've never even *seen* your mother."

Kusi stabbed at the dirt with his top. "She's the Qoya. She doesn't have to see anyone she doesn't want to see."

"So why does she hide in her rooms? She ought to be running our father's household. Why does *my* mother have to do all the work?" Now I have him, Orqo thought, as he watched Kusi's face darken like a thundercloud. Suddenly he wanted to hurt Kusi, hurt him so that he would not forget.

"Maybe she's not just lazy," Orqo went on. "Could it be she's ugly? Maybe she's a dwarf or a hunchback like her servants."

Kusi leaped to his feet, his hands in fists. Orqo felt a thrill of pleasure.

Kusi's eyes narrowed. "Is not! She's beautiful, just like your mother! And—and—she's not just beautiful. She talks to the gods! Can your mother do that?"

Orqo reveled in his newfound power. "Prove it."

Kusi stood for a moment with his shoulders hunched and his fists like knots on his legs. Then he grabbed Orqo by the wrist and pulled him across the courtyard, through one room and another, through another courtyard, then another, through an alley, and into a part of the palace Orqo had never seen. Orqo was vaguely aware of people pausing and turning their heads, but no one tried to stop them. Finally, two tall men jumped aside to let them through a doorway, and two more men no taller than Orqo's waist shouted greetings to Kusi and likewise made way. Kusi pulled Orqo past them into a dark chamber.

Orqo found himself face-to-face with the palest woman he had ever seen. No wonder they called her Mama Runtu, Mother Egg. Her face glowed like the moon in the darkness, and her jaw moved constantly. At first Orqo thought she was trying to speak, then realized she must be chewing *kuka* leaves. He had heard that she slept with them in her mouth. At her elbow sat a plate bearing a whole *qowi*, untouched. The scent of the roasted guinea pig filled the air and made Orqo ravenous.

The Qoya betrayed not the least surprise, but merely nodded toward a pile of blankets, much like that on which she herself reclined. Then she waved at a shadowy figure in the corner who was playing a flute. The music stopped, and the woman who had been playing limped painfully from the room, nearly doubled over by the hump on her back. Orqo felt ill.

"Welcome, Orqo." Mama Runtu's voice was light and musical. "Please sit. Are you hungry?" She offered him the *qowi*.

He shook his head and groped for the blankets. "You know me?" he stammered.

"I watch," she said simply. "Or *they* watch for me." She glanced to her left, and Orqo saw that their meeting was being observed by a crowd of some eight or ten attendants, none of them the size or shape of a healthy adult person.

"No need to stare," the Qoya added. "We are all injured by the gods. In some of us, the wounds are visible. In others, they are not."

Orqo flushed, and looked at the floor in front of Mama Runtu. She was stranger than he had imagined, though she did have an odd beauty, with her pale skin wreathed in wild black hair. Her *lliklla* looked plain of fabric but glittered with many jewels.

The Qoya patted the blanket next to her, and Kusi sat down, his chin lifted with pride. They did not touch, but Orqo felt something strong between them, something that frightened him. He wondered what his father would think if he could see them all there together. Orqo knew that Wiraqocha spent little time with Mama Runtu. Enough to make sons, but no more.

"I am glad to have a good look at you," she said smoothly. "The next Inka. I am honored. I think your father would remind us all to remove our shoes." She smiled and slipped her sandals from her feet with one hand. Her attendants did the same. The gesture made Orqo nervous. He wanted to go, but he couldn't give Kusi the pleasure of watching him run. Perhaps he could find a way to leave with his pride intact.

"My father is expecting me," he said.

"No doubt." The Qoya leaned back. Her eyes studied him closely, with such intensity that he had to look away again.

"Give me your hands," she said suddenly. Orqo stood to approach her. He felt like a giant. When he reached her, he sat on the floor and held out his hands. He wished they wouldn't tremble.

"Ah." Mama Runtu pressed his hands together, then held them to her face. Gently she rubbed his palms against her cheeks. He had never felt skin that soft, not even—he felt a traitor to think this—his mother's.

The Qoya released his hands and looked at him with motherly concern. "Take care, Orqo. Your hands hold your brother's fate. The *wankakuna* told me. Whatever Kusi will become, or not become, is up to you."

Orqo tried to shrug off her words. Why would the sacred stones talk to Mama Runtu? And why would they talk about him?

She sighed. The brightness of her face dimmed, as if a thin cloud had passed over the moon. "Your father must be waiting," she said. "Kusi, show him the way."

Kusi looked once at Orqo, a glance of pride and triumph that Orqo did not understand. Hadn't Mama Runtu just said that he held Kusi's fate in his hands?

But Kusi did not seem at all disturbed by her announcement. With a light step—but without speaking—he raced Orqo back to his own part of the palace.

The chill of the water ate into Orqo's bones. But he knew he had to endure the river's cold for as long as he could, to swim as far as possible from Kusi's reach. He squinted at the mountains. Had he passed Tampu yet? Kusi must have soldiers at Tampu. If he could swim far enough below Tampu he might have a chance to escape and regroup his forces. Wiraqocha still commanded some loyalty.

Mama Runtu was mad, he thought. I don't hold Kusi's fate in my hands; he holds mine in his.

But mad or not, the Qoya, like Kusi, had won the hearts of Qosqo's people, while they maligned the faithful Qori Chullpa. Orqo found it hard to understand. Mama Runtu never showed her face outside her palace, never attended a feast or a ceremony. The people never even saw her. And yet they said of the Qoya, *What a fine mother! And so kind to her poor servants! No wonder Kusi is thoughtful and generous. Look how gently he speaks to the crippled beggars—just like his mother does. And a skilled young warrior, too! The* amauta-kuna *never cease in their praises.* Then they would whisper, *Ah, what an Inka he would make! Why is Wiraqocha so blind?*

But of Orqo's own mother, who faithfully managed her husband's household and who actually spent more time with Kusi than did Mama Runtu—of her, Orqo had never heard a kind word spoken. He had lain awake at night, seething with anger at the whispers he had overheard. *Qori Chullpa never bathed Orqo in cold water; no wonder he looks sickly. She picked him up and held him whenever he cried; no wonder he whines and insists on his own way. She gave him toys and indulged his every whim; no wonder he spends his days eating and drinking and dressing himself in fine things. Qori Chullpa ruined Orqo—and now Wiraqocha asks us to accept him as our lord?*

Orqo swam hard again, his anger renewed. Yes, it was true that he had spent much time in feasting and merrymaking—what else would his father allow him to do? And he wore the best cloth, the finest sandals and pins and earplugs. His father insisted.

The people, they didn't understand. Let them try to live his life. Let them live the life of the heir and favorite son of Wiraqocha.

In any case, when *he,* Orqo, was Inka, the gossip would stop. Anyone who spoke ill of Qori Chullpa would die. And he would expose Mama Runtu's madness to the world. Hear the *wanka-kuna*? He might as well claim that he heard them himself!

The current slammed him into a rock before he had time to swim around it, and his shoulder burned. Damn you, Mama Runtu, he thought.

But Kusi, now, that was another question. His mother was right about Kusi—he was different. Did *he* hear the *wanka-kuna*? Did the gods and the stones and the ancestors speak to *him*?

Kusi had tried to show him, once—

"Ssst! Orqo!"

Orqo awoke to a voice no louder than the buzz of a fly.

"They're all asleep," Kusi whispered. "Let's go!"

Orqo rose from his bed, leaving his sandals. Qori Chullpa lay at the other end of the room, and a few younger siblings sprawled in the space between. Even the *qowi-kuna,* the guinea pigs, slept huddled in a corner, instead of running about and disturbing people's sleep.

Kusi was already at the doorway. The men who sat on either side, facing the courtyard, had indeed nodded off; this was a rare opportunity. Orqo tiptoed between them, then ran after Kusi toward the garden. His heart thudded, making it difficult for him to listen for others who might be up and about, and report an errant prince to Wiraqocha. But they reached the small grove of *qewña* trees without seeing anyone. The front entrance of the palace, Orqo knew, was flanked by guards who would not fall asleep, but Kusi had assured him that the trees offered a way over the wall.

"Watch me." Kusi mouthed the command and then swung himself up on a branch. The tree looked barely strong enough to hold his weight, but with his feet halfway up the trunk, he could lean over and just catch the top of the stone wall with his hands. He pulled himself up and scrambled over the top.

Orqo, conscious of his greater size and clumsiness, climbed as high as he dared. The peeling bark scratched his bare legs and arms. But he could not turn back. He leaned for the wall and managed to put his arms across the top. For a moment his legs swung wildly, but he found a crevice with his toes, and finally he was over.

How would they get back in? he wondered. But Kusi tugged at his hand, and they ran through the streets of Qosqo lit only by the stars—Mama-Killa, the moon, lay hidden that night. They met only the occasional late-night traveler, too hurried or too drunk to care about a pair of mischievous boys. When the last house lay behind them, Kusi ducked behind a rock. Orqo crouched next to him, panting.

"How far is it?" he whispered.

"Not far."

"Do you know who it is?"

Kusi shook his head. "I've never heard anyone speak of it. It is very old. Perhaps one of the first."

"First what?"

"Inkas."

Orqo fell silent, suddenly oppressed by the enormity of what they were about to do—visit an ancestor, alone, in the darkness.

Then Kusi sighed. "I didn't tell you," he whispered.

"What?" Orqo trembled. "What, Kusi?"

Kusi's thin fingers closed around Orqo's arm. "It spoke to me. No one else was there. But I heard it."

Orqo stared at the rock. So this was why Kusi was so eager to sneak out and risk Wiraqocha's fury.

"What did it say?" Orqo asked.

For a long moment, Kusi did not answer. What terrible thing had he heard? Orqo wondered. An omen of doom?

Again Kusi sighed, and he looked up at the brilliant stars. "It called me Inka." He shook his head and turned to Orqo. "But I'm not to be Inka. You are."

A cold chill gripped Orqo. "I think you should not tell me this."

"Who else am I to tell? Father? My mother?"

Orqo remembered the pale face of Mama Runtu, and Kusi's pride in her—and that she claimed to hear the gods and spirits. "Why not your mother?"

Kusi stared silently at the ground, but Orqo heard his breathing, labored and slow as if he gathered strength, or courage. "I am afraid of what she would do. I don't want to cause trouble. I don't want to *be* Inka." Then he looked at Orqo with luminous eyes. "But if anything happened to you, Orqo—to you and Father—I would work hard to be a good Inka. I would protect our people."

Orqo's stomach knotted. "Kusi, don't—"

Kusi let go of Orqo and jumped up. "Come. You must hear, too."

Orqo followed him into the darkness, inwardly cursing the stones that jabbed at his feet. He always wore sandals—Wiraqocha insisted—and his feet were not as tough as Kusi's. But Kusi must never suspect weakness. So he bit his tongue.

Orqo was limping by the time they reached the mouth of the cave. Tucked behind a boulder, and visible only as a sliver of shadow in the starlight, it would have been nearly impossible to find even in the day, Orqo thought. Indeed, when he squeezed in after Kusi, he had to let out all his breath, and still the rock raked his back like a puma's claws. He sighed. Any chance their adventure would go undetected had just vanished.

Inside it was so dark and silent he felt he must have fallen into Pakariytampu, the cave from which the four Inka ancestors and their sister-wives had emerged onto the earth. Kusi's sudden whisper made him jump.

"Here, Orqo. Touch it." A hand bumped into him, felt its way down his arm, grabbed his wrist. Orqo had to lean over as Kusi pulled his left hand down, down toward the cave floor. At about the height of his knee, his palm met something dry and dusty-feeling—cloth, Orqo realized, the ancestor's clothing.

"Your other hand, too."

Reluctantly Orqo knelt and lifted his right hand, inching it into place next to his left. Something stringy brushed his fingers, and he suppressed a scream. This hand rested not on cloth but on something dry and wrinkled, like a maize husk. Skin, he realized, and the strings were hair. He must be holding the mummy's shoulder. His own skin trembled as if ants crawled all over his body.

"Are you touching it?" Kusi asked.

Orqo nodded, then realized the gesture was useless in the darkness. "Yes," he whispered. The mummy's skin felt warm under his hand, and the darkness was so complete he wondered if he would go blind. Kusi said no more, and the silence became unbearable. Orqo tried to think of an excuse to leave.

"Shouldn't we offer it a sacrifice?" he said.

"I brought one."

For a terrible moment Orqo wondered if Kusi meant *him*—then he felt a bit of fur against his arm, and a soft plop as it fell to the ground.

"*Qowi,*" said Kusi.

"Is it enough?"

"Last time I brought nothing."

Nothing? Surely that settled it, Orqo thought. No ancestor or god or stone would talk to someone who brought *nothing*.

He heard Kusi settle himself on the floor. The warmth of Kusi's body radiated across the space between them, though they were not touching. "What do we do?" Orqo whispered.

"Wait."

So Orqo waited. He continued to shake, and he hoped Kusi could not feel his tremors. Coldness seeped from the floor of the cave into his legs. He could see nothing, and hear nothing save his own breathing and Kusi's.

Then Kusi's stopped. Orqo held his own breath to listen for his brother's, and just as he thought he might faint, Kusi moaned, then screamed. He fell onto Orqo, Orqo yelled, and they both scrambled for the way out of the cave. Kusi found it first, and Orqo pressed after him. For a moment he felt stuck, and he thought perhaps the mountain would squeeze him to death in punishment for trespassing on sacred ground. Then Kusi pulled on him with both hands, and he stumbled into fresh air.

Kusi ran. Orqo followed his shadow, tripping and stumbling all the way back to Qosqo. Finally the walls of the city loomed before them.

"Stop!" Orqo called. "Wait, Kusi!" His ribs hurt, and his feet felt torn to shreds; but also he knew that once they returned to the palace it would be hard to talk.

Kusi paused and turned. His eyes glinted. But even in the starlight, Orqo could see his expression, and it was one he had never seen before. Kusi was afraid—but not of the mummy. He was afraid of Orqo. Indeed, he kept moving his eyes so that he would not have to look Orqo in the face.

"What did you hear?" Orqo asked.

Kusi shook his head.

"I heard nothing," Orqo insisted. "What is it?"

The fear on Kusi's face turned to sadness, a horrible sadness. "You did not hear?"

"No."

Kusi fell to the dirt with his head in his hands. He moaned. Orqo waited.

Kusi finally whispered, "It isn't just the mummy, Orqo. Stones. Water. The gods in the temples. They all speak to me."

Orqo's mouth felt dry. "What do they say?"

"The same. *Pachakuteq Inka Yupanki,* they call me."

"So that's what the mummy said?"

"Not this time. This time it said—it said, beware of Orqo. Beware. He is no brother to you." Kusi looked up imploringly. "Would you hurt me, Orqo? Are you not my brother?"

Orqo felt as if his feet had grown one with the ground. He could not move, and when he tried to speak reassuringly, the words stuck in his throat. He reached toward Kusi, and Kusi flinched. Finally he mumbled the only words he could muster: "I don't know."

At that, Kusi leaped up and ran again, and Orqo chased after him. When they neared the palace they found that sneaking in undetected would have been impossible, after all, for they were scooped up by Wiraqocha' s guards and carried bodily into the palace. Qori Chullpa tended their scrapes and bruises while Wiraqocha lectured them on the danger of the next Inka running around unguarded at night like a stray dog.

Their skin wounds healed soon enough. But as the days passed Orqo knew that Kusi would never look at him with brotherly trust again. Not because of what the unknown mummy had said—but because of what Orqo had not been able to say.

Orqo felt he had been swimming forever, when he glimpsed ahead a bridge swinging high over the Willkamayu. Tampu—he must be approaching Tampu. If he floated under the bridge, he thought, he would surely be seen. He swam to the riverbank to continue his journey on foot. His wet sandals still clung to his feet, but they slipped so treacherously on the stones that he finally took them off and flung them into the current. If they were seen, he might be presumed dead, and so much the better.

The sandals bobbed on the ripples. "For you, Mayu-Mama," he said to the river spirit, half in jest. "A sacrifice."

A sacrifice.

Orqo froze. What was that? Had a god deigned to speak to him? Or were his ears playing tricks?

He licked his lips. What did one say in return? He looked into the water, not knowing whether he appeared reverent or absurd. "Did you speak to me?"

But the river ran on, absorbed in its own thoughts. Orqo shook off the moment. The last thing he needed was to be distracted by imaginary voices from the gods. He had to get past Tampu. He jammed his mace into his belt. He saw that his knife and sling still hung there as well, and he felt encouraged. At least he had his weapons.

Orqo climbed quickly into the rocks at the river's edge. He kept one eye on the bridge as he crept along, and though he saw no one pass, he tried to stay well hidden. With the bridge behind him, however, he returned to the river. Travel by foot was devastatingly slow. He had a better chance of escape if he let the Willkamayu carry him.

The brief walk had warmed him, and the icy water took his breath away. He kicked to keep himself afloat, and wondered about the voice he thought had spoken to him. Was that the sort of voice Kusi had heard? Quiet, almost breathless, seeming to come more from within than without?

If he made another sacrifice, would Mayu-Mama speak again?

At a bend in the river, he saw a narrow stretch of white rapids, and in the middle of them, a large flat stone. He swam for it, though the waves nearly drowned him before he pulled himself onto its surface. He coughed and caught his breath, then sat up and considered what he had. Precious little; but then, his sandals had not been much.

He pulled his sling from his belt and threw it onto the dancing water. "May it please you," he said.

The world seemed to hold its breath. Then he heard it again, the whisper that came from the water and from nowhere.

Thank you.

Relief washed over Orqo. He had not been hearing things. He was no longer out of favor. The gods spoke, and they spoke to him.

"Help me, Mayu-Mama," he said.

More, said the water.

More? Orqo was loathe to give up his club or his knife. Then he knew what to do. With shaking hands he untied the belt and removed his loincloth—woven by his mother, of course, fine fabric worthy of any holy thing—and tossed it into the water.

"Can you help me?" he shouted, not bothering to whisper any longer.

Perhaps, the water said. *More.*

Yet more sacrifice? The relief Orqo had felt vanished. The river was insatiable. He had only his mace and his knife; without at least one he would be defenseless. But the mace was the finer object, he knew, and now was no time to be stingy. He tossed it into the water and tried to remember where it landed. If Mayu-Mama failed him, perhaps he could retrieve it.

More. Yet more.

Orqo pounded the rock in frustration. The river toyed with him. Would it demand next that he jump in and drown himself? "What do you want?" he shouted.

Silence answered him.

He grabbed the knife. First he hacked off his hair; then he gritted his teeth and slashed his arms and legs until the blood ran over the stone and into the river. The pain made his eyes water. Finally he threw the knife into the waves, and tossed his belt after it.

"This is all I have," he shouted, "unless you would take my life as well."

No, said the river. *It is enough, Orqo son of Wiraqocha. What do you wish to know?*

The rapids quieted; the water seemed to wait. Orqo shook violently. He was not sure now that he wanted to know anything. But he whispered, "Can I save myself? Can I become Inka?"

He thought the river laughed. *At a price,* it responded. *At a great price.*

Orqo gulped. "What price?"

Only the glory of the Inka people.

The glory of the Inka people? What sort of price was that? Surely Mayu-Mama toyed with him, Orqo thought. Or tested him.

"I would never bargain away the glory of my people," he said.

Then you choose to die.

Orqo nearly wept with frustration. "No, I do not choose to die," he shouted. "You tease me with riddles."

No. No riddle. Lie down.

Orqo hesitated.

Lie down.

The river's voice was irresistible. Orqo lay on his back, with his palms pressed against the cold, wet stone. He closed his eyes.

A warm wind swept through his body, and he clung to the rock to keep from being pushed off. Then he was spinning and he could not tell where he was or where he might be going, and he gave himself up to the river's whim.

A vista opened before him, and he darted over it like a bird—he realized he was looking at Qosqo, not Qosqo as he knew it, but a cleaner, grander Qosqo, with gold-encrusted temples and people from the four quarters of the earth mingling on its streets. The wind lifted him, and he saw roads stretching into the distance, full of travelers and pack llamas, and many bridges across the rivers, and people working on terraces and in well-kept fields.

Then he fell toward Qosqo again, where an old man stepped into the plaza, to the cheers of the people. *Pachakuteq Inka Yupanki! Pachakuteq Inka Yupanki!*

Kusi.

Orqo's heart hardened within him. The scene vanished, then opened again. He still hovered over Qosqo, but this Qosqo was smaller, dirtier, unfinished. The wind dropped him nearer, and he saw his own people scurrying fearfully through the streets, while walking among them, slow and arrogant, went many Chanka men with their thin mustaches and finely braided hair.

Then that scene, too, disappeared, and Orqo found himself returned to the stone in the river's heart.

He opened his eyes to assure himself he was alive. A condor drifted overhead. Orqo lay still, wishing he could pretend that he had seen nothing, for the river's meaning seemed clear. If he lived, the Chankas won. If Kusi triumphed—

No, he would make the river say it.

He sat up, too quickly. His head spun and he thought he would faint. But the world righted itself, and he looked out over the river.

"Tell me what this means."

You know.

"Tell me."

Water rushed by in a huge sigh. *Swim to Chupalluska. Kusi's men find and kill you. Kusi becomes Inka and builds a great empire, an empire that astonishes peoples whom you do not know and of whom you have not dreamed. But pass Chupalluska, and the war continues. Kusi dies in battle. You rule Qosqo for a time, but the Chankas challenge your descendants. The Inka people disappear from the earth.*

The water's voice dwindled to murmurs. Orqo held his head in his hands. He felt stabbed to the heart.

He groaned, and then raged, "This is no choice!"

But the water flowed mutely by.

Again he shouted, "How do I know this is true?"

Mayu-Mama offered no answer.

Orqo howled and leaped to his feet. "*I* will do it! *I* will build the empire!"

A wave lapped over the rock and washed blood into the river. *It is not in you, Orqo.*

"I will! I will!" He jumped into the waves, embracing the water that stung his self-inflicted cuts, and swam desperately. But when he passed the rough water, and let his tired and blood-drained body float and rest, a certain knowledge surfaced from deep within him. Mayu-Mama was right. It was not in him to build an empire. He would have work enough just ruling a distrustful Qosqo.

Besides, he had seen the fire in Kusi's eyes and, just as formidable, the confidence—indeed, the worship—in the eyes of Kusi's followers. The river spoke the truth. Only Kusi could build an empire. Only Kusi could save the Inka people who so despised Orqo.

For the first time in the whole wretched, bloody campaign, Orqo wept.

It was mid-afternoon when Wiraqocha's scouts finally sighted Kusi and his army entering the valley below Hakihawana. Orqo hurried to array himself in the finery commanded by Wiraqocha: his best tunic and mantle, arm bands of gold, new fine sandals made of leather from the neck of a llama, a feathered headdress, his golden earplugs, and a disk of engraved silver around his neck. This last he tried to cover with his mantle, for it signified bravery in battle, and Orqo knew that it would draw only scorn from Kusi. But Wiraqocha had told him to wear it, and he must.

His head ached from all the *aqha* he had drunk since the news of Kusi's victory had arrived from Qosqo. Wiraqocha continued to insist that Kusi could not have defeated the Chankas, but Orqo was not so sure, and he was not ready to face the truth with a clear head. He fumbled with the knot on his mantle. An attendant straightened his headdress. Then his bearers helped him into his litter—his father had insisted on that, too, even though they were traveling no further than the fortress gate—and he rode to join Wiraqocha, to await the defenders of Qosqo.

The Inka sat at the gate with Qori Chullpa in their own resplendent litter. Its gold and silver adornments sparkled in the sunlight, and the curtains were pulled back so they could watch for Kusi. Wiraqocha wore finery similar to Orqo's, except that he had donned his own battle helmet and the *maskapaycha,* the red royal fringe that hung across his forehead and marked him as ruling Inka. Age had shrunk him, Orqo knew, but he looked a king in blood and bone, still in command of himself and his people. Orqo relaxed slightly. Even Kusi could not fail to respect their father. In his younger days, as a warrior, Wiraqocha had more than earned the gold and silver disks that glittered at his own neck.

Orqo watched with growing unease as Kusi's troops flowed like a river through the hills below the fortress. At the head of that river of soldiers someone rode in a royal litter. Orqo swallowed his sudden anger. Riding in a litter as if he were already Inka—had Kusi's arrogance no end?

Wiraqocha's army stood silently both within and without the gate, but the noise of Kusi's procession rose to their ears. Music, joyous shouts, the rattling of weapons—Orqo saw Wiraqocha set his jaw stubbornly and shake his head. "We shall see," he said.

"You still do not believe Kusi won?" Orqo asked.

"When the Chankas lie at my feet."

The din of voices and instruments approached, becoming merely loud, then deafening. Finally the curtained litter halted but a few steps from the place where Orqo and Wiraqocha waited. Someone flung open the curtains from within. Without even waiting for the bearers to lower him, Kusi leaped to the ground and stood before Wiraqocha, his face solemn but his eyes sparkling. His clothes were blood-stained, his silver earplugs small—and he barely old enough to stretch his earlobes for them—but he stood proudly, and behind him, a troupe of musicians played flutes, beat drums, and sang loudly of the great victory.

Kusi turned to his followers and lifted his arms. Someone blew a conch shell. At the loud blast, the shouts and the music ceased. Kusi turned back to Wiraqocha, removed his sandals, and bowed.

"Lord and Father," he said, loudly enough for those behind him to hear. "I bring you the Chankas."

The musicians parted, and between them the warriors dragged one after another of the painted and mustached Chanka soldiers, shoving them to the ground in front of Wiraqocha. Yet other Inkamen came, bearing armloads of weapons, and finally a group of eight with a large, costumed lump on a litter. Orqo's stomach lurched, and not only because of the *aqha* he had drunk.

The mummy of Osqo Willka, the Chanka ancestor—the shrunken figure could be no other, unless Kusi had somehow stolen a mummy to fabricate the victory. Orqo glimpsed dry, dead skin where the rich clothing did not quite cover it, and his fingers felt again the shoulder of the unknown mummy who had spoken to Kusi.

What would Wiraqocha do, he wondered, now that proof of the victory lay before him?

The wrinkles in his father's face seemed turned to stone. Kusi, likewise, did not move. Then the soldiers began to shout and to cheer, and their cheers became as a single voice, "Pachakuteq! Pachakuteq! Pachakuteq!"

Earth-Shaker.

Orqo stared at his brother. The litter was one thing—presumptuous but perhaps excusable, since Kusi had ridden occasionally as a member of the royal entourage. But had he also dared to take a new name? Surely he had not claimed the rest of what the gods had called him—*Inka Yupanki*—as if Wiraqocha had already abdicated. No, not even Kusi would be that bold. But perhaps there was now no limit to his audacity.

Still Wiraqocha sat motionless. Then he moved his hand, and an attendant was immediately at his side. Orqo barely heard his whisper. "Bring the Chanka envoy. Immediately."

So, thought Orqo. Still he is not satisfied.

Waman Waraka arrived almost before Orqo finished the thought. He must have waited nearby, Orqo surmised, to learn the fate of his people. The envoy stood in front of Orqo and Wiraqocha for just a moment before his face crumpled and he fell to the ground, shrieking. The Inka people's shouts intensified. Wiraqocha's shoulders sagged, briefly. Then he held up his chin.

"Well done, Kusi, my son." He raised his arms and gazed at the cheering thousands. Then he clapped once, and they fell silent.

Kusi straightened and looked Wiraqocha in the face. Still he did not so much as glance at Orqo. "The Chankas are driven from Qosqo, lord," he said formally. "I bring prisoners and spoils that you may walk upon them and claim your victory."

Wiraqocha looked down at Kusi. His eyes narrowed, then his face relaxed. He smiled, and nodded to Orqo. Orqo felt an impulse to flee. His head pounded with pain.

"I am old," said Wiraqocha. "My remaining days as your lord are few. Let Orqo, he who will soon be Inka, claim the victory." He signaled to Orqo's bearers, who lowered the litter so Orqo could step out. The motion made Orqo dizzy, and he held tightly to his chair.

But Kusi stepped forward and grabbed Wiraqocha's ankle. The nearest soldiers gasped. "No! Not him!" Kusi hissed.

Wiraqocha broke Kusi's grasp with a quick twist of his foot. His voice was low and menacing. "He will soon be your lord. Give him this honor."

"Him? The deserter? The coward who ran from the Chankas like a frightened *qowi?* He is no brother of mine, and he will never be my lord!" Kusi finally looked at Orqo, and the anger in his eyes made Orqo flinch. But he did his best to meet Kusi's gaze. Kusi already thought him a coward; Orqo would not prove him right by refusing to look him in the eye.

Wiraqocha squared his shoulders and gazed straight ahead. "It is decided. Orqo claims the victory." He nodded to Orqo.

Orqo climbed from his litter and took a hesitant step toward the nearest Chanka. But Kusi leaped in front of him, and they stood chest to chest, not a finger's breadth between them. Orqo still stood the taller, by half a head, but Kusi's shoulders were broad and muscled.

"No, Father," said Kusi. "Only warriors claim victories."

Orqo looked sideways at Wiraqocha. Kusi was adamant, surely he could see that.

The Inka crossed his arms. "You are young, Kusi. We will discuss this again. You and your generals will join us for a victory feast when the sun sets?"

Kusi looked from one man to the other, then stepped back. "Yes, Father." He turned to Orqo. Barely moving his lips, he whispered, "You deserted Qosqo. You left my mother to the Chankas."

"Not only I," Orqo protested.

Kusi leaned toward Orqo's ear. "Father is honorable, but old. He would not have abandoned Qosqo without persuasion. I know who the real cowards are. *Both* of them." Then Kusi looked at Qori Chullpa and spat on the ground.

Orqo shook with the injustice of his accusation. But Kusi was gone, swallowed up by his admiring troops. Orqo could only return to his litter and follow Wiraqocha. It took all his concentration to sit upright. Once they were well inside the fortress, his father irritably ordered the bearers to set him down. Orqo did the same. Wiraqocha whispered some quick orders to one of his soldiers, then took Orqo's arm and led him toward their private courtyard. Qori Chullpa touched him reassuringly before going to see that the feast would be ready.

"So Kusi won," Orqo said. His mouth was dry as sand.

"Yes," Wiraqocha admitted. He cleared his throat and put a hand on Orqo's shoulder. "I have decided. When we return to Qosqo, I will give you this." He touched the fringe on his forehead. "I have been Inka long enough. It is time for you to begin your reign."

Orqo swallowed. "The people will not accept me as Inka, not while Kusi lives. They loved him before. Now he is the hero of Qosqo."

"Don't worry." Wiraqocha removed his helmet and rubbed his head. "I have already sent men to take care of him."

"You mean—"

"An ambush."

Orqo shuddered. He needed more *aqha*. "And the people who love him?"

"The people are changeable. They will learn to love you, too, when they have no choice."

"And the gods?"

Wiraqocha did not reply.

The crag called Chupalluska was one of the few landmarks on the river that Orqo knew—and that knowledge he owed to Kusi. After the failed ambush, Kusi had returned to Qosqo, claimed the title of ruling Inka, and declared that Orqo was forbidden entry into the city until he recognized Kusi as ruler. Of course Wiraqocha would permit Orqo to do no such thing, and Orqo had traveled widely to find warriors willing to fight for him. He had passed Chupalluska more than once. Now he saw it loom in the distance, and his heart froze within him. He swam for shore to rest before his decision.

But the river was impatient. *Now,* it whispered. *Go now. Or there will be no choice left.*

"What do you mean? Will I die or not?" Orqo responded impatiently.

The river ran silent.

He could almost bear it, he thought, if only he could tell Kusi—if only he could watch his brother's face as he learned that he owed it all, his empire, his riches, his victories, to his despised brother Orqo. To die unknown, unacknowledged, was unendurable. But the thought that the Inka people would disappear from the face of the earth was more horrible than anything he could imagine.

Mama Runtu had been right. He held Kusi's fate in his hands—but much more than Kusi's.

One last time he turned to the river. "I want Kusi to know," he said.

Mayu-Mama laughed. *Very well.*

Orqo could not believe it. "He will know? How?"

Trust.

"Why should I trust you?"

Have you a choice?

Orqo paused.

Go.

He plunged into the water, kicking and paddling just enough to keep from drowning. He could think only of the proud, hate-filled face of his brother, spitting on the ground as he refused to let Orqo claim the spoils.

As long as Kusi knows, he thought. *I can bear this as long as Kusi knows.*

He will know, Mayu-Mama whispered, almost inaudibly. *He will know.*

The crag neared. Orqo felt weak, and his wounds burned. He swam toward the shore and death.

And so it happened that Orqo, son of Wiraqocha, met his fate at the hands of his brother's soldiers at the crag of Chupalluska on the Willkamayu. Kusi had Orqo's body cut to pieces. Wiraqocha's grief, however, knew no limits, and some of those faithful to him carefully gathered up Orqo's limbs and head and put them in a sacred place.

Kusi, as Pachakuteq Inka Yupanki, built an empire that grew in size and in wealth until an army of white men with metal armor and their diseases struck it down. Pachakuteq, however, died an old man before the strangers arrived, and his mummy was lovingly guarded by his descendants. Wrapped in fine cloth, wearing new eyes of beaten gold, Pachakuteq continued to watch over his empire.

But time and space do not exist for the dead as for the living, so when the jaw of Orqo spoke gloatingly in its secret cave, the mummy of Pachakuteq in its shrine heard with maize-husk ears.

I made you, the jaw would say. *You could have been nothing. You owe it all to me.*

Then the jaw would shiver and laugh as the mummy of Pachakuteq, Earth-Shaker, flashed its golden eyes and ground its teeth.

The earliest record of the Myrmidons, soldiers renowned for their industry, thrift, and endurance, comes from Homer's Iliad, *in which they fight under the command of Achilles. Centuries later Ovid, in his* Metamorphoses, *reached back to the days of Achilles' grandfather Æacus to explain their origin and their name, "Ants." Entomology—and etymology—being undeveloped disciplines at the time, Ovid overlooked one crucial detail of Formicidae biology. Larry Hammer, in his poetic epic, has not.*

The Myrmidons

The plague came out of nowhere. No one knew
What god or goddess sent it, and the signs,
When not ambiguous, were all too few:
The oak leaves still, the livers whole and fine,
From left and right the birds flew in straight lines,
And worst of all, the tea leaves all refused
To form a pattern readers could have used.

And so Aegina suffered under doubt
As well as spotted fever. Amid the death
And raw despair, a couple souls were stout
And tended invalids to their last breath;
But others, I report to my regret,
Were drunken, rowdy, riotous, and rude—
In short, a bacchanalic rout ensued.

The harbor, drunk with sailors, caught the mood,
And soon from there the tide of riot spilled
To sweep depopulated streets in flood
Until the city plain was all but filled,
A violent lake—except where good sense stilled
The fires round two places, islanding
Plague houses and the palace of the king.

King Æacus was long since past his prime
And, not as strong as once, in youth, he'd felt,

He couldn't stop the carnival of crime.
His sons? Off heroing with club and pelt
And so no help with troubles he'd been dealt.
  They're only known today for being hid
  In family trees, and not for what they did—

For *hero* means "he scatters wide his oats,"
And heroes' brats are strewn across the nations,
Like jetsam tossed from overloaded boats.
Son Tenon apprenticed that vocation
With the greatest of the generations:
  No lesser man than he—a drum roll please—
  The man, the myth, the legend—Heracles.

Soon after Telamon had helped the Herc
To conquer Troy, he spawned the Ajax who
Would later try to replicate that work.
Young Peleus sacked as well a town or two
Before he gave a fateful goddess woo;
  His son Achilles had his song of rage
  That still is read in this descendent age.

Thus, sonless, Æacus was forced to handle
The crisis, and he too old to wield a sword—
Which added to his shame, for the scandal
Of crumbling state will always hurt a lord,
Since he is judged by his domain's accord.
  And so, as when mere anarchy is loose,
  He did what monarchs do, and prayed to Zeus.

During a lull, he climbed the island's peak
Alone (though leaning on the shoulder of
His—valet of the chamber), there to seek
The god's will in his place—for there above
Aphaea's temple is a sacred grove.
  He tottered in and settled in the shade,
  Then after catching breath, he slowly prayed:

"Dear father—so my mother says you are,
And I think well enough of Mom that I
As king renamed this island after her—

Help us or the city soon will die:
What plague has left, the riots have made fly.
    We ask in whatever name you wish we use,
    Help us—the city dies if you refuse."

The sun beat down. Summer's cicadas chirred.
Some ants marched up a tree. A gecko found
A hidden moth. At last the old king stirred
And from an empty sky, with dreadful sound
A bolt of lightning struck and fire crowned
    The Thunderer's most sacred oak—a sign
    Unerring of assistance that's divine.

The crack set Æacus's head to ringing.
"Give me—" he started, feeling full of awe,
"Give me—" he thought he heard the acorns singing,
"Give me—" alas! slow thinking was his flaw,
"Give me—" he took the first thing that he saw,
    "As many citizens, replacement folk
    For losses, as the ants upon this oak."

Leaves whispered to a wind not there, then stilled.
The king correctly heard that message too,
And toddled home, secure that Zeus had willed
His realm reborn, his populace renewed.
He was so heartened, he decided to
    Go past the citadel down to the city,
    Nod, smile, clasp hands, be seen, and do the pretty.

For being seen at being king is, more
Than judgments, generaling, or golden throne,
The greater part of kingship. Even for
The weak, an order makes a leader known.
A word stopped refugees from leaving town:
    "It all will turn out right now," he assured.
    The sailors looked askance, but none demurred.

To fully play the part, back at the castle
He ordered up a feast in celebration.
The palace cheered—except, it was a hassle
For servants, fixing quickly the collation.

That night, the castle's total occupation
  Was fun, both eating hard and drinking deep,
  Which led to—not more riots—heavy sleep.

In deepest night, the hour of Hecate,
The quiet of the world rolled out before
The city and the stars. The king's oak tree
Shook branches like maids stretching after chores.
Ants fell to ground, and got up ants no more:
  They lost two limbs, stood upright straight and strong,
  A formic horde become a human throng.

When Dawn rose from her lover's bed to light
The east, 'twas well before the better folk,
But after early servants. To their fright,
The mountain side was moving—was it smoke?
No, it's descending, like a falling cloak.
  The growing light revealed to servile classes
  A ragged stream of strapping naked lasses.

For myrmidian workers—soldiers, too—
Are female; they're the only ones who swarm,
While hustling for the food they bring back to
The queen and drones in their below-ground dorms.
'Twas these upon the oak who were transformed,
  And those who change partake of prior nature
  For what you were before will shape your fate here.

The past is—not the present—present in us;
We aren't slaves to it, but as we grow
We have its habits and, as mirrors twin us,
It gives us shadow selves we cannot disavow:
What we have done informs what we are now—
  But if I keep digressing from my topic
  My story line will end up microscopic.

The servants, startled, finally woke the guards;
A guard, the king: "Your majesty, come see!"
He came, he saw, he rubbed his eyelids hard,
And mumbled, "What the ———!" (I am not free
To print the word). But then, with gravity,

The king went out to greet what for the nonce
We'll call "ant girls"—in Greek, the myrmidons.

He met, midst smoking ruins by the wall,
This unclothed cohort causing a sensation
And hailed them, thanking Zeus for, most of all,
His answered prayer—this in explanation
Of what was going on to the staring nation.
It worked, for just a few men hit upon
These women—who ignored them and walked on.

This shrug-off irked the men, who started grousing,
But then a charred beam shifted in the dust,
Reminding people soon they'd need more housing—
Although new clothing also was a must.
Before ancestral voices had discussed
The tasks, the women from the ant collective
Just dusted off their hands, and turned effective.

Burials first. They learned that, during the clashes,
The plague had burned itself out, once refused
New fuel, on quarantined survivor ashes.
The obvious conclusion from the clues:
The cure'd been carried by the girls from Zeus.
Their epidemiology was slight,
But their theology may well be right.

The girls received the kingdom's reverence
With calm good grace, then started reconstruction.
Some city men with vast experience
Tried giving all these newborns some instruction,
But ants and building need no introduction;
Relations with the townsmen turned uneasy,
For all that they were Greeks and civilisé.

Continued nakedness too caused a snit—
While some, the outside workers, took to clothing,
The others, never having needed it
Before, rejected its constraint with loathing—
And there is, for a hide-bound elder, no thing
That signals civic ill-health like the crudity
Of unselfconscious public nudity.

The king worked soothing old men's ruffled feathers,
But who'd soothe his? His issue was, despite
Their civic efforts, one of duty: whether
As subjects they'd obey him, king by right.
They didn't hear his orders—no, not quite;
  They listened, but then didn't seem to heed him.
  It was as if they didn't really need him.

They did it well—'twas several days, at least,
Until he noticed he had been deflected
To planning the next sacrificial feast
And not the new defense to be erected—
A skill that came from practice: they'd protected
  Drones' fragile egos from all things that vex
  To keep them trained on their sole purpose—sex.

That's not to say they didn't value It—
Indeed, with drones reserved for royal thirst,
They prized it more because 'twas illegit.
The habits of hands-off were kept at first,
Confusing many men, when they conversed—
  They didn't understand that going nude
  Says nothing for how easily you're screwed.

But then an ant tried it, and soon all learned
That every woman is a queen to men—
Once homage has been horizontally earned.
They took to having sex like sailors when
On shore leave, if you credit that—but then,
  According to the deeply held male credo,
  There's nothing, nowhere, stronger than libido:

Sex drives our species: for our procreation,
We do all that we do that is outstanding;
Sex drives our drive for wealth: it marks our station,
And nothing's sexier than social standing;
Sex drives the arts—not just love songs' demanding,
  For all the Muses are invoked to aid
  Success for artists hoping to get laid;

Sex drives our social structures: "Marry me";
Sex drives our mores: in our mating dance,

Without rules for the steps of he and she
The rituals turn discordant, askance,
As partners lurch about and don't advance—
  As soon our sex-mad ingenues found out
  When their stumbling turned the ball into a rout.

The girls' miscues were bad enough—their chase
Also tripped on sexual disparity:
They had replaced one third the populace
(Those dead or fled), so men were one in three;
While two on one might seem a fantasy,
  When the two women both are too voracious
  And squabble over you—now that's hellacious.

Their own behavior shocked each myrmidon—
Were not they all from the same city/nest?
Hadn't they worked together, fed the young,
Dug tunnels, gossiped, eaten as a mess,
Defended colony, and all the rest?
  As sisters, they were sickened by their fighting,
  But shock alone won't make you do the right thing.

Without a queen or history to guide them,
They quarreled—when provoked or just because
The ones who could have helped now evil-eyed them:
Surviving wives and widows, their angry buzz
Provoked by these replacement thieves of hus-
  bands, widowers, and bachelors—worse, the bitches
  Had focused most on those with well-filled britches.

Through all this, reconstruction still proceeded—
The unrest wasn't civil, but erotic—
And yet, the more that Æacus softly pleaded
For moral self-restraint, the more quixotic
His toothless campaign seemed—and life, chaotic.
  He persevered, for he was not a quitter,
  But still, at times, he almost could feel bitter.

The worst part was his saviors—all those good,
Hard-working girls—brought this domestic flu,
Infecting subjects with their attitude
Like some new plague—which told him what to do:

The first was cured by gods, so this one too.
  But prayers sent to Zeus would here depart amiss—
  For these unmarried women, go to Artemis.

The temple of Aphaea on the hill
Was sacred to a nymph who, by that name
Or as Dictynna or another still,
Attended the wild goddess who they claimed
Was that great huntress giving Delos fame—
  As Artemis, or also Hecate,
  Aeginetans revered her specially.

For Greeks, you understand, were not so anal
As all those tidy myths make them appear,
Which turn religion into something banal.
Cults of Olympians were not so dear
As local shrines, or graves that gave them fear—
  There is more power in a nearby ghost
  Then all the gods of heaven's distant host.

Her temple offered rites of incubation—
That is, a vigil overnight to pray
The goddess helps you with your situation.
The king climbed up the mountain, sans valet,
And after ritual cleansing, groped his way
  Into the darkened sanctuary where
  He lay upon a deer-hide, solitaire.

He listened in the quiet for her veiled
Small voice—but silent night was too well heard—
The crickets cricked—the nightingales engaled—
The itch was out of reach—at times he stirred
To ease his joints—his focus always blurred.
  At last, he found the still point and could keep
  Composed enough to hear . . . and fell asleep.

He had no dreams, but, waking—there—a sense
Of what to do, that seemed to linger on.
He left the temple with some confidence
And, slipping past his keepers in the dawn,
He hailed the first new girl he came upon,

The leader of some hunters: "Come with me."
She waved her troop on with alacrity.

Her deference came from, the king inferred,
His air of firm command. But while he'd sought
Some goddess aid, a myrmidon had heard
A townsman call him "Queenie" with a pout.
The word ignited, like a spark in drought,
The tindered consciences of myrmidons:
"A queen? Not drone? He'll know where we've gone wrong!"

He passed throughout the city, picking here
A trainer in the new palaestra, yonder
A wife directing husband-fetching, there
A building foreman, on a harbor wander
A female stevedore, and when he found her
His new ant steward—he pulled this human tide
Up to the temple and locked them all inside.

These leaders made by local acclamation
Were not allowed to leave till they created
An answer for the domestic situation.
Thus: New girls and survivors were equated,
And every man of age to would be mated
To one of each, with this constraint: all three
Must live in mutual fidelity.

Because the tripling method must be fair
To all, before anyone else could try,
The girls had organized a system where
A weighted choice of mate could modify
That first informal rule of thumb, whereby
A husband, if all three of them connived,
Could have two town- or oak-born as his wives.

The news was greeted with relief—for here
Were rules for their sex ratio that seemed
Both equally (un)fair and not austere.
The plan was more complex than the king had dreamed,
But Æacus could grasp this fact: the scheme
Required king and castle to be listed
Among potential grooms—the girls insisted.

Alas for Æacus! He'd gotten heirs,
And duty done, he wanted his delayed ease
In arms of—well, in casual affairs;
And now both he and his were given ladies
He'd rather not have—that is—he—oh, *Hades!*
  I see I'll have to tell you all the sordid
  Specifics of the household, clearly worded.

I'd hoped to gloss this over, but such is fate.
By now, the chance I'll get a PG-rating
Is slimmer than a draw for inside straight,
What with the girls promiscuously mating,
So there's no point in prudish hesitating—
  Besides, a poet who won't tell what's true
  Not only lies, but is a scoundrel too.

The king liked boys—or young men, I should say.
He'd married young at duty's harsh direction
But when his first wife died, without delay
He indulged his paedic predilection
Learned from a mentor held in fond affection.
  That "valet" was a pretty teen, well-bred,
  Who dressed him, yes, but also warmed his bed.

No more though—no more sleeping in his arms;
No more watching youth turn, with the days,
Into a man; no more his boyish charms
Nor his hard body that led thoughts astray;
No more teaching a young protégé—
  For Kallimorphos, when he could contrive,
  Abandoned Æacus for his twin wives.

These childhood friends together had planned his break
From royal duties. The king, not knowing this,
In private cursed how Chance made him forsake
His chance for happiness—exchanged for his
Two ants. At least his had good statuses:
  Two leaders, both negotiators, who'd
  Grown fond of this old man who wasn't lewd.

The chief of huntresses, blonde Cyrene,
Thought from her dawn encounter that the king

Was as quick-witted as leaders need to be.
Lampito knew, from daily stewarding
His castle, otherwise—while valuing
  That all he did he did with good intent,
  And, too, his pliancy to management.

When she'd arrived, the management was needed—
Old steward dead of plague, staff disarrayed;
She'd started giving orders; they were heeded.
The king'd ignored his household while it frayed
To dodder round his country—which dismayed
  An erstwhile ant who pined for household order;
  The queen's house and the state had shared one border.

Between his servicing two wives (while jealous
Of his valet) the king could hardly stay
Upright. At least Lampito was less zealous
Near Cyrene, who balanced out her ways,
But by first light, her co-wife went away
  On hunts, which left him in Lampito's hands,
  Her energy, her strength, and her demands.

The other men had no advice for him:
The elders, even those remarried, all
Had older wives who cut their juniors' trim;
The youngsters, on the other hand, could call
Upon their energy. These national
  Small compromises they were fashioning
  Were different for the commons than the king.

Which goes to show that every permutation
Of bodies and of beds both can and will
Be tried—through all the times and nations
A marriage party usually is filled
Per balance of the sexes. It's hard, still,
  Because of claims from old religious quarrels,
  To keep in mind conditions make our morals.

But such is life, distractible and local—
Like fights that have become their own excuse.

The king retreated into bland but vocal
Pigheadedness, pretending to be obtuse
On issues they debated—from the use
  Of palace funds, to plans for his domain:
  Not dredge the channel—repair the harbor chain.

"Without good trade, there'll be no revenue,"
She argued, "and defenses cost too much."
What can a wife (and former steward) do
When her good sense has been ignored? She clutched
Her righteousness, and upped demands a notch.
  He thought he'd reached the depths of his dismay—
  Then Cretan Minos rowed into the bay.

This ruler soi-disant of all the seas
Had wrested Crete from regent brothers, all
So he and his could do just as they please—
Wife's tastes were bestial, son's beastial,
Which worked, for his were architectural.
  He'd heard of small Aegina's plague and flight
  And thought he'd conquer it without a fight.

Alarms! Excursions! Mobilize our forces!
War ships in harbor! Enemies have come!
King Æacus was filled with all remorses—
He'd let the stubborn fight distract him from
Those critical defenses. He felt numb,
  Especially when the ultimatum came:
  Immediate submission or the flame.

Lampito realized, as her husband claimed,
Expensive walls and weapons were really needed;
The thought she'd weakened the nest left her shamed.
As men's and myrmidons' demands exceeded
Her rationed swords and shields, her hopes receded,
  But with her co-wife gone—off hunting things—
  'Twas left to her alone to aide the king.

Each side's commander soon received reports:
Aegina's rocky shores were all secure,
With no place for a landing but the port—
But there, alas, defensive works were poor.

The myrmidons were news, unknown before,
  But Minos didn't do a double-take.
  "More women? Ha! They're nothing." Big mistake.

Formalities: Aegina spurned surrender.
Thus answered, Cretans landed on the quay,
To find that they were fighting either gender:
The men were trained, but women meaner—they
Threw all their strength and numbers in the fray,
  All weapons raised against invading males:
  Swords, brickbats, pointy sticks, teeth, fingernails.

At first they held their ground. Their viciousness
Unnerved the Cretans—myrmidons fought hard,
Ignoring danger, to protect their nest,
And men, to save their wives. Thus caught off-guard,
They were confined and couldn't gain a yard,
  But with good armor and their better training,
  The Cretans forced a breech, and soon were gaining.

They battled house to house, result too clear,
Till Cyrene at last came from the hills
With all her huntresses, each armed with spears—
All former soldier ants fresh from the kill.
Resistance stiffened under her—but still,
  The Cretan front kept rising up, not falling:
  The death rate of defenders was appalling.

The myrmidonic tactics were the cause:
Their sense of strategy was mass attack
In crowded interference, without a pause
To make sure that reserves were at their back.
Retreat on purpose? The thought took them aback.
  King Æacus soon realized that while he
  Was not obeyed, they'd follow Cyrene.

But she was in the deepest thick of things
And wouldn't back out either. It was hot,
But shielded by Lampito, our brave king
Worked through the battle din to where she fought—
Which made the ants who saw him quite distraught—
  And once he caught her and her sole attention,
  He then explained his tactical intention:

That first, Aeginetans in front fall back
To draw the Cretans out, then sides sweep in
Behind their rear, now open to attack.
The plan was good, but Cyrene didn't grin—
She saw a flaw, much to the king's chagrin:
  "What keeps our enemy, while we retreat,
  From pressing on to finish our defeat?"

Lampito, with her managerial skills,
Knew what: unused material for planned
New houses could make barricades to fill
The streets, behind which fighters could safely stand.
The work was quickly done at her command,
  And Cyrene then plunged where battle pressed
  To give the word: fall back, sweep round, invest.

They fell back in good order; with fighters freed,
As quick as knives her counter then attacked
The Cretans. Minos missed what happened—he'd
Blinked—suddenly, instead of helpless city sacked,
He'd lost his landing party. His wrist smacked,
  He soothed his ego with an easy crime
  And went to bully Athens one more time.

They held a sacrifice in celebration—
This after clean-up—during which they mourned
And newly dead were given their libation.
That done, while some remarriage plans were formed,
They partied hard—though Æacus was scorned
  By Kallimorphos. Thrown into a funk,
  He was consoled by getting rather drunk.

The skills of both his wives were sorely tested,
Cajoling him through the dregs of his expense—
Hung over, he was crabby and congested.
At least each thought well of the others' sense
(Their organizing, his experience)
  And mutual respect—domestic grease—
  Is the sole basis for a lasting peace.

History, at least thirty-nine of its countless elements, began with Sumer, or so Samuel Noah Kramer would have us believe. The origins of history are being continuously reglossed, even as we are perpetually revising our view of our relationship with the past and our own place in the present—and what, in fact, history *actually is. Despite the uncertainties in our knowledge of the past (and the present), and the subjectivity of our interpretations of either, there are constants, however much their particulars and primacy might be argued. There have always been, will always be, work and play. Suffering and healing. Firsts and lasts.*

Gregory Feeley here offers a meditation on "the end of history," both as fearfully anticipated and as complacently announced

Giliad

Trent's pleasure in being asked to βeta-test *Ziggurat* deeply annoyed Leslie, who watched without comment as he slid in the CD but left when summer-movie music began to vibrate from the speakers as cuneiform characters appeared on the screen and slowly turned into the company's name. She was in the kitchen when he called her to come see something, and had nearly finished preparing lunch when he appeared at the door. "No, I'm not interested," she answered, ignoring his crestfallen expression. "Go role-play as Sargon, but don't tell me it's history. And that anachronistic Greek letter is pretty dumb."

"They're just showing off their HTML," he protested, hurt. "You say you hate not being able to underline in e-mail." He took a sandwich, an act he made seem like a peace offering. "Was there really a king named Sargon?"

Leslie sighed. "Yes and he's certain to appear in the game, since his name sounds like someone out of *Star Trek*." Trent laughed. "You know what else they'll put in?"

"Gilgamesh?" he guessed after a second. Trent hated being made to feel he was being tested.

"Beer," she answered, handing him a bottle. "The Sumerians invented it."

"Really?" His pleasure at some bauble of fact was unmediated, like a child's. "And there were seven cities vying for supremacy?"

"In Sargon's time? I don't know." Leslie thought. "Uruk, then Kish . . ."

"Nippur, Eridu, Ur, Lagash, and Umma." Leslie looked skeptical, and he added, "I know, it depends on when."

"These are independent city-states? Then this would be before Sargon, or sometime after." She sighed. "I'll look it up, okay? But I don't want to deal with your game."

When she entered the office, however, a color map of the Tigris-Euphrates valley was glowing on the monitor. Trent was nowhere to be seen. Leslie pulled down her *Cambridge Ancient History,* and as she turned back toward the desk a half dozen cities appeared within the lopsided gourd formed by the two rivers. She stepped closer and saw that the symbols marking the sites were ragged-sloped triangles, ziggurats. Kish was nearest the stem, with the rest farther south; but after a second a constellation of features began to appear: the word AKKAD materialized just beneath the bottleneck, while stylized inverted Vs, ominous as the peaks of Mordor in Tolkien's map of Middle Earth, rose to the east and became *The Zagros Mountains*. ELAMITES, AMORITES, and GUTIANS threatened from the periphery. Leslie glanced at the speakers and noticed that the volume had been turned down.

Not wanting to sit with her back to the monitor as it cycled through these changes, she took her book into the bedroom. She could hear tapping from the living room, where the laptop was plugged in by the couch. She sat in the armchair—the squeak of sprawling across the bed would doubtless bring Trent—and browsed through the pages on Mesopotamia.

Reading history will send you repeatedly to the bookcase to consult other sources on the subject, unless the author has managed to catch you in the spell of his narrative (which means you are not reading history). This volume was so introductory that Leslie would have found herself standing up with every page, save that she did not own the books to consult. Finally she went to the back hallway and searched the double-shelved rows to locate an old paperback, *History Begins at Sumer*. Anecdotal and lacking an index, it led readers by the hand through successive "firsts"—first library catalogue; first farmer's almanac—with little discussion or analysis. She wondered whether the game designers had quarried it for local color.

Returning the books to the office, Leslie saw that the screen now showed a stylized face with dark holes for eyes and the corrugated beard of an Assyrian sculpture. She recognized it as a bronze head thought to be of Sargon, with its damaged eye-hole digitally restored. The image stared out at the viewer, its probable accompaniment muted.

"That's somebody," said Trent, who had appeared at the doorway.

"True enough," Leslie replied. "Ancient statues don't bear plaques, but they always turn out to be of specific gods or individuals—never some generic woman or warrior."

"How about epic heroes?"

"You mean like Gilgamesh and Enmerkar? They were probably historical figures."

"Enmerkar?" Trent said, startled.

"Sounds like Earwicker?" asked Leslie, smiling. He was already going to his shelf, pulling down the *Third Census* and the *Concordance*. After a minute he reported, "No . . . no references to Enmerkar or Gilgamesh. Rather surprising, when you think of it. Isn't the poem about the search for immortality and bringing back the dead?"

"No, not really. Is that what fantasy writers think?"

Trent flushed at this, then sat down to consult one of his reference works. Leslie picked up the book on Sumer and tracked down the chapter on Gilgamesh ("First Case of Literary Borrowing"). Kramer's précis did make the poem sound more about seeking immortality than Leslie remembered. As Trent was doubtless about to find corroboration of this, she decided to withdraw the remark.

"Hey," she said suddenly, "pause that." She was pointing to the monitor, where the image of a desert landscape dominated by an enormous crumbling mound was undergoing digital transformation. By the time Trent had turned and clicked to freeze the image, the mound had risen into angular prominence, like an ice sculpture melting in reverse, and the surrounding wastes had sprouted small buildings. With a keystroke Trent restored the original photograph, and they gazed at the massive ruin, so decayed that the eye first saw it as a natural formation.

"I've seen that picture," said Leslie. "There's a modern structure on top, built by archeologists. It looks like a Crusader's castle."

"Really?" Trent drawled. "They must have edited it out."

Leslie explained that while the later Babylonians incorporated the various Gilgamesh poems into a single sequence that did include a quest for immortality, the Sumerian originals—composed during the period in which Trent's game seemed to be set, around 2500 B.C.—told a different story, in which Enkidu is physically detained in the netherworld and Gilgamesh merely seeks to get him back.

"But it's the Babylonian version that everyone knows, right?"

"Well, yes." Leslie thought irritably that Trent was crowing, but he looked back to his reference book—an encyclopedia of fantasy, she saw—and she got it.

"That's right, the great man wrote about immortality, didn't he?"

It came out sharper than she had intended, but Trent didn't take offense. "He always insisted it wasn't immortality, simply an extremely prolonged life span," he said mildly. "He was far too obsessed with the end of things to preclude its certainty."

And you had to be similarly obsessed to write his life, thought Leslie. Most of Trent's enthusiasms—*Finnegans Wake,* the works of James Branch Cabell, Wagner's *Ring*—were those of the great man, whom he was seeking, through a kind of literary archeology, to understand. That this required the intentness of the scholar rather than the enthusiasm of the dilettante was for Leslie its primary value.

"He would have hated computer games," Leslie pointed out.

"Certainly *these* games. He would have hated postmodernism's embrace of pop culture and mass media; he still believed in great modernist masterpieces rising above a sea of trash. Yet look at his best work: commercial SF novels, his 'serious' efforts unpublished. And his narratives are fragmented and decentered, mixing prose with verse and embedding texts within texts like—" Trent looked at the monitor, where overlapping windows had opened atop one another, and laughed at the too to-hand analogy.

Trent had been gesturing unconsciously toward the top shelf, too close to the ceiling to hold any but small-format paperbacks, and Leslie glanced up at their titles. "If you want to write about pomo sci-fi, why not the guy who wrote *The Simulacra*?"

"He's not as interesting," Trent said in a conspiratorial whisper, as though broaching heresy. "*My* guy isn't trendy; he's still out in the margins."

Images were appearing one after the other on the screen: an ancient map of Nippur, an artist's rendition of the walls of Uruk, a detailed relief of charioteers riding into battle. Scenes of war, which the city-states waged incessantly upon each other until they were conquered from without. Was this how players would busy themselves? An image of naked prisoners in a neck-stock was followed by a stele fragment of soldiers dumping earth over a mound of enemy dead.

"How do you win?" she asked. "Conquer everyone else, or just stay on top of your own small heap until you die of old age?"

"I'll let you know," he said. The screen was once more displaying the entire region, and Trent leaned forward to study it. "Why do they call it a river valley? The land between the rivers is wide and flat, with mountains on one side only."

"It's an alluvial plain." Except for the levees that gradually build up along the banks of the river and any canals, the land appears perfectly flat. But the basins defined by these ridges, too wide and shallow for the eye to discern, would determine the flow of water as it floods, an issue of gravest consequence.

"Annalivia, Annaluvia," Trent mused.

"Yes, dear." Outside, Megan's shout echoed off the tier of condo balconies across the grass, and she looked out the window. "Beta-testers *play* with the product, right? They don't work at it."

"Not exactly, but I take your point." Leslie was already heading for the door, where Ursuline was blocking the threshold, evidently to alert her to anyone coming or going. She stepped over the sleeping Labrador and padded quietly down the hall, leaving her book on the table outside their bedroom. Through the back screen she could hear the children's shouts, none pitched to the pain or alarm she was always listening for.

Four kids were visible or audible through the dining room window, circling each other on the trimmed lawn. Their game seemed improvised yet intuitively understood, and even the fluid shifting of rules that Leslie observed provoked neither confusion nor protest. What games did children play in the ancient world, without structures designed for their edification? Would the diversions of ancient Greece be more familiar to us than those of early Sumer, a culture twice as old and incomparably stranger?

Leslie took chilled coffee from the refrigerator, added ice, and stood watching out the kitchen window, a few degrees' different perspective. Without a ball or demarcated spaces, their game seemed the frolic of will in a field of limitless play, the impulse to sportiveness before it has touched a limit.

At one point the four children were all facing one direction, paused before a prospect invisible to Leslie. Something in their hesitancy immediately reminded her of the scene, shown earlier in this Kubrick's year on living room DVD, of the killer apes crouched warily before the slim featureless monolith. "It looks like the World Trade Center!" cried Megan, still weeks shy of her eighth birthday. "Where's the other one?" Trent had laughed, anticipating the coming scenes depicting life in 2001. "You'll see," he said.

The sun retained the brightness of midafternoon, though it was after five and Leslie, had she not taken a half-day from work, would be on the train home by now. The resumption of school still left what seemed an entire play day for Megan, who would go back outside for more than an hour after dinner. This plenitude, possible only in the first weeks of the school year, possessed the transient glamour of enchantment: one layer of time folded over another. Partake while the feast is before you, she wanted to tell her daughter, who consumed her good fortune with youth's grassfire prodigality.

She brought a glass in for Trent, who had called up another map of

Mesopotamia, this one showing the network of canals running between rivers and cities. "It's all connect-the-dots on a flat surface," he said in mild surprise. "I bet news traveled by boat and canal path, along these lines. Like a computer chip," he added after a moment.

"Watch it with the cute conceits," Leslie warned. She wondered whether the map's density of crisscrossings (which seemed to include all the thirty or so Sumerian city-states, not just the Big Seven chosen for gaming purposes) was largely imaginative reconstruction. How many of those first distributaries could still be discerned beneath millennia of subsequent history, flooding, and war? Perhaps through satellite photography, of which the last decade must have seen a lot.

Trent, angling his head to regard the map northside up, seemed to be thinking along the same lines. "The entire region is now part of . . ."

"Iraq, yes." Where children now perished for the imperial ambitions of their leaders, as had doubtless happened five thousand years ago.

Trent grimaced. "At least Great Games never pandered to the help-kill-Saddam market." He was reminding her that he had refused to get involved with a project called *The Mother of All Battles* nearly ten years ago, when turning down assignments was hard to do.

Leslie recognized that she was looking for a reason to dislike the game. "Ancient Sumer was such a strange culture, you're not going to gain an understanding of it by playing geopolitics."

"I don't think this is all war gaming," Trent replied as he clicked through a series of menus. "Here's a module on the economy of mud bricks. Look, you have to bake the ones that go into the bottom rows, or they will draw moisture out of the ground. And you need wooden frames to make them, which are expensive."

"That's not a mud brick," Leslie pointed out. "It's a clay tablet."

"Whoa, you're right." Trent backed up to restore a rectangular image that had appeared as a sidebar. "That might be a bad link." He scribbled for a moment on a clipboard next to the monitor.

Leslie leaned forward as Trent, exploring the program's architecture, followed a series of links that brought up more cuneiform images: tablets, cylinders, a pieced-together stele. "Wait, stop," she cried. The clay square on the screen was evidently small, as it contained only five rows of text. "I remember that one from college. See the first characters of the top three registers? They are 'Day 1, Day 2, Day 3.'"

"Really?" Trent studied the pictograms—a pair of curved lines, suggesting sunrise over the saddle between two hills, with one, two, and three vertical slashes beneath—while Leslie explained that the tablets dated from 3000 B.C., the dawn of writing, and that these three characters were for a long time the only ones on the tablet whose meaning was known. She had seen a slide of it in a history lecture, and when the teacher asked the class to guess she felt a thrill at the unmediated transmission of meaning, like current, across five thousand years. "How many hash marks till the base number?"

"The Sumerians had a sexagesimal system, based on factors of sixty, but their place notation progressed in alternating tens and sixes. It was very complicated."

"Hey!" Trent looked delighted. "So their system partook of both hex *and* decimal."

"Watch it," she repeated. "I didn't say hexadecimal." But Trent had already returned to the computer and was searching the game's list of tables.

Any history game that gave an explanation of the Sumerian notation system had a good chance of positioning itself out of the market, Leslie reflected as she returned to the living room. This one would have a tough time in any event, with *Civilization III*, the industry's 900-pound gorilla, about (she remembered Trent saying) to burst onto the scene. She wondered whether games that big paid their beta-testers.

The living room window looked onto the front yard, away from the angled patterns of the condo complex behind them. Their lease allowed the owner to terminate on two months' notice if he sold the house to the developers, who evidently had plans to expand the complex next spring. This agreement reduced the rent but also, they learned, discouraged the owner from maintaining his property.

"History begins at Sumer." And ended, presumably, a few years ago, at least according to that silly book her dad sent her one Christmas. Leslie worried less about inhabiting a posthistorical world than a postboom one, which seemed now to be fully upon them.

Trent was clicking rather than tapping, evidence he was venturing deeper into the game. Fair enough, late Friday afternoon in early September; it was anyway Leslie's turn for supper. She plugged in the laptop's phone jack and went online, and spent the next twenty minutes (the ingredients for salad were already prepared) browsing through the pages that a search on *Sumer, Akkad, Mesopotamia* brought up.

Gamespace isn't textspace, which tilts the plane to create page, tablet, screen: upright to the eye like the drawings that words once were. Gamespace models the earth, a field of play for agents, not the gaze, to move through. Battlefield means battleground, its participants grounded as text never is. Sumer was a plain, even as its texts, lying forgotten beneath the successive accumulations of history, eventually became. You may claim equivalence, each plane perpendicular to its opposite, but the fallen tablets make clear which one subsumes the other.

Perhaps the computer game holds out the promise of genuine space, the three dimensions produced by intersecting planes. A surface isn't space at all, though references to "the white space" between words or "floor space" underfoot may seduce us into thinking otherwise. Leslie is undressing for bed, whose flat cotton expanse (it's too hot for blankets) extends unbroken almost to fill the room. Pulling a fitted corner back over the mattress, she causes a spray of rills—converging on an adjacent corner like improbably straight ridges—to widen and disappear. Every bedsheet is a landscape.

Sumerian scribes held their tablets at an angle while writing, as an old stele shows. So the act of writing takes place in space, even if it is read flat? Leslie plans to be asleep before Trent joins her; she is halfway there already. She can hear him in Megan's room reading about Greeks besieging Troy, with occasional glosses. There are probably also excisions of repeated lines, although Leslie can't hear them.

Scribes excised lines with a wet finger, rubbing the clay to blankness. Dried clay couldn't be altered, but fresh material was plentiful; Mesopotamia left no palimpsests like the scraped parchments of the West, too precious to discard. Leslie blanked texts at a stroke, words with no physical fixity dispersed even from the dance of forces that had briefly held them. Drawing the mouse across its pad, its faint drag pacing the highlighting she extended across the page, Leslie unworded the clumsy locution, restored the soothing emptiness, ready for words better chosen, as a child might smooth the surface she had scored. Scribes prepare their own tablets, but merchants are too busy, and Nanshe could push the set clay into the frame's corners with stronger fingers than her brothers, who preferred to scoop mud and hurl. She was not allowed to cut reeds but could bring them to her father, who let her lift the damp fabric and make marks on the pristine square so long as she smoothed them before he needed it.

A female scribe would be laughable, but women in merchant families were often taught to read. Nanshe plied needle, dowel, and chopping knife—awkwardly, but she could still hold a reed better than either brother. Carefully she positioned it between her fingers so that the nib was angled correctly, then sank it cleanly into the surface. The tactile pleasure of its yielding was intensified when she lifted the stylus to see the sharp wedge she had made. Twisting her fingers slowly, she added diagonal and perpendicular strokes: syllables, a word. She yearned to match her father's fluency, but the pride she took in producing a recognizable "wheat" swelled her heart, and she drew the cover back over the tablet without effacing it, a secret message for him to find.

Dampness fled swiftly in the midday heat, and Nanshe stood up with the two frames in her arms and began to pick her way to the upper bank. Enannatum could bear them faster, but he and his friends were busy diverting a stream past their walled mud city, which would soon suffer attack from rival fortifications. Atop the rise, where a footpath paralleled the straight-ruled canal, Nanshe could see across leagues of fields, orchards, and low shaded houses. It seemed readily plausible that if she set down her frames and climbed the nearest tree she would see, wavering on the horizon, the walls of the enemy.

Writing, trade, and a premonition of the consequence: endless warfare and eventual destruction. Ineluctable modality of the geographical, the scribe thought as he rolled a fresh sheet into the platen; at least that if no more.

He was a half dozen pages into a science fiction story, about a nuclear war fought with long-range bombers. Given time, the Soviet Union would doubtless be able to fire rockets halfway round the world, children of the V-2 with H-bombs as warheads. At the moment it didn't seem the world would wait that long.

"There's panic buying in the streets," called Cyril from the front hall. The scribe heard the clink of bottles in the paper bag, and the sound of the door being kicked shut. He realized that he had been unconsciously listening to the elevator ascending, and had set down the book and returned to his story in anticipation of Cyril's entrance.

"Just closing time for the liquor stores," he said calmly. "They're not open Sunday."

"I know panic when I see it." Cyril came in with a pair of bottles and an opener. "There will be fistfights in the grocer's, old ladies trampled in the crush."

"Well, we'll be sure not to hoard." He flipped off the bottle cap and took a deep swig.

"Whoever imagined Armageddon would arrive through the Suez? Hungary was galling enough. What's this?" Cyril lifted the book off the chair and read the cover. "*From the Tablets of Sumer.* A subsidiary of Pfizer?"

"You know very well what Sumer is," the scribe retorted. "And the tablets are dried clay."

"My people used stone. Actually, we took whatever God handed out."

"And look where that got—" said both men together. Cyril grinned blackly and tossed the book onto the desk. "Not a great title," he remarked.

"They'll probably change it for the paperback." The scribe typed the rest of his sentence, a brief rattle, and pushed his chair back.

The elevator began to descend back to the lobby, a rickety hum that did not register when he was typing or listening to music, but would start up during a lull to remind him that he lived in a hive. He had moved his family to Milford expressly to get outside the blast radius, and here they were back again, just across the river from Manhattan as Western Civilization seemed to be entering its death throes.

The basement shelter in Milford, with its blankets, chemical toilet, and emergency provisions, seemed in his imagination to lie still underwater. The image, literary and unreal, could not be contemplated in the intolerable present: it belonged to some other category of time. He imagined the occupants of a New York apartment building crowding down into the basement in the minutes before attack.

Cyril was leafing through the book. "Firsts?" he asked curiously. "Sumer was the beginning of civilization?"

"As we are its end. Great cities whose literate class is kept busy producing official documents, and so don't distract their masters. They found the Gilgamesh epic among thousands of temple inventories and official genealogies."

"First tame writers, eh?" Cyril commented. "Guess that's why they also had to invent beer." His own bottle, the scribe noticed, appeared to be bourbon.

"In their beginning is our end," he murmured.

"It's a cute idea," said Cyril, meaning that's all it was. "Is there a story in it?"

"I don't really feel like mining it for story potential," the scribe replied, a bit waspishly. Which wasn't really true, he realized: without thinking about it, he had been doing exactly that.

"I suppose you've been digging for references to Sumer in that damned thick square book," Cyril continued.

"It's not square; it's circular," he protested mildly.

"Found some already, I'll bet. Care to read me one? Go on; you know you want to."

With only a show show of reluctance, he pulled out the big book, supple-spined as a dictionary from frequent opening, and found the marked passage.

"Behailed His Gross the Ondt, prostrandvorous upon his dhrone, in his Papylonian babooshkees, smolking a spatial brunt of Hosana cigals, with unshrinkables farfalling from his unthinkables, swarming of himself in his sunnyroom, sated before his comfortumble phullup-suppy of a plate o'monkynous and a confucion of minthe . . ."

"A bigshot," Cyril commented. The scribe blinked at this, and jotted *lugal = bigshot* on a pad beside his typewriter. "Lots of bug imagery:

drone, cigals, papillon—this is the ant and the grasshopper story, right?"

The scribe nodded. Cyril would love the *Wake* if he allowed himself.

"Dhrone also meaning throne, meaning the crapper. The great man's preoccupations never recede far, do they? I can bet what the 'unthinkables' are, but what about the 'unshrinkables'?"

"Pajamas, I think," the scribe replied. His mind flinched away from *unthinkable*. "There's a later passage, which contrasts 'Summerian sunshine' with 'Cimmerian shudders.'" Cyril looked about to smirk, and he added sharply, "Not Robert E. Howard's, but the land of shadows."

Cyril nodded wisely. "Sumer is igoin out," he said. "Lhude sing Goddamn."

There was nothing the scribe could add to that. The faint whine of an overhead jet, some 707 bound for Idlewild, reached them faintly through the window. The scribe looked at the pane, thinking about shutters. Flying glass; blast sites in the financial district, the naval shipyards. Apartments with a view of the Manhattan skyline might prove less of a premium.

"You're thinking story ideas." Cyril became very acute, not to say accusing, when he got drunk.

The scribe flushed. "The greatest temptation is the final treason," he began, then stopped: he seemed to have no more control over his words than his thoughts. "I was thinking about shutters."

Cyril laughed, then finished the bottle and set it on the floor. "Well, tell me what you decide."

The scribe's bottle was also empty, and it occurred to him that when Virginia took the kids to a movie so he could entertain in the tiny apartment, he should be quicker in realizing that he had to go to the kitchen himself. Indurate though he was to alcoholic remorse, the scribe felt a stab of grief, that he had brought his family back to the targeted city, now near the endpoint of history.

And Cyril, who sometimes seemed to read minds (but likelier knew to follow one's stream of consciousness to where it pooled), said, "There's your title: *Last and First Gravamen.*"

The scribe found he could not bear to contemplate the word *gravamen*. He was standing in front of the refrigerator, looking at containers of the juice, whole milk, condiments that he usually saw only at table. The quart bottle was cool in his hand, its heft comforting, but the hum of electricity and wisps of Freon-cooled vapor seemed fragile to evanescence, and the emanating chill breathed a message that he hoped not to hear.

Leslie was halfway through an aggravating Monday afternoon when Trent called with his proposal. "That game?" she said distractedly, waving away a colleague who had poked his head into her cubicle. Trent had fooled around with it all weekend, reasonable behavior for someone who spends his workdays editing documentation, but was expected to set it aside for Monday.

"I have been exchanging e-mail with the developers, and they're planning a series of novel tie-ins."

"Novels? You mean, like Dungeons & Dragons books?" Leslie had seen such paperbacks in Barnes and Noble.

"Not gaming novels, but novels set in the game's era. They would be packaged to tie in with *Ziggurat* but wouldn't follow its storyline or anything—it doesn't have one, of course. Three novels, each one long enough for a slim book, and historically authentic, which is a selling point. But dealing with wars, trade conflicts, dynastic succession: just like the game."

Leslie didn't like the sound of this. She had met friends of Trent who had worked on such projects, which seemed a good way to earn six thousand dollars in four months rather than four weeks.

"What are they offering you?" she asked.

"They want to see a proposal, maybe two or three outlines. I told them about your history background, and said you would be involved."

"In writing a *novel?*" Leslie was sure she was misunderstanding something.

"I'll do the work, I just need input for the outlines."

"Trent, this makes no sense." Her phone began blinking, a call routed to voicemail. "Isn't this game coming out in November? There isn't time for all this."

"It's been pushed back till spring; they're afraid of the competition from You-know-what. This repackaging is kind of desperate, and they need the books fast. I can do that, I just need to get the contract."

Leslie sighed. "We'll talk tonight, okay?" A second coworker appeared, and Leslie waved her in. Another light went on, and she jabbed at the button, too late. "Sit down, I just need to check my messages."

On the way home Leslie returned the weekend video rental to the library, where she checked the 930s shelf for books on Mesopotamia. She brought back several, which Megan studied curiously while Trent made supper.

"These must be very old people," she remarked. Then she added confidingly: "Daddy is reading me the oldest story in the world."

"The Sumerians were around long before the Trojan War. They probably invented the wheel."

Can something so obvious be startling? Megan evidently pondered the matter until dinner, when her parents' conversation brought it to the fore.

"Their civilization was stranger than those game designers realize. You can't write a popular novel about it without distorting everything."

"Oh, come on—how strange can their motivations be? The cities fight over resources and influence, their churches slowly turn into bureaucracies, and individuals pray for solutions to their personal problems and worry about dying. Sounds familiar to me."

"That's a gamer's-eye view. A novel would have to go inside the heads of one of these characters, and their value system—it's as far from the Greeks' as they are from us."

"They invented the wheel, so they *wanted* to be like us. The Pequots didn't have wheels, and Ms. Ciarelli read us a book about *them*."

Both parents stared at their daughter.

"That's an excellent point, dear. The Sumerians even had chariots, which they used in their battles just like the Greeks. Did I show you the images of them on the computer?"

"Not yet. Do they look like the ones the Greeks rode around the city walls?"

"We don't actually know what Greek chariots looked like," said Leslie. "But Daddy is right, there are actual pictures of Sumerian ones."

"Even though they're older?" Megan thought for a moment. "I guess if you *invented the wheel*, you'd want to make sure everyone knew it."

Trent showed Megan images of Sumerian carts and chariots while Leslie washed up, then took her to the library to get a video. Leslie spent the hour reading about early Mesopotamia, the laptop beside her for taking notes. The glow of domestic contentment—the parents' eyes meeting after Megan said something wonderful could spark the most luminous serenity—still suffused the otherwise empty house, and this, plus perhaps the fact that she generally curled up in this armchair with a novel (the glass of wine also helped), shifted something within her, and the customs and practices of *kalam*, "The Land," began to suggest the most familiar and comfortable of stories: a Mystery (turning upon a former scribe's ability to enter a darkened chamber and read the clay tablets with his fingertips), a Melodrama (legal records told of wicked uncles challenging the legitimacy of their dead brothers' sons), a Gothic (involving the Sumerian custom of burying the family dead within one's house), and even a Romance (a marriage contract could bring the future bride, sometimes still a girl, into her husband's household without specifying who the husband will be, so that she grows up wondering which brother she shall marry). How easily the third millennium B.C. could be shaped to the varieties of the twentieth-century (or nineteenth-century, if Leslie is honest) novel, the template of bourgeois sensibility.

Trent came down the stairs, hardcover in hand, with the careful tread of one leaving a child just asleep. Leslie smiled and waved. "Still on Book III?"

"For every category of ships I omit, I have to add an explanation for something else. She has already suggested that the story may last as long as the war."

Leslie laughed. "Switch to the *Odyssey,* fast! I'm surprised you've kept her interested so long in a story where no one travels."

"I suspect she's waiting for the captive princess to be rescued and flee toward home." Trent dropped into the couch opposite Leslie. "Raymond Queneau once said that all novels are either iliads or odysseys. He wrote one, *Odile,* that was intended to encompass both modes."

"As its title suggests?"

A look of astonishment spread across Trent's face. "I never thought of that."

Leslie shook her head fondly. "But does this rule apply to pre-Homeric literature?"

"Good question. The Gilgamesh poem would be an odyssey, wouldn't it?"

"Maybe the later versions, not the Sumerian one. No descriptive journeys but lots of dialogue and social clashes."

"Huh." Trent pondered this. "So what do you call a Gilgamesh-Iliad? A Giliad?"

"Go to bed, Trenchant. I'll have something for you later." It was only after he had left, a grin on his face, that she realized what he was thinking.

He was asleep when she finally came to bed, the reading lamp on and a splayed book beside him on her pillow. *Hamlet's Mill: An Essay on Myth and the Frame of Time.* It was one of Trent's endearing qualities, that he fell in love with the assignments that were tossed to him: gave them his heart, which got bruised when they were kicked into some chute and later mashed flat in a change of plans. Entering the realm of novel tie-ins, land of the flat fees, he was already resolved to do more than asked. She shifted the book to the bedside table and slid in beside him, feeling an affection that flared brightest at the sight of her daughter's features visible in her sleeping husband.

As she pulled the sheet over her and darkness expanded beyond the bedroom walls, Leslie found herself thinking of the *Iliad,* seemingly more modern than the *Odyssey,* beginning with the war it treats already in progress and ending before its conclusion. Megan must already know the story of the Trojan Horse; will she be upset to hear of the burning towers, the slaughtered populace, and what awaits the victors who set out on triumphant returns? Gilgamesh was an iliad in that respect, too.

It is the last night of the end of history, and Leslie—who had been reading of the three tiers of cultivation in Mesopotamian farming—dreams of Nanshe climbing a tamarisk: emerging above the lower canopy of citrus and pomegranate to look across the grove, the date palms standing like aloof grownups surrounded by crowding children. Nanshe's playmates, feet planted among the cucumbers and lettuce, stood looking up as she scrambled higher, the breeze unimpeded in her hair. The sound of men raising the sluice gate carried clearly from the canal, and Nanshe imagined the water, trickling through the channels and branchings into the orchard, reaching at last to wet their toes. Their startled shrieks would rise like birds, and Nanshe would laugh and hurl down twigs.

"Your faces are tablets," she once cried, exulting at her friends' alarm, "I see what you really feel!" Father had been explaining to Enannatum how a man's expression and posture can disclose his true feelings, vital skill for any merchant. Invisible in a corner, Nanshe listened. Now every visage contained characters effaced and rewritten, yet legible to her questing eye. The canopy is a face, where stirring leaves bespeak Ekur's stealthy efforts to climb. The horizon is a register, the line where dust storms, the winter rains, attacking armies will first inscribe themselves. The world is a tablet, a stele, the frameless burst of meaning that Nanshe, alone between the fruit trees and the unforthcoming sky, resolves to see hear feel for her own.

The rentals were returned unwatched; Trent's redaction of Helen and Paris's rapprochement was left dangling. Cubicle workers stared transfixed before streaming video; officials disappeared into shelters; the skies fell silent. In the shocked still evening, the intolerable images replayed.

Connecticut, untouched by war for nearly two hundred years, got an upwind look. Leslie and Trent lived closer to Stamford than to Bridgeport, but it was toward the older city that Leslie traveled each day, to a thirty-floor gleaming wafer whose daily occupants flowed in and out on the nearby commuter trains. That afternoon, in response to a whispered comment by an ashen coworker, she rode up to the roof and looked out west. It was there: a low smudge on the horizon, widening as it spread on its own terrible winds into Brooklyn and New Jersey.

No work was done the next day, and the weeks that followed were traversed in a cloud of dazed grief. Megan, who had gotten (they later realized) a good dose of live coverage while her parents stood white-faced before the TV, had scary dreams about jets. Trent took a long time completing his assignments, then found new ones hard to get. It was somehow still that Tuesday, so violently nailed to history one could not pull free and move on.

"They now say less than ten thousand." No real numbers known at all, just vast uttered estimates, to be slowly refined by counting absences. From the hole in Pennsylvania, perhaps a salvageable black box. Amid horror, Leslie found herself yearning for story: a cockpit transcript, defiant last letter, jubilant claim of victory. Which of you have done this? The loathsome Taliban of Afghanistan denounced the attack, Saddam Hussein hailed it.

Work resumed, though badly. Leslie had to tell her tech staff not to go to CNN.com so often. She came home to a consistently clean house, sign enough of how Trent wasn't spending his days. Megan's school held its postponed Open House, and they stood before her cubby and examined her activities book, album of drawings, and her daily journal. Leslie turned to the journal entry for September 11, and they read:

> *Today somthing is going on but I don't know what. Marry came in and said somthing is getting wors. Somthing aubt a plane. But what that's the onley quchin I have. I'm probley going to ask her to tell me the ansor becas quechins are ejacashnal.*

Trent shook his head. "You couldn't make up something like that," he said. Leslie looked at him with annoyed bemusement. Who said anything about making things up?

Their first trip to the City was a rainy Sunday excursion to the Brooklyn Museum of Art, where an exhibit on Japanese *anime* was about to close. They were quiet as they crossed the bridge to Queens, which afforded them a good look at the south Manhattan skyline. Trent perked up as they entered the lobby, however, and led Megan off to the fifth floor while Leslie checked the map for the Assyrian collection.

Most of the Mesopotamian exhibits were Babylonian, but Leslie found one extremely strange artifact from the era of *Ziggurat*: a teapot-sized terra-cotta jug bearing a chicken's head and four clay wheels. She stared at the thing, which looked more Dada than Sumerian, then read how such vessel carts could be dated to the mid-third millennium, but that scholars were divided as to whether they had been built as toys or for temple rituals. Leslie thought that the saucer-sized wheels were too crude for religious purposes, and noticed something that the description hadn't mentioned, a half-ring emerging from the front of the vessel, from which a rope could be tied to pull the device. Of course it was a toy, though she could not imagine why wheels had been put on a pouring jug (it had two openings, one for filling from the top and a spout in front) rather than a chariot.

More compelling was a copper statuette on the opposite wall, of a man wearing a helmet with long curving horns and strange boots that curled up extravagantly at the toes. His pointed beard and wide staring eyes reminded Leslie of a medieval devil, a conceit that would give pleasure to a fantasy writer or a fundamentalist. The text noted that the horns resembled those of a species of ram found in the mountain regions, whose present-day inhabitants wore pointed slippers. So perhaps the figure had been made there: no one knew.

". . . It wasn't the actual film at all, just the video projected onto a big screen, so we saw the clamshell version with its sides trimmed off." Trent was talking about a kid's movie that had been shown as part of an exhibit. It was raining on the ride back, and Leslie was concentrating on the road.

"So what were these creatures like?" she asked dutifully. She was trying to get onto the Whitestone Bridge, but the lane for the turnoff was stalled as a stream of cars, most bearing American flags, passed on the left to cut in just before the exit.

"They were mammals, I guess. furry, with serene expressions. You couldn't tell from the dubbing whether *totoro* was a made-up word or the Japanese term for a forest spirit."

"Like Huwawa?" Trent was always gratified when she remembered an earlier subject of interest to him.

"Hey, maybe. Huwawa fought back, but then the *totoro* were never attacked. They *did* have enormous teeth."

Leslie wanted to ponder the nature of wheeled vessels, but consented to discuss Gilgamesh and Enkidu's journey to the Cedar Forest to slay its guardian. The strange passage held more interest than *Ziggurat*'s political macaronics, and spoke (in some way) of the distances Sumerians had to travel to get wood for their roof beams and chariots.

"Huwawa was supposed to be evil," Trent mused. "An odd quality for a forest guardian."

"It was Gilgamesh who called him that," Leslie pointed out. "It seemed pretty plain that he wanted to kill him for the glory. You will recall that Enkidu, closer to nature, hated the whole idea."

"A *totoro* wouldn't kill anyone for the glory," Megan observed from the backseat. "They don't need glory."

Her parents exchanged glances. "Good girl," said Trent. "More people should think that way."

After dinner Trent showed Megan a game board on his computer. "Archeologists called it 'the Royal Game of Ur,' because the first boards were found in the Ur royal cemetery. But other versions were found elsewhere, even drawn on paving-stones, so it wasn't just for kings."

Megan studied the irregularly shaped board, which comprised a rectangle made of twelve squares and another made of six, joined by a bridge two squares long. Each square was brilliantly colored with one of several complex designs. "How do you play?" she asked.

"Nobody really knows. Some rules were discovered for a much later version, and it seems that each player threw dice to move tokens around the board. The two players each move in opposite directions, and can land on each other's tokens and bump them off, especially along the narrow stretch here."

Megan reached out and traced her finger down the board's side. "Can we play it online?"

Trent shook his head. "Sorry, this is just an image of the original board. It wouldn't surprise me if there was a website somewhere to play it, though."

"Maybe the designers should add that feature to *Ziggurat*," he said later to Leslie.

"They know their audience better than you do," she replied. "You know what they would say? 'There's no place here for a *game*.'"

Trent laughed. "True enough. I like the narrow defile, though. It compels the player to move his tokens along the equivalent of a mountain trail."

"No mountain trails in Sumer. Were you hoping to give players a pleasant suggestion of the Khyber Pass?"

That night Leslie opened a file on her laptop and began to organize her notes on Sumer into something that could provide the outline of a novel. War had to be the theme of at least one book, Trent had said, and present in the background for the other two. Leslie decided to think about agriculture and water rights, a likelier cause for conflict than the poems suggest. Even a prosperous landowner would have no reason to read, but Leslie suspected that a middle-class audience would have problems with an illiterate protagonist, so she invented a younger son who was intended to become a scribe. Worldly doings would dominate the action, but it was the kid sister who would prove the novel's secret protagonist, and not merely for Leslie. *Women always constitute more of these books' audience than the men realize,* Trent had told her. You craft the book to please them, like the baby food that is flavored for the mother's palate.

She sketched out some paragraphs about a girl who helped her younger brother prepare practice tablets for school, while the older brother learned the family business with their father. Nobody knew how the clay tablets were made, though she could make some obvious guesses. Nobody knew the location of Agade, Sargon's magnificent capital. Leslie was tempted to set the novel there, though of course she realized she should use sites that readers would find in *Ziggurat*.

In fact . . . Leslie padded into the office, where the flexing trapezoids of Trent's screensaver moved silently across their bit of darkness. Trent used her own machine's better speakers to play music, so had left the *Ziggurat* CD in his drive, its icon present (she saw after tapping the side of the mouse) on the task bar at the bottom of his screen. She twirled the volume knob, then brought the cursor gliding down to click on the tiny pyramid. As the game instantly resumed, she brought the volume up to the lowest audible level, and the clashing sounds of battle faintly reached her.

Leslie clicked rapidly backward, undoing whatever war Trent had gotten himself involved in, then paused in the silence to examine the lists of artifact images. Might as well use implements actually pictured in the game, if you're going to write a tie-in. But the subdirectories showed few agricultural or domestic tools (the designers favoring scenes of splendor or warfare), and she found herself studying the gorgeous works of art, museum photographs—had the producer cleared the rights for these?—of enormous-eyed statuettes; gold jewelry of exquisite workmanship; goddesses carved of alabaster and serpentine, the later ones of Attic accomplishment, the earlier ones deeply strange.

What kind of culture could carve these stone figures, hands clasped reverently and eyes like saucers, and place them in their temples, presumably as stand-ins for individual worshipers? Their gaze was neither submissively lowered nor raised toward heaven; they were *looking at* their gods, with an alertness Leslie knew she could not understand. Did the temple's divine statues—made certainly of gold, meaning leaf covering perishable wood, which was why none had ever been found—gaze back, or were they intent upon other matters? The gods were sometimes taken from their temples and transported to other cities;

vase paintings and cylinder seals showed them being poled along the river.

These were "idols," Leslie supposed, but it was foolish to conclude that they were literally worshiped, any more than those statues of the Blessed Virgin that Connecticut Italians still carried to festivals. Carved images of supplicants stood before gilt representations of divinities in an enactment doubly signified, creating a field of force no instruments can measure.

Trent couldn't use this, though he might be interested in the "sacred marriage" hymns, which made clear that the new year's ritual ended in sexual consummation between the city's ruler (who assumed the role of the god Dumuzi) and a priestess who represented divine Inanna. More metonymy, although perhaps the gods were recognized as physically present in their surrogates.

Same with the food, she wrote in a file she was compiling for Trent's use. *Everyone knew that the food set out for the gods was actually consumed by the temple staff. Nothing is stone literal; it all hovers between levels of mediation, and we can't tell where to draw the line.*

This was evasion, and Leslie knew that Trent would brush it impatiently aside. The "Stele of the Vultures" was so named because one panel showed vultures flying off with the heads of slain soldiers, and there was no reason to believe that Sumerian armies showed mercy to their captives in any of their endless campaigns. Prisoners who could not be ransomed were killed or mutilated, and what else could you expect? The ancient world did not have POW camps. Trent's novelizations could not gratify the gamers' zeal for battles without acknowledging this truth.

The textbooks gave few women's names, but Leslie remembered a goddess known for mercy named Nanshe, and decided in the absence of evidence to the contrary that Sumerians sometimes named their children after minor gods. She added some more lines about the girl and her family, spent a few minutes reading news updates (a habit now faintly obsessive, but she couldn't help it), then took herself to bed. Drifting past shoals toward sleep, she thought of Nanshe, who spoke sometimes with the water-carrier, a great-shouldered man baked like a brick by the sun, who had been captured and blinded during a war years ago. He stood all day drawing water from the levee and carrying it along the road to the village square, the thick pole with buckets swaying at either end bowing across his back like an ox yoke. Mudu, the kids called him, as he had apparently said it once when asked his name.

"Were you a farmer?" Nanshe asked him as he walked back toward the well, buckets and pole slung easily over one shoulder. She felt pleased to have inferred this after watching his practiced motions with the shaduf—when temple servants were sent for water, they slopped and wasted effort.

"*La-ul,*" the man replied curtly. The intensifier suggested disdain for the question.

Nanshe was taken aback. "You weren't an artisan," she guessed after a moment; a blind potter or weaver could still ply his trade, or at least serve as assistant.

"*Sataru,*" he said simply. The verb meant to have incised, but Nanshe was slow to understand.

"You mean you were a scribe?"

Mudu didn't turn his face toward her, which was a relief, since his gaze was frightening. "Palace, not temple. Records."

His calloused hands did not look as though they had once held a reed. Nanshe looked at his powerful arms and back, which she had supposed had been his since youth. Various thoughts contested within her, but her merchant's thrift won out and she protested, "Scribing is a valuable trade."

The man grunted. The sounds of men working the shaduf on the levee had evidently reached him, for he turned without pausing onto the path that led to the well, where he set down the pole and began to tie up the first bucket's handle. The polished crossbar over which the rope was slung squealed as he let the bucket drop, and he stretched his arms while they listened to the splash and then the glug of its sinking.

"Water is heavier than clay," he said suddenly.

Nanshe looked up at him, puzzled. "That's not true," she said. She started to say something more, then realized that speaking betrayed her location. She took a step back, and added, "Clay tablets will sink."

Mudu turned and began drawing up the rope. It occurred to Nanshe that he was probably saying that scribes do not carry loads all day. She was still trying to work out why the Palace hadn't ransomed him to his city, or set him to work keeping its own records, or otherwise turned his tangible value to account.

"How many years ago?" she asked. It occurred to her that he might have had children.

A shout carried faintly across the open air. Nanshe turned and saw an adult waving from the path bordering the adjacent field's far side, her mother's cook. She set off at a run, then whirled round to call "Good-bye!" to the slave. If Mudu had once been a palace scribe, he was something other than she had thought.

"If you like dallying at the well, you could bring home some water,"

Cook observed. She could not discern detail at a distance, or she would have cuffed Nanshe for speaking to the slave.

"You didn't send me out with a bucket," Nanshe observed. Then, "How long ago was the war with Umma?"

Cook laughed. "You sound like a tablet-house instructor." Nanshe scowled, and Cook pretended to flick water at her. "Which war do you mean?"

Nanshe began to say *When they brought back all the slaves,* but thought better of it. Sitting in the courtyard with a basket of legumes, she watched Cook cleaning a turtle with a small bronze knife, and wondered whether scribes impressed into battle for their city fought with better weapons than laborers. The household's other knives were flint, while vendors in the market sliced their wares with blades of clay. Was Mudu's weapon also carried back in triumph to Lagash; did it serve Ningirsu in his temple today?

Later Nanshe retrieved her doll from Sud, whose tiny clay soldiers had overrun it. Sitting in the shade of the poplar that arched over the house, she took a reed she had cut and positioned it beside Dolly's arm, as though it were a spear. The figure now looked like Inanna—Nanshe could not imagine an armed woman otherwise—and she reflected that if she took Dolly out to the house they had made for her in the tamarisk brush (Sud had helped, under the impression that he was building fortifications), then the knee-high mud-brick structure, its thatched roof removable to disclose partitioned rooms within, would become perforce Her temple. Nanshe, who knew nothing of any temple's inner chambers, was thrilled at the thought of now gazing upon them.

As she lay that night with Dolly in her arms, the reed spear forgotten under the tree, Nanshe wondered whether she could recruit her mother's assistance in making Dolly a new dress for Festival. Attired like a prosperous merchantwife, Dolly would certainly

This isn't what my readers want. The plot must conform to a gaming scenario; any novelistic texture must grow in the cracks between.

Your readers? They are the game's readers; you're just brought in to entertain them.

Okay, I'm sorry. But if they're reading something I wrote, can I think of them as mine, even if the copyright isn't? At least for as long as they hold open the pages?

This is only a brief scene. Even a novelization can't be incessant action.

I'll give it a paragraph. One can introduce new themes in that little space, establish a counterpoint, okay? If I write more the editors will cut it.

Clay soldiers stood atop the house's perimeter, like invaders breaching the city walls. With an annoyed cry Nanshe swept them clear, but the point returned to her as she lay remembering: Sud thought in terms of armies because the lugals did; the cities did—it was the way things were. Perhaps the gods did.

War with Umma precluded trade with Umma, but Umma (Nanshe's father often said this) produced little that Lagash did not, and competed with Lagash for trade elsewhere. If the arrogance of Umma's people regarding water boundaries roused Ningirsu's ire, there was no reason why Lagash's merchants should question the will of the city.

Shock troops thunder across the plain, impossibly loud, each chariot drawn by two onagers. Lugal Eannatum's chariot commands *four*, and the songs will declare that it moved twice as fast. They far outpace the infantry, which disappears behind boiling clouds of dust, emerging seconds later, a forest of speartips glinting above their helmets, like figures marching out of a mountainside. The enemy ranks break and scatter, and though the chariots do not run them down as in song, no soldier stands fast to attack as they sweep through the line, causing spearmen to drop shields, spring away like panicked grasshoppers, trample each other. Umma's own chariots, fewer and slower, have not yet reached the advancing Lagashites, who see the rout, roar terrifyingly, and present spear tips to the spooked Umman onagers. The plain dissolves into a swirling chaos of smoke, noise, and trembling earth, but the contest is already over.

The sickle-sword in Eannatum's hand would be portrayed in stelae and (now lost) wall paintings, the implicit metaphor—of his enemy falling like wheat before him—apparent to the most unsophisticated viewer. Sumer's plains, where nothing stands waving in ranked thousands but the wind-tossed stalks, themselves compel the image. Shall Ninlil, goddess of grain, bow down like grain before warlike Inanna?

As her city did before Inanna's. That is the story—Gilgamesh of Uruk's—he wants most to write, the wordstring that will reach from inscribed clay to etched polycarbonate. Beginning with young Gilgamesh's defeat of Agga's army and ending with the elder king building a shrine in subjugated Nippur, it will bracket the period (a few years, presumably, of his early maturity) when Gilgamesh gained and lost Enkidu, and so *must* deal with it, though in terms a gamer will not balk at. If Gilgamesh's triumphs over Kish and Ur are dramatized with suitable élan—Trent accepts that there must be several battle scenes—then the reader will sit still for the journeys to the Cedar Forest and the netherworld: perhaps even in the less familiar Sumerian versions. The harmonics of mythopoesis, echoing even from this profoundly alien culture, can inform any story, however strong its appeal to gamers.

He is trying to decide whether *The Epic of Gilgamesh* and the earlier poems can be considered either iliads or odysseys. Declaring the *Epic* an odyssey is banal but probably unavoidable, just as "Gilgamesh and Agga," the only Sumerian Gilgamesh poem not to have been incorporated into the *Epic*, is an iliad in every respect. Role-playing games are all iliads, since they deal with battles, depict societies primarily in terms of their ability to sustain a war effort, and see individual psychology only through the lens of fitness for combat.

Longingly he thinks again of Enmerkar, the figure not in the carpet, whose presence in the *Wake* he yearns to discover. He suspects that Enmerkar and his friend Lugalbanda were the models for Gilgamesh and Enkidu, but the fragmentary nature of the few surviving tablets leaves this unclear. For these oldest of texts Queneau's schematic dissolves, and we are confronted with the stuff of myth, which Trent wants to rub between his fingers, raise to his nose. O show me the substrate of meaning, psyche's bedrock.

What did Lugalbanda cry when he awoke and found that his companions had left him for dead? The steppes of Mount Hurum, dry and desolate, must have seemed the Sumerian underworld; did he realize at first that he still lived? The tablet here crumbles into powder, the rest of the story is lost.

Enmerkar and the army commanded by his seven heroes succeed in subjugating Aratta (the poem could hardly have gone otherwise), and they return to Erech along their original route, intending to reclaim Lugalbanda's body and bear it home. Upon reaching Mount Hurum,

1. They find Lugalbanda, who has been roaming the steppes in despair. He
   - 1a. is overjoyed to see them, or perhaps reproachful, but accepts in the end his retrieval by his peers and his return to the land of the living.
   - 1b. rages and does not forgive; the story becomes one of irreparable breach.
2. They do not find Lugalbanda, who
   - 2a. has wandered deeper into the wilderness.
   - 2b. has been taken away by the gods.

Trent imagines more pathways, a thorough exploration of the branching possibilities that, like books opened in dreams, can appear but not actually be read. Some he knows can't work: it's the Greek gods who take up petitioners *in extremis* and turn them into constellations. Nor can Lugalbanda break with Enmerkar; Sumerian myths don't deal with character conflict in that way. So Enmerkar and Lugalbanda are reunited; the ordeal of Lugalbanda abandoned is a wound that heals up by poem's end.

Such wounds make us feel what we can't understand: that's what myth is. Niobe, still weeping for her children though turned to stone, or the centaurs' anguished thrall to wine and lust, retain their power to claw at the reader. The *Wake* doesn't claw, though the great man, a lesser writer in every other way, knew enough to.

Untitled, obscure in meaning, often fragmentary, the two or three dozen narrative poems that exist in Sumerian versions seem too blunt and odd to move us as the Greek myths can. Except for the line about mankind being created from "the clay that is over the abyss," the only tale that Trent found deeply affecting was Lugalbanda's abandonment on Hurum and his undescribed reaction.

Mount Hurum is not on *Ziggurat*'s map—no one knows where it is—and Trent recognizes that his novels must reside within the game's geography. He hovers above the plain, watching the words IRAQ and BAGHDAD fade away and the coastline press inward until it is resting against the city that now labels itself *Ur*. Trent begins to fall, slowly at first, then faster as the land below grows larger and more detailed until it tilts abruptly away, like the view from a plane pulling out of a dive, and he is skimming above a landscape that has lost its lettering and cartographic flourishes and assumed almost the realistic detail of a desert seen in the opening shot of a nature documentary.

A ripple breaks the horizon's flatline, and at once the ground flashing below is not sand but cultivated fields, divided by roads and levees. The structures ahead swell and gain definition, a great wall bristling with towers, its ramparts topped only by the central ragged pyramid. The viewpoint circles the city center, temple and palace readily identifiable (Trent remembers close-ups of them) and the ziggurat's corrugated slopes rendered in vivid detail, then swoops down to alight in the central square.

The city is full but empty, for Trent knows (with the logic of dreams) that moving crowds would strain the resources of role-playing games: yet this is the Uruk of *his book,* anchored to the CD-ROM yet ranging freely, ungameably peopled by people. Trent moves through the throng in this confidence, secure in his characters' imaginative reality even as their bodies pass through him, or perhaps his through them. Cinched tight by the city walls, the crowded buildings radiated heat—unrelieved by winds—and a terrible stench, electronically imperceptible but evoked, made real in the mind's nostrils, by the twining long molecules of words, complex chains that twist to do anything, like wisps of smoke weaving themselves into firewood.

Stinks and gritty skin, heaped refuse and open water glimpsed from ramparts: immaterial perceptions, electrons are too crude to trace. Why are words finer than particles, which are older than anything? The meaning of Sumerian myths elude us, but not because their tablets are fragmentary or our grip on their language infirm. Every word sprouts wings, turns metaphor, and flits off at an angle we hadn't seen. These angles are not ours, they disregard our geometry. This unbegetting language, spoken by no one, is hardware that only ran thoughts now incomprehensible, their myths a food our minds cannot digest.

No single stuff of myth, then, no wellspring feeding every people. To work in the digital realm is to accept this: the sentences you construct do not pretend to be transcriptions of spoken words, nor do your images seek validity as representations of nature, judged by their fealty to something. Music—always disconcertingly itself, especially when not giving tune to words—still plays while you play, but no longer serves only as dramatic accompaniment. Word, image, and tone alike emerge from the difference between 0 and 1, the contrast between fields of force that needs, can have, no touchstone.

Game-players don't know this; they blithely enter these regions (paying for admission), thinking them flat, directional. Assume our forest is merely your path; cheer yourselves after walking its length. Contention is stranger than you know, gamers, who strain at the lines we draw round you, roar at the points we dole out, and imagine yourselves at play in the fields of the board.

Trent frequently checked the online news outlets, a practice he justified on the grounds that it kept him at his desk instead of sending him into the living room to turn on the radio. Some days he merely glanced for new headlines; others he read to the bottom of what stories were available, searching for hints of the attack that was surely coming. He knew that Leslie was doing the same from work, and sometimes imagined them sharing a second in the pages of msnbc.com/news or www.bushwatch.net, invisibly present to each other.

When it came, the websites gave it headlines, although there was nothing more than reports of rocket bombardments. "It has begun," he said aloud. What someone had told him a dozen years ago, coming out of a late movie to students gathered on the sidewalks and word that Baghdad was under attack.

They ate dinner before the TV news: few facts, much commentary.

"Word from halfway round the world," Leslie murmured, her thoughts on a different track than Trent's. "How long have most people waited for news of distant battles?"

"We're not getting much," he replied. Anchormen, bleating helplessly, were being replaced one by one with roundtable discussions. Trent cycled through the channels once more, then left it on public television.

"True; I was thinking of information reaching the strategic command, not the sorry populace. Do you think reporters will make it in before they flatten everything?"

"Afghanistan isn't Kuwait," Trent replied. "It's a big country, mountainous; far from the sea. You can't pulverize it from aircraft carriers."

"I don't know," said Leslie. She was sick with hatred for the Taliban, whose recent demolition of two immense Buddhas seemed their only assault upon something not living. But George W. Bush had declined to distinguish between them and al Qaeda, as though playing to a constituency that would regard such nicety as treason. His demands had been provocative and insulting, impossible to meet although the Taliban seemed to have tried. Yet had the Western nations invaded Afghanistan in the spring, she would have cheered.

"Is the President our foe?" Megan asked while Leslie was loading the dishwasher.

"In what sense?" she said, startled.

"I just heard Daddy on the telephone, and he was talking about our 'foe president.'"

On his desk Leslie noticed a photocopied page, with several sentences highlighted and scribbled dates and numbers in the margin. She squinted at the text, calling upon her grad school French. *Il y eut une attaque. Les villages insoumis . . .* There was an attack. The unsubdued villages illuminated themselves in turn, marking the progress of conquest, like the little flags in commercial cafes.

A shadow from the other side darkened the sheet, which she turned over to find a sentence in Trent's handwriting. *The resisting villages burst alight one after another, illuminating the path of ?victory, like the ?snapping banners of a streetside cafe.* The photocopy had been made with their scanner, his usual practice when he wanted to mark a passage from a library book.

"I hear you likened our President to Dario Fo," she said as they were getting ready for bed.

"I did?" He thought about it, then laughed. "He could be played by Dario Fo."

Reaching to turn off the light, she saw a book on the floor and turned it over to see the title. Her lips quirked: there was nothing to smile about, but confirmation of her husband's nature prompted an odd comfort. The photocopy had pleased her more than the notation of his daily progress, as though the assignment he had sought were a ditch to be measured in linear feet dug. He should have been writing books all along—books that encompassed history and literature, like the biography he had begun, rather than novelizations, mixing non-history with non-literature as though he was afraid to pull free of this world well lost. Could that last tug hurt as much as Trent seemed to fear?

She spoke of Trent when reluctant to speak of herself, her therapist had once noted, but wasn't she supposed to voice her cares? Trent had moved on, getting tech work and even a small grant, but privately raged, rejected (at least in his own mind) by a profession he should have rejected. It was only after tearing free, Leslie explained, that the wound could begin to heal.

"Do you think he is still suffering from that 'wound'?" her therapist asked.

"I'm sure he does." Leslie shifted slightly in the armchair, away from the view of Long Island Sound, and let her gaze rest on the pottery lining the book case. "It gnaws at him, that some people believe it, and that others won't declare they don't."

"Do you believe it?"

"No." This time she spoke firmly. "I've met her, remember? The whole industry is full of misshapen people who design games because they don't have the social skills to work in other environments. I mean—" she laughed— "I've got computer nerds reporting to me; I know about badly socialized people. But my guys don't claim creative temperaments. He shouldn't have been working for someone who lived with her boss, however stable she seemed."

"Does the fact that you believe him offer some solace?"

"You'd think it would." Leslie thought. "I guess it does, but not enough. He wanted to write a book called *Complicity,* a study of why people side with their peers' oppressors. I told him to stop it."

"And this was when Tobias was ill?"

"Right before he was born. It was still going on, afterward. Maybe that's . . ." She shrugged, her eyes suddenly stinging.

"That was four years ago," her therapist observed delicately. "This dispute may have exacerbated matters for Trent, since it struck directly at his role as a family man." She was reminding Leslie that she is not Trent's therapist. "That might explain his continued anger over professional problems that, by now, are ancient history."

Four years ago Leslie had been in bad shape, and the return of what she now recognized as clinical depression threatened to wash away the ground gained since. She began doing things only when she had to, and didn't pick up *Ancient Mesopotamia* at the library until they threatened to send it back. Trent made oblique comments on her listlessness, and even word that a Florida newspaper office had been contaminated by a rare form of anthrax—another grotesque intrusion from the world of techno-thrillers—failed to jar her out of numbed and ringing stillness.

Was everybody hurting? Leslie supposed so: the avidity with which her coworkers followed the war news smacked of self-medication. Updates rarely came during the workday, but she knew they checked regularly. Trent glared at the TV news, bitter and conflicted, while Megan, unselfconsciously mimicking the familiar Texas accent, asked about "the War Against Terra." Afghanis, caught in the erruption of renewed warfare as winter began to close the passes to their underprovisioned villages, experienced a brief rain of brightly colored food packets.

She sat on the couch, the household still after Trent had gone sullenly to bed, and considered her new book, whose full title proved to be *Ancient Mesopotamia: The Eden That Never Was*. It compared favorably with *Sumer: Cities of Eden*, the pretty Time-Life volume that the library already had on its shelves. *History Begins at Sumer* was unaccountably absent, but Kramer had contributed the text for another Time-Life title, *Cradle of Civilization*. Leslie was annoyed with Kramer for his tendency to make judgmental distinctions between "conquerors in search of booty" and "peaceful immigrants eager to better their lot," as though migrating populations' worthiness to move into a land depended on their adherence to some United Nations–like ideal of peaceful coexistence. Did that notion represent the spirit of the mid-sixties, or the spirit of Time-Life Books?

In the absence of Kramer's own tome, the earliest volume in Leslie's modest collection was A. Leo Oppenheim's *Ancient Mesopotamia: Portrait of a Dead Civilization*. Its forthright subtitle intimated Oppenheim's contention that Sumerian-Akkadian-Assyrian civilization was extinct and should be studied for its own sake rather than for its supposed value as the seedbed of human progress. Leslie found she preferred this austere honesty to the pious melioration that saw Gilgamesh, cuneiform, and the Code of Hammurabi as the first toddling steps of mankind's march.

The weeks that followed pulled Leslie in opposite directions: toward the fixity of the past and the lunacy of a fantasy future. She read with disbelief the mornings' news of anthrax spores mailed to TV studios and the nation's capital, with senators' offices contaminated and postal employees dead. The conclusion was inescapable: the United States was under attack by biological agents. The twenty-first century was turning out just as her teenaged sci-fi reading had predicted.

"They say it's Saddam." Trent was following the links from news reports on the spores' surprising sophistication to declarations by "fellows" at right-wing institutions that Iraqi responsibility was certain.

"Well, it certainly isn't the Taliban." The medieval theocrats who were regrouping in disarray under assaults from their warlord adversaries and miles-high bombers seemed poor candidates for the invisible attack that sent the world's superpower into panic, though perhaps (pundits mused) al Qaeda's penchant for low-tech operations staged within the target country had led them to obtain a cache of Soviet-era war germs. Such a theory did not require the hand of Saddam, but Leslie found it hard to push the reasoning further. The idea of pestilence blooming in the nation's nerve centers like sparks falling on straw left her disoriented. She did not fear for her own safety, but felt the axis of her being tilt vertiginously, a slow tipping into boundless freefall.

There were no further attacks, although a Manhattan woman with no traceable connection with the contaminated mails died of inhaled anthrax in Manhattan, and then another—a ninety-four-year-old widow named Ottilie—in central Connecticut. Midway geographically, Leslie wondered if she should feel her family was in the crosshairs. She didn't, taking comfort in statistics. Word that spores might cling to letters that came through New Jersey moved Leslie to discard all junk mail at the curb.

A week later a letter was delivered sealed in a plastic wrapper containing a notice that the U.S. government had discovered traces of anthrax on the envelope and had subjected it to irradiation: it should be discarded unopened if it was believed to contain food or camera film. Leslie and Trent stared, unwilling to tear through the wrapper (the letter within was indeed junk mail) or to throw it away. It was an undoubted historical document, but to save the thing would make it a relic. Trent carefully photographed both sides with their digital camera and sold it on eBay for $85.

Cries for retaliation rose, angrier for being balked. Since Afghanistan could not be attacked twice, other targets were deemed plausible, usually Iraq. "Look at this," said Trent angrily, gesturing at his screen. "They're all so sure of themselves."

"I don't know why you're reading that at all," Leslie replied. "The chat boards of wargame fans isn't a place for political insight."

"These are my potential readers; I should know what they're thinking."

"I don't even believe that's true." Trent was clawing for a toehold, anxious for demographics that the Web couldn't give him. He showed more self-confidence with work that he respected.

Later she glanced at her screen and found a window open to the posts that had enraged him. Vaunting and aggressive, they bore the signature of angry, powerless guys desperate to be knowledgeable. *Let's do it right this time* and *Next time we nuke the K'abah* and *It's time we revisited The Land Between the Rivers.*

By this point Trent was convinced that the anthrax attacks had not been the work of Islamic militants at all. He suspected rogue forces within the American "bioweapons community," which had secretly developed the strain of anthrax. "Even the administration has admitted that the spores belong to the 'Ames strain,'" he argued, link-clicking deeper toward the documentation he sought. Leslie found his explanations painful to listen to, and she shrank without looking at those windows he left on her screen: laparoscopic images of warblog, like lab reports of current pathology.

Had Sumer suffered from pestilence? Though Leslie recalled no references to the plague, or even to disease as something contagious, it seemed incredible that cities of thirty thousand people, which created standing bodies of water and relied upon wells for drinking, were not periodically ravaged by pandemics, especially during wars. Perhaps Nanshe loses much of her family to cholera during a siege; it was a more plausible involvement than engaging her somehow in the business of battle.

No Sumerian myths mention plague; none of the images of piled dead picture it, nor is it mentioned in legal records. Mortality is ubiquitous, but the index entries for DEATH in Kramer's *Cradle* show an exclusive interest in the Sumerian afterlife, while those for *The Eden That Never Was* focus on the archeology of grave sites. Gilgamesh showed no fear of catching Enkidu's fever, nor Enmerkar of Lugalbanda's. Death did not leap from victim to victim like a flea; each mortal possessed his own, patient and implacable. Whatever the hero's achievements in life, in the Land of No Return he wandered naked, like all the other dead, hot and eternally thirsty.

It was stifling on the second floor, the day's unseasonable warmth undispersed by the mild evening, and Leslie kicked away the damp sheets to rise and open windows. She continued through Megan's room and the baby room, now choked with books, opened the bathroom window (the tiles were barely cool beneath her soles and the toilet seat actually warm, as though someone had preceded her on it) and thence to the end of the hall, where the far window would allow a cross breeze. From there it seemed natural to descend the stairs, for the screened patio doors admitted the night air and she could walk around freely in the unlit rooms.

Opening the refrigerator would illuminate the uncurtained kitchen, and an attempt to fill a cup in the dark clattered the stacked dishes so loudly that she jumped back. Leslie wandered instead toward the front of the house, slowly—she sank her bare foot into the warm furry side of Ursuline, too torpid even to stir—but guided by the faint light coming from the office. Her own computer adjoined an open window so she sat at Trent's, where the monitor's low setting cast just enough light to see by. Trent never kept loose papers on his desk, but she could make out a page of his handwriting lying between *Odile* and *History Begins at Sumer*. She turned the light up slightly, and saw the journal Megan had given him for his birthday, blank sheets bound in dyed silk, held open between the two volumes. He had written in it with his fountain pen—another gift—and weighted the pages flat to dry.

If it had been a paragraph, manifest Dear Diary prose, Leslie would not have bent forward to read, but the two lines were centered like aphorisms, and there was something odd in the lettering. The monitor brightened slightly as the screen saver turned some corner in its workings, and the words leaped up at her.

βeta-testing for βeta males? And underneath: *Real men write their own βooks.*

The Mont Blanc rested in the gutter, a third object to disturb if she wished to turn back the page. Leslie sat back, feeling her face redden in the cool air. Seeking refuge for her gaze, she smacked lightly at the mouse, and the saver vanished, presented her a vista, dim in the darkness, on a burning city. Only the flames actually moved, the fleeing populace and spear-waving invaders caught as in a frieze, but the central building, one side lit by the conflagration, was a recognizable stepped tower, which its builders called "unir" and the successors to Sumer knew as "ziggurat."

Leslie moved her hands to the keyboard, hesitant lest she disrupt the game in progress. Within a minute, however, she had slipped past the undisturbed scenario and was reviewing Trent's interaction with the program, which proved to be the only one open. She checked the system documentation and saw, with a start, that the game had been running for days.

It was the work of a moment to settle in front of her own screen and search its flotilla of icons for Trent's preferred word-processing program. She ran it and found a list of text files: research on Sumer, downloaded online data, and *Ramparts.txt,* which proved to contain

The Ramparts of Uruk, 56,917 words, last revised that afternoon. Trent had moved his work files onto her computer, presumably (it seemed obvious after a second) to allow *Ziggurat* to run unimpeded on his older machine. She had forgotten what gluttons for RAM these new games were.

The image was poignant: Trent keeping his writing files in a crevice between her hard drive's enormous programs—nothing takes up less room than text—while abandoning his own machine to the demands of *Ziggurat.* Doing his work at Leslie's desk, getting his e-mail through the laptop, returning at intervals to his own computer where *Ziggurat* flourished, like a cowbird's chick, to consult with the creature to ensure that his own work not exceed it in grace or wit: this was austere to the point of penitential. Was Trent setting burnt offerings before the thing?

She clicked on another file, *BookTwo.txt.* It appeared to be mostly outline, but there was a title, *Wheels for Warring.* Leslie shook her head. It was just like Trent, to start with a safe title and have a better one ready for the next book.

The outline was followed by notes, which Leslie scrolled through idly. Some comprised bits of research that she had passed to him; others surprised her. *Only two types of personages are portrayed naked in Sumerian art: humiliated prisoners, and priests engaged in sacred ceremony. Why no sexual connotations?* Leslie shifted her bottom on the wicker chair and smiled. For Trent all nudity held sexual connotations. The dogwalker outside, glimpsing screen light falling on her breasts, doubtless felt the same. *Fragments of those statuettes of worshipers were found incorporated into the floors of the Inanna Temple. I.e., these objects remained sacred, even when no longer used?*

That lone blue eye in the display at the Met: they often used lapis lazuli for eyes (look at the blue-eyed ibex in the next case!), though they could never have seen such features. A legend of men with blue eyes?

"No, Jurgen, you must see my palaces. In Babylon I have a palace where many abide with cords about them and burn bran for perfume, while they await that thing which is to befall them." Epigraph? (No.)

Afghanistan is the opposite of Mesopotamia: a land crumpled into inaccessibility. Geographical barriers everywhere, the bane of invaders; while Sumer was open to all armies, the "Kalam" as flat as a board game.

Title for Book 3: A Game Without a Name. *Problematic because the Sumerians of course knew its name; we don't. The game as metaphor for war; if it was also used for divination, then a guide to the Sumerian cosmos & psyche. Historians call it the game "of Ur" since that is where the first boards were found; if I call it the Ur-game can I make allusions to the original FORTRAN "Adventure"? How many of Ziggurat's players were even alive in 1975?*

Leslie created a new file, named it *Book3.txt,* and began to type. *Trent, you don't want to construct one of your novels around that board game. You are appealing to an audience that won't spend its money on books.*

You want to write about a female protagonist, preferably young and, though not herself powerful, able to glimpse its workings. If you must include that game, you can show her watching it played: it was laid out in the streets, remember? A little girl can watch almost anything unnoticed.

Women bring food, nurse the wounded, bury the dead. You want an aperture on war? Don't use the viewpoint of a young soldier; soldiers see almost nothing of the totality of war, they are brought in like a load of rocks and then hurled. Women see everything, and when it is over, they are often what is left.

The wind blew the smoke roaring through the streets, blinding the fleeing villagers and lofting scraps of glowing reed to settle like fireflies on the roofs not already burning. Scattered soldiers came at them, whom Nanshe first saw terrifyingly as the enemy, then realized with a greater shock were the defenders of Lagash. One flung away his shield as he sprinted past.

They had sought to watch the battle from the rooftops, but the wheeling armies had raised a cloud of yellow dust, immense as those seen in the sky, which obscured everything. The city wall was lined with spectators, who enjoyed a better view of the action, although the settlement across the canal was closer. Perhaps they saw the flank of battle shift then spill into the barley fields, concealed from the village by stands of date palm and poplars; perhaps the waving cityfolk had been trying to warn them. Nanshe could remember little of that disordered hour, of anxious inquiry between adults who blocked her view, the surmises and cries, people swarming down the ladders to shout questions, to call for their families, and finally to run.

Nanshe had become separated almost immediately, buffeted by legs and swinging arms. She tried to head home, but a cry to make for the city gates sent the crowd rushing against her, and by the time she emerged from the side streets she could smell smoke. Someone lunged for her, not the person she later saw stabbed with a spear, though events seemed alike unreal save what was happening now, grit biting her legs where she crouched. She could see Sud lying in the road, and started repeatedly when a large scrap caught in the rubble waved like a sleeve.

Smoke spattered the sky, and when night fell she thought it another gout from the burning market, to recede after some minutes.

At some point she found herself stumbling over littered ground, eyes stinging in the darkness. Unnatural sounds reached her, a loud snap or the crash of walls. A groan from somewhere, and for an instant she imagined the slave moving confidently through the blackness, eyeless and unsmarting, calling out in an accent the marauders would recognize.

A shift in wind pushed aside smoke to disclose still-burning houses, flames from their collapsed roofs flickering through doors like glowing ovens. Occasionally Nanshe could hear a faint shout call down, and so knew the direction of the city walls. Lips cracked, she groped across open ground to the well, which she discovered surrounded by corpses. Desperation drove her to the exposure of the levee, where at last she fell forward to drink.

It is Gilgamesh come to subjugate Lagash, if you like, or else the Gutians sweeping out of the hills. Better perhaps a Sumerian enemy, for Nanshe had been assured that the armies would clash on the plains beyond the cultivated fields, or else before the city gates, and that soldiers would only kill soldiers. Hiding in the tamarisk brush, Nanshe understands only that what the boys had said about war was not true. She is not pondering the implications of this, any more than she is thinking about her parents or their smoldering home, for she is in a kind of shock. Alert to any movement in the brightening morning, she knows that nothing around her will proceed as she had been told.

Can you tell that *story? The vaunting steles do not, nor any poems that officials preserved.*

It cannot be reduced to a game, nor presented in terms of one. The metaphor itself is immoral.

A wail floated down the stairs, its eerie pitch catching the agelessness of the dreaming mind. Leslie left the room at once, negotiating the darkened floor's furniture and doorways with intimate familiarity. At the top of the stairs she heard it again, wavering between frightened and querulous, and went to her daughter's room. Megan was asleep but in distress, her head turning from side to side in the faint moonlight as her mouth shaped half words. As Leslie approached, she saw the dim glint of open eyes.

"It's all right, honey." Experts advise that children having nightmares not be wakened, but her parents had learned how to offer Megan comfort without disturbing her. Leslie stroked her daughter's hair and murmured that everything was okay.

"I heard the plane and it scared me."

"Plane?" The Bridgeport Airport was a few miles away, and corporate jets sometimes landed late at night. Leslie tried to recall whether she had heard a plane a minute before.

"It sounded like a jet," Megan said lucidly.

Leslie doubted that her daughter had ever heard a nonjet engine overhead, but she took her true meaning. Storm-tossed but hearing the lighthouse, she realized with a pang that her misery did not matter, nor Trent's professional tribulations nor his baffled fury, but only her daughter's well-being, which she had heeded but not enough. "It's all right," she said, leaning forward and touching foreheads in the dark. "No more bad planes."

What is wrong cannot soon be put right—at least not what lies in the mind, which occupies not two or even three dimensions, but the infolds of a space no one has mapped. Leslie began attending her daughter more closely, reading to her at night (no Homer) and stopping with her for hot chocolate on their way back from the library or soccer practice. Megan worried about the school's winter pageant, holiday plans, a classmate's parents' divorce. She mentioned the World Trade Center only when discussing an assignment to summarize the week's news. What more concerned her was an image she had come upon while searching the Net with a friend's older sister: a condemned woman being forced to kneel while a Taliban executioner put a rifle to her skull.

"It's a horrible picture," Leslie agreed. She was furious that her daughter had been shown it.

"The people who did that . . ." Megan spoke with unaccustomed hesitancy. "They belong to al Qaeda, don't they?"

"Not exactly." If you want to get technical. "The Taliban let al Qaeda stay in their country, but they did not help carry out the attacks. The President insisted that they turn over Osama bin Laden, which they probably couldn't do, so he launched an invasion."

"I don't care," said Megan firmly. She was staring into the middle distance, where the woman kneeling facedown was visible to both of them. "I'm glad he's dead."

He wasn't the only one, though. As the death toll from the September attacks steadily dropped from the initial six thousand to just more than half that, a reciprocal number, of those killed in Afghanistan, rose to match it. The first, dwindling value was widely followed and subtly resented—one couldn't actually accuse those compiling it of unpatriotism—while the second, swelling one was neither: its extent (reported only on dissident websites) unacknowledged and enjoyed.

Leslie spoke twice with Megan's teacher, and even rejoined the listserv of women who had become pregnant the same month she had, which she had dropped four years ago. She read online reports of children experiencing anxiety and bad dreams, spoke to her therapist of Megan rather than herself, and watched her daughter: eating breakfast, doing homework, asleep. When troubled Megan was before her, she ignored everything else.

Rumblings from the shocked economy sounded dimly from work and home. Great Games, losing market share, canceled its plans for a line of *Ziggurat* novels, and Trent (midway through the second book but not yet paid for the first) slid from stunned rage into depression. Leslie comforted him distractedly. Truckloads of rubble filed by the thousands, like a column of ants reducing a picnic's rubbish, from the still-smoldering wreckage of Ground Zero to Staten Island's Fresh Kills landfill, where it was sifted for personal effects and body parts. Troops of the "Northern Alliance" (a cognomen worthy of *Star Wars*) drove the remains of the Taliban into the mountains, which shuddered beneath the impact of enormous American bombs called "daisycutters."

Leslie wanted to spend the hour before dinner with her daughter, but Trent finally protested at cooking every night. Coming from the kitchen, she heard them sitting in the office together, discussing return trips to favorite movies.

"Dumbledore is kind of like Gandalf," Megan was saying matter-of-factly, "except I don't think Gandalf would be very good with children."

"He treated those hobbits like children."

". . . But Sauron and Lord Voldemort are even more similar, aren't they?"

"Well, it's hard to put much spin on evil incarnate, isn't it?"

"Incarnate?" Leslie could hear her taste the word. "Is that what they call the 'evil-doers'?"

Trent groaned softly. "How I hate that term."

"Because *they* don't think what they're doing is evil," said Megan wisely. Leslie stood outside the doorway, leaning forward slightly to see them. "They think that God wants them to do this."

"That's right. And our culture—what the President calls 'Western Civilization'—believes that *we* are doing what God wants, though the government is careful not to say so in as many words. In the real world, your enemy doesn't oblige you by acting like Sauron or Voldemort."

"Or Darth Vader." Megan has a happy thought. "We'll be seeing Part Two of all three movies next year! Too oh oh too!"

"It must be the age of sequels."

"And the age of *Evil-doers*."

Trent laughed. "In movies, yes. In real life, it would be better if people were more careful about using that word."

"Or 'cowardly.'"

"Indeed." Trent looked at their daughter closely. "You still think about that?"

Megan shrugged. "Julie's dad almost got killed." She paused, then asked, "Did Gilgamesh represent Western values?"

"Gilgamesh? He lived before there was a West, or a Middle East."

She is changing the subject, Leslie wanted to cry out, but Megan turned to face her father and said, "I'm sorry your book's not going to be published."

Trent blinked. "Heavens, dear, don't worry about that. Maybe someone else will publish it. Maybe I was writing the wrong book." He extended an arm, and Megan slipped under it. "That's an awfully tiny problem, if you think about it."

Lying awake, Leslie listened to her husband's steady breathing and wondered at the loss of his dream, the rout of the last ditch. He had told her in college that prose narrative was dead, that they stood at the end of its era just as the—had he actually said ancient Sumerians?—stood at its birth. Science fiction was the mode of the era, but its future masterpieces would not come in strings of sentences. The Web—he had charmed her by admitting that he too had reflexively read *www.* as "World War Won"—had blossomed in their college years from jury-rigging of dial-ups to a vast nervous system, and Trent's vision of nonlinear, multimedia fictions—richly complex structures of word, image, and sound, detailed as Cibachrome and nuanced as Proust—seemed ready to take shape in the hypertrophied craniums of the ever-cheaper CPUs.

Trent seemed untroubled that the point of entry to this technology would be through electronic games, which were being developed solely for audiences uninterested in formal innovation and poststructural *différance*. He expected not to retain copyright to his early work, which would be remembered only as technical exercises and crude forerunners of the GlasTome. Its form would emerge by pushing against commercial boundaries from the inside. Even product, he told Leslie, could be produced with a greater or lesser degree of artistry.

When asked to reconcile this conviction with his love of novels, Trent replied that he also loved verse dramas. Reading the draft chapters of his biography of the great man, Leslie wondered at the wretched fellow's dogged attempts (remorselessly documented by Trent) to traverse the swamp of commercial fiction and pull his soles free of it later. Better to emulate the great man's own master: subordinate all to your work, let creditors and family wait upon your genius? Perhaps, as with the intervening James, fame will greet you anyway!

Lie down in bogs, wake up with fees. Trent had ended his unhappy sojourn in the land of the games without copyright or royalties, footloose into the barrens. *But we have our daughter, dear.* The occasional classes he taught, the magazine articles and the tiny fellowship, offered no visible path back to the realm where word and image alike danced in the flux of Aye and Nought. *But what you do is valued, and I love you.* An old colleague had offered the chance to beta-test and Trent had obliged, poor hopeful fool, been sucked in and spat out. *Write something about ancient Sumer.* Your banishing Eden beguiles then betrays you, leaving you stunned with grief, lost to truer pleasures, deaf to your lover's cry. It is the fracture of the unmalleable heart, the oldest story in the world.

It is Christmas Day, "a celebration of great antiquity," as the great man once put it. Dinner with Leslie's sister in Riverside Heights, their first trip to Manhattan since summer. Megan balks at going (she has heard some report of a possible "terrorist attack" over the holidays), and must be reassured that Caroline lives on the other end of the island from Ground Zero. Despite Christmas carols on the car radio and a half hour of *The Two Towers* on tape, she is moody and withdrawn.

"Are you still reading *Odile*?" Leslie asks, seeing the book resting in Trent's lap.

Trent picks up the book, studies a passage, then translates rapidly. " 'For years I have deluded myself and lived my life in complete error. I thought I was a mathematician. I now realize that I am not even an amateur. I am nothing at all. I know nothing, understand nothing. It's terrible, but that's how it is. And do you know what I was capable of, what I used to do? Calculation upon calculation, out of sight, out of breath, without purpose or end, and most often completely absurd. I gorged myself on figures; they capered before me until my head spun. And I took that to be mathematics!' "

Leslie glances sidelong at him; she isn't sure if this is the point where Trent had stopped reading or a passage he had marked. "So is the novel both an iliad and an odyssey?" she asks carefully.

"Not that I can tell. I asked an old classmate, who wrote back last night: he says that the novel was written years before Queneau published that theory and that the title was likelier a play on 'Idyll' and 'Odalisque.' "

"Oh." Leslie frowns. "Academics exchange e-mail on Christmas Eve?"

"Why not? And now I can't remember where I read that claim—probably online."

"Did you search for the site?"

"Can't find it now."

Leslie gets her brooding family to the apartment of her sister, whose husband speaks with zest about the coming assault on Iraq. Caroline and Megan exchange whispers about presents in the kitchen, while Trent politely declines to be baited. Kubrick's film, sound muted, plays on the DVD; Leslie can see the second monolith tumbling in space. Sipping her whiskeyed eggnog, she thinks about 2002, the first year in a while that doesn't sound science-fictional.

On the third day Lugalkitun rode out to survey the damage, striding angrily through the village that had been destroyed when the battle overran its intended ground. Vultures took wing at his approach, though with insolent slowness, and a feral dog fled yelping after he shied a rock into its flank.

Beside the fields of an outlying farm he regarded the body of a girl, sufficiently well attired to be of the owner's family. Her clothing had been disturbed, either before or after death, and the king turned away, scowling. If the enemy had enjoyed the leisure for such diversions, they would also have paused to contaminate the wells.

Caroline asks Trent about a news item that appeared a few days ago announcing that a quantum computer, primitive but genuine, had successfully factored a number by using switches comprising individual atoms, which could represent 0 and 1 simultaneously. Is this still digital? she wonders. Trent, who was examining his gift—a new hardcover edition of the great man's *Cities in Flight*—offers a wintry smile and tells her that the spooky realm of quantum physics will make software designers feel like the last generation of engineers to devote their careers to zeppelin technology.

They go outside, mid-November weather of the warmest Christmas in memory. Down the street a circle of older women are singing, some of them wearing choir robes. A wind off the river blows the sound away, and Megan, looking anxiously upward, does not see them.

Near the burned house he came upon a toy cart, intact among so much rubble. Its chicken head stared as though astonished to find itself upended, and the king righted it with the tip of his boot. He had seen such contrivances before, and they vexed him. Miniature oxcarts and chariots he could understand, they were copies for children; but the wheeled chicken possessed no original—it stood for something that didn't exist. Set one beside a proper boy's clay chariot and you irresistibly saw both at full size, the huge head absurd in a way that somehow spilled onto the chariot.

The toy's wheels, amazingly, were unbroken: it rolled backward from his pettish kick. It never occurred to Lugalkitun to crush it; a shadow cast by nothing is best left undisturbed. He looked at the ruins about him, pouring smoke into and summoning beasts out of the open sky. Neither emptiness above nor crowding below concerned him; his brown gaze ranged flat about his own realm, imagining retribution in full measure, cities aflame, their people in flight across the hard playing ground of The Land.

The wind shifts, and the last strains of melody—a gospel hymn—reach them. "Let's go listen," says Caroline, taking her niece by the hand. By the time they cross the intersection the choir is singing again, in a mournful, swelling contralto that courses through Leslie like vibrations from a church organ.

There is a balm in Gilead
To make the wounded whole;
There is a balm in Gilead
To heal the sin-sick soul.

Megan begins to cry. "I don't want a bomb," she sniffles, pressing her face against her mother's side.

Leslie and Trent exchange bewildered expressions. The notes soar into the air, fading with distance. Leslie pats Megan's shoulder, feeling wet warmth soak through her sweater. *My daughter is not well,* she thinks, deeply disordering words. Their wrongness reaches through her, and she furiously tells herself not to cry, that composure will calm her child. But the stone of resolve begins to crack, and two beads of moisture seep through, welling to spill free—their path will trace the surest route—and carve twin channels down her face.

—August 2001–July 2002

Sometime around 1160 B.C., Hekla, the most active volcano in Iceland, erupted, with dire consequences for northern Europe and beyond. Even before the cataclysm, the harsh conditions of the Orkney Islands, off the northern tip of Scotland, demanded adaptability from their human and animal habitants. The archaeological record preserves evidence that the ancient breed of Orkney sheep met those demands in a peculiar way (and continues to do so today). As Laura Frankos shows us, Hekla, having rallied the oppressive forces of Father Winter, also pushed the people of these islands to the limits of their bodies and especially of their spirits.

The Sea Mother's Gift

LAURA FRANKOS

Dett stood on Western Isle's cliff, ignoring the thousands of birds wheeling and shrieking above him, even when some spattered his deerskin cloak with their droppings. He studied the sky as the sun dipped toward the horizon, as he had done these past few months whenever the clouds lifted enough to see the sunset. That wasn't often; the Islands usually spent the summer months wrapped in fog, and this particular summer had been especially cold. What he saw unnerved him. *These colors are wrong,* he thought. *Too red, too orange, too yellow—like fire. I have never seen sunsets like this before, yet ever since the Day of Darkness in late spring, they have all looked this way. Why have the sunsets changed? It must mean something. But what?*

He turned his gaze upon the waves pounding the sheer cliffs below him. Guillemots, kittiwakes, and auks, unafraid of the power of the Mother of the Sea, darted in and out of the water, seeking fish and crabs. His eye was accustomed to their rapid motion, likewise, to that of the seals hunting their prey. Then, at the base of the cliffs, he spied a strange sight amidst the seafoam.

A blood-red figure—its color much the same as the queer skies—broke through the billows and stretched a long red arm upward, grasping, but catching nothing. A powerful wave knocked it back under, but only for a moment. It surged up once more, allowing Dett a glimpse of a gigantic head with a gaping mouth, before another wave, as strong as if pushed by the Mother herself, overcame it.

Dett watched the same spot for more than an hour, but the thing did not return. The wind that tore at his hair and clothes and chapped his lips didn't bother him. He would have noticed it more if the wind had stopped. Gust-blowing demons continually plagued the Islands, sometimes banding together to create a terrific gale in hopes of pleasing their lord, Father Winter.

"Dett!" A deep, resonant voice called him. He turned to see his brother Mebaw ascending the slope to join him at the cliff's edge. Mebaw was wiry where Dett was stocky, but they both had the same oval faces and high cheekbones, the same warm brown eyes.

"Jolpibb thought you'd be up here," Mebaw said. A broad smile appeared in a thicket of dark brown whiskers. "What do you hope to find here, brother? Saving birdshit, of course."

"Answers," said Dett. "Instead, I found another question. Perhaps it is a blessing that you are here, for you are the Mastersinger's Second, and learned in signs and portents. Look down there, by that slanting rock with the four seals and the cluster of terns. Do you see anything? No? Let me tell you what I saw." He described the sighting, and Mebaw's jolly face creased into unfamiliar frowns.

"The elders must hear of this, brother, but I fear it sounds like Klevey. This could be very serious, for there are few monsters on land or sea that can wreak destruction as Klevey."

Dett shuddered. "That is what I thought, too. I came up here, as I have for many weeks now, seeking the reasons why the sun has hidden its face. This is the height of summer, yet we have had as many weeks of freezing clouds as when Lord Father Winter reigns. And behold the sunset! The sky seems touched with flame as the sun goes to its rest. Do you think the reddened sky is a sign that Klevey is near? The red flesh I saw thrashing in the surf was much the same color."

Mebaw's bony shoulders moved in a shrug under his sealskin cape. "Nothing in the songlore connects Klevey with oddly colored skies. He is a creature of the ocean, not the heavens."

"I fear that red sky means something is wrong in the heavens."

"Do you remember that trader who came some years ago, the one with the so-sharp metal knives? He thought the air of our Islands shimmered, and seemed different from the air of his native land in the distant south."

"And Grandmother Glin told him it was because the Seafolk ground pearls to sprinkle on the fishladies' tails, and must have tossed some into the sky," laughed Dett. "But the trader, for all his fine wares, was a fool to believe that. A shimmering! Bah! It is nothing but the sea salt in the air. You can taste it; you can see the crystals catch in your beard.

But if you go far from the sea, where the trader has his home, or into a sheltered place, you cannot see any floating sparkles."

"Perhaps it is because the Seafolk cannot throw the pearl dust into such places," Mebaw said with a wink. "Besides, who can go far from the sea in the Islands? No one but mad adventurers like Father and Uncle Talloc on their boats!"

"Ah, Uncle Talloc," said Dett with bitterness. "I am sorry he was named to the elders' council. Not that I doubt the wisdom of his years, but I am his least-favorite nephew because I am no sailor. Father made allowances for my terrible seasickness—why couldn't Uncle?"

"I am fortunate the Mastersinger chose me for his Second, saving me from a life at sea. No one, not even Uncle Windbag, can argue with the Master."

The pair stood silent for a while, staring down at the waves. Mebaw finally spoke again, "The cliffs and rocks below are of red sandstone. Is it possible, brother, that you mistook a rock for the monster?"

"No," Dett said firmly. "I am not versed in lore, but my eyes are keen."

"Then we shall present your sighting to the elders. They meet in three days' time, when the moon is full. For now, brother, let us go home. Your wife is waiting."

The two brothers turned away from the sheer red cliffs and trudged down the sloping hills. Soon they passed some of their fields of barley and wheat. "Look," Dett pointed. "The fields do poorly because the weather has been bad ever since that day when the skies became as black as night. Our harvest will be a small one this autumn."

"How cheery you are today," Mebaw said. "Can you not find something pleasant to say, such as, 'My brother, your singing has improved of late. How many verses did you manage last night—sixteen? No, twenty!' "

"Of course your singing has improved. It could hardly worsen. The auks are in better voice, or the sheep. Harken at them; they're doing the chorus, you can chant the verse."

A rise, sprinkled with hundreds of small pink flowers, shielded the sheep pen from their sight, but the bleating of the lambs and the reassuring calls of the ewes penetrated the ever-present growling of the surf. They also heard a piping voice swearing amidst the other sounds.

They crested the rise and looked down. The enclosure was protected on one side by the steep rise, and bordered on the others by stone walls with a single wooden gate. The foul words came from the direction of the gate, where a small figure in a dark cap was shoving a gray ram back inside. The boy was soaking wet and shivering. The ram's gray fleece, recently shorn for the summer, was also damp, though the beast showed no sign of feeling a chill.

"Trouble, son?" Dett called out. He and Mebaw walked down to the flagstone wall his great-grandfathers had built, or so said Grandmother Glin. It was a strong and sturdy wall, not unlike Glin herself, the oldest woman on Western Isle. They leaned on it, watching the lad struggle with the animal.

"Father, this one should be *named* Trouble!" cried the boy. He slammed the gate shut. "He's done it again, cursed beast! I grow tired of his games."

"What games, Fummirrul?" asked Mebaw. "I love to play games."

"Not these games." Fummirrul heaved a shell at the ram's backside. The animal twitched at the impact. He turned his horned head and appeared to scrutinize the young shepherd for a moment, then walked toward the small stone barn.

"One of the other sheep was grazing next to the wall. Trouble saw her there, leaped on her back, then sprang over the wall. The other two new rams have done this trick, too, whenever another sheep goes close by the wall. Not the ewes, for which I am thankful, for there are many more of them. Two mornings ago, when I came to take the flock to pasture, all three rams were outside the pen."

"Ho ho!" Mebaw chuckled. "Father's prized sheep are trying to go back to their southern homeland."

"Yes, Uncle Mebaw. For they *do* go down to the shore."

Mebaw looked astonished that Fummirrul had taken his joke literally. Dett, who had heard his son complaining of the new sheep, was not surprised. He asked, "And did they do the same as before?"

"They did. They grazed upon seaweed. Whenever I lead the flock to the farther fields, these stupid new animals keep trying to run to the shore. I spend my days chasing them and bringing them back to their more obedient cousins. But there is even worse. Today, after Trouble escaped, he saw me running after him, and the wretched creature *swam out to the rocks*. I do not jest or tell untruths. Father, Uncle, I swear that ram was laughing at me from his perch. I had to wade into the arms of the Mother of the Sea to drag him back to shore." His youthful face filled with indignation. "Our old sheep do not behave like this. What am I to do with them?"

"What any man does when faced with a dilemma: do what you think is best to cope with it. So our father told us. So I tell you."

Fummirrul grimaced. This bit of paternal advice was not the solution he sought. He muttered something about drowning them all the next time they went swimming.

"Did you hear me, son?"

"Yes, Father. You said to do what I think best."

"Let us go home, that you may have a hot meal and dry clothes."

"May I run, Father?" At Dett's nod, he pelted down the trail, the dark cap and the pale crook bobbing with every step.

"The new sheep *are* funny sheep," Dett murmured. "And clever. To use another animal as a stepping stone!"

"Father and Uncle Talloc said they ate seaweed on the trip home from the south, after their supply of grain ran out on the long voyage. Nor did they seem harmed by it."

"They must have acquired a taste for it. Don't suppose a little can hurt them; after all, we eat the stuff, too. But for my poor boy's sake, I am glad the old sheep and the new ewes do not play runaway."

"Heh, for all we know, the new ewes might be frisky, too, but for their new lambs," Mebaw said with a malicious grin.

"If you want to remain my son's favorite uncle," said Dett, "I advise you keep that observation to yourself."

Dett's village, which nestled in Western Isle's best harbor, numbered around one hundred and forty people. Most, like Dett and Mebaw, farmed and fished and hunted, but there were a few—including their father, uncle, cousins, and two brothers-in-law—who sometimes ventured farther in their boats, trading goods with nearby islands and catching fish that lived in deeper waters. On several occasions, under the guidance of the Mother of the Seas, they traveled an even greater distance, past the Small South Isles to the Great Island. On their last trip there, they discovered a village put to the sword by sea raiders, save a girl and a boy, both young shepherds. After many arguments, they decided to bring them all—sheep and children—back to the Western Isle, though it perilously crowded their vessels. Seven sheep and the boy died on the way, but the girl now lived in Talloc's house and would wed his youngest son after her monthly courses began. Now called Gefalal, or "stranger," she had yet to learn more than a dozen words of their language.

As the brothers entered the village, they spied Gefalal sitting before the doorway of Talloc's house, carding wool from the recently shorn flock. She leaped to her feet at their approach and bowed her head in respect. Whether her people were naturally more deferential or she still felt ill-at-ease after several months in her new home, Dett did not know. He only knew the children of Western Isle tended to be more outgoing. Fummirrul, for one, never seemed still unless sound asleep. Dett nodded politely to Gefalal as he passed; she bowed more deeply.

The sight of the stranger girl brought a question to Dett's mind. "Has Father mentioned when he and the others will go back to sea?"

Mebaw frowned. "He and Uncle Talloc are uneasy about sailing farther than the nearest isles because of the weather. They don't like the cold and clouds any more than you do, Brother Sky-watcher. Our brothers-in-law want to go anyway, this being summer—well, a sort of summer—but the elders urge caution. I suspect they will be even more reluctant to put to sea if they think Klevey lurks beneath the whitecaps."

"I hope they will say I was mistaken in my sighting. Still, it is wise to be cautious. Father says the currents between the islands are treacherous enough in good weather, and many lack safe harbors such as ours. Better to proceed with care than lose ships in an unexpected storm." He turned back to face the western horizon, where the setting sun glowed like an ember. "Sleep well, brother. I intend to wake you early to help me hunt. It is time we had a feast at the Pit."

"You are cruel. The nights are too short as it is, and my wife is after me to make her another storage box."

"If you spent less time singing and more time working . . ."

Mebaw brushed off this scolding and headed for his house at the eastern end of the enclave. Dett entered his home nearby, where the usual din prevailed. His oldest daughter, Joloc, was spooning barley porridge into the next-to-youngest, who was humming as she gummed each mouthful. His wife, Jolpibb, was changing the wrappings of the cranky baby, and Grandmother Glin was singing charms over the bed of the feverish four-year-old, Orrul. Fummirrul, now naked but for a wool blanket, was squabbling with Rarpibb, his six-year-old sister. He teasingly held her doll, a blobbly lump of sealskin stuffed with a handful of wool, above her outstretched hands.

"I am glad Mebaw dragged you from your high perch," Jolpibb said over the baby's howls. "You spend so much time gazing at the heavens, I sometimes fear you will forget what happens here on the ground."

"I know what happens here on the ground," Dett said. He plucked the doll from Fummirrul and tossed it to Rarpibb, who cuddled it. "Nothing grows well in the ground but weeds. From above, the sun stares down on us, clothed in vermilion and yellow robes. And today, in the froth at the cliff's base, I saw something else, something I must report to the council of elders."

"For you to propose such action sounds serious," Grandmother Glin said from the little one's bedside. "You are not given to speaking rashly."

"Would that I were!" Dett cried. "Then everyone could dismiss my worries as they did those of old Telley, who saw disaster everywhere and omens in every least little thing!" He spoke with such vehemence that everyone shut up, even the baby. For a moment, the only sound in the close, smoky room was Orrul's harsh, labored breathing.

"Is something wrong with the sun, Father?" Rarpibb asked, a slight tremor in her voice. "Can you put it right?"

"No man has power over the sun, little one," Dett said. "Our place is here on the earth."

"The sun went away before, when I was little, like Orrul," Rarpibb said, "but it came back, and now it hardly ever is gone, though sometimes it is hard to see in the clouds. I am glad, because I do not like the darkness."

Dett, Grandmother, and Jolpibb exchanged wry looks. To a child, the long nights of winter must have given the impression the sun had indeed left for good. Rarpibb was too young to understand the cyclical nature of the seasons.

"I do not like the darkness, either," Dett said. "But I would like some porridge."

Dett and Mebaw and several other men went hunting the next day and managed to kill two red deer stags. They also spied a doe with a fawn, but let it go to fatten for the fall. They dragged the carcasses to the Pit outside their village, where many of the women were waiting. They exclaimed over the men's success, for deer were not plentiful on Western Isle.

The Pit lay beside a small lake, their principal source of fresh water. A great heap of blackened soil, rocks, and ash stood next to it, the remains of decades' worth of meals, according to Grandmother Glin. The Pit itself was huge, and lined with clay and stones, capable of cooking several deer at once, or even enormous chunks of whale. A steady parade of youngsters with buckets began filling the Pit with lake water as the men set to skinning the stags on the flagstone workplace. The women tending the Great Hearth made certain to keep clear of their keen-edged stone knives.

"It's always at this time I think of that trader," said Mebaw. "The one with those metal knives." He sighed, as if longing for a beautiful woman.

"We do well enough with what we have," said Dett. "His price was too high."

"But I'd never seen the like, not before or since!" cried Mebaw.

Uncle Talloc nodded soberly. "Sharp as Klevey's teeth, they were."

"And what do you know of Klevey?" snorted Grandmother Glin.

"Your skill is with boats, not song lore. You are as empty-headed as the Pit, Talloc."

Mebaw came to his uncle's defense. "And is the Pit so empty? It is near full of water, and then you women will drop in the heated stones."

"I confess to being wrong in that respect, grandson. However, your head *is* like the Pit: full of rocks."

The work continued for a time, then Talloc called out, "This is drudgery. Give us a tale, Grandmother, to entertain us while we labor."

"Willingly," she said. "The younger women can heat the stones for the Pit. I will sit and rest my aching bones." She eased herself on a pile of flagstones near one end of the workplace. From the orderliness of them, Dett suspected they once had been part of a wall, the remains of which were long gone, perhaps used when his ancestors constructed the Great Hearth.

"I shall speak of Klevey," she announced. Dett sorely wished she had chosen differently, but as he had not presented his sighting before the council, he saw no way of stopping her.

"Klevey dwells in the sea, and there is no more monstrous creature to be found under or above the waves," said Grandmother. "He is oath-brother to Lord Father Winter, and sometimes they work together, bringing ruin and devastation to men."

Rarpibb, who had been toting a bucket, asked, "If Klevey lives in the sea, why doesn't the Mother of the Sea control him, as she does the Seafolk?"

"Foolish girl! Does not the Mother have enough to do, battling Lord Father Winter every year?" Grandmother retorted. "How she struggles with him every spring, so fierce you can hear them roaring! How she binds him to the seafloor, and brings back the warm waters for us! How he cunningly breaks free in the autumn, to banish the Mother in turn, and afflict us with storms and plague us with his shrieking wind demons! Until at last, the Mother returns, to confront the chill Master once more and chain him yet again."

Mebaw bent his head over his skinning and suppressed a grin, but Dett saw it and knew the reason for it: Grandmother had just given a short account of one of the clan's most famous songs, "The War Against Winter." Barely three months ago, during the height of the spring gales, Mebaw sang all fifty verses without error. The Mastersinger showered him with praise, and he was puffed with pride for days.

Rarpibb, however, grumbled something about why the Mother couldn't manage things better, and so keep Winter chained. Fortunately, Grandmother's poor hearing caused her to miss this cheeky observation.

The old woman continued: "But we do beg the Mother for protection from that dread menace, Klevey, for she alone can keep him satisfied and prevent him from prowling the lands of men. Aye, the Mother, and good, fresh water—those are the only things that Klevey fears."

"What does he look like?" Rarpibb asked.

"His head is gigantic, with a mouth like a whale's, from which the most foul and venomous reek spews forth. When he breathes, any nearby living thing—be it man, beast, or plant—perishes from his poison. He has no—"

In the midst of his carving, Dett came over queer, as if the ground tilted beneath him, or he had eaten something that made him ill. "Enough, Grandmother!" he cried.

She stopped. "What is amiss, Dett?"

He reeled away from the bloody carcass, trying to keep down his nausea. He snatched a bucket from the foreign girl, Gefalal, and dashed cold water on his face. The queasiness receded, but the uneasy feeling did not. It was similar to what he sensed on the cliffs while watching the strange skies, but much, much stronger.

He glanced westward, toward the distant cliffs. Standing there, stark against the gray skies, was the red figure he'd seen before, swaying slightly on its flipperlike legs. "There!" Dett croaked. "Look to the west! Klevey comes! Do you see him?"

The villagers turned to stare, but the gods had granted the sighting to Dett alone. Unable to gaze at the monster any longer, he collapsed, retching. When he managed to look up again, Klevey had gone.

Beside him, Gefalal shivered with fear. He nodded, hoping to reassure her, then turned to the others, who were also staring at him in dismay. Dett was sober, quiet, and not given to displays, unlike his flamboyant brother. They didn't know what to make of his behavior.

"A sighting, nephew?" Uncle Talloc asked in tones clearly hoping for a denial.

"My second," Dett whispered. "I saw the Red Scourge yesterday, at the cliff bottoms. I planned to tell the council of it."

"It is true," Mebaw said. "I spoke with Dett not long after the sighting."

"This was worse. He stood on our land, though he was there but for a moment," said Dett.

Grandmother pursed her wrinkled lips. "Well! This will be a more interesting council meeting than most. Enough so, I suspect, to make me yearn for boredom. Under the circumstances, I shall tell a different tale, for fear my words bring back the Red Scourge."

"But I want to hear—" Rarpibb began, but fell silent at a sharp gesture from her mother.

"I shall speak of the swimming dances of the Seafolk, held in their glittering underwater palaces." As she related the simple story, the others returned to work. Dett listened anxiously as he hacked at the carcasses. It took a long time for the awful wretchedness inside him to abate. By evening, when the chunks of meat had simmered to perfection in the Pit, the families ate well, but Dett had to choke down nearly every bite. The fresh meat tasted foul, as foul as Klevey's breath.

That night, as Dett slept beside his wife and children, Klevey walked through his dreams. At first Dett thought it was just Orrul's wheezy rattle, which had recently worsened. Then he realized his mind's eye was seeing his well-tended fields of barley and wheat, and beyond them, the flower-sprinkled rise that marked the sheep enclosure. His mind's ears heard the sheep calling frantically while that hoarse coughing grew louder. Dream-Dett climbed the rise in the same place he and Mebaw had climbed when they stopped to check on Fummirrul. He looked down on a scene of horror.

Woolly corpses littered the pen. Klevey, his huge chest heaving as he struggled to breathe air, lumbered after the surviving sheep on his awkward flipper-legs. Not that he needed to go near the animals to cause them harm. Some collapsed from sheer fright. Those close enough to smell the noxious fumes from the monster's mouth died in writhing agony, while others were felled by blows from his clublike fists. He popped an entire lamb in his gaping mouth; his daggerlike teeth shredded it, and blood trickled down onto his torso.

As dream-Dett watched, frozen in terror, he noticed two things that gave him hope: Fummirrul was not in the pen and the new sheep were escaping. As the older animals huddled near the wall, the new beasts, in almost orderly fashion, leaped on their backs and vaulted to safety. Even the ewes and lambs made it out, though it seemed impossible that the little spindly creatures could jump that high. Led by Trouble, the largest ram, the entire flock trotted north along the shoreline and disappeared from sight. Dream-Dett could only hope his son had vanished with them.

Klevey soon decided he was done tormenting the sheep, so he lurched to the wall nearest to dream-Dett, and heaved himself over with his massive arms. Dream-Dett threw himself behind a boulder, hoping Klevey's single red eye had not noticed him. The Red Scourge followed the path to the tilled fields, and plunged into them. His flippers trampled the young plants; what he didn't crush, his venomous coughing destroyed. The tender green and golden shoots blackened and died; the skies grew darker and the air colder.

When all the fields were smoldering, Klevey finally stopped. The destruction was taking a toll on him. Spasm after spasm racked his broad chest. Klevey was skinless, yet his exposed red flesh glistened moistly as though his exertions had made him sweat. Black blood pulsed through the yellow veins crisscrossing his frame.

After what seemed to dream-Dett an eternity, Klevey stopped barking and wheezing. He rested a moment, knuckles pressed into the turf, then turned toward the village.

Dream-Dett knew it was futile, but he tried to scramble around the boulder to stop the monster. He slipped on the wet grass and found he couldn't get up, for something was pinning down his tunic. He wheeled around to free himself, only to find a large gray seal had the cloth in his mouth—nor did it appear ready to let go. It stared at him with eyes unlike any he had ever seen in a seal before. There was intelligence behind the dark pupils. No ordinary seal, then, but one of the Seafolk.

"You must let me go," dream-Dett pleaded. "Klevey is attacking my village!"

The seal, or, rather, Seaman, its mouth still firmly shut on the tunic, shook its head. Its belly and sides were encrusted with wet sand and a long tendril of seaweed was draped over one flipper. This gave it the appearance of having only just crawled out of the sea . . . except there were no tracks of its passing behind it, only the grassy heath, with the virgin shore some distance further.

"Have pity! Or are you in league with the monster?"

It shook its head once more, its wide eyes wet with tears.

"Is there nothing we can do?" he wailed, fully expecting the creature to shake its head a third time.

It did not, but released him so abruptly he stumbled onto the grass. When he turned back, the Seaman was gone, leaving nothing behind but the seaweed and a few smears of crusty sand on the grass. Dream-Dett ran into the village, but he was too late. Klevey had gone—the tracks of his flippers quite plainly ran through the entire community and down into the harbor, where they disappeared into the surf. A resounding silence met Dett, filling his ears until he thought his head would burst.

Then he awoke and found the silence in his own house was real. Orrul was dead, his painful wheezing forever ended.

The village elders, when summoned by Mebaw for an urgent council, listened to Dett's account of his dream in an aura of concern. All were shaken by Dett's queer comments at the Pit and by the death of Orrul while his father was witnessing Klevey in his mind's eye. They tried to interpret what Dett had seen.

"Klevey means death and destruction," said the Mastersinger. The gaunt old man knew more songs and tales than anyone in the village, save perhaps Grandmother Glin. "He has not walked among us in long years. This dream is a sign he has come again."

"No doubt of that," said Mebaw. "My nephew's death is but the first, and Dett has feared for some time that the strange skies portended ill."

Uncle Talloc pulled on his dark beard. "But what can we do? Nothing!"

"No!" said Grandmother Glin. "If we could do nothing, then the Seaman would have let dream-Dett die with the rest of us. After the Seaman released Dett, he disappeared. Where? Back to his home in the sea, of course. Therefore, we must beg the Mother of the Sea for protection. She alone can keep Klevey in the sea where he belongs, and away from our lands."

The Mastersinger nodded sagely. "And do not forget the monster's dread of fresh water. We should place buckets of lake water beside the door of every house."

Mebaw laughed. "And we should hope the weather stays bad! It is so cold and rainy, the enemy will dare not surface from the depths, for fear the raindrops might sizzle his skinless flesh."

"My brother, watch your tongue," Dett said with great weariness. "You would not speak so lightly had you seen Klevey's hate-filled red eye."

Mebaw, for once, had the decency to look embarrassed.

Later that day, they put small Orrul's body to rest in the barrows beyond the village, then prepared an offering to the Mother of the Sea. They went down to the harbor, ignoring the icy drizzle, and everyone—even Gefalal the stranger girl and Fummirrul, who had left the sheep alone to participate—placed a pinch of grain in a bowl. Then Dett's father and uncle took their boat a short distance into the bay where they dumped the bowl and a chunk of venison, in hopes the Mother would find it pleasing. The Mastersinger, accompanied by Mebaw, sang many verses in praise of the Mother while Orrul's closest relatives made an offering for his safe journey to the world of the dead.

Although Dett grieved for the loss of his small son, his spirit felt lifted by the devotions. And it helped that the heavy rain clouds blocked out the dread, red skies.

Unfortunately, the offering did not please the Mother, for there soon followed the coldest autumn and winter anyone could remember, even

Grandmother Glin. It truly seemed as if the Mother had lost her strength, and Lord Father Winter reigned supreme. A snowfall ordinarily lasted a day or so, but now white drifts blanketed the island. No sooner did one melt than another covered the land once again.

Klevey was working in tandem with his oath-brother, for his vile touch was evident in the stunted wheatstalks, the frost-damaged vegetables, the withered and brown grasses. With the cold and the failing crops came the deaths, leaving no family unaffected. Uncle Talloc was hardest hit, losing a dozen family members to different ailments. Only his oldest son, now a widower, and Gefalal survived. Dett's wife, Jolpibb, and the baby died before the solstice, and only Grandmother Glin's skillful nursing saved Rarpibb from a deadly flux. Grandmother herself seemed undaunted, save she walked more slowly and her back was more bent. Otherwise, she was as enduring as the red cliffs, taking punishment from the pounding waves, yet still standing.

Fummirrul, on the other hand, no longer smiled and joked, and his slim frame seemed bonier than ever. He had ceased complaining about the pesky new sheep and treated Rarpibb so tenderly the little girl wearied of it. One night, she tried pinching him to provoke him into teasing back. He simply moved away to the other side of the hearth and continued sewing a seam in his trousers. That was usually women's work, but the only woman in Dett's household was Joloc, and she was sorely overburdened. Under more ordinary circumstances, Grandmother Glin would have stayed to help Joloc; Glin had no permanent home, being related to everyone, but moved where she was needed. As the most skilled healer, she was in constant demand that season. It would have been too selfish of Dett to insist she stay after Jolpibb died, not when others needed her care.

Rarpibb, small as she was, helped where she could. Her sister was teaching her homely skills, but she was still clumsy at sewing and weaving and weak from her illness. Dett hoped Rarpibb would stay healthy and learn more, for the day would come when Joloc's courses would begin, and she would eventually wed and move into the house of her husband's family.

But that was still several years distant. For now, Fummirrul's somber ways were a more immediate burden on Dett's mind as he and Mebaw worked to repair a hole in Mebaw's roof. "It's as if Fummirrul's spirit is being crushed by all the deaths. He has not laughed in days. Every week, he reports we've lost another sheep, and Joloc counters that another villager has died. How long can Klevey plague us?"

Mebaw barked his knuckles on a chunk of flagstone and swore mildly. "Well, Grandmother insists that your encounter with the Seaman means that at least some of us will survive. The elders agree with this interpretation. I'd even go so far as to say that *you* have something to do with our chances."

"Me? I'm nobody special. It's men like Father and Uncle, the bold ones, who accomplish things."

"But the Seaman appeared before *your* mind's eye and did not deny you when you asked, 'Is there nothing we can do?' "

Dett laughed bitterly. "Here's what I can do: patch a roof."

"Fine. Maybe that will prevent the rain from soaking my family, and thus we shall not freeze. You have saved perhaps nine people."

"Always joking, brother."

"I am not joking. You may have already helped us prepare for this cold reign of Lord Father Winter, with your clucking over the strange skies. My wife, matching your worries with her own, was especially frugal with our grain this summer. Thanks to her foresight, we will have enough to last till spring. Other wives did the same."

"Jolpibb among them," Dett said, tears welling up in his eyes.

"Ah, but I have spoken with men from other villages on Western Island. Some of them are already starving, and Klevey's culled their flocks the way he did in your dream, right down to the last lamb. Your boy Fummirrul may mourn our losses, but we've still got a decent-sized flock, and promise of more come spring. I went by our pasture yesterday, and that troublesome ram was humping the ewes like a woolly bridegroom on his wedding night. Made me feel proud to be male, he did, and the other ram, the brown one, was having his share of the ladies, too."

Talk of the sheep made Dett feel uneasy. "All the same, it is easier to be frugal when there are fewer mouths to fill. I imagine there is plenty still in Uncle Talloc's storebins, as there is hardly anyone to eat it in his house."

"Hush! Here he comes, his own self, and he looks angry. Greetings, Uncle!"

"Greetings, Nephew Mebaw. I would speak to you a moment, Nephew Dett. A matter of concern between our families." Talloc drew his sealskin cape across his barrel chest—he was built like Dett—and waited for the younger man to slide down from the rooftop.

"Something wrong, Uncle?" Dett asked.

"Your son, Fummirrul, has been spending time in the company of the stranger girl, Gefalal. He has been doing so for many months now."

"If this has been so for many months now, why do you sound annoyed by it?"

"At first, I did not mind. Fummirrul has helped her learn our tongue. Perhaps she learned more from him because he is nearer her own age. I am grateful, for her position in my house has grown in importance since Klevey has taken so many of mine, including wife, daughters, and daughters-in-law. It is good she knows simple words and commands. But he must not come near her any longer."

"Why? Where is the harm? They are but children."

Talloc kicked a loose stone, sending it ricocheting off Mebaw's house. "Because she is now meant for Glinaw, my last remaining boy! I do not want anyone, not even a grandnephew, taking her and planting his seed within her!"

"How absurd, Uncle!" said Dett. Clearly, grief had rattled the older man's wits. "She is still unbloodied, and Fummirrul has not yet sprouted his man's hair, nor had his first dreamtime wetness. He's a boy still, with the slender shoulders of youth and a high voice like those of the shorebirds. As for his manhood . . ."

"I care not that Fummirrul's manhood is as yet unripe. If he stays any longer by Gefalal's side, he will know what to do as soon as it is ripe, and he will desire to do it with her.

"Gefalal could start her courses any time. She is a woman in shape, no longer the ragged stick-child we rescued last spring. Her hips have widened, to prepare for bearing my grandchildren. Her breasts have rounded, the better to nurse my grandchildren." Talloc's breath came a little faster, puffing white in the cold air, and he shifted his feet, as if suddenly uncomfortable. Dett had not seen enough of Gefalal to realize how much the stranger girl's body had changed over the seasons, but clearly Talloc knew it in detail. Dett suspected his uncle's lecture had two goals: to protect Gefalal for Glinaw, or, if Glinaw died, to save her for himself. Glinaw had the same wasting cough that had taken many of the villagers in the last month. And Talloc was still virile, though getting on in years: his wife had died in childbirth not long after Dett's dream.

Dett said, "As you wish, Uncle. I shall speak to the boy, though I am sure you are worrying needlessly."

"You would worry, too, had you been as afflicted as I! At least three of your children still breathe! Even those daughters of mine who dwelt with their husbands are gone, and all the grandbabes with them." He choked up, then abruptly walked away.

"Well!" said Mebaw from above. "That was an unpleasant performance."

"He is shaken by grief."

"Shaken by lust, if you ask me. He's just waiting for the stranger girl to ripen, then *he'll* pluck the fruit. Glinaw doesn't have a chance; he must have breathed plenty of Klevey's fumes."

This uncomfortably echoed Dett's own thoughts, but he said nothing out of respect for his uncle's position and sympathy for his losses. It sometimes seemed Mebaw respected nothing.

"I must speak to Fummirrul," Dett said. "This news will only make him gloomier, I fear. He enjoys talking with Gefalal."

"Go, then. I can finish this myself."

Dett pondered. "It grows late. He should be putting the sheep back into their enclosure soon. I will wait for him there, if he has not yet returned from the pastures."

He began trudging through the village, noting house after house and remembering those who had died. Icy slush covered the ground; Dett could feel the chill creeping through his boots. As he made his way past the silent fields, he realized he had been avoiding the sheep pen ever since his frightful dream. He knew why: he didn't want to see the place where Klevey had run rampant before his mind's eye. Even now, ascending the rise, he felt uneasy, though the harsh winter landscape differed significantly from the green grasses of his dream. The tiny pink flowers were long gone.

He heard the sheep baaing as he approached, but not the frantic calling he remembered in his dream. Nor, when he looked down, did he see ruin and destruction. The sight, however, was sobering: perhaps a fourth of the flock had died, and some of the remaining beasts were sickly. By some weird twist, all of the animals taken by Klevey thus far had been from the old flock. The new southern sheep, for all their frisky and peculiar ways, seemed in far better health.

Fummirrul, a sleek figure in black from his cap down to his mittens, was in the far corner of the enclosure with one of the new rams and several ewes. It might have been Trouble, but Dett wasn't quite sure. Fummirrul jumped with alarm when his father called his name.

"Why do you start so, my son? Are you up to some mischief?" asked Dett. "I have important news. Your great-uncle Tal—what is that stuff? What *are* you doing there? Have the wind demons swept all sense from your mind?"

Dett advanced purposefully on his son, who cowered beside the wall. At his feet was a large pile of seaweed, which Trouble and the ewes were munching. "When you told me these animals had a fondness for seaweed and even leaped the wall to get it, I took it as a joke. You children, when mere tots, would often unknowingly place yourselves in danger, trying to get something forbidden to you. So, I thought, it was with these sheep. Being ignorant creatures, they do not know any better. You, the shepherd, like a parent to a wayward child, would teach them the right way to behave.

"Now, in this time of troubles, I find you have abandoned your duty and have given in to the whims of these beasts, supplying them with what they crave. Likely they will all die, thanks to your foolishness! What made you think you could do this?" Dett did not often shout, but he did so now, frightening the sheep and sending a nearby flock of gannets flapping into the sky.

"Father, *you* gave me the idea!" Fummirrul blurted out. His face, like Dett's, was red with suppressed emotions, but he had ceased his trembling.

"I? I never said a word!"

"That day when you stopped by the pen with Uncle Mebaw, you said a man must do his best to cope with a dilemma. My dilemma was that the sheep kept eating seaweed on the shore. How could I deal with it? Building the wall higher would only stop them while they were in the enclosure, but they were constantly running off when I took them to the pastures, too. Tying them up didn't work—they chewed through every rope I tried. So I thought to ask Gefalal what they did with the sheep on her southern island. You remember, she and her brother, the boy that died on the boat trip, were shepherds to this very flock of bothersome sheep."

Dett blinked. Until this moment, he had forgotten his original purpose in coming to the pen. "Gefalal. Yes. What then?"

"I'd talked to her before, Father. It's so interesting to know her people have many different words from our own. For instance, she calls the ocean—"

"You stray from your story. Uncle Mebaw and the Mastersinger would scold you for rambling. What did she say of the sheep?"

Fummirrul rubbed the head of a nearly grown lamb as it butted him with affection. "It took a while to understand enough of her words. We learned more from each other when I brought her out to the pastures. She is very good with the sheep. Father, you will never guess what she told me! These southern sheep eat seaweed nearly all year long, save the summertime when the ewes are lambing. When the young lambs are a few months old, they too eat the seaweed. See this rascal here? He likes it as much as his father does." The lamb was now taking delicate nips of the seaweed at the boy's feet. Trouble, nearby, took far larger mouthfuls, as did the ewes that had ambled over, now that Dett had stopped shouting.

"At first, Father, I didn't know what to think. It seemed stupid. But then Klevey walked in your dream, and the Seaman appeared, too, *with seaweed draped over his flipper.*"

"And he left the seaweed after he vanished," said Dett, thinking hard. "Do you think he left it for us to feed the sheep?"

Fummirrul shrugged. "I am just a boy. I don't know much about interpreting dreams. But it seemed to make sense. So I used that—and Gefalal's advice—to convince myself that it was all right. Father, it must be all right! For the grasses have grown poorly and there is not enough grain for the village, let alone the flock, but there is still seaweed. The old sheep are starving, but I have lost but one of the new flock, and that a swaybacked lamb."

Dett didn't reply at first. Only minutes ago, he and Mebaw had been discussing the meaning of his dream. His brother thought he, Dett, would somehow help save the village from Klevey's destruction, and maybe he was right. Well, partly right. Dett did not see how he could be a savior when all he had done was fuss and fret. He was a confirmed worrier. Jolpibb used to tease him about it. But perhaps his cautious ways had saved lives.

Fummirrul, on the other hand . . . He had interpreted an elder's dream and taken action on it—a bold thing to do for a mere boy, but the interpretation *could* be a valid one. Dett's gaze passed from the weak older sheep to one of the new ones. Most were gray, but this was the brown ram, and he stared back with bright brown eyes. *The brown was having his share of the ladies, too,* Mebaw had said. The sheep's robust condition—and that they were intent on breeding—certainly seemed to vouch for the validity of the interpretation. Come spring, the Western Islanders who had lost their flocks would lack wool and mutton, but Dett's village would not.

"F-Father?" Fummirrul sounded anxious. "*Is* it all right?"

"Yes, I think so," Dett said. "I will talk to the council about it. Grandmother may be irked to realize that you may have interpreted an important dream more accurately than she or the Mastersinger did. My son, if you have a talent for such things, perhaps you will be Mastersinger after Uncle Mebaw."

Fummirrul wrinkled his nose in distaste. "I want to go to sea with Grandfather and the uncles. That is why I want to learn Gefalal's tongue. Then, if we go to the Great Island, I can speak to the people there, and trade for their things." He scratched the lamb's ears, looking wistful. "But, of course, someone else would have to watch the flock."

This intention surprised Dett only a little; Fummirrul was a restless spirit, not given to staying in one place, growing grain and gathering seabird eggs off the cliffs. Dett believed his son would do well as a fisherman-trader, especially if he made the effort to learn other people's tongues.

But that was all yet to come. "You have done well with the sheep, but when you are a man, some other clever youngster will take your place as shepherd." *That youngster might have been Orrul. Or the baby.* "However, I fear you must wait some time before learning more of Gefalal's language. Great-Uncle Talloc has forbidden you to see her." When Fummirrul began to cry out in protest, Dett raised a restraining hand. "I do not agree with him, but as she is in his household, I cannot countermand his desires. He may change his mind, given time.

"Look. It is beginning to snow again. I will help you move the sheep into their barn, and then we will see what messes little Rurpibb has made for us, eh? That mutton stew last night was so tough, I thought she'd cooked her doll."

That won a sly grin from his son. "True, Father! Say, if I hid her doll and pretended to eat it, that would make her squeal indeed. May I play such a joke?"

With that, Dett understood that Klevey's rampage had caused only some of Fummirrul's low spirits. The rest came from worrying about his feeding the sheep.

"Indeed you may. It will be fine to hear her squeal again. I have sorely missed that sound."

The elders readily accepted Fummirrul's interpretation, once they had inspected the old and new sheep, and heard from Gefalal that the creatures did thrive on seaweed on the Great Island. Klevey and Lord Father Winter continued to torment the islands for another year. Illness took more lives during the second winter after the Day of Darkness; Glinaw, the Mastersinger, and even Grandmother Glin succumbed. The elders, however, took care that no one starved, carefully doling out precious mutton as needed. Talloc, in particular, readily shared what his depleted family would not need. It also helped that they were better prepared for Lord Father Winter's fury; everyone had plenty of warm woolen clothes and thick blankets.

As the community dwindled, new unions formed to take the place of the old. Dett married again, to Aip, the widowed sister of one of his brothers-in-law. Aip was a pleasant woman, not as lively as Jolpibb, but kind-hearted, with a young son who regarded Fummirrul with awe and eagerly helped with the sheep.

Everyone rejoiced when the first warm spring days returned. Mebaw, now Mastersinger, sang "The War Against Winter," and there was a feast at the Pit to celebrate the binding of the Chill One to the seafloor. They dined on a whale that had beached itself, but Dett found himself savoring the fresh cheese made from ewe's milk nearly as much as the whale-meat. He had a dream that night, as he did after the feast of venison, but it was an enjoyable one. He saw his dream-self walking on the shore with dream-Fummirrul. The pair of them found tracks in the sand running down into the sea—ones that matched those of Klevey. Dream-Dett surveyed the horizon and rejoiced to see a distant red smudge vanish into the waters.

He turned to tell dream-Fummirrul, only to discover the boy was crouching, eye-to-eye with the gray seal. "Hail, Seaman," dream-Dett said. "Have you come to tell us the Red Scourge has returned to the Mother?"

The seal nodded, and then nosed at the sand just in front of their feet, partially uncovering something. It jerked its head at the object, so dream-Dett pulled it out: a beautiful metal knife, like those the southern trader had. The moment he touched it, the Seaman vanished.

"A treasure of the south, my son, and a gift of the Seafolk," dream-Dett said. "I present it to you, in gratitude for your youthful wisdom." With that, he gave the valuable thing to his dream-son, who beamed with pleasure.

That morning, he went to relate his dream to the elders, not wanting to wait until the next council meeting. They rather hurriedly brushed him off, being occupied in casting charms over the fishing fleet, which would set out with the tide.

"This dream clearly does not portend any grave disaster," said his father. "Rather, it is a good omen, for Dett saw Klevey return to the sea and the Seaman confirmed he is gone. As for the knife, I interpret it as meaning if Dett stumbles across something rare from the south, it is his. Do you all concur?"

The elders, including his brother the Mastersinger, readily agreed, and returned to their chanting.

Several days later, Dett was weeding in the fields when his little stepson ran up, urgently calling his name. "Father Dett! Come quickly! There has been a disaster."

"What has happened?"

"Klevey reached up through the waves and smashed Great-Uncle Talloc's ship! Talloc, Klebaw, and Nerrul have perished!"

Thoughts raced through Dett's mind. "Does anyone else know?"

"No, I just found out because I was gathering shellfish at the harbor.

I saw Grandfather's boat come in. Everyone is busy helping Clett, for he was near to drowning. I came to get you right away."

"Good lad. Go tell your mother. I will come shortly." After the youth pelted off, he ran also—to the sheep meadows, not the village.

Fummirrul was there, as always, tending the sheep. The remaining dozen old sheep grazed on grass; the new sheep chomped contentedly on their seaweed. Dett quickly told his son the news, and the pair hurried to the village, where they burst into Talloc's house. They startled Gefalal, but Fummirrul managed to make her understand Talloc was dead. She showed no remorse, which did not surprise Dett.

They swept her belongings into a heap; Fummirrul proudly carried the bundle himself, muscles straining under the shirt he had clearly outgrown. Dett's new bride Aip looked on with interest as they piled everything in a corner. "She is to stay here? I do not mind, but perhaps your father will want to claim her. She is a comely girl."

"He has two other daughters-in-law still living. Besides, I have the backing of the elders on this," Dett said with a grin. "For they agreed I should keep a southern treasure if I could find one."

"Ah!" Understanding swept over his wife's face. She glanced at Fummirrul, who was a trifle slower to comprehend.

"A southern treasure?" he asked, then blushed as he remembered the rest of Dett's dream, in which dream-Dett gave the treasure to dream-Fummirrul. "Oh, Father, how grand!"

"Interpretations aside," Dett said, "I thought it best to settle her here before anybody else got any ideas. As you say, she is comely, though too thin." Dett privately thought Talloc—blessings upon his spirit—did not treat the girl as well as he might have. He was more eager to share his extra grain with the village than feed the stranger girl. Small wonder her courses had been delayed. No matter. Fummirrul still had a few years till manhood himself.

Gefalal clearly wasn't understanding what was said around her. Her fingers nervously played with her skirts.

Dett was wondering what to say, how to put the girl's new circumstances into simple words, but his son spoke first. He took Gefalal's hands, then said something that sounded like gibberish. Gefalal smiled broadly and nodded. She squeezed Fummirrul's hands.

"What did you say, my son?" Dett asked.

Fummirrul grinned. "I do not know her word for 'welcome,' so I said, 'This is home to you.' I think she understands."

Perhaps no event of the Bronze Age is better known than the Trojan War, and this is also one of its most famous puzzles. Homer's Iliad speaks of the sack of Ilios—of Troy. Heinrich Schlieman found the remains of a destroyed city in western Anatolia, a city contemporary with the Hittite empire farther to the east. The Hittite palace archives speak of "Wilusa" and the "Ahhiyans." Could they mean "Ilios" and the "Acheans"? Historians and archaeologists can only speculate if the Hittite kings might have come to know the Trojan War centuries before Homer sang his first verse. Lois Tilton, wise to the true nature of war, speculates how.

The Matter of the Ahhiyans

LOIS TILTON

So now I am to be a spy.

Well, I have been many things besides a scribe in the service of the Great King Tudhaliya, ruler of the Land of Hatti, and his father before him. I have traveled to many foreign lands to set down the terms of the treaties made by his ambassadors. I have gone with him to his wars, writing accounts of his battles and victories for the palace archives.

Now the king of Wilusa has written to plead for aid against the sea-raiders from Ahhiya.

Priamos King of Wilusa to the Tabarna, the Great King Tudhaliya, the Sun, Lord of the Land of Hatti:

You know for how many years I have been your loyal servant and obeyed your commands, for how many years I have sent tribute to you, of gold and silver, and of high-necked horses, how I have sent soldiers to serve in your distant campaigns. Now my domain is threatened with destruction. The king of the Ahhiyans has come in his ships to lay waste the whole land of Wilusa. He has burnt my cities and carried off my people into slavery. My palace at Taroisa is now under siege.

Now if I have ever been the Great King's loyal servant, I beg you to come at once with your chariots and your footsoldiers to drive these invaders back into the sea, or else the land of Wilusa may be lost.

When I finished reading this letter, the Great King cursed the Ahhiyans. "Always, they cause trouble! Even in my father's day and his father's day they were always raiding our lands and inciting insurrection among our subjects, even when my father wrote to the Ahhiyan king as an equal and a brother, offering a treaty. They pledge their good faith, and at the same time they are conspiring with our enemies. Whenever our armies meet them on the battlefield, they retreat in their ships and we cannot touch them. We can drive them into the sea, but always they come back to make more trouble in our lands!"

Indeed, I knew the truth of this, for I had been on campaign with his father when he fought the Ahhiyans over the matter of Wilusa, years ago. Yet as I reminded Tudhaliya, we were now supposed to be at peace with Ahhiya. Perhaps this was the moment for diplomacy, not armies.

So I set down the words of the Great King, using the language of the Ahhiyans:

I, the Great King Tabarna, the Great King Tudhaliya, the Sun, Lord of the Land of Hatti, to Agamemnon King of Achaia:

King Priamos of Ilios writes to me saying: The king of the Achaians has attacked my lands. But the king of Ilios is my servant, and his lands are my lands. Why therefore have you attacked my lands? Are we not at peace? Is there not a treaty between us? Are we not as brothers?

Now if Priamos has given you just cause to make him your enemy, then tell me of it, and I will send my army to punish him. But if you have attacked Priamos without just cause, then know that I, the Sun, will come with my whole army, my chariots and my infantry, to drive you back into the sea.

This was the letter the Great King sent to the King of Ahhiya. But to me privately he admitted, "Hantili, you understand the problem I face in this matter. I dare not risk sending my army so far west as Wilusa, not now."

I understood his reasons well. In the east, Assyrian armies were on the march in the borderlands near the Euphrates. In the north, the Kaska tribes were raiding again, probing for weakness. He dared not withdraw his armies from these borders just to repel a few sea-raiders from Wilusa, so far away from Hattusa, the center of the kingdom.

Yet if the Ahhiyans took the citadel of Taroisa, they would be in a position to control all the sea traffic through the straits into the Black Sea. They could strangle our trade. They might even make an alliance with the Kaska tribes along the coast. The Great King knew he could not allow this to happen.

In due course there came a reply from the Ahhiyan king Agamemnon:

Indeed I am at peace with the Land of Hatti, my brother. I have only attacked Priamos at Troia because the gods require me to avenge a great sacrilege. Paris, son of Priamos, has violated the guest-friendship he had with my brother Menelaos, king of Sparta. He came to the palace of Menelaos and stole from the altar the golden figure of the goddess Helene. He took with him also treasure and women from the palace. The gods would destroy me if I ignored such a crime.

I have taken a sacred vow to punish Priamos and restore the golden goddess to her altar. But let this not be the cause of war between us, my brother, between the land of Achaia and the Land of Hatti. My quarrel is only with Priamos and Paris his heir, not with my brother the Great King of the Hittites. In token of my good will I send you these gifts, a gold and crystal flask of scented oil and a two-handled silver cup, embossed with images of the Wine God.

When I had finished reading the letter, the king was greatly troubled. "Sacrilege. This is a grave charge. But how can I be sure of Agamemnon? Gifts are no guarantee of the truth." He turned the silver cup in his hands, admiring its workmanship.

"Yes," I replied, "it is a gift fit for a king, but I have to wonder—was it looted from one of your subjects in Wilusa?"

"There is one way to find out," he said finally. "Hantili, I send you now to Wilusa so you can report to me on this matter as you see it with your own eyes. I know it may be hard to make such a journey at your age, but there is no one I trust more to tell me the truth. Let me know: Was there truly sacrilege committed by Priamos's son Paris? Have the Ahhiyans attacked in force? With what strength—how many men, how many chariots? Do they come for conquest or only for revenge? Tell me whether I need to send my army to Wilusa."

Now I am in all things the servant of the Great King. I go at his command.

By the time I arrived at the citadel of Taroisa in Wilusa, Agamemnon and his Ahhiyan sea-raiders had already sailed away, taking the spoils of their raids onto their ships and returning to their own lands in the west, across the sea. Men here tell me, men who know the sea, that contrary winds and the risk of storms make it impossible to set sail into open waters once the summer has come to an end.

Men here in Wilusa speak the language of the Ahhiyans, whom they call *Achaians*. Many of them have Achaian blood. In the past, in times of peace, much trade with the Achaian lands has passed through this harbor, making Wilusa a rich land and ripe for plunder.

Men tell me the Achaians were raiding up and down the coast, sacking the towns, carrying off the horses and livestock, carrying off the women into slavery. They say they struck the nearby islands, as well—

Tenedos, Lesbos, Lemnos—though I have not seen these places with my own eyes. But with my own eyes I have seen the homesteads of Wilusa in ashes, the fields and groves despoiled. I have seen the orphans and the old people starving at the roadsides, begging for bread. This seems to me as if Agamemnon was more interested in plunder than in avenging sacrilege.

At Taroisa, which men here call *Troia,* the evidence of war is everywhere. I myself have seen the tar-stained marks at the shoreline where the Achaian ships were drawn up out of the water—a great host of ships, and men tell me that each one can hold fifty men, to row and to fight. This was a large force! I saw the earthen rampart, also, that they threw up to protect their ships, though the men of Troia have by now demolished it. They seem convinced the raiders will return in the next season.

Troia has the look of a place long besieged. It is evident that the hardest fighting has been on the plain that lies below the walls, between the city and the sea. The land there has been trampled to dust by the two contending armies, the hooves of their horses, the wheels of their chariots, the feet of their infantry. And there is the stench of the city, of too many bodies crowded together behind walls for too long. It is not a thing a man forgets, once he has known it: the odor of war, the odor of death.

Yet Troia's walls still stand. They are strong walls, well-built walls. I recall that the citadel fell in the time of the Great King Hattusili, but it is apparent that the ramparts since have been rebuilt, stronger than before. The citadel occupies the summit of a hill, and the walls rise above it, thick and well-sloped. There is a good, deep cistern inside the walls, and an ample supply of grain put by in the king's storehouses. I do not think Troia will fall easily.

All this I have seen myself, with my own eyes. But on the question of the sacrilege Agamemnon has claimed he must avenge, it is harder to discover the truth. Some men insist that Agamemnon lies and Paris committed no theft. Others tell me it was not the golden figure of Helene that he took from Menelaos, but Menelaos's wife, who was named Helene for the goddess. A few others say that Helene the wife of Menelaos is the goddess herself, but of course this is the sort of foolish notion that a man will hear if he goes seeking information from strangers in the marketplace and the harbor.

As far as I can tell the truth of it, this is what I have learned: Of all the sons of Priamos, and there are many, only two have ever been considered as heirs to his throne—Paris and Hektor. Paris is the elder, but he was passed over because of an unfavorable prophecy at his birth.

Most men have always favored Hektor to be king after Priamos.

But several years ago, an oracle proclaimed to Paris: *When golden Helene comes as a bride to Troia, then will her bridegroom take a throne.* Or at least Paris claimed to have such an oracle, and Priamos believed it, for when Paris returned from his raid on the palace of Menelaos with the golden figure of Helene, the king named him heir and gave him the wife of Menelaos as his wife. Other men say it was Priamos who had this prophecy in a dream. In any case, say the supporters of Paris, the theft was the will of the gods, no sacrilege at all.

But the men who favor Hektor deny this, and many of them curse Paris as the cause of this war.

The people here are hungry and full of fear. The fields, the orchards and groves surrounding the city have all been despoiled, the herds all driven from the pastures. I have seen a few ships in the harbor, bringing grain, now that the Achaians have finally sailed away. But of course the price is high. The poorest people are already reduced to selling their children or themselves to buy food. So it is always in a siege.

But Priamos is still rich, and men say that he has sent word to the kings of nearby lands, offering them gold and silver if they will come to his aid. For men all say the Achaians will return in the spring to renew their attack on Troia, as soon as the winds allow them to sail.

I have found a house here and a couple of slaves to keep it, a woman and a boy. Now that the Achaians have returned to renew their war, they have plenty of captives to sell, and the price is low.

I deal in these matters with Agamemnon's steward, a man named Glaukos, a man of my own kind: men who write and keep accounts, the records of what goods have been taken and distributed to the soldiers in camp; men who know the price and cost of things. I have decided to set up as a merchant, a dealer in the spoils of war. This will give me a chance to observe the Achaians without arousing undue suspicion. I expect I will make a good profit from it as well, for the Achaians can only transport home as much plunder as will fit into their ships. The rest they must sell.

I have spoken with Glaukos over a cup of wine that should have gone to the king's table. The painted cups are really very fine work. There used to be an extensive trade in Achaian wares through this port. I would like to get more of such cups before I leave this place, for they would be worth a great deal in Hattusa.

Glaukos tells me that Agamemnon has brought to Troia not only his own army but soldiers from many other lands of the west. There is a company of soldiers here from Knossos and one from Rhodos, and many others from places I have never heard of. These seem for the most part to be his allies, not his subjects. Agamemnon is not a Great King, to command the obedience of other kings. Still, they follow him here, and it is a great host, many times outnumbering the army of Priamos, which Hektor leads. And Glaukos says they are more men this year than the last, more men joining them to reap the spoils of war.

"Some men say," I suggested, "that your army has come here more to plunder the palace of Priamos than avenge the crime of sacrilege."

"How can an army make war without plundering? How else can they eat, unless they take cattle from the enemy?"

"And what of the men who say this war is only being fought to take back the wife of Menelaos?"

"I tell you this," said Glaukos. "There is only one cause that would bring all the men of Achaia together in this way, and it would not be a woman! But we make a common cause when it comes to offenses against the gods."

So we finished our wine and our bargaining, and I took my newly purchased captives away. The nearest large slave market in this region is on the island of Lesbos, but I can offer a better price, without the trouble of transportation by sea. I mean to send them overland, perhaps as far as Hattusa, where I will be able to get a good price.

Of course the real profit from war captives is in ransom, not sale. Despite the war, the nobles of Wilusa are still rich, and fathers still have storerooms full of gold which they will pay to spare their children slavery or death. But even a shepherd boy may have a father willing to part with a sheep if it will redeem his son, and I will not turn down such an offer if it is made. These are after all no strangers, but subjects of the Great King.

The war does not go well for Priamos and the soldiers of Wilusa. I should rather say, it does not go well for Hektor, the Troian war-leader.

Some of my slaves—common men who cannot afford a ransom—say that if Hektor were king, he would repudiate his brother's crime and offer to make restitution. But Paris always refuses to give up his prize, the golden goddess Helene. It would mean relinquishing his claim as heir to Priamos's throne.

Even the Achaians seem to have respect for Hektor, as warriors will always respect a worthy enemy. Even they say he is to be feared in battle. None of them have anything but curses for Paris.

Yet even Hektor cannot defeat the vast numbers of the Achaians by himself. The men of this country are skilled with horses, skilled charioteers. But the vast host of the Achaian footsoldiers overwhelms them on the battlefield with spear and sword. The Achaians prize Wilusan horses as spoils of war. Their quality is renowned, and it would appear that Achaia is not a good horse-breeding land. But I wonder how long the men in Troia will have fodder to feed their animals, both the horses and the cattle kept inside their walls.

The situation for Priamos's citadel is grave. I fear that Troia may fall if reinforcements do not arrive.

I have written to Hattusa to advise the Great King in this matter: *While I do not believe Agamemnon intends the permanent conquest and occupation of Wilusa, he has called in allies from far and wide, from lands as near to your kingdom as Rhodos, and as mighty as Knossos. The citadel of Troia is under siege by an overwhelming force of the enemy, and I fear it cannot continue to withstand their assault for long.*

My king, if you wish to save Priamos and his city, you must send an army to his relief. But if it is not possible to send your own army because of the press of other military commitments, then I advise you to write urgently to your servants in the west, to the kings of Mysia and Lykia, and say to them: Send soldiers to the relief of Troia, and Priamos will reward you with silver and gold.

The news from Hattusa is not good. The Assyrians have dealt the Great King a severe defeat. Tudhaliya engaged the Assyrian chariots in battle at Nihriya and was driven back with heavy losses. Now the enemy presses harder along the Euphrates and the lands to the north. The Great King must marshal all possible resources to guard the Land of Hatti against a new Assyrian assault. He has made great sacrifices and prayers to the gods, that they may reveal the reason they have inflicted this defeat on the Land of Hatti.

I think it is well that he did not follow my advice and weaken his armed might by sending an army to Wilusa at the end of last year.

This year, the war goes well for the Troians, now that allies have come to join them on the battlefield. The Mysians have come in force, for the Achaians have been raiding into their lands as well as the Wilusan lands. Also men have come from Lykia, Karia, and Phrygia, as well as smaller places such as Maionia, where they breed fine horses below Mount Tmolos. There is even a company of soldiers from Melitos, which I had not expected, since Melitos has always been an Achaian colony, even when it has nominally submitted to the authority of the Land of Hatti.

At first I said to myself: Now the Achaians will learn what it means to invade the territory of the Great King of the Hittites! For I credited my letter to Tudhaliya, suggesting that he order the rulers of these lands to send soldiers to aid Priamos. Yet I have since learned that soldiers have come here as much for the reward and for spoils in battle as in obedience to orders from the Great King. Still, their presence has stiffened the resolve of Troia's defenders and turned back the invaders from its walls.

There was a recent truce in the fighting when Hektor arranged a single combat between his brother Paris and Agamemnon's brother Menelaos, king of Sparta, leaving the gods to choose between them. But Paris refused to come out from behind the walls and fight. He claims the golden goddess Helene reached out her hand and held him back from the battlefield.

Men have reviled him as a coward for this, men on both sides. And indeed I wonder how Priamos can still defend his heir against the charges of both cowardice and sacrilege. I think also that if it had not been for the appeals of Hektor, many of the newly arrived allies of Priamos would have returned to their homelands in disgust rather than fight for the cause of Paris.

But Hektor rallied them, and they pressed the Achaians hard until the invaders were forced to fall back and defend their ships.

So for this season, at least, I think that Troia may not fall. I will write to the Great King with a list of the lands who have sent soldiers to relieve the siege, at his command.

Every year, this war expands. I begin to wonder how the Achaian camp can hold all the men who come here hoping to sack Troia. There is hardly room for their ships on the beach, drawn up so close together a man can barely walk between them without getting his garments stained with tar. The stench is ripe in the summer heat, of garbage and ordure, of cookfires and the smith's forge. A man trying to pass through the camp must make way for soldiers in helmets and bronze armor who refuse to step aside, even for an old man such as I.

At the moment, the entire Achaian army is seething with excitement at the arrival of a new company. When I finally reach Glaukos in his place by the ships, he tells me that their leader is a famous warrior and that Agamemnon has promised him a share of the war spoils larger than any other man, excepting his own.

"It was an oracle," he says.

Another oracle? I wondered silently.

"The oracle said Agamemnon would never take Troia without the aid of Achilleus, so he sent ambassadors to promise Achilleus anything he wanted if he'd sail to join his army at Troia. Now that he's here, Priamos's walls won't stand for long!"

"Surely, with more soldiers, there will be less booty for each man," I remarked casually.

"They say that when we finally sack Troia there will be more than enough for everyone. Me, I wonder how much treasure is left in Priamos's storehouses. At least I won't have to be the one to divide it up between the leaders. Of course Menelaos will finally get his wife back, though by now she must be an old woman. But they say Priamos has twelve daughters, all beautiful as goddesses. So who will get which one of them as his share? That's Agamemnon's job, and he's welcome to it. He'd just better not slight Achilleus—there's one man who's quick to take offense!"

"Speaking of dividing the loot . . ." I suggest, but Glaukos has to apologize that he has such scant takings to offer for sale. With more fighting men arriving to join in the war, more merchants are following them, eager for a share of the spoils. They are driving prices higher.

But there are also more men joining the Wilusan side of the conflict. Men say that a large company of warriors have come across the straits from Thrace to get their share of Priamos's silver.

"Much good it will do them in their graves," Glaukos says boastfully, "after they meet Achilleus and his Myrmidons in battle."

I will say that Glaukos was right about this Achilleus—his presence has rallied the Achaians, and they press harder at the defenses of Troia. He was right, too, about Achilleus being quick to take offense. Already, he has been quarreling with Agamemnon. "Over women, what else?" says Glaukos.

These disputes within the Achaian camp sometimes made me wonder if the various factions might be made to turn on each other, which could only be to the advantage of Hektor.

I must consider a scheme which could bring this about.

Now plague has struck the Achaian camp.

Such diseases spread quickly. The sickness is striking down kings and common men both, great warriors and their captives. I hear rumors that both Agamemnon and Achilleus are afflicted, that they lie groaning with fever in their huts. "The anger of the gods," men are saying fearfully. The

Achaians are making great sacrifices and prayers in an attempt to appease whatever god has sent this affliction.

But I have seen such plague in many camps where soldiers are crowded together for long periods of time, as they are when conducting a siege. I cannot say this outbreak was unexpected—by me.

Yet perhaps the plague is indeed the answer the gods have finally decided to give the Wilusans after their many prayers and sacrifices. Now I wonder how they will take advantage of this gift.

Hektor has acted quickly, as I expected. With the Achaians stricken by plague, he has mounted a counterattack with all the forces he commands. His chariots have again driven back the Achaians from the walls of the citadel, back toward the sea. It is desperate battle. The Achaians, despite their weakness, defend their ground savagely. The Wilusans and their allies have to pay in blood for every spear's-length gained on that battlefield, but at last the invaders have found themselves with their backs against the rampart guarding their ships.

It is night now, as I write this. The plain is glowing with fires lit in both camps as sentries keep watch for the movements of the enemy and other men lie sleepless, waiting for dawn and the resumption of battle. I am not there with them in their camps, but I know it is so, for I have seen many battles in my lifetime.

The Achaians have retreated to their ships, behind their rampart and ditch, but I can see no sign that they mean to retreat farther, to abandon the siege and sail away to their homeland. For Hektor, this is the chance for victory finally granted him by the gods. Tomorrow's fighting may end this war at last.

All day the armies have battled at the earthen rampart protecting the Achaian ships. It is the invaders who are now forced onto the defensive, to fight from behind their walls. The ships—they are the prize. If the Wilusans can manage to burn the Achaian ships, Agamemnon's army will be trapped on the shore with no way of escape. But the Achaians defend them with fierce desperation.

All day the battle has gone first one way, then the other. At least once Hektor's men broke over the wall and began to set fire to the ships, but the Achaians threw them back, at great cost in life to both sides. Savage fighting! The Wilusans have left their chariots behind in their camp. This is close combat, where a man will find his face spattered with his enemy's warm blood and trample his companion's entrails underfoot as he struggles to press forward. Men use their shattered spearshafts as clubs, they pick up rocks from the ground to shatter the skulls of their enemies.

There will be no captives for sale at the end of this day's fighting. There will be no ransom, no quarter given, no mercy. No one would hear such an appeal over the din of clashing bronze, the screams of wounded and dying men.

Such a terrible thing is war!

Now it seems that the gods have turned against the people of Troia. Their great war-leader Hektor is dead, and once again the Achaian forces are at the walls of the citadel.

Even before dawn, the sound of men arming for war could be heard across the battle plain. All through the night, I could hear the groaning of dying men as they lay in the dark with the stiffening corpses of companions and enemies who had gone ahead of them into death. So hard the fighting had been, so long, that the armies had not been able to gather in all the bodies.

Then at dawn came the Achaian charge. The Wilusans had again kept their chariots in the rear, anticipating another day of close fighting. But the Achaians put their chariots at the spearhead of the attack, led by the formidable Achilleus. They cracked the Wilusan line, with the great mass of their footsoldiers rushing in behind.

Men who have been in battles know this moment, when the line breaks, when men see their companions falling on either side, and others fighting beside them begin to look nervously toward the rear. A man can hold firm then, he can take a tighter grip on his sword or spear and call to his companions to stand fast against the enemy. He can press forward, hoping they will follow. Or he can turn and run.

This is how armies die, when men panic, when they try to flee death. Rout is the older brother of defeat.

At the center of his line, Hektor tried to rally his soldiers, he strode forward to meet the Achaian charge. But the force of the Achaian assault was too great. One after the other, the men who had followed him fell to the spears of the enemy, and Hektor was forced to give ground.

The army of Troia broke and ran for the citadel, but few of them ever reached the safety of the gates. Behind them in their chariots came the vanguard of the Achaian host in bloodthirsty pursuit. One after another, men fell with Achaian spears through their backs.

Some of the Wilusans, cut off in their retreat, turned to flee across the river called Skamandros to what they imagined was the safety of its far bank. But Achilleus pursued them, he and his men cutting down so many that the bodies dammed the sluggish summertide flow and the river became a lake of blood.

As the panicked survivors of Troia's army fled through the gates, a small company of brave men, led by Hektor, made a fighting retreat, attempting to hold back the enemy. One by one they fell into the dust under the feet of the Achaians battling their way forward. At last, as the enemy was almost at the western gate, threatening at any moment to break through, the men inside managed to swing it shut and bar it.

Trapped outside with the wall at their backs, Hektor and the few companions with him tried to flee for the south gate in hope they might still win their way through to safety. But the Achaians swarmed over them, stabbing with their spears and swords.

When I heard them raise the triumphant shout: *Achilleus! Achilleus!* then I knew that Hektor was killed, and the hope of Troia with him.

I must write to the Great King to tell him all these things. If he does not send his army, then the citadel will certainly fall, and all Wilusa will be lost.

But now I see that the river has broken the dam of corpses, and a crimson floodtide is rushing to the sea, bearing the bodies of the dead on its crest.

The remaining allies of the Troians left them at the end of the last season, and they have not returned. For a brief time then, when Paris killed the great Achaian captain Achilleus, the Troians had hope, but no more. The city's defenders still fight from its walls, yet they must know the end will come soon. Their enemies are relentless. Last month, after Paris was killed, Priamos finally sent out heralds to Agamemnon offering to return the golden figure of Helene and all the treasure in his palace besides, but the Achaian king sent back word that the time to make restitution had passed.

I observe that the battering ram moves closer to the western gate, despite all the Troians can do to prevent it. The Achaians have covered the framework with wet hides and armored it with bronze, so that the men who propel it forward are protected from weapons hurled down from the walls above. A ram is what we call such a machine in the Land of Hatti, but men here name it a horse.

I have set my slaves to packing up my goods, everything I will be transporting back to Hattusa. There is no more reason for me to stay. The Great King has sent me his answer with a copy of his latest letter to Agamemnon:

My brother, I am willing to accept your oath as you have written it to me. In exchange I, the Sun, grant you your vengeance on Priamos and his heir for the sacrilege they have done. Before all else, men must respect the gods.

If you can take Priamos's citadel of Taroisa, all that is within it is yours. I will not send my army to prevent you or to defend the city against you. Out of respect for the gods I do this, because of the crime the king of Wilusa and his heir have committed against the gods.

But as you have sworn your sacred oath, then when you have taken Taroisa and all its goods, you will go to your ships and depart from my land of Wilusa, nor will any force of yours remain there, nor will you return to the lands that are mine. And if you return to Wilusa, breaking your oath, or to any of the lands that are mine, then I, the Sun, will send my chariots and my footsoldiers to destroy you utterly without mercy.

Now the Storm God of the Land of Hatti and the Storm God of Ahhiya are witness to your oath, and they have seen your words. And if you fail to keep your oath, then shall the Storm God of Hatti and the thousand gods of Hatti destroy you and all your household and all your servants, and the Storm God of Ahhiya and all the gods of Ahhiya shall destroy you as an oathbreaker and a man hateful to all the gods.

So the Great King has written. I have to suppose that Tudhaliya has relied at least in part on my own reports in making his decision. I pray to the gods that it was the truth I told him.

Now the killing is finished, the ashes of the citadel are cooling, the taint of smoke is finally leaving the air. The Achaians have packed their tarred ships to the rails with their spoils of war, and many of them are already sailing away with weeping captive women stretching out their white arms toward their homeland as they see it fade out of sight.

But Agamemnon, at least, is keeping his word about leaving the Great King's lands.

I have my own goods packed and ready to leave, but I found myself first compelled to go one more time to the ruins of the citadel, to stand as a witness to all that has happened in this war. Men will say the end of Troia was the judgment of the gods on the crime of Paris, son of Priamos. Perhaps—yet brave men died here, men on both sides.

But what I saw today in the ruins . . .

Now I will not report this to the Great King. I may not ever speak of it to any man. But men do say that the golden figure of the goddess stolen by Paris was never recovered from the ashes of Priamos's citadel. Agamemnon had the palace searched before it was put to the torch, and all the city, but the golden goddess was never found.

Yet today in the ruins of Troia, I came upon a woman, one who had survived the sack of the palace, or so at first I supposed. A golden woman, with burnished hair and skin that glowed with softness, as a man would imagine a goddess. Before I could think, I blurted out her name: "Helene?"

The woman smiled at me, and though I am an old man, I felt the sap stirring in my veins at the sight of her. "You call me Helene? But Menelaos already has his wife again. She sits in his ship, weeping for dead Paris, sailing back to his palace in Sparta."

I had to take a breath before I could speak. "I did not mean Helene who is the wife of Menelaos."

She beckoned me closer, and her face glowed with her beauty. No man could fail to desire her. No man could not want to carry her away. Her voice, so compelling . . .

"My name is Eris. I used to belong to Paris, but I can be yours now. Will you carry me away with the rest of your captive women to Hattusa?"

It may be that it was my old age which let me resist her temptation. If so, I am glad of it. "No, Lady. I will not."

I left the ruins. I went back to my house and gathered my possessions to depart that place without looking back.

For I know her. Even before I knew her name, I knew her. And now I know how poor dead Paris was deceived, the real reason the citadel of Priamos was doomed to destruction.

I only pray to all the gods that the Land of Hatti is never likewise visited by Strife.

For the ancient Greeks, the bronze Age was the third generation of humanity: the first was the golden. Literature too has its golden ages, science fiction being no exception. During the golden age of science fiction the motifs, themes, and conventions of the genre, in forms seminal or conclusive, flourished: the imaginations of these authors, blossoming in the 1930s and '40s, were like the earth in the days of the Greek golden race, bearing fruit "abundantly and without stint." But they are, and were, science fiction's first generation, and only the gods are deathless.

At about midnight on July 31, 2001, one of the great heroes of the golden age passed away. Poul Anderson had enjoyed a life of seventy-four years and a writing career of more than fifty. In that half century Poul's works ranged from hard science fiction to high fantasy, exploring technological and social implications on the level of society and, especially, of the individual. He did so with a wit, sincerity, and insight that we deeply miss.

But eras rarely end with a definitive period. They tend to transform gradually, as what follows them comes from them. Poul knew this as well as any of us can.

The Bog Sword

POUL ANDERSON

For a moment I hesitated, suddenly half afraid. Sunlight played in the crowns of trees along this quiet residential street and spilled warmth across me. A neighboring lawn lay newly mown, not yet raked, and a breeze bore me the scent. In a few hours Jane would be through work and bring Myrtis home with her from day care. Next month we'd vacation by the sea. Just planning it was joyous. Did I really want to risk any of that?

I'd been warned, I'd signed the waiver, but it was still possible to turn away.

No. I straightened my shoulders, strode up the walk to the porch of the big old house, mounted the steps, and rang the bell.

Rennie himself opened the door. "How do you do, Mr. Larsen," he said. "Welcome. Please come in." His formal courtesy had struck me a little strange at first, something out of another, more gracious age, coming as it did from an explorer on the frontiers of reality; but it had helped me trust him. Well, of course he was quite old by now. He led me to a living room lined with full bookcases and offered me a seat. A smile made further creases in his face. "Let me suggest we relax a bit first and get slightly better acquainted. If you don't think the hour is too early, would you care for a glass of wine?"

"Why—" I realized that I would. "Yes, thank you." His tall form moved off. "Uh, can I help?"

"No, no. I like to play host. Take your ease. Smoke if you wish. I'll be right back."

Not even a maid? I wondered. *And him a full professor.*

For a moment I thought that it fit the pattern. An emeritus should have the use of more university facilities than just the library, if he was still doing research. Certainly people throughout academe did who pushed ideas more controversial than his—sometimes harmful or downright crazy. Besides being a good teacher, Rennie had done respected studies of brain electrochemistry. But soon after he commenced on his psychophysics, he moved that work to his home, where it had continued ever since. I suspected pressure quietly applied. Not only did most scientists look askance at it, but a few of his subjects reported findings that didn't sit well with true believers in several creeds, especially political. And, of course, any administration would be afraid of legal liability. Thus far the dangers had been subtle, and nobody who suffered had sued, but you never knew.

Widower. He's got to have a housekeeper who comes in and maybe cooks most of his dinners, at least. And he does apparently have friends in town, and sees the children and grandchildren once in a while. But otherwise a lonely man. Also in his work. Yes, very much so in his work. Nobody else has ever managed to replicate his experiments with any consistency, no peer-reviewed professional journal has accepted any paper of his for decades, and he wants no part of the crank publications.

He returned carrying a tray with two glasses, set it on a coffee table before me, and lowered himself into the chair opposite. "Are you Danish, Mr. Larsen?" he asked.

"My father's parents were," I said, "and I've explained that I've been over there quite a bit, and hope for more."

His white head nodded. "A charming country." He lifted his glass. "Let me therefore propose '*Skål*' and request that you forgive my pronunciation."

We clinked rims and sipped. It was a good Beaujolais. His manner, though, did more to loosen the cold little knot of fear in me.

We chatted for maybe ten minutes, then: "Let's be honest," he said. "This is a gamble on your part, with nothing whatsoever guaranteed. Do you really want to take it? You have a family."

"Not much of a personal risk, is it?"

"No, no physical hazard, and nobody's suffered a nervous breakdown or anything like that. However, I trust it was made quite clear to you that some of my subjects have found the experience . . . disconcerting. In a few cases, almost shattering. They've been haunted for weeks afterward, depression or nightmares or— Frankly, I suspect one or two never entirely got over it. The past is, for the most part, no more pleasant than our world today, often less. Or—emotional involvements—I respect their privacy and haven't tried to probe. But it's not like being a tourist, you know."

"I do, sir. Generally, your people have come through all right, haven't they? Shaken up, sure. I expect to be, myself. However, the odds are, it should be well worth whatever it's likely to cost. My wife and daughter are prepared for having me broody a week or two."

Rennie chuckled, turned serious again, and said, "And you hope to advance your career as a promising young archaeologist. You certainly will, if you come back with priceless clues to what to look for and where. But—I'm staying stubbornly honest, albeit perhaps boring—you do understand, don't you, the odds strike me as being against it? Hasn't Scandinavia been thoroughly picked over?"

Eagerness stirred in me, the same that had made me apply for this. "You never know what'll turn up. Anyhow, way more important than physical objects, some insight into how people lived, thought, worshipped, everything. We have written records from southern European and Near Eastern countries, sort of, but nothing from the North."

Rennie raised his brows. "I fear your colleagues won't necessarily take your word for what you witnessed. What proof will you have that it wasn't a hoax or, at best, a delusion? On the whole, mainstream science finds what I do no more acceptable than psionics in general."

"I know that, too." I took a full swallow of the wine and leaned forward. "Sir, I didn't come in blind. I asked around, got in touch with several of your people, and *I* think you're on to something. So maybe all I come home with is just an, an experience. Okay. I'll nevertheless have been there, lived it. I'll have interpretations of the evidence to offer; and what that might lead to, who can say?"

"Ah, yes. Your application and our interviews, official though they've been, have certainly roused my interest. The Scandinavian Bronze Age, centering in what's now Denmark, was rich, extraordinarily creative, and generally fascinating, wasn't it?"

"It had to be. Copper and tin aren't found there. So they had to trade widely across the known world, which means awareness of what was happening elsewhere. An aristocratic society, yes, like every society in its Bronze Age, but peaceful, to judge by what's been uncovered—not like the Stone Age before or, absolutely, the Iron Age afterward. How'd that come about?"

Rennie frowned slightly. "You do realize you'll have only some hours, while your body lies unconscious for the same length of time here? Of course, the one yonder will have his or her own memories of earlier life, and many of those should come to mind. Please understand, too, that my control over the point and moment to which you return is quite uncertain. It could be off by hundreds of miles and hundreds of years. I've only groped my way gradually to any targeting at all. And, finally, under no circumstances will I ever send the same person back twice. Given the hazard in each single venture, ethics forbids."

Impatience almost snapped: "Yes, I've been through this often enough."

He leaned back, lifted his glass, and said ruefully, "And, no doubt, the rather far-out theory behind everything. I merely want to make sure. You'd be surprised at what surprises I've had along the way."

Yes, theory, I thought. *I've tried to grasp it. General relativity. A world line as the path through space-time of a body, like for example a human individual. Except that it doesn't commence at birth or end in the grave. At the moment of conception, it springs from the joining world lines of the mother and father, and when we beget our own children, their world lines spring from those moments. What Rennie's discovered is that the mind—or the soul, or some kind of memory, or whatever; nobody, including him, knows—can be made (persuaded?) to go back down those branchings and for a while—not exactly be, but share the mind of an ancestor. Why we can't go likewise into the future, he doesn't know either. It suggests a lot about the nature of time, maybe even of free will. But his work isn't scientifically respectable. Easy to see why. So complex, so tricky, so much in need of exactly the right touch.*

Maybe he can help me a little. And maybe afterward I can help him a little.

We talked onward for a while. He mainly wanted to put me more at my ease, but how he did it was interesting in itself. At last we agreed to start. He took me upstairs and had me remove my shoes and loosen my clothing before I lay down. The pill he gave me was simply a tranquilizer, the meditationlike exercises through which he led me simply to establish the proper brain rhythms. Then he turned on the induction field and I toppled away.

As the short, light night, that is hardly night at all, whitens toward day, my lady and I follow the trumpeters up onto the hillcrest. There I look past two plank-built crafts a dozen logboats drawn ashore, westward and outward. Already the water gleams like molten silver. Across it, Longland and, farther off on my right, Yutholand are still darkling. Clouds loom huge and murky beyond them. A stiffening wind whines and bites. It has raised chop on the straits. Even this early, the seafowl, gulls, terns, guillemots, auks, are fewer than I have formerly seen. Their cries creak faintly through the wind.

Will a rainstorm drench the balefires—again?

We turn around and take our stance, the trumpeters side by side, I on their right with a spear held straight, Daemagh on their left with fine-drawn gold wrapped about the holy distaff. Now I am looking east, widely over our great island, past the massive-timbered hall and its outbuildings, past the clustered wattle-and-daub homes of my folk, past their grainfields and hayfields and paddocks, on to the forest. Thus far the sky yonder is clear, a wan blue from which the few faint stars of midsummer have faded, and treetops shine with the oncoming light.

Below the hill, the people stand gathered, not only those of the neighborhood but outlying farmers, herders, hunters, charcoal burners, and others, some with their women and small children along, come together for the blessing and the fair, the feasting and dancing, merrymaking and lovemaking and matchmaking that ought to be theirs. As yet I cannot make them out very well, but I feel their eyes. Several are my guests at the hall, the rest have crowded in with kinfolk; all, though, are Skernings, and today one with me.

The sun rises above the forest. It sets the disc-shaped trumpet mouths ablaze like itself. My lady's bronze beltplate shines as bright, her amber necklace kindles with its own glow, and my cloak of Southland scarlet becomes a flame. Kirtles, breeks, blouse, skirt, headgear, the best we have, taken from their chests at times such as this, lend their softer hues to the sunrise. The trumpeters set lips to mouthpieces; the deep tones roll forth, hailing the sun at her height of the year, overriding the wind.

Suddenly—it has happened before—I am not altogether Havakh, son of Cnuath, nor is Daemagh altogether my wife and mother of my children. These are not altogether Saehal and Eikbo between us, who have been taught and hallowed to play at the holy times but are otherwise a farmer and a boat-owner. As they stand here with the trumpets curling mightily over their shoulders, one left, one right, and above their heads, the gods take us four unto themselves.

The sun swings higher on the tide of the music.

It ends, ringing off to silence. I lift the spear, Daemagh the distaff. We cry the words that were cried at the beginning of the world.

The wind seems to scatter them.

And then we are merely the lord and lady of the manor and two men. We start back down to carry out the rest of the day and the following night.

By now the light overflows, though somehow it is as unseasonably bleak as the air. I see all too clearly how thin the millet, emmer, and barley stand in the fields, the grazing kine and sheep not fat; and I know all too well that the pigs have lean pickings in the woods. *Let the weather hold till tomorrow, only till tomorrow,* I pray. But I do not promise an offering if it does, for such vows have done little if any good in the past score or worse of years.

Maybe it will. At least this isn't as bad as the spring equinox. Then, when I plowed the first furrows, wind, rain, and sleet lashed my nakedness, I could barely control the oxen, my left hand shook so, holding the reins and the ard. Leaves were scant on the green bough in my right hand. After I came home, I shuddered between sheepskins for a long while.

Fears ill become the lord of the Skernings. I straighten my shoulders and my heart and stride downward with my companions.

Men mill around and greet me. I reply to each by name, and ask those whom I seldom see how they have been faring. There is more to being a lord than leading the rites, taking the levies, judging disputes, sustaining the unfortunate, going armed against dangerous wild beasts or the rare evildoer, and otherwise upholding the peace and honor of the domain.

Savory odors drift to my nostrils as I near the hall. Now my lady and I shall provide the morning feast. Afterward come the giving and receiving of gifts. Both will be meager, set beside memories of past holy days. Even the king's yearly procession around Sealland is less showy than it used to be, and no longer lavish. Still, no one is in dire want, my own coffers and storerooms are far from empty, and—at least this year—the folk need not crowd inside out of the rain but can spread themselves over the grass in the sunshine, freely mingling while they enjoy the meat and ale.

"Happy morning, Lord Havakh."

The hoarse voice jars me to a halt. There stands Bog-Ernu. How long since he last trudged the weary way here to take part in anything? I reckoned that a sullen pride kept him away. He was too poor to bring more than a token gift. When I gave him something better in return—which I must, of course, not to demean myself—it would lower his standing further yet. Men might not openly mock him, but their eyes would. So he, his woman, his children, and a few others like them have stayed apart. Three or four times a year, a trader or two comes by for the peat they have cut and dried, and maybe dickers for some pelts they have taken; else they are mostly alone. They hunt, trap, gather, and herd pigs in the forest, they grow a little grain in grubbed-out plots, and whatever Powers they offer to are not likely our great gods.

It has not always been thus with him. A tide of memory rises in me.

My words seem to come of their own accord. "Happiness to you, Ernu—old crewmate—" They break off. Another man has thrust forward from behind his broad back.

A snaggle-toothed grin stirs Ernu's unkempt, greasy beard. "You know Conomar too from those days, nay?"

How could I forget? Conomar the Boian says nothing, only stares straight at me, but the hatred in that gaze has not changed.

"Well—well, he shall partake, since he's with you," I answer lamely.

Glee throbs. "You'll be glad, my lord."

They stand there in their stinking wadmal and birchbark leggings like a clot amidst clean, well-clad, well-groomed people—these two, and three more, younger, whom I suppose must be Ernu's sons. Flint knives at the belt are common enough among commoners, but theirs are crudely homemade. Despite the ban on killer weapons at folkmeets, the staves they grip could easily shatter skulls. Nevertheless they are Skernings, with that much claim on my hospitality and justice—except for their captive wolf—and once Ernu fared and fought at my side.

I give him a nod, turn, and continue to the hall, unheeding of anyone else. Memories are overwhelming my soul. Why? It is almost as if something beyond myself is calling them up, seeking to understand.

Oh, we were young when we set forth, all of us except Herut, and he just a bit grizzled. However grim our goal might prove to be, for us the venture began joyously. New lands, high deeds, fame to win and maybe wealth to regain!

But we were not callow. As the second son of Lord Cnuath, I was of course in command. Yet I meant to heed the counsels of Herut, a skipper who had thrice made the first part of this journey as well as plying our more usual trade routes. Besides, I'd already been on a few voyages myself. Mainly they were short, among the familiar islands or to Yutholand, but one went across the Sound and north along the coast yonder as far as anybody lived who shared our ways, while another went clear over the Eastern Sea to trade with the colonies.

About half my followers had had some such experiences, being of well-to-do families. Most of the rest had paddled logboats as far as needful for fishing, sealing, or taking birds' eggs. A few had not, Ernu among them; their sort had all it could do scratching out a bare living inland. I supposed—then—that none of them came along for anything more than the reward he was offered or gave the meaning of our emprise any more thought than would an ox. However, their backs were strong, and if we must fight, their flintheaded axes and spears should be almost as good as sharpened bronze.

Sixty men in two ships of twenty-four paddles, we left behind cheers and wellwishings. The aftermath of yestereve's farewell carousel buzzed in us like bees. The wind soon blew that out. It was not unduly high, nor were the seas ever violent. When anyone got sick, he suffered chiefly from the jokes of his comrades. Back in those years, the weather seldom turned truly evil. Old folk did say it had been worsening throughout their lifetimes. But more often than not it was still mild. The question that troubled us until it prompted this expedition was: What had gone wrong in the far South, and what must we look for in time to come? What should our kings *do*?

I could not feel fearful now. The water sparkled, the wind bore salt and tang and enough cold to rouse the blood, the sky was full of wings, bird-cries and wave-whoosh mingled with the paddle-master's chant, keel and sheer horns traced our path before and abaft our hull, curving up toward heaven, while withy-bound strakes slipped through the waves as lithe as a dancer.

Thus we went onward, north along Yutholand until we rounded its tip and bore south again. At the end of each day, we'd beach our craft and make camp for the night, unless we came on a settlement. When we did, we were received gladly. A small gift or two from our stock of trade goods was enough for such villagers. Sometimes after the dining and drinking, some girls, low-born but pleasing, would wander off into the meadows hand in hand with some of us leaders. The nights of late spring were shortening and lightening toward summer, and the moon turned full just then.

We did not linger. Before long the shore bent west. Shortly thereafter we reached the estuary of the River Ailavo and started up it.

I have heard that it is a torrent in the mountains from which it rises. But that is far south—far indeed; somewhere beyond them, bordering seas warmer and gentler than ours, lie the lands of such peoples as the Hellenes, which to us in this shrunken age are almost fables. Once in the lowlands, the river runs broad, slow, often shallow, northwesterly through a distance that it might take an unhindered man half a month to walk, until it empties into the Western Sea. Paddling against that current wasn't hard, but sometimes we had to jump overboard and manhandle our ships across sandbars.

This is a land of vast and gloomy forests, dominated by the oak, but one finds much clearing and a few settlements along the stream. The dwellers are akin to us, though there is less wealth among them. Livestock are plentiful but small and scruffy. Men often wear no more than a leather cloak, and anything else is likely to be skin also; however, women usually have coarse linen undergarments and are always long-skirted, never bare-legged in warm weather. These people burn their dead like us, but still raise mounds over chieftains. Not even those men go clean-shaven in life, though all who are free do trim their beards and coil their hair up in a braid. Yes, chieftains; there is no king over any tribe, let alone over several, and each tribe is scattered in single farmsteads or tiny hamlets through a large territory. Maybe it is their backwardness that makes them so apt to wage war on each other.

However, traders have little to fear, unless that too has changed by now. They have always been traveling on the Ailavo, from both the North and the South and back again. The riverside folk have long since learned that leaving them in peace means more goods than their back-country cousins can hope for. I think that meeting strangers, hearing new tales, getting some ongoing knowledge of the world beyond these woods, enriches their lives still more. Certainly a visit delights them.

I recall one especially, because it came to matter very much to me. We had been on the river for several days, the fog and tidewater of the coast lay well behind us, when, following Herut's advice, we stopped at a village called Aurochsford. It was the biggest we had seen and the farthest he himself had ever reached: for it was a staging post. Few men have made the whole distance between North and South, none in living memory, and it is said that they went by sea, steering clear of mountains, wildernesses, robber tribes, and alien languages. By far the most wares have gone overland, year after year, from hand to hand, the exchanges usually occurring at time-honored meeting grounds such as this. Not everything passed all the way, of course; cattle, slaves, and the like began and finished their journeys at places in between. But amber, furs, train oil—and copper, bronze, brightly dyed cloth, finely wrought cauldrons—flowed from end to end of a network of routes across the whole known world.

So had it been. So was it no longer.

We drew our boats ashore where, I could see, traders were wont to. Townsfolk flocked eagerly around. Nevertheless we left a guard, our thirty-odd commoners, camped nearby. They would have been ill at ease anyway, unused to foreigners as they were. The tongue spoken here was so changed from ours that I myself, who had ranged abroad somewhat, could follow it only slightly and with difficulty and say almost nothing. I put my young kinsman Athalberh in charge. Somebody high-born must be. He sulked, but a duty is a duty.

The headman, named Wihta, invited the rest of us to feast. There was barely room in his house for so many. Herut, I, the captain of our second craft, and two more sat benched with him and a few others at a trestle table which was brought in. Most were crowded wherever they could find a space, mainly on the floor. Come night, they would be quartered in humbler homes. Not that this one was any better than a fairly well-off farmer's in Sealland—nothing like my father's hall, where hangings decked the walls, gold and copper gleamed, the carven pillars seemed well-nigh alive. Nor were we served a meal to boast of—game, cheese, barley bread, with never an herb to season it. *I can tell Athalberh that he's missed very little,* I thought with an inward grin.

The trenchers had been cleared away and the women were going around with jugs of ale to refill horns when Wihta wondered aloud, "Few have come to us straight from their homelands; yet you tell us that you mean to go on. Never have I seen traders traveling in two boats at once, or ships so big, yet you have filled them much more with armed men than goods. What is your intent?"

This is how I remember the talk. It really went slowly and awkwardly through Herut, the interpreter. He glanced at me. As commander, I ought to reply.

"We seek to learn how it is that no more wares are coming from the South," I said. "That's a grave matter, especially the metal."

"Why, you've got to have heard. Wild tribes with terrible weapons have poured in from the Southeast, plundering, killing, taking the land for themselves. Who would be so mad as to try carrying riches through?"

"Yes, we know. Tidings have reached us, piece by piece, year by year. And we know the weapons are iron. Somehow those folk have learned to smelt and work the stuff. Maybe renegade southerners taught them the art, maybe their gods did—who can say?" A shiver went through the company. I groped for workaday words. "First they'd have to find the ore, whatever it looks like. My father thinks it must be plentiful in their homeland, wherever that is. Be this as it may, suddenly they are as well-armed as Hellenes or Persians or, or any of the nations that live in . . . *cities*?" I knew only tales of huge and wonderful settlements where there were gleamed buildings of polished stone, and wasn't sure whether I had the name right.

Belike Wihta had never heard it. "We haven't thought so deeply." Well, they were simple tillers and woodsmen here. They had no ships trafficking from the Eastern Sea gulfs to the Tin Isles and the Island of Gold in the far West. They actually saw little of the merchandise that formerly went to and fro and sometimes was bartered at this very spot, because they could not afford it. His admiring tone harshened. "There's begun to be talk of our tribes getting together to build earthworks, lest we too be overrun." He gulped his hornful down and beckoned for another. The ale was soothing him a bit. "But they're still far off, the wild men, and have more to gain by attacking countries ahead of them than struggling through our forests. Don't they?"

"That's one thing we want to make more certain of than you are," I said.

He blinked. His friends gaped. "You're bound yonder—to them?"

"Yes. As scouts, if nothing else."

"They'll kill you!"

"We trust not. We may even be able to talk with them, if we can get an interpreter."

"Or two or three, each translating for the next," remarked Herut wryly.

"What would you talk *about*?" protested Wihta.

"They may number some who can see farther than a bowshot," I explained. "They may come to agree it will pay them to let the traders pass through for a toll. Not that we suppose our party can by itself make such an understanding firm, but—"

The door darkened. Athalberh stumbled through. "Quickly, come quickly!" he shouted across the crowd. "A fight's broken out. A brawl—They don't heed me!"

He was hardly more than a boy, who needed the razor maybe once a month. I sprang to my feet and pushed through the sudden uproar. "Stay behind me," I ordered. A battle between the high and the low would be ruinous. I stopped only to grab my sword, leaned against the front wall with other weapons, and unsheathed it as I ran out. My heart galloped, my mouth dried, sweat trickled cold down my ribs. I too had never dealt with this sort of thing before. *I must not let it show,* I told myself over and over, a drumbeat in my skull.

The sun had slipped behind the trees on the opposite bank, but the sky was still blue and the river shimmered. A nestbound flight of birds crossed overhead, gilded by the unseen radiance. Air lay cool and quiet. Outrageous amidst this, snarls and curses ripped from among the men at the campfire. Most stayed aside, unhappy, but two had seized arms and squared off. Four or five behind either stood tensed, glaring, fingers knotted into fists, about to fly into the fray.

I didn't immediately ken the two. They were from the second boat, burly, shaggy, coarsely clad, the poorest of the poor. One held a flint ax, the other a spear.

Even as I plunged toward them, the spearman yelled and jabbed. More skillful than I would have expected, the axman parried the thrust. He jumped past the shaft, swinging his great weapon aloft.

I arrived barely in time. "Hold!" I roared. My blade whirred between them. They checked, gasping. Their partisans milled back. Someone among the onlookers uttered a faint cheer.

"What is this?" I demanded. "Has the Ghost Raven snatched your wits?" By then my followers were on hand and I knew the trouble was quelled. A wave of weakness swept through me. I hid that also, as best I could. "So help me Father Tiu, whoever started it will rue the day."

"He did," growled the axman.

"No, he did, that scum-eater," said the spearman. Sullen mutterings chorused from their friends.

"Do you hear, master?" cried the axman. "He called me worse than that, the son of a maggot, and did me worse at home. Kill him!"

"Be still, both of you," was all I could find to say.

Herut stepped forward. "I think, young lord, if you feel the same, we should straightaway hold a meeting, ask witnesses what they saw, and get to the truth," he proposed.

I nodded. "Yes," I answered. "Of course. At once." When I thought nobody was looking, I threw him a smile. We understood that he had rescued me.

Dusk fell over us, the earliest stars blinked forth, an owl began to hoot, while I sat in judgment. Herut's shrewd questions helped move things along. Nevertheless the wrangling and the tiresome stories tangled together, dragging on and on. That was for the better, though. Tempers cooled, men wearied, they grew glad to have an end of the business.

It came out that the quarrelsome pair and their abettors—kinsmen—were from the marshlands around Vedru Mire. Few though the dwellers and scattered though their huts be in that outback, they are often at odds. Lives so wretched and narrow must make it easy for dislike to fester generation after generation, now and then bursting into murderous clashes. When my father's messengers bore word of the venture everywhere around the Skerning country, these descendants of two different, otherwise forgotten men had offered their services as much to get equal gains as for the rewards themselves. It was a mistake to put them in the same hull, but who of my kind and Herut's knew that much about them? They had kept a surly peace until this eventide. Then a lickerish wish uttered by one as a woman of the village walked by, and a sneer at his manhood by the second, turned swiftly into a slanging match, and then they went for their weapons.

"That you were full of the beer our hosts handed out earns you no pardon," I declared at last, after a short, whispered consultation with Herut. "To make such a showing before them was as bad as trying to spill blood when we may need every man to keep all of us alive upstream. You would-be warriors have forfeited the bronze tools and good clothes promised you when we return. You who were about to fight have forfeited half. Maybe you can redeem yourselves as we go. Maybe. We'll see. Meanwhile, the two lots of you will serve apart."

The spearman hight Kleggu, the axman Ernu. Because Ernu had not truly pleaded but grumbled his case somewhat less badly, I chose him and his cousins for my ship. In the morning we departed with our slightly rearranged crews. We had meant to stay a day or two, less for rest than in hopes of learning more. A dwindled and impoverished trade did still move along the lower Ailavo, bringing news with it. But the incident had shamed us—I think more in our own eyes, the eyes of Skerning gentlemen, than in Aurochsford. We would try elsewhere.

I have kept no tally of time, but we were always aware of it, the summer slipping away from us at home. Let us learn whatever we could, do whatever we could, turn around, and paddle back out of this darkling land. Nobody threatened us in the next several days, but we lost two of them when weather forced us to ground our ships and huddle ashore beneath the rain and lightning, amidst the thunder. Therefore we pushed on without stopping until we reached a thorp called Suwebburh—I suppose from the tribe in whose territory it lay. Wihta had told us that it was the last of its kind. Beyond it were only some isolated steadings, and then the country held by the Celts.

Again folk received us hospitably, although less gladly. I marked at once that trouble weighed on them. When we sat in the headman's house, much as we had done before, I heard bit by awkward bit what it was. And yet at first it seemed as if some god bestowed luck on us.

Fewer men were on hand, for this house was smaller. I can't quite remember the headman's name—something like Hlodoweg. All our heed was soon on another of his guests.

Gairwarth lived here, a man of standing and, what mattered, a man with the knowledge we needed. It began with his being able to speak the language as it was spoken farther north, yes, as far as the estuary. That enabled me as well as Herut to talk with him fairly readily and, through him, with the Suwebi. Stocky, a bit paunchy, his brown hair braided, Gairwarth from the first slipped shrewd questions of his own into the interpreting. At length he said slowly, "Then you're bound for Celtic country, eh?" He shook his head and clicked his tongue. "I'd rede otherwise. You've chosen an ill time."

"What do you mean?" I demanded.

"Why, you'd have heard much the same from anyone, but I can tell you the most. The Boii are lately on the move again, and all wildfire is breaking loose."

The headman and his fellows frowned. Gairwarth made haste to bring them into the conversation. Did he want to head off suspicions that we might be plotting against them? I could well-nigh feel the uneasiness everywhere around us. They added their warnings to his. But I need not recall such breaks in discourse.

"Do you know the—the Celtics so well?" asked Herut.

"As well as is good for a man, if not more," replied Gairwarth. "I'm a trader, taking my boat along the river, sometimes clear down to the sea, sometimes clear up to the Boian marches. I've dealt with them if and when they were in the mood for it. Sometimes I've been a go-between on behalf of some of my own folk, as it might be there'd been a fight and we hoped to settle things before the trouble got worse. The Celts aren't always raving mad. Not always."

"So you speak their tongue?" I blurted. "How did you learn?"

His small eyes probed at me before he explained: "From my mother. Her kin lived not far from the Boii. A gang of them came raiding when she was a little girl and carried her off together with two or three siblings. She was raised among them, a slave, though not too badly treated. Years afterward, when she was turning into a woman and my father was a young man, he came that way trading. Like I said, it's not been unbroken war. We've stuff to offer, like honey, fine pelts, or amber when it's reached us from the North. They get wares from the South and East—kettles, jewelry, little metal discs stamped with pictures, and what all else. Once a chieftain's taken you in, you're under his protection till you've left his domain. And some men on either side know some scraps of the other tongue.

"Anyhow, my father liked the maiden's looks, bought her, and took her home. She could never be his real wife—no family left, been in foreign hands, never learned his language well—and must have felt lonely; talked much to me when I was a boy. That's how I got my Boian, and it's stood me in good stead."

He finished bleakly: "I got to know that tribe, too. I tell you from experience, you'd better turn back."

"Why?" I cried, and Herut asked more quietly and wisely, "What's happening?"

Gairwarth sighed. "I can't say for sure. But word runs from steading to steading, through the woods to the water. More and more raids. A few dwellers get away, with nothing left to them but the tidings they bear. Rumor goes that those who lived nearest the Boii saw big warbands gathering. That may or may not be right. Still, it's enough to keep me here, with my boat ready to carry off my household and me if they come this way." He paused. "Oh, I'm no coward. I'll stand with our men. But, between us, I'll know it's hopeless, and when we break, I don't aim to flee blindly."

Herut sat thinking—my own head was awhirl—before he murmured, "Why do you say hopeless? I gather the Celts have no fleet of boats. They'd have to go overland, and I wonder how many at a time can get through these forests."

"They needn't be very many," Gairwarth said. His mouth tightened in the beard. "Their weapons are iron."

A shiver passed through me. I had heard something about iron, that it was not only stronger and kept a keener edge than bronze, but was far more plentiful. The Southfolk had long made use of it, and then the knowledge spread to the wild tribes north and east of them, who were soon hewing their way west. But I had never seen any. A vision rose before me, a sword with a blade that shone flamelike.

"Two or three times I've tried to bargain for one, even just a knife," Gairwarth finished low. "The owner would not part with it."

"Was he afraid you'd turn it against him?" gibed Herut. "Small use, a single piece, when you have no way of making more."

"No, it's that they believe their weapons have souls, somehow bound to theirs," Gairwarth answered. "A strange folk, fearless, reckless, spendthrift, yet if a man thinks he's been wronged, he may well brood on it for half a lifetime, planning his revenge— They have holy men, deeply learned in their lore, who stand higher in their eyes than do their kings, yet they sacrifice captives to their gods. I don't really understand them myself. I can only tell you to turn around, go home, before it's too late."

"No, we can't!" burst from me. "Slink off like dogs at a mere word? We're Skernings!"

Herut shook his head at me slightly, made a brief silencing gesture with his hand, and said, "We welcome your counsel and wish to hear more. You'll find us not ungrateful." Whereupon, aided by the roundaboutness of translation, he got talk going in other directions. The Suwebi were glad to set their worries aside and hear about our journey and our homeland.

After the meal, as evening drew in, he said that he and I had better go see if all was well in the crew's encampment before we returned here for more drinking and then sleep. While we strolled off over the muddy ground, among the scattered huts, he told me, "What we need in truth is to speak together quietly. If honor forbids we give up the quest this easily, mother wit bids us give heed to what we're told and make use of what tools come into our hands. Havakh, we must have that man along with us. I think the gods may have seen to our meeting him."

What gods? I wondered. *Have we not left ours far and far behind us?* I looked around me. Beyond the squalor of the hamlet, the forest lifted, its crowns goldened by the setting sun, and through the stenches drifted its sweet breath. Mighty ahead of us, the river gleamed. *Surely,* I thought, *if none else, whatever these people call her, Yortha is here also*, the Mother for whom the maidens at home dance when the hawthorn blossoms. My heart steadied.

Our feet dawdled while our tongues ran hurriedly through ways and means. Nevertheless, we soon came to the boats, which we must for appearances' sake. As before, the men squatted or sat cross-legged around a fire, where they had heated food the villagers gave them. I did not await more than a glance and maybe a few words. It was a surprise when a big fellow got up and lumbered over to us.

I recognized Ernu of the bog and stiffened, though he had paddled quietly enough. Nor did he now pose a threat. He bobbed his shaggy head and rumbled, "Lord, a word, by your leave?"

I nodded, puzzled. Staring at the ground, he said, "I'm sorry about the fight. Not but what that Kleggu toad— Well, I got him and his kin not talking to me and mine no more, nor us to them." I saw that the two factions sat on opposite sides of the fire. "But we're all at your beck, lord."

"That is well," I answered almost as awkwardly.

Did a sly grin steal through the beard? "We'd not get home without you to lead us." He lifted his gaze to mine. "First, though, lord, we're going on into danger. The wild men, right? What I want to beg is your leave that my kinsmen and me, we make an offering for luck."

"What kind of offering?" snapped Herut, as I should have done. Who knew what might please or might anger the gods of this land and the river?

"Oh, a poor little thing. We're poor men. We'll go into the woods and . . . give blood. Our own blood. Just a few drops on the ground. With a few, uh, words."

I glanced at Herut. This must be some uncouth rite of the outback. He thought for a heartbeat before he shrugged. "You may," I said.

"Thank'ee, lord. I wouldn't want you to think we were running away or anything. We'll be gone a while tomorrow, but we'll come back. We'll feel better, bolder. And it's for you likewise, lord. Thank'ee." Ernu slouched off toward the fire.

Too many eyes around it were upon me. I turned and strode from them, Herut at my side. After a while he murmured, "That man surprises me. Uncouth, but not witless."

"Why, do you suppose his spell will be of any help?" I asked.

"Belike not. However, I don't look for it to do any harm, and—he's right, it ought to brace them. The thing is, he thinks ahead."

I wasn't used to believing that of anyone so lowly. Nor did I care, then. "We were talking about Gairwarth," I reminded him.

"Yes. What will it take for him to come with us? He's a trader, he'll have his price, but he'll start by demanding all the goods we're carrying, and we'll need plenty for gifts, if we can meet with a Boian chieftain. How to bargain Gairwarth down without seeming to demean him—"

I laughed. "That's for you."

"Be on hand," he urged. "Be gracious. Pay close heed. Those are skills you ought to learn, Havakh."

I felt a flicker of offense, I, a son of Cnuath, lord of the Skernings. I caught a breath and stamped on the feeling. Herut was also well-born, and he was right. In the years afterward, as ever more of our olden strong world has failed us, I have often harked back to that sudden insight.

But there's scant use in calling up the whole of the next two days. We stayed at Suwebburh and dickered with Gairwarth. In the end, we loaded a goodly treasure aboard his boat, for his trusty man to guard and take away with his family if the worst came to the worst, and we would give him as much again if we returned here safely. Him on my craft, we set forth at the following sunrise. I remember how mists swirled and eddied in the chill and the enormous silence. The villagers clustered on the riverbank, gaping, half terrified, were soon lost to sight. The sounds and sweat of paddling were very welcome. Then a flock of ducks winged noisily off the water and life awakened everywhere.

Now, when the memories and ghosts crowd in on me as I walk to the hall of my fathers, until it is that which seems unreal, now my yearning is to recall this last short while of peace and half-hopefulness. I would see water shine murmurous, a thousand hues of green on either side, clouds tall and dazzling white against blue. I would feel cool shadows where we camped at eventide, and share merriment with my friends until the stars overran heaven—for we were young, proud, unaware that our boldness sprang from our not truly understanding that we could die. But the few days and nights blur together, go formless, like land seen through one of the snowstorms that come over us in these winters. Today I have met Conomar again, and there was victory behind his eyes. Our first meeting overwhelms me.

As when lightning smites an oak—

The land was rising, less and less level, the current faster and the paddling harder. Once in a while, where the banks were too steep for trees, we glimpsed what must be mountains, afar and hazy to the south. Once we passed an open spot where a riverside steading had been. Only the charred wreck of it was left, already weed-begrown. The sight did not give us much pause. We knew that an always uneasy peace had been breached again. We were outsiders, with no quarrel here but, rather, good things to offer. Besides, we were not so few, and well-armed. What we did not know was that our faring was being followed, scouts slipping through the woods to peer from cover and speed their messages back.

Where the river swung around a high bluff on our left, it shoaled. Hulls barely cleared sandbars; water swirled and gurgled around us. "Hai, hoy, stroke, stroke, stroke!" and we toiled onward. As busy as we were, paddlers, steersmen, lookouts squinting to find channels, the sight beyond burst upon us.

Here was an end of forest. A few groves remained on the east side, still high and gloomy, but broad, rolling reaches had been cleared—slashed and burnt, I think—to make grassland, grazing. I spied two or three herds of ruddy cattle in the distance; smoke rose from scattered huddles of huts and one larger cluster at a distance that might be a hall and its outbuildings. This was only at the edge of my awareness. A band of the Boii waited ashore.

They numbered maybe two score, warriors all. Their leader stood with his driver in a chariot drawn by a pair of restless horses. His spearhead glowered aloft, a gold torque circled his neck, and he wore breeks and tunic of fine, colorful weave. Beneath a horned helmet his hair was pulled back in a queue, his cheeks and chin shaven, while a mustache fell nearly to the jawline. The others poised in loose array, afoot. They were mostly tall, fair men like him, though their garb was seldom more than a kind of blanket thrown over one shoulder and wrapped about the waist. Their gear was as simple: spears, slings, and swords. *Iron,* rammed through me. But those blades were not flamelike, nor even as bright as bronze. They were dark, almost brown. Nor did they have the laurel-leaf curves of ours; they were long and straight, barely tapered at the ends.

My hand dropped to the hilt of my own. Several among the crews yelled. Paddles rattled to the bottom of the boat. Those who had not been paddling snatched for weapons and shields. Standing beside me, Herut caught hold of my shoulder. "They don't know whether we're friendly," he said fast.

His strength flowed into me. "Easy!" I shouted, loud enough to be heard in both boats. "Keep station! Gairwarth, tell them we're peaceful!"

The Boian leader shouted, flung his spear at us, and drew sword even as he sprang from the car. His followers howled and dashed forward. A slingstone whizzed by my ear. I saw a man in the hull crumple, skull smashed asunder, brains spilling out on a tide of blood.

For a trice, I think, each one of us stood unmoving, stunned. The Celts splashed into the shallows. It comes back to me how the water swirled and glittered around their calves, knees, thighs. "Get away!" I cried. I felt us scrape bottom. The current had borne us inward and we sat fast. The foe were hip-deep when they reached us. Their blows and thrusts crossed our low freeboards.

I remember the battle as a wild red rainstorm, formless save when a lightning flash brings a sight forth searingly bright. I had learned the use of arms, as every high-born youth should, but never before had I wielded them in anger. Since then—too often, when stark need in the worst of these worsening years has raised packs of cattle raiders, and lately we must beat off an assault greater and fiercer than that— Harking back, I can piece together the jagged tales I heard after this affray, and see the shape of it.

At the time, all that I knew to begin with was a face glaring at me, a mustache like tusks over bared teeth and red stubble, a blade lifted slantwise, and the fleeting thought that that blade seemed endlessly long. Blindly, I stabbed my own at the throat beneath. It missed when he shifted deftly aside, and I stumbled, half falling against the strake. My clumsiness saved me, for he swung. Not thrust, swung. The whetted iron flew inches past my shoulder and bit deeply into the wood—how very deeply!

Herut edged close. His point reached. I saw it go in one cheek and out the other. Ferret-swift though he was, I saw how the Boian pulled his sword free before himself. That movement took him past our upward-curving prow. I know not what became of him. Belike he returned to the combat, wound and all. Maybe he lived, maybe he died.

What I remember next is another of them there, and that his hair was black and his nose crooked. He must have appeared quickly after the first, but by now everything was one uproar. His sword whirred past Herut's and cut into the neck. It nearly took the head off. Blood spurted and gushed, weirdly brilliant. It spattered over me. Herut sagged down, jerked, and lay still, sprawled at my feet. I felt nothing, just then. It was as if I stood aside and watched another man tread on the body, forward, to thrust into the Boian before he could recover. I watched the bronze enter beneath the chin. More blood spouted. He toppled out of sight.

No, wait, I did feel Herut's ribs crack beneath my weight and the . . . the heaviness of metal piercing flesh.

Next I remember standing on the sheer horn, clutching its end, so I could look the length of the boat. Struggle seethed, not only alongside. Boii who found or made a clear space were hauling themselves up. A pull, a squirm, a leap, and a man stood in the hull. Once there, he hewed about him with the iron blade that was deadly from hilt to point. We outnumbered them, but their weapons made each of them worth two of us. The dead and the wailing, groaning wounded thickly cluttered the bilge.

My soul still icily clear, I saw what might save us, filled my lungs, and bawled the command through the racket, over and over. Gairwarth, amidships, was fighting skillfully. It was not his first time. He used a spear to fend off blows, yielding enough that the sword did not cut the shaft in two, then jabbing in before the foeman was again on guard. That checked the onslaught, at least. He heard me and understood. He passed the order on to those near him. They obeyed, bit by bit and blunderingly, but doing it. When men are desperate, their single great wish is for a commander.

Take paddles. Push us off this sandbank. Or else stand by and protect.

Next in my memory, I was fighting my way aft. That seemed to be the only duty left me. But I did not really fight much. I pushed against the crowd packed into the narrow room, forcing myself among crewmen. Once, I think, a foe came before me, and I stabbed and may have hit, but others, Skernings, roiled between us, and he was gone. Afterward I saw that it would have been better for me to keep my place forward and help repel boarders. What happened is unclear to me. Mainly I remember the sharp stench. When a man is killed he fouls himself.

And then we were free, drifting north on the river. We had not been hard aground. I hope it was I who called for paddlers to get us out beyond the enemy's depth. Maybe it was Gairwarth, maybe both of us. At first just a few were able to man the sweeps, but that served.

In truth—as I, astonished, saw after a while by the sun—the battle had been short. No more than a handful of Boii had scrambled aboard. They had reaped gruesomely, but now several slashed a path to the side and sprang back over.

I learned that later. Suddenly one broke out of the press that hindered him and charged forward. His cry ululated, not a wolf-howl but a strange song. Drops of blood flew fire-hot from his lifted sword. Somehow I had been forced clear of the struggle and stood again in the bows, shakily, alone. I knew it was my death coming for me and raised a blade too short and soft to stop it.

Behind him, Ernu surged from the crowd. He had dropped his ax;

a red gash gaped on the right forearm. But he threw that arm around the Boian's throat and clamped tight. They tumbled down together, Ernu underneath, still throttling while his left fist pummeled. The Boian went limp. Ernu rolled over on top, sat astraddle, and laid both hands around the throat.

"Hold," I gasped. "Don't kill him. Not yet. Keep him quiet."

Ernu grinned. "Aye," he rasped. The Boian stirred. Ernu cut off his breath for another bit.

I have often wondered why I wanted this. Yes, a fleeting thought that we could learn something or gain something from a prisoner—but hardly a plan, there and then in the tumult. Did a god slip it into me? If so, to what end? On this midsummer day I wonder anew, and a chill strikes into me.

On that day, there was too much else. I looked behind us. Already we were rounding the bluff. I barely glimpsed our other boat. It had not broken loose. Maybe it was stuck too fast—for none of the crew could have gone into the water to push, with rage all around them—or maybe no one had gotten our idea in time. The Boii were swarming into it.

Young Athalberh was aboard.

And Herut lay dead at my feet, a horror to see, Herut who told me and taught me so many things in my boyhood, whose quietly spoken counsel guided us along our way through a foreign land, who had been closer to me than my own father—I know not which was the greater grief. Both choked me.

I pushed them down, blinked the stinging from my eyes, and squared my shoulders. Later I could mourn, we could all mourn. Right this now, with work to do, it was unworthy of a lord.

I went from prow to stern, giving men orders and words to hearten them, my voice sounding eerily calm in my ears. We had lost some paddles, broken underfoot or thrown overboard in the fight, but a few spares lay stowed, and presently enough were swinging to carry us at a good downstream speed. We dared not stop yet, but we laid out our five dead and bound the wounds of our half dozen most sorely hurt as best we were able while afloat. I set those few who were more or less hale and otherwise unengaged to cleaning off the blood and filth. Even in midstream, a cloud of flies was buzzing nastily about us. We never got all the stains out of the timbers.

There were three Boian corpses. One looked as though somebody had slit his throat after a blow stunned him, but—I didn't inquire—maybe not, for the only weapon of theirs we found was a dagger sheathed at this man's waist. Dying, each seemed to have cast his sword into the river, or else a comrade did it for him. I sent those bodies after their glaives. Ravens flew from the woods and wheeled above our wake with guttural cries.

The sun was westering through air gone hot and still when at last Gairwarth and I could draw a little aside and talk. "Are they mad yonder?" I asked. "Would they not at least hear what we had to say?"

"They are what they are," he answered. Though his tone was as dull as mine in our weariness, the trader wits were again busy. "Plain to see, now, the signs and rumors of unrest amongst them bore truth. I'd guess they're at war with each other, or, anyhow, a feud's begun and been spreading, as feuds do. Well, when a Celt is in battle rage, he's dangerous to everybody. That's how they're raised to be. And the rage can smolder just under the skin, always ready to burst into flame. I'd also guess the fellows we met lost a fight not long ago, got driven off the field, are still full of fury and pain about that. Here we came, somebody to strike at—our powers unknown to them, save that craft like ours had never been seen in these parts before, so we must be strong enough that honor could be won by beating us. And loot; but honor, what they call honor, meant much more. If the chief had listened to us and invited us to land, we'd have become his guests, our persons sacred while we stayed. So he didn't."

I shook my head. "You may say it's their way of thinking. I say it's madness. And yet—did they throw away the swords to keep us from having them? That sounds like forethought."

"No, I'd guess, instead, they didn't want the weapons, which they believe have souls, to become captive, any more than they'd want a brother taken for a slave." Gairwarth sighed. "Those few wouldn't make a markable difference to us, would they? I see naught for you now but to return home. What you've gained is the knowledge that there'll be no dealing with them for a long time to come."

"Yes." I tried to tell myself that that was something to show for our losses and deaths. Suddenly I stiffened. "We have a prisoner!" With all else there was to do, I had quite forgotten.

Gairwarth nodded. "I noticed. *And* his sword, for whatever it may be worth." He grinned. "If the poor dog is still alive. That's a hefty weight squatting on him."

I hastened forward. Yes, Ernu held the Boian fast. His hands remained at the throat, though he had eased their grip once the warrior understood that otherwise there would be no breathing. He looked over his shoulder as I neared, Gairwarth beside me. "Can I let go now, lord?" he asked. "My knees are sore, my legs are nigh gone asleep, and we're both wet from when I had to piss."

A laugh like a crow's broke from me. I drew my blade; Gairwarth lowered the spear he had taken again as I started off. Ernu clambered to his feet, grabbed the iron sword, and lurched aside. *Yes,* flashed through me, *Gairwarth was right, he does have a yokelish canniness.*

The Boian croaked and sat up. We peered. He was somewhat shorter than most of those we had fought, a little bandy-legged, but his upper body and arms were heavily thewed. Blanket, sandals, and a scabbard hung slantwise across his back were his only garb. Ruddy hair was braided behind a round head. A mustache of the same hue bristled on a long upper lip below a snub nose. Blue eyes glared. His neck was badly bruised, and at first he could barely utter a few hoarse words.

"He'd attack us and die like a warrior if he had strength," Gairwarth explained. "Instead, he asks us to kill him. Nothing less than death—his, since he can't give us ours—will make good the indignity he's suffered."

Ernu half raised the iron sword. "Want me to do it, lord?" he rumbled with a leer. "I'd like to try this thing."

"No," I decided. "Better we keep him and question him. Our undertaking was—is for the sake of learning about his folk."

"Safer to keep a wolf or a wild boar," Gairwarth warned.

"I know—now." My thoughts had sharpened themselves afresh. They were as bleak as our winters have become. "Tell him this. We'll hobble his wrists and ankles with thongs. We'll tie a rope around his waist and secure the other end about a thwart, so if he jumps overboard we can at once haul him back. If he nonetheless misbehaves, we won't kill him, we'll blind and geld him."

Ernu slapped his thigh. "Haa, good!" he guffawed.

Gairwarth was more troubled. "That does not seem much like you, Havakh."

I stared aft. We had spread bedrolls over our dead. I had myself set Herut's head straight, closed the eyes, washed the body. Yet there he lay, and others with him, and already it was clear that one of the gravely wounded would soon die. As for our second boat, I could merely hope that Athalberh and the rest had fallen. Yet it was not hatred that replied, it was will. "I swore to do what I can." Now, though, entering the hall of my fathers, I think it was also a foreshadowing of the cruel years ahead.

Gairwarth grimaced, then shrugged. "Well, I understand. But I'll have to put it to him less bluntly, not all at once. What may I offer him?"

"Oh, if nothing else, a livelihood among us after we're home, if he's behaved himself," I answered indifferently. "Maybe someday his freedom, if he somehow earns it. Take charge of him. See to his needs. And question him. Belike I'll think of questions of my own later, but do you begin." I paused. "I suppose you can deem how trustworthy he is."

"It'll take time and patience to draw him out," said Gairwarth, "and maybe a few small kindnesses. However, I see no reason why he should lie, and indeed that's unbefitting a Celtic warrior."

"I'll tell off men to stand by as guards." I turned to go. Bone-tired I might be, but so were my crew, and I had become their skipper. I stopped. "Give me that sword, Ernu."

The bog dweller handed it over. "A good thing to have, hey, lord?" A slight whine slipped into his growl. "I didn't do so bad by you, did I?"

"No," I acknowledged. "You saved my life, and afterward you were useful. You shall have the reward I promised when we return home. And more," honor made me add.

"My kinsmen, lord? They didn't start that squabble, nor me. It was Kleggu and his breed, lord. And they're off to hell now."

I frowned at the unseemly gloating. He swallowed it. "Yes," I felt I must give him. "We'll pay your kinsmen too." I cut off his thanks—can a bear fawn?—and sent him back to work. Thereafter I set about discovering duties of my own.

We camped briefly that night, with sentries posted, and surely everyone's sleep was uneasy and dream-haunted. At dawn we swallowed some food and paddled onward. Again things blur together for me. It is enough that we went onward.

And that when we came to the clearing where folk had lived, we drew ashore, gathered brushwood, cut logs, and burned our dead: for this was right, rather than they bloat and stink, waiting to be set free. We did it as properly as we were able, bearing in mind that we were few and must keep watchmen out and be ready to escape pursuit. Those who could danced around and around the blaze while I, for lack of anyone and anything better, cast amber and sweet herbs into it and bade the souls a joyous faring home to the sun. We stayed overnight, letting the ashes cool, then in the morning gathered what pieces of bone we could find and buried them.

And onward.

Meanwhile Gairwarth dealt with our prisoner. He continued after we reached Suwebburh, where we rested a while—and burned and buried two more men—with increasing success. He learned that there was no danger of an invasion anytime soon. The raids in the south had been simply that, spillover from widespread violence, gangs with their fierceness kindled who had nowhere else to take the fire until the next real war. A fresh wave of wandering was going through the Celts. Tribes eastward, fast-breeding, hungry for new land, pushed west. This stirred no few of those who had settled ahead of them and were, after all, themselves becoming many, to move on. It was not peaceful. Wars went like backflows in an incoming, wind-driven tide. But the tide itself was sweeping ever higher, it still is, and I know not when or where it will finally ebb.

Our captive hight Conomar, as nearly as I can voice the name. I never troubled to remember the names of his father or his . . . clan? In everyday life he was only a grazier, but he boasted that his brother was a smith and that he had sometimes helped that highly respected, slightly feared man.

When I studied his sword, I myself could well-nigh believe there are unhuman powers in iron that touch those who work it. Long, lean—gaunt, I almost thought—and darkly shining, the weapon weighed less for its size than mine, as if the more ready to leap. Where the fight had left mine battered and blunted, in need of hammer and file, this thing seemed well-nigh untouched, the keenness barely off the edge at a few places where it had hit something hard. The guard did not curve down, it was straight; the pommel was not much rounded or decorated; the grip was riveted oakwood, which I could see had often been clutched in a sweaty hand.

I tested it a number of times, as did several other of our well-born, hewing at a block or, after duly begging pardon, a tree. But we gained no skill. That would have taken years and been of scant use when we had only the one and nothing of the mysterious art that had gone into the making.

Most of what new knowledge we got was from Conomar, after we continued our journey. Having found that his home would be safe, Gairwarth was willing, for pay, to keep on with us as far as the river mouth. He earned that pay. Sullen, snarling, at first the Celt refused food. Among his people, if a man has no other way of getting justice or revenge, he can lay terrible shame on his enemy by starving himself to death. Gairwarth patiently—and, I am sure, cunningly—brought him to see that this means was always open to him but before thus giving up all hope of release it would be better, yes, manlier to bide his time, watchful for any opening. Thereafter, bit by bit, he coaxed more of an account forth. He told me he did it oftenest by provoking boasts and threats.

"Not that Conomar is witless or unwitting," he said. "I begin to think that behind that fiery, hasty heart is a mind with depths I cannot sound. However, the Celts are a talkative as well as proud race, two strings from which notes may be plucked." He shook his head. "I'm glad, though, that he's in bonds."

They whom we had thought of as merely wild are in reality a people of much accomplishment. Their priests are living storehouses of lore. They honor their poets almost as highly, and the lowliest herdsman has a share in that heritage, however small. Some of the wonderfully made things that had reached us in the North were from their own craftsmen; this had been forgotten or misunderstood over the long trade routes. When I looked closely, I saw that Conomar's blanket was finely enough woven to be worthy of a king among us.

Quarrelsome, warlike, they nonetheless have a good awareness of the world around them. News travels swiftly from end to end of their lands. It spreads to everyone at the councils and fairs they hold throughout the year. Thus Conomar could name tribes far to the east of his Boii, and others well to the west. Some had settled in great mountains, from which they were spilling south into a land of cities. Some were crossing a river mightier than the Ailavo. All this movement sent tides clashing to and fro among the Celts themselves. Gairwarth's guess had been right, the Boii were at odds with their neighbors on either side, in no mood to make terms with anybody.

Today I am not quite sure whether I found out most of what I am recalling then or later, as shards of knowledge—and often, I suppose, mistakenness—have come to us here at home. Nor do I care. What stands before me is our last encampment with Gairwarth. On the morrow we would reach the estuary settlement and leave him to take passage back with whatever fellow traders touched there. He had become our friend. We broke out the last ale aboard to drink with him. Night fell while we did.

It is as if we sit again around the fire, mingled without regard to birth, for we had become so few and shared so much grief. Horns, filled out of the clay jugs, pass from hand to grimy, calloused hand. Light flickers red across us, then loses itself in the huge dark or the resin-sweet smoke. Wood crackles, spitting sparks. I remember nothing we said, only that it was slow and comradely, save for this: Gairwarth leaned toward me and asked, "What will you do with him?"

The prisoner sat apart, still hobbled, now leashed to a tree. At Gairwarth's rede we gave him a share of the drink. He surprised us by muttering a sort of thanks. He had already begun to pick up our tongue. "Keep him," I answered. "What else?"

Gairwarth lowered his voice. "Do you think kindlier of him than before?"

"Well, not very, but we can find work for him, and anyhow, I wouldn't butcher a helpless man."

"He isn't. Havakh, do not, not take him into your household, whether as slave or freedman. He's grown more careful, but—I know his breed, and I've gained some feeling of him as a man—he lives for revenge. Someday, somehow, after as many years as need be, he'll take it, on you or on someone dear to you."

I shivered slightly, though the night was forest-warm. "Do you truly think so? Then how should I handle him? Let him go? Wouldn't that be to loose a wolf on the dwellers along his way?"

While we spoke softly, to make sure Conomar wouldn't guess what we said, others nearby heard. Ernu broke in. "Ah-um! Lord, why not give him to me? I'll take good heed of him, I will."

We stared at him. He grinned. "Away off in the bogland, how could he hurt you or yours, lord? We've use for every pair of hands, we poor folk. If he took flight, he'd soon be lost, but we'd track him down, and if he'd killed, we'd make him sorry. Not that I'm afraid he would. Better a life amongst us than penned up at the great hall, no? Why, he might earn himself a woman."

I glanced toward Gairwarth, who spread his hands to show that he couldn't judge.

"You promised me reward, over and above those bronze tools and cloth, after I saved your life, lord," wheedled Ernu. "This'd be a lordly gift, and rid your dear ones of a danger too, I make bold to say."

Yes, shrewd, I knew. *He listened closely indeed.* My gaze sought to the captive. Dooming him to such wretchedness—and yet not to full unfreedom—a vengeance of my own, of which I need not be ashamed? "I will think about it," I said.

But when at length I agreed, I had so much else on my mind that it was almost carelessly.

We did not linger after we left Gairwarth off, for there was a tide we could catch and a hunger in our hearts. The sea voyage was hard only because we were undermanned. When at last we drew up on our own strand and saw our own folk eagerly gathering to meet us, it was such an utterly lovely late-summer day that for that short span I, at least, forgot this was a sorrowful return.

Sunlight struck dazzlement from water and tall white clouds. Surely nowhere else in the world were grass and leaves as green. Wavelets clucked, fowl mewed and cried, and on the holy hilltop the trumpeters sang welcome. In the gentle weather, several well-born maidens had put on a garb seldom worn anymore, close-fitting knit bodice, bronze beltplate disc, and string skirt ending well above the knees. Great sheafs of fair hair tumbled over their shoulders, down past their breasts. Suddenly, shakingly, I kenned one among them, daughter of a goodly house, Daemagh her name.

I have always been glad that my lady can talk with anyone, man or woman, high or low, readily and wisely. Never has this served us so well as today. Lost in memories, I am barely half aware of the feast and the company, barely able to give some kind of reply when somebody speaks to me. Her flowing words and sun-bright smiles draw their heed. Thus I dare hope that they little mark my withdrawnness.

She does. I see her glance flit across me whenever it can without betraying the trouble in her. She wonders what has gone wrong. I do myself. Why should a small surprise, the appearance of Ernu and Conomar after all these years, during which I scarcely ever gave them a thought, why should it cast my soul back through time? Does something in me—a ghost out of the Otherworld?—sense that this meeting may be fateful, and seek to learn how it has come about? I sit cold and alone, hosting the sun-feast.

Yet it clatters on, horns and trenchers, chatter and laughter, gossip and tales, while youths and maidens look at each other and forward to tonight, and meanwhile sunlight streams in the open doors to glow on gold and amber and brightly dyed garb. And slowly the spell on me fades, like dawntide fog giving way to clear morning. Little by little I come back to myself and the now. It is as if I must call up each happening of long ago, but once I have done so, it lets go its hold on me.

Or could it simply be that when I was reminded, that wakened a powerful wish to recall? Old men dwell much on the past, and I am no longer young. Surely a high holy day is a time for remembering friends who are gone: Herut, Athalberh, my elder brother who had so briefly held this seat that was our father's—

The guests rise, the trestle tables are cleared away, a hush falls. I go to the hearthstones and bless the dying fire. Two of my daughters bring a tub of ashes from former years. With beechwood scoops they gather today's and the embers and bear them off. At sunset I will make our needfire, and with a torch from it light the balefire, as balefires will be lighted everywhere over the land. The great and solemn moment sets me wholly free of my ghosts.

Daemagh and I return to the high seat. "Are you well?" she murmurs.

"I am again," I reply, also softly. "I went . . . dreamy for a span, but that's over with."

Her forefinger draws the branching sign of Mother Yortha. "May it never come upon you again. I was afraid for you."

"I don't believe it was anything to fear," I tell her and myself. "This is a good midsummer. Not like those our forebears knew, but better than many we've seen. We can hope it bodes well."

We take our seat, side by side. Our guests bench themselves along the walls, cheerful and expectant. Their gifts have been laid there, often wrapped in cloth, and now most of them take these things onto their laps. Serving wenches go about refilling their horns. Manservants bring mine in and stand holding them. I say my words, Daemagh says hers, and the giving begins. One by one, in order of rank or, for equal rank, age, the heads of households come up for their little speeches and their presentations, amber lumps, pelts, hides, carved tokens, meaning that a horse or a cow is tethered outside—no surprises, merely the best they can offer in these lean times. Mine to them are likewise traditional, bronze knives and ornaments, cloaks, tunics, well-made harness, a goblet from abroad that the dwindling trade has carried this far—the best I too can bestow, meager though my father would have reckoned it. So do we renew the ties that have held us together from of old.

Meanwhile the humbler folk have gathered outside. My steward steps forth to let them know it is their turn. By twos and threes, some shyly, some brashly, they come in, stand before me, utter a few awkward words, and set down whatever they are carrying. I say thanks, Daemagh gives each one her smile, and I beckon a servant to pick the thing up and another to fetch over whatever I deem is a fair exchange—for a ham, a useful bronze tool; for a sheepskin, a small brooch; for a straw basket full of hazelnuts, a comb— It goes on. Making so many quick judgments is not quite easy. But it is part of being a lord.

All the while, I am inwardly wondering what Ernu will bring, and why, and how I shall deal with it. If he gives me, say, a foxskin, a crock of honey would be a generous return, maybe overgenerous. But Conomar is with him—

How I wish I had kept better track of them. I did at first, inquiring of peat carters and suchlike men when they came by. Ernu had taken a strange and dangerous slave into his hut. If Conomar did anything untoward, I wanted to know, and set matters right, hunting him down if I must. But the word was that he had settled in, seemingly without the men of the bog having to break him with beatings, and the two of them worked together. There were rumors of witchcraft, and presently news of a second hut built nearby. Others shunned the place. However, Ernu had never been very neighborly, and after his voyage he kept more and more to himself. He raised his brood to do the same. When they did meet with other folk, they talked surlily and no more than was needful. Yet the bog dwellers suffered no worse ills—sickness, injury, and the like—than they had always done. Whatever wizardry Conomar tried, and Ernu tried to learn, was either harmless or lacking in force at this distance from its homeland. As for that new hut, it was known that Ernu had given him a daughter early on, and it was said he got the others too when they became fit, if they lived. Anyhow, Ernu never turned them over to anyone else. So maybe Conomar had cast a spell on him, at least.

I disliked hearing of such things, they posed no threat that I could see, and the gods knew how much else was pressing itself on my heed. After a while I stopped inquiring, then well-nigh forgot about it.

Now, all at once—

The last and lowliest of my people gives his gift, takes his gift, and leaves us. Ernu's bulk darkens the doorway. He shambles forward, bold as a bear. Conomar strides beside him. Both have gone gray and lost teeth. Well, so have I, and even my Daemagh. The bones stand sharp in Conomar's face above a thicket of beard. His eyes are the same wintry blue, defying me.

The hall goes silent. A breath of strangeness has blown through it, and everyone sits taut, watching. The pair stop before the high seat.

"Welcome again," I say lamely. "It's been a long time."

"Have you missed us, lord?" asks Conomar in our own language—mocking me, but I had better not respond. It would look as though I were afraid of him. Breath hisses between Daemagh's lips. Otherwise we keep still and wait.

"Well, we took a long time making a thing for you," says Ernu. "The two of us. We wanted it should be great." He holds it to his breast, bundled in a mildewy hide.

"That is . . . well thought of." *Unless this be a curse*. "Both of you?" *I know no cause for Ernu to love me, but neither for him to hate me. Conomar, though—*

The Boian takes the word. While his speech is rough, bog-dweller speech, it flows, and a Celtic lilt is in it. "Lord Havakh, once we fought, and you fought bravely yourself. It's bad luck that caught me, and you did not do as ill by me as you might have. You passed me on to a man who's become my friend, and sure but the friend of my friend must be mine too."

Does he mean that? I wonder.

Daemagh knows the story, of course. As often erstwhile, she asks the right question. "Has it not been a poor and lonely life for you?"

"That it has, my lady." His smile and his tone charm, but the eyes are unwavering. "Yet it could have been worse. When Ernu here and his house listened to my tales, poems, songs, I was no longer alone, not really. Homesick I have been, but not alone like a fish caught and thrown on the riverbank to wait for the beheading."

This has made it easier for them to keep their backs to the outside world, I understand. *They've had a bard with them. And what else was he, is he? Oh, indeed I have underreckoned both the warrior and the bogman.*

"And he listened to more than that," Conomar goes on. "We've come to work well together, the pair of us."

"I'm . . . glad to hear this," I say for lack of better.

Ernu sweeps a hand through the air. He fairly swells with his own importance—which is not just in his head, I know now. "At last, lord, we can bring you a worthy gift," he booms. "You remember that sword we—you took when we fared yonder?"

I can only nod. I gave it to the king when he came through on his yearly procession, and I believe he has kept it in his treasury. Since then, I also believe, some few iron knives and the like have trickled to the North, though I have not seen them.

"Well, lord," Ernu says, "this'n's not so good, not yet, but it's ours what we made for you, and there'll be better to come."

He unrolls the bundle, tosses the skin to the floor, and reaches the thing up to me. It is an iron sword.

Crudely done, yes. Already, holding it, staring at it, while gasps and mutters go through the hall, I can see it's inferior to a good bronze blade, less sharp, dull-hued, the marks of the hammer everywhere on it—but it is long, a weapon not to thrust with but to hew with; it is iron.

"Where did you get the metal?" is all I can find to ask.

"From the bog, lord, the bog," Ernu tells me victoriously. "Conomar knew to poke down with a stick and find the lumps of, of, uh, ore. He knew to make a kiln, and heat the stuff and pound it and, uh, quench it— He didn't know the whole thing, lord. We worked it out together, year by year, the how of it. There's much yet to work out, yes, I won't say otherwise, but I will work it out, and already I can do tools and things worth swapping for. Already I'm a blacksmith."

And thereby a man of power, a man who may reforge our world.

I force the eerie thought aside. Is it not high time that we in the North began to gain these skills? First, however— "This is a great gift," I hear myself saying. "It's hard to know what I can give back."

"We've thought on that—" he begins.

"My freedom, my freedom," Conomar croons. "A boat that takes me to the mainland, a weapon, a little gold or amber so I can pay when I need to, and I'll make my way home. Is that too much, lord?"

"No. You shall have it," I must say. "And you, Ernu, shall have honor and a home here," he and his family and their uncouthness, well rewarded for each new discovery he makes, because he is now a blacksmith. I can only hope that soon there will be more.

Yes, they thought far ahead, these two.

I should be glad. Why do I find vengeful joy in Conomar's eyes? He is a poet, it seems, and poets are seers. What foreknowledge may *he* have?

I woke instantly, but lay for minutes bewildered. So much, so much—Rennie sat by the bed. The sight of him and of the objects around us, chairs, a desk, a computer, an Ansel Adams landscape framed and hung on the wall, a floor lamp lighted against the dusk gathering in the windows, those gave me back my reality. I was again the one I had always been. Jane and Myrtis were waiting for me at home.

It was not like rousing from a dream, though. I remembered what I had been as clearly as I remembered them, with none of the vagueness and illogic of dreams. I loved them, but I had lived longer with Daemagh and she had borne me more children.

No. She was Havakh's. I must be clear about that.

"Are you all right?" Rennie asked quietly.

"Yes." I got up. My feet were steady. "Just, well, overwhelmed."

"To be expected. Come on downstairs and relax awhile, start sorting your experiences out, then we'll call either your wife or a taxi." He had advised me not to drive here.

Already my scientist thoughts were busy. Yet sorrow was rising and rising. When he poured me a glass of wine, I drained it indecently fast. Doubtless I wasn't unique, for he had left the bottle on the table and gave me a refill without commenting. Instead, he let me brood while I sipped more slowly and the alcohol began to ease me a little.

"Was your experience helpful?" he asked at last.

"I learned a lot," I mumbled.

"I'd be fascinated to know. You're not obliged, of course, and in fact you'll probably take weeks to assimilate and organize your memories enough to write them up in even a preliminary fashion. But if you're willing to send me a copy, I assure you it'll have one mighty interested reader."

His commonplace words were exactly the sort I had want of. I realized that he knew it. "Sure, be happy to." He must also know that need as well as courtesy would make me tell him a bit here and now. "I did enter the Northern Bronze Age. Not its glory days, the way I hoped. Its decline. The beginning of the end, in fact."

"I'm sorry. You know the system is poorly calibrated."

"Yeah. A matter of luck. And I know you won't let me try again." I managed a smile of sorts. To absolve him was a comfort to me, a slight easing of my sadness. "Not that I'd apply. You're right about the risks."

"History isn't melodrama. It's tragedy," Rennie said low. I had the impression that that was a quote. "And prehistory. Was your experience terrible?"

I shook my head and slid more wine over my tongue, down my throat. "No, actually not. That is, while I was there I, uh, remembered some pretty grim events. But—" The knowledge surprised me; I hadn't thought of it before "—to the ancestor I shared the mind of, they'd happened long ago, and to him, in his culture, they weren't, well, they weren't shocking. Regrettable, but not, uh, traumatic. Kind of like a veteran nowadays recalling combat. The actual hours I spent were quite peaceful."

His look sharpened, though his tone remained gentle. "Just the same, it's touched you rather deeply, hasn't it?"

I sighed. "Yes. More and more, the more I hark back. I saw the end of a thousand wonderful years."

He sipped from his own glass while he arranged his words. "Not to push you, Mr. Larsen, especially right now. Explain at your leisure, if you like. In spite of studying your application, I'm afraid I'm basically ignorant in this area."

How good it was for me to go prosaic. "Oh, infinitely complicated, like every other subject. Still, I can give you a rough outline, what you'll find in popular books."

I drew breath. "Copper and tin aren't too easy to come by. Anyhow, they weren't in the far past. So bronze was expensive. Not very many families could afford a full panoply of up-to-date arms and armor for a fighting man. They became the aristocrats. That didn't necessarily mean tyranny. Sometimes they maintained a reasonably just rule of law. Minoan Crete seems to have been pretty happy, for instance. Like, later on, when the technology had gotten there, Bronze Age Scandinavia.

"Iron, though, iron's everywhere. It's harder to extract and work on, but once you know how, anybody can. Barbarians learned, and swarmed forth. They brought Mycenean Greece, for instance, down into a long dark age.

"When the Celts learned, they came out of their Danubian homeland and overran central and southern Europe, as far as Galatia in Turkey, Cisalpine Gaul in Italy, France, Spain, and the British Isles. Meanwhile they developed quite a remarkable culture. At last the Germans stopped them, later the Romans conquered most of them.

"But I—I was back sometime in, I guess, the late sixth or early fifth century B.C. The Celts were cutting off the trade routes and the climate was going bad. Then the arts of ironworking reached Scandinavia. Danish bog iron isn't awfully good, but it was a start, and Sweden has first-class ores. Eventually a peasant could have weapons almost as good as a noble's. Between them, these changes spelled the death of the old order. For better or worse. I'm not saying which. The Celtic influence became so strong in the North that archaeologists define a Celtic Iron Age, before the Roman and the Germanic ones. Certainly some magnificent artwork got created. For a while, society was at least a bit more democratic, the Thing meetings and such. But—it was an age of upheaval, violence, even human sacrifice. And the violence went on and on and on, for two thousand years and more."

I stopped, exhausted, drained my glass again, and slumped, staring into it. "I see," Rennie murmured. "Or half see. Let's call for your ride home."

I nodded. Yes, best to get back and begin coming to terms with my grief. It was not Havakh's, it was mine. He never really knew what was coming. But I had been him, and I did.